IT'S

C0-AWW-046

Exercise Caution

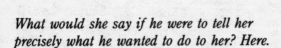

What would she say if he were to tell her precisely what he wanted to do to her? Here. Now.

"Okay," he said, aware of the boyish uncertainty she created in him. "I've told you my name. Won't you tell me yours, Miss . . ." When she failed to reply he said, "Where's the harm in that?"

She weighed her response. "Mrs.," she said. "Mrs. Geneva Sharps."

Married. The wide gold band on her left hand told him that. Told him even more. Studded as it was with finely cut diamonds, all those expensive points of light under a ceiling of neon tubes. Mr. Sharps, whoever he was, did very well, whatever his line of work. Certainly he made a great deal of money. But there was more to a marriage than money.

ASPEN AFFAIR

BURT HIRSCHFELD

Harper Paperbacks

Harper & Row, Publishers, New York
Grand Rapids, Philadelphia, St. Louis, San Francisco
London, Singapore, Sydney, Tokyo, Toronto

This is a work of fiction. The characters, incidents, and dia-
logues are products of the author's imagination and are not
to be construed as real. Any resemblance to actual events or
persons, living or dead, is entirely coincidental.

Harper Paperbacks a division of Harper & Row, Publishers, Inc.
10 East 53rd Street, New York, N.Y. 10022

Cover photography by Herman Estevez

First printing: September, 1990

Printed in the United States of America

HARPER PAPERBACKS and colophon are trademarks of
Harper & Row, Publishers, Inc.

10 9 8 7 6 5 4 3 2 1

ASPEN AFFAIR

The Beaver Man

T H E Y had been formed by the stress and pressure exerted by an earth undergoing massive and radical changes, the long rugged range of high peaks and alpine valleys. Changed by a roiling sea that five hundred million years earlier had covered the earth, by ponderous glaciers that squeezed the land, crunching rock formations into random shapes that closed off the horizon. Eventually trees grew on the steep slopes and grass and flowers in the protected meadows, and minerals and metals were concealed under the rough landscape. That range came to be known as the Rocky Mountains.

Later, hundreds of years later, when the weather became more hospitable and the high valleys more accessible, wildlife in all its astounding variety drifted up into the high country. And human beings; the Ute Indians made their way up the Western Slope. The dramatic vistas, so stark and pristine in the winter, so softly green and lush the rest of the time, assured those early Americans that the Great Spirit had smiled upon the land and had blessed the Ute people.

The Utes existed in harmony with the earth. With the bowls and ridges and peaks of the mountains, with the animals, with the trees whose leaves quivered like jittery tendrils in the slightest breeze. They lived from one season to the next, taking from the mountains only what they needed in order to survive. There was always water in the gushing streams. There was always wood for their campfires. And meat to fill their bellies. They lived out their lives unhurriedly, unmarked, in a never-ending, graceful cycle, at peace with themselves and the land.

Until a white man finally found his way up into the high valley. He began to trap beaver—of which there were so many—along the river that one day would be known as the Roaring Fork. The Utes watched him from a distance and decided he offered them no threat, this solitary trapper, who lived very much as they lived, and so they tolerated his presence. They could not imagine that his coming marked the beginning of the end of their idyllic way of life and the beginning of the white man's way in that part of the world.

1

*D**EVLIN** had been expecting the boy. Not *this* boy—his name was Alain—not this particular boy. But someone designed as this boy had been designed, with all his very delicate and special specifications. Someone younger than Devlin was, and better looking. At least not so marked and weathered by the sun and the cold and by time. Someone who had yet to develop those lines around the eyes, someone without those leathery creases in his cheeks. Someone whose dark hair had not yet begun to show signs of thinning, without those patches of silver at the temples. Someone whose eyes still glittered with hope and optimism.

Only a younger man could measure up. One relatively untouched by any of life's harsher realities. To whom defeat was merely a rumor, an unacceptable suggestion of things to come. Certainly it meant someone who had not acquired the scars of body and spirit that so plainly marked Devlin.

But did he have to be this young? This bland and unformed youth, it surprised Devlin, and for a fractured moment of time he resented the boy—not Alain, particularly—but anyone Barbara might have brought home.

Alain was almost as tall as Devlin, slighter in build, too soft to be any kind of an athlete. This was not a person of violent temper, not dangerous physically. But a threat nevertheless. Even more, Devlin reminded himself ruefully; Alain was the living personification of another defeat in a growing line of defeats. He was tired of coming out on the short end of things.

Devlin acknowledged Alain with a handshake and a quiet, "Hello." The younger man's hand was too soft, his mouth never still with a nervous smile, his eyes swinging from place to place. Alain said he was pleased to meet Devlin, but Devlin doubted that very much.

Barbara, in tennis whites, prescription sunglasses pushed back on her thick auburn hair, watched the exchange with the pride of possession. Of authorship. And why not? She had invented them both, in a manner of speaking, and had surely composed this quiet, obligatory scene, so fraught with drama. This was Barbara's way, always in control. It occurred to Devlin that too often had he subordinated his own life to someone like Barbara, making a partial surrender of personal sovereignty and will. That was something he'd have to consider, when he had the time; explore his motives; and change things. But not now. This was Barbara's time, and she was speaking.

"Isn't he beautiful, Dev? Alain, I mean."

"I know who you mean." He spoke in dry, flat tones, determined to conceal the unease he was experiencing. *Alain* . . . The way she pronounced the name might have caused a casual listener to believe the boy had recently stepped off the Concorde from Paris, France. Barbara always said it that way: Paris, France. Lest anyone confuse the City of Lights with Paris, Texas, or some other town by that name. Barbara had an abiding love affair with things French; the clothes, the food, the wines, the men. Especially the men.

"The French are superior lovers," she liked to say, suggesting a firsthand sexual knowledge of a substantial number of Frenchmen. She actually called it "french kissing" and "frenching" it, as in "I want you to french me now."

"Where you from, kid?" Devlin said, masking his resentment. None of it was Alain's doing. Not his fault. Alain was the embodiment of the inevitable; the phrase pleased him, and he managed a restrained, decent smile.

"Key West, sir."

The "sir" jarred him. Had he aged *that* much? Oh, what the hell, he had a good twenty years on the boy. He shifted around to confront Barbara and showed his strong white teeth in a smile limned with self-mockery. She gave nothing back. Her meticulously made up face was grave, that petulant mouth painted a fire-engine red, as always disapproving. Barbara, Devlin had decided months before, approved of nothing and no one in the world. Unless they happened to live in, or come from, Paris, France. Or Palm Beach, Florida, where she made her home.

"Almost perfect, isn't he?" Devlin drawled. He stepped across the room, stiff-legged and deliberate, his knees not nearly what they used to be before the operations became necessary. He paused at the bar alongside the French doors that opened onto a carefully tended garden, a liver-shaped swimming pool, and the Atlantic Ocean beyond; all that separated Barbara from her beloved Paris, France. He looked back at the other two out of eyes the color of an unsettled sea, faded, somewhere between green and gray and clouded with ghostly memories. His nose was lean and dominant, as was his jaw. He had a wide and flexible mouth, sensual without being too fleshy. The kind of man who ages well, advancing deliberately through life's stages, never looking quite like anybody else. Always his own man.

Barbara answered for the boy. "Alain doesn't drink."

"That'll keep your booze bills down." Devlin deliberately filled a crystal tumbler with thirty-year-old Glenfiddich. He raised his glass in silent toast and drank. Any further conversation was unnecessary. Still . . .

"Where'd you find him?"

"He means," Barbara said to Alain, "where did we meet? Dev has a way of putting things that is not always desirable or polite." She made a motion with her slender hand, at once dismissive and commanding, indicating her displeasure. An almost regal annoyance. A way of letting it be known she was concerned with more pressing matters. "I'd like to talk to you in private, Dev." Ever so polite, Barbara. "If you don't mind, Alain, dear?"

Alain didn't mind.

Barbara moved off toward the bedroom wing of the house. Devlin emptied the rest of the Scotch in his glass and refilled it. Mustn't react too quickly. Obedience had never been his strong point. No way he intended to let on that in this house Barbara alone called the shots, that he was only an animated element in the decor, an incidental bibelot meant to entertain and decorate. Why spoil it for the kid?

"Stay loose, Alain," he said, and went after Barbara.

She was waiting for him in the bedroom, standing near—not too near—the great round water bed of which she was so fond. Two pieces of luggage rested on the bed. Soft black leather replete with straps and buckles, clearly very expensive. A brown envelope rested on the larger of the two bags.

Barbara went to the door and closed it. Discreetly. Firmly. All that money. All those years of subtle and overt training. The generations of ancestors, of accumulated wealth and authority, the transcendent belief in one's own natural superiority. Only such a person could close a door with the well-bred finesse and finality Barbara managed. He was almost smiling when he turned to face her.

"There's no need for a scene," Barbara began, establishing the rules of the game.

"You always do that," Alain said mildly. "Determine how things are to go."

Her elevated brows put a distressed expression on her classical features; it surprised her that he had no-

ticed. She'd never thought him that clever or perceptive. Not that it mattered, not now.

"We are adults, Dev. I want you to act as one."

She was doing it again. Weariness wrapped itself
around him, laced with uncertainty and a modicum of
fear. Well, why not? A man closed in on forty, certain
fundamental changes began to take place. A diminish-
ment of strength, for example. Both moral and physical. A loss of energy and drive. An increasing need for
solitude and a concomitant reluctance to be alone.
Changes and contradictions. When had he ceased to
believe that his way was the best of all possible lives?
When had he stopped caring? When had fear become
a key element in the equation?

"No prior warning?" he said, voice tipped with
irony. He knew better; Barbara was concerned only
with her own well-being. Consideration for others was
not a sentiment she ever entertained.

She watched him with a feral alertness. As if he
might turn on her without warning, cause her irreparable harm. Looking at him now, she wondered what she
had ever seen in him. He was much too old for her
needs, worn down by life, soon to pass over into utter
worthlessness, from her point of view. He had become
a burden. An intruder. She wanted him gone as quickly
as possible.

"This was inevitable," she said. She made it sound
like an accusation, as if he had caused this moment to
come into being. "Sooner or later," she added for emphasis.

Inevitable. Devlin allowed the word to roll around
the inside of his skull. Barbara and Alain. An inevitable

confluence of beings, not an honest emotion existed between them.

Was he much different? He preferred not to consider the implications of the question. "Where'd you find him?" He slurred the words.

"You're repeating yourself, Dev. No need to make things sordid. If you've learned nothing from your year with me, surely I've taught you the value of good manners."

"Is he the gardener's son?" Devlin persisted. "Or is he out of the carwash? Where you take the Rolls?"

She shook her head in disappointment. "No grace at all. Very well, if you must know. Alain was working at the Farmer's Market . . ."

"Bagging groceries?" He could not keep from laughing.

"It's honest work."

As if Barbara had the least notion of what the phrase meant. She had never done a day's work in her life. "I should've known, you always did enjoy squeezing the fruit."

"There you go, crude again." She indicated the large round bed with a slight movement of her chin. "Those are for you, a going-away gift."

"Luggage. An appropriate touch, Barbara."

"I thought so. And a few dollars to ease your way."

That accounted for the brown envelope. Barbara thought of everything, leaving no room for debate, denial, or delay. "When?" he said.

"As soon as possible, if you don't mind. Alain will be moving his things in this afternoon. He'll need the bureau and the closet space."

He drank the remainder of the Scotch and put the glass aside. "Now, you mean?"

"Now." The absolute sound of the word left no room for argument.

And if he refused her? Refused to go. At least not with such precipitous haste. Dismissed like a common hustler, paid off after delivering the goods. A hustler; what else was he if not a hustler?

"I don't suppose you'd care to give me a reason, running in the second string this way." He grew angry at this display of weakness, this plea that she reassure him, tell him that he'd performed up to standard during these last twelve months. Christ Almighty! What had he allowed himself to become?

She stared at him disapprovingly. Those ice blue eyes, so clear and so still, socially correct eyes, was the way he thought of them. Passed down over the generations by Germanic ancestors. The kind who owned castles and estates all across Europe and factories in a dozen different countries. The kind of blue eyes that only money could buy.

"I thought you knew, Dev." She released the words in a voice cramped with displeasure. "You're past your prime, dear heart. Almost forty, aren't you?"

"And Alain, he must be all of eighteen."

"Seventeen, darling. And under my tutelage, he'll age well. He's quite beautiful, don't you think?"

Thirty-eight, he almost said aloud. I'm only thirty-eight. But he restrained himself; his position was indefensible, his short-range destiny already decided. "I'll need some time to pack."

"Have you thought about it, where you'll be going?"

He suppressed a grin, answered solemnly. "Fear

not, dear lady. I'll be moving on. Palm Beach and eternal sunlight, I've had my fill of both. Maybe back to the mountains. Snow; cold, clean air. It will be good to get back on skis."

"Yes. Well. You know best, Dev. Where your interests lie."

She went back to where Alain was waiting and left Devlin to do his packing. To deal alone with his discomforting thoughts and uneasy emotions.

2

W E A R I N G tight-fitting slacks and a dark wool sweater, hair pulled back off her forehead, and without makeup, Peggy Pearce looked younger than her twenty-five years. There was a feline grace to the way she moved, her body strong and well shaped, her stride confident and purposeful, as if she knew precisely where she was going. She exuded competence and dedication as she maneuvered around the Burnside house, vacuuming, dusting, checking the washer-dryer in the mud room, folding clean, dry loads as they became ready.

Three people besides Peggy were on the team; she was in charge. The others followed her lead, accepted her authority without question, came to her with their problems. In four hours the job was completed, includ-

ing polishing the wood floors. Windows were the prov-
ince of specialists who showed up once a month;
Peggy, and her people, were on a once-a-week schedule.

The job done, she drove the Apex Cleaning Company van into Aspen, drawing to a stop in front of the
company office on Smuggler Street, only a few steps
from Triangle Park. Inside the storefront office she
made her report and turned over the payment check
to Harvey Latham, her employer. He was a stocky
man running to fat, with layered chins that jiggled
when he spoke and a large midriff that signaled his
coming before he arrived.

"Things go okay?" he inquired, making suitable en-
tries into a ledger.

"Always do."

That was the truth. Peggy Pearce was his best su-
pervisor; she was smart and hardworking and never
caused problems nor demanded any special treatment.
She was also the best-looking employee he'd ever had.

"Anything else for today?" she asked.

He shook his head, and his chins swung from side
to side. "You're clear, Pearce. Go skiing. Rush down
that mountain out there. Break your neck and have a
good time." Harvey Latham believed all skiers were
brain-damaged; spending all that time out in the cold,
sliding down those steep and dangerous hills, risking
life and limb. He certainly didn't want Peggy Pearce
to do damage to any portion of her exquisite body;
what a waste that would be. What, he wondered,
would it be like to be in bed with a woman like that?
One so beautiful and perfectly formed, so athletic.
More than he could handle, he conceded grudgingly.

Probably launch him into cardiac arrest. Maybe she'd meet him for a drink some night, some night he was able to get away from his wife. He waved a pudgy hand in Peggy's direction. "Go! Go!"

Back outside, Peggy dismissed her crew and located her Isuzu Trooper, black and silver, glistening in the winter sunlight. The Silver Bullet, she called it. Started up immediately, as always. The best car she'd ever owned. She turned the Trooper toward Glenwood Springs, no more than twenty minutes away.

She was one of the lucky ones. Only two rooms in the boarding house had private bathrooms, and Peggy laid claim to one of them. It was her pride and the source of much pleasure. A large, tiled chamber with a deep, old-fashioned tub on claw feet. As soon as she arrived she stripped off her clothes and ran the tub. She soaked for nearly an hour, letting the hot water run periodically to keep the temperature up. Sweat formed on her brow and she closed her eyes, head back, pillowed on a folded towel, mind searching for answers to her questions.

Did she have what it takes?

The nerve?

The intelligence?

The ability to plan ahead and foresee any difficulties?

Would other people follow her lead?

Some questions defied her ability to answer them; only when put to the hard test of experience would she learn the truth about herself. She sighed and soaped her body, let the water drain out of the tub, and used the shower to rinse off. Hot and cold. Hot and cold. Reinvigorated and convinced it was time to move ahead, she donned a wool robe and put through a phone call to the number in Denver.

To her surprise, a woman answered. "I'm trying to reach Mr. Evan Larson."

The woman, whom Peggy took to be a secretary, asked for her name and told her to hang on; a long silent interlude during which her uncertainty grew. She resisted the urge to forget all about it, to hang up. Until Evan Larson came on the line.

"Peggy Pearce," he began. "Have we met?"

"No, sir. I'm a friend of Tony Chase. Tony said if I ever needed certain kinds of advice, I was to call you. . . ."

He didn't answer at once, and that caused her nervousness to increase and at the same time gave her confidence that she had·not made a mistake in calling. She approved of people who thought before they spoke, who considered their responses, who were cautious and thorough. People very much the way she was.

"Miss Pierce," he said at last. "In your opinion, is this going to be a lengthy—make that complicated—conversation?"

"I would say so."

"Well." Another pause, another silent delay. "How well do you know Tony?"

"Very well. At least I used to know him well."

"Where was this, that you knew him so well?"

"On and off, for a year in Cleveland. And before that, for about six months in Kansas City."

"I see. I'm not comfortable with extended conversations on the telephone, Miss Pearce."

She replied at once. "I'll come to Denver."

"When?"

"I'm in Aspen. I could fly out in the morning and—"

He broke in. "Make it tonight. Let's say eight o'clock. We can have dinner together. I dislike eating by myself. The Sunset Tavern. You might say it's my home away from home. There's a plane leaving in about an hour. . . ."

"I'll be on it."

"Good," he said, and hung up.

She did the same and was dismayed to discover that her hand was trembling.

Sunset Tavern was in an unfashionable section of downtown Denver. At this hour the streets were virtually empty and most of the shops were closed. Outside, false wooden beams gave the tavern the solid look of an old English pub. Inside it was poorly lit, in need of painting, and sparsely patronized. All eyes swung her way when she appeared, and the barman examined her speculatively, elbows on the bar, his voice disapproving and rough.

"You want something, lady?"

"I'm Peggy Pearce. I'm supposed to meet—"

The barman interrupted. "In the back, middle booth on the right." He busied himself polishing glasses.

Evan Larson was a surprise. A tall man with courtly manners, impeccably dressed in brown tweeds and a black turtleneck. Silver hair flared out over his ears, matching a neatly trimmed mustache. He came out of his booth at the sight of her, hovering over her hand as if about to kiss her knuckles, making him seem like British royalty, only slightly out of place in this rundown bar and grill.

He wore round, gold-rimmed glasses behind which his small, quick eyes seemed to hide dirty secrets.

"Welcome, welcome, Miss Pearce. How lovely you are. How young. How pleasant a surprise." He ushered her into the booth and took his place opposite.

As if on silent command, the barman appeared. "Ah, Teddy. A refreshment for my young friend. What is your preference, Miss Pearce?"

Peggy decided to keep a clear head. "A Coke would do fine."

"Coca-Cola," Evan Larson said. He waited for the barman to leave before speaking again. "It isn't often that a man my age and disposition gets to enjoy the company of one so young, so beautiful. You've made my day, Miss Pearce. May I call you Peggy?"

Smooth, she observed. In a way none of the men she knew ever were. Smooth and practiced, a generational attribute, an acquired skill; she wondered if the old man could still get it up. And wondering, she decided that, if necessary, she'd come across. She needed him more than he needed her.

"I'd be flattered if you would," she said. "It's really Elizabeth, but no one ever uses that."

"Peggy fits you, Peggy. Do you like Aspen?"

"I've been there about a year. I ski a lot."

"Naturally. It's not my sport. Tennis, squash, they're more up my alley. As you can tell from looking at me, I'm a conservative man, with conservative tastes. A conservative philosophy that colors every project I undertake. Attention to detail. Caution in all things. Avoid unnecessary mistakes. Keep risk at a minimum. And, believe it or not, listen to other people talk whenever possible. One learns much more that way. What did you want to talk to me about, Peggy?"

All at once it sounded silly to her, silly in the silence of her own thoughts, silly that she could present herself to this worldly and experienced man as someone of command and deviousness. But here she was, seated opposite him, and he was waiting for her to begin. It was too late to change her mind.

"What I do in Aspen," she said. "Besides ski, that is. I clean houses. I'm a crew chief for Apex Cleaning Company. The thing is, not many people in Aspen have full-time servants, no matter how rich they are. It's easier, cheaper, more efficient in the long run just to hire a service like Apex. A good crew can zip through a large house in a few hours. Carpets, drapes, floors, the works. We even change the linen on the beds. In and out and the people have their privacy again. The point is—"

"The point is," he put in, "you have legitimate access to many homes in Aspen."

"And Snowmass, throughout the area."

"I've been told there are many outstanding homes in Aspen."

"The town's become a rich man's playground. Wealthy people by the hundreds. Famous people. Jack Nicholson, Don Johnson, Leslie Wexner—he's chief of The Limited. Maybe you heard of them, they sell women's things."

"I heard of them."

"Jerry Cross, the movie star. John Denver. Lots of people like that. An average house these days, they cost almost a million dollars, and some of them go as high as—"

"You've made your point, Peggy. Rich people in Aspen. And rich people means lots of expensive jewels and furs and other fine items."

"It's gotten so that ordinary people, people like me, we can't afford to live in town. Most of us rent in one of the nearby towns. I myself am in Glenwood Springs—" She broke off, aware that she'd begun to chatter, made jittery and unsure by the distinguished tranquillity of Evan Larson. He continued looking at her through the round glasses, his handsome mouth pursed quizzically, waiting for her to continue. She was grateful when the barman arrived with her Coke.

She sipped it through a straw until they were alone again. "The point is, I do have access to many of those houses. I spend hours in each one, at least once every week. Steady customers. As well as the occasional job. I have freedom to move around as I see fit. Nothing is off limits to me. No room. And most of the time, I am left alone. To make notes. Drawings. Sketches of where things are kept. Floor plans."

He shifted forward, his cultured voice softer now. "Would you know an alarm system when you see it?" She nodded once. "And the power source? Have you been able to locate them?"

"Some of the homes I work don't have alarms. It's as if those people can't imagine anyone daring to lift a hand against them. As if they're unreachable."

"Yes, the wealthy can be as careless and foolish as the rest of us. Tell me precisely what you have in mind, Peggy."

The risks grew exponentially from this point on. Exposing herself to Evan Larson. Giving herself over to this stranger. But Tony Chase had vouched for Larson, said he was a good man, trustworthy. But then Tony was not the most acute judge of character she'd ever met; what choice did she have?

"Tony Chase spoke very highly of you, Mr. Larson."

"Tony's in jail. Did you know that? Back east, in Connecticut. Some stupid little job with minor rewards. Not worth the doing. Still, Tony did it and got caught. Three to five, I understand, with very little chance of parole, his record being what it is.

"You're asking yourself, Is Larson to be trusted? How do I know he won't cheat me? Or betray me to the law. That's the chance you take. You've come to me. You need me. Without a proper fence there's no point in any of this, is there.

"Very well, let me qualify myself to some degree. I own a jewelry store here in Denver. And a second shop in San Francisco. Quality items only. I deal only with people who have lots of money to spend. I also own a small trucking company which gives me immediate and unlimited transport, when required. There are other businesses, largely cash enterprises where the turnover is rapid and the opportunities to make swift adjustments to a changing market are many.

"All of this means I have available to me large sums of money, ready to be paid out at odd hours of the day and night. It also means that I have the connections to get goods moved across the country or conceal them in one of my warehouses, should the occasion arise. To all outside observers, I am a circumspect businessman, low key, attracting no attention, dealing only when it is in my interests to deal."

"You've convinced me."

"There's more you should understand. What I've told you, my business interests, results in a substantial overhead. Expenses. And, should the law ever become curious about me, I could be extremely vulnerable. All of which means that—"

"That your cut is going to be bigger than I anticipated."

"You are a clever young woman, Peggy."

"How much?"

He adjusted the round glasses on the bridge of his elegant nose. He worked a filtered cigarette into an ivory cigarette holder. He placed the holder between his teeth and used a gold lighter to light his cigarette. He grinned at Peggy Pearce, the holder snapping up into a jaunty angle. He reminded her of photographs she had seen of Franklin Delano Roosevelt.

"Fifty percent."

She never hesitated. "That's outrageous."

"You think so? Despite what I told you about overhead, expenses, the costs of operating in somewhat shadowed areas. Fifty percent and you'll receive your share upon delivery of the merchandise. Cash in hand, dear lady. No one else in Denver will cut you a better deal."

She rocked her head from one side to the other. "Forty percent."

He blew smoke out of his nose. How long had it been since she had last seen anyone do that? A trick from a bygone era. "My dear, we have reached an impasse. Return to Aspen. Enjoy the mountains. The fresh air. The skiing. Put this other matter behind you."

"I do not intend to be cheated."

"If you feel you might be, look elsewhere for help."

She assessed him steadily. As far as she could tell, there was no room to bargain; his price was set. She had hoped for a more advantageous division of the spoils; it was not to be. Perhaps at a later date they might renegotiate their agreement, once she had established her own reliability and the value of her merchandise. Until then . . . "All right," she said. "Fifty percent it is, cash on delivery."

He offered her his hand, and she took it. "You've made yourself a good deal. You won't regret it. How soon can I expect the first delivery?"

When she hesitated, he leaned back, his eyes dark and mean in the dim light. "That's just it, I need help. A crew . . ."

"You don't have anybody." It was an accusation, clear recognition that he had been misled. "Nobody at all."

She responded rapidly. "The way I see it, it's vital that I separate myself from the break-ins. Both in distance and in time. Just as you do," she added in a lowered tone. "If the police should become suspicious of me, it would be over then."

"You," he said, "and how many others?"

"Three, I thought. Two inside people and a driver waiting outside in a car."

"Yes. Three will do. Men, preferably. Should there be a need for a swift physical response, men do best. Have you considered weapons?"

"Guns, you mean! Good God, no! No guns. No weapons of any kind. If things go the way they should, there'll be no need."

"Things don't always go the way they should. Still, guns do have a tendency to go off unexpectedly. Murder arouses the police to extraordinary efforts. No guns and no trouble, if at all possible."

"Then you'll help me find a crew?"

He pulled at his nose and looked past her. "There is a man. Experienced and nervy. With good skills when it comes to electrical systems, alarms and the like. How long were you planning to stay in Denver?"

"Overnight. I'm booked out on a midday flight."

He slid out of the booth, towering and erect, so very proper and handsome, a benevolent presence. "Be here at nine o'clock tomorrow morning. We'll breakfast together, and perhaps the young man I have in mind will join us. . . ."

At about that same time, Sam Daly decided to make his move. Stationed in an alley between two frame houses: one occupied by a beauty salon, the other a shop that sold old movie posters, comic books, and baseball cards. He rocked from foot to foot against the cold and pounded his gloved fists against his brawny chest and stared at the lighted windows of the apartment on the second floor of the house across the street. Behind drawn shades, in warmth and camaraderie, the game continued. Dealer's choice—five-card stud, seven-card stud, five-card draw—nothing wild. A no-limit game. Populated by serious players, men who played for only one purpose: to win. Every one of them had been too strong for Sam Daly.

It had taken him most of the evening to read the other players. Each man's betting patterns. And by then it was too late. He lost three-quarters of his stake before he realized that no one at the table ever tried to run a bluff. These were straight-on players; when a man raised, he held cards. When he raised big, kept bumping the pot, he expected to win.

Daly had expected to win. Convinced he was going to have a big night. He felt lucky; winning hands all the way. But he had never accepted the notion that luck had very little to do with gambling. Especially poker. Daly had yet to learn to keep his mouth shut at the table, not to antagonize the other players. Nor did he know much about money management; his betting was erratic, tough and aggressive at all the wrong times. Too soft when the stakes really got up there. He lacked the patience to sit back and wait for a good hand when the cards were running against him, repeatedly throwing good money after bad. A consistent loser.

Busted flushes and low straights. Two pair when another player held three of a kind. Betting the come too often, driving up the pot for the eventual winner. His pile grew steadily smaller as the evening wore on, leaving him with a rising desperation and light pockets. He was at the table for only three hours and he lost two thousand dollars.

Now, in the alley, he could hear their mocking voices when he'd had to quit. Made him out to be a lousy gambler. Said he was too dumb to win in a game of penny-ante. Said he was a born loser.

Mo Curry was the worst of them. With that big, fleshy face of his, that taunting laugh, those cutting words. "Dumb Mick," Curry had started out, as if signaling the other men to join in the verbal assault.

"Poker's not your game."

"The fool ain't got a game, except losing."

"Born to lose," Mo Curry said, shuffling the cards for a new deal. "Comes to cards, your brains are in your asshole."

That drew a big laugh around the table.

Ready to depart, Sam Daly thought about busting Mo Curry's face for him. A couple of well-placed shots; crush cartilage, break a bone, draw blood. How good it would have felt.

The thing was, Daly raged silently. Mo Curry was the big winner. Seemed he always won, as if he owned the deck. Daly had himself convinced: Mo Curry cheated. A man who'd cheat in a friendly game of cards deserved no mercy.

He changed his post in the alley. From one side to the other. He tugged his coat collar up around his chin and stamped his feet some more. Checked his watch one more time.

Until Mo Curry appeared. With two of the other players. Laughing, talking loud in the night. Exchanging confidences. Mocking him, Sam Daly was sure. Enjoying a good laugh over his bad luck. Well, laugh it up, boy. For the last time.

The men separated, Mo Curry swinging down the block toward the municipal parking lot where he'd left his Mercedes roadster. A beautiful vehicle, sleek and low-slung, white as the snow of winter. Must have cost Mo fifty thousand, maybe more. Paid for, Daly reckoned, with Curry's poker winnings. Money won from Sam Daly. Well, Mo Curry's run of luck was over. He waited until the big man had turned the corner and went after him.

Caught up just as Curry turned into the parking lot. Deserted at this hour and dark, only a handful of cars waiting to be picked up. Daly tippy-toed up behind Curry and hit him hard behind the right ear. Down he went, and Daly went after him, both hands pumping ferociously.

To his surprise, Curry fought back. Squirming, rolling, kicking out like a woman. Landing unexpectedly strong blows to Daly's face. Blood began to flow; it tasted salty back in his throat. Enraged by this insult to his person, Daly drove his stiffened thumbs into the other man's eyes. Mo Curry screamed and tried to roll away. No use. Daly's big fists pounded at him, even after he had slumped into unconsciousness.

Breathing hard, Daly searched through Curry's pockets until he located his winnings. A thick stash, neatly arranged and held in place by a thick rubber band. Satisfied, he hurried away.

Back in his room, he counted the money. He was surprised, shocked, confused. There were only a few hundred dollars, in fives and tens. Where in God's name was the rest of it? Had Curry secreted the rest of his pile on that big body of his? How could he have missed such a big amount? He considered returning to the parking lot, going through Curry's pockets one more time. He dismissed that as a bad idea; besides, by now Curry would be up and away in the Mercedes. Just went to show, when a man's luck ran bad it kept getting worse.

Questions began to plague him. It was always thus, after a fight or a job. So many questions, tantalizing and too often unanswerable. Why was it the questions never came to mind beforehand, before he went into action? Giving him time enough to consider their implications. Time enough to remedy any problems.

Had Mo Curry recognized him? Even in the dark of the parking lot, that was possible. Just his luck to have Curry and some of his goonish friends come after him. Curry was a mean sonofabitch. Ruthless, it was said, in his quest for revenge. And relentless, it was also said, in his pursuit of an enemy.

Daly conceded the point; Curry was tougher than he was in ways Sam could not always understand. Tougher and smarter. Even if he hadn't seen Daly's face, he would put it all together, conclude correctly who had assaulted and robbed him. And seek Daly out.

The moment to leave Denver had come. Clear out for safer, more congenial surroundings. Maybe go south and get some sunlight. Where the girls went around in flimsy dresses and short shorts, advertising their wares. That was one area in which Daly was confident, his ability to attract pretty young women. Which is what he needed now: a loving woman. One to ease his concerns and draw the tension out of his big body. To turn back the fear he was feeling.

That's it, then. He was on his way. Out of there. Good-bye, Denver and Mo Curry. It was time for a change of scenery and a change of luck. Only one question had to be answered.

Where to go?

3

D U N C A N Turner Sharps spent no more than sixty minutes with the woman. In her flat on Curzon Street. A surprising location for someone in the life. Very fashionable. Very expensive. A street containing some of London's finest private clubs and residences. All of which suited Sharps, who had developed a singular taste for quality.

The woman was tall, taller than he, with aristocratic features and a good, strong body. Not slender like Geneva. Not one of those model's bodies, long and fragile, with an absence of good flesh. No, this one was solid and resilient, built to last, he told himself. Built to take it.

She said her name was Vivian, and she spoke quietly, with an upper-class accent that had been carefully cultivated. She offered him his choice of liquor or champagne or tea.

"When in England," Sharps said, making a joke, "do as the natives do. Make mine tea."

She managed a reluctant smile and went after the tea. Served in expensive crockery along with buttered biscuits. He nibbled and sipped and inspected her openly across the small serving table that separated them, as if she were a new piece of equipment for one of his construction companies or a complicated machine for one of his factories. Sharps prided himself on his ability to judge equipment, men, and women with exceptional acuity.

She was, it was plain to see, a remarkably attractive woman. Dark of hair and eye, she was olive-complected, with a full-lipped mouth that promised an infinite variety of sensual delights. Italian blood, he decided. Or maybe Spanish. Yes, Spanish. With roots going back to one of the survivors of the Spanish Armada who made it onto the Irish coast and implanted his dark seed in so many of those pale Irish and English maidens. Sharps allowed himself to dwell on the images he'd conjured up.

"You have been extremely well recommended," Vivian said politely. Her way of letting him know that otherwise he would not be sitting here drinking her Twinings tea and chewing on her delicate biscuits. She sat in a straight-backed chair, knees held primly together, erect and unyielding, her chin raised. But easy in her own skin. Sure of herself. "You will let me know when you want me to begin, Mr. Sharps?"

He shifted around in his chair, as if screwing himself into place. He was a solidly constructed man with powerful shoulders and large, strong hands. His head, shaved clean, gleamed in the soft light as if deliberately brought to a high gloss. His face was strong, a series of planes and aggressive thrusts, his eyes, set deep behind prominent cheekbones, were tilted slightly, in reminder of some Oriental ancestor. A wide black mustache curling around the corners of his mouth added to that impression.

He had hoped she would simply enact her role according to the instructions earlier conveyed, make the visit, her performance and his own, natural and seamless. Real. Well, almost real. But it never went that way. Always there were these introductory moments, an almost romantic ritual played out for the woman's satisfaction, which was the last reason he had come. He swallowed the last of his biscuit and put his tea cup aside.

"Let's get on with it," he said in that edged, hard voice of his.

She stood up, her expression vaguely disapproving. "As you wish."

"You know what to do?"

"Really, Mr. Sharps, I'm a professional. I may improvise on the theme, but I know my job."

"Just making sure, is all. I want to get things right."

She undid the top two buttons of her loose white blouse, exposing a substantial portion of her full, heavy breasts. She worked her fingers through her hair, mussing it, and went to the entrance of the sitting room.

"If it's all right with you, Mr. Sharps, I'd suggest the love seat. It allows a little more freedom of movement and gets us away from the tea set. It has a certain sentimental value, and I wouldn't want it to get broken."

"Okay." He got himself situated on the love seat. A book lay on the end table, and he picked it up, opened it randomly, pretending to read.

"Perfect," she said. "Very well, to begin. It's late at night, quite late, much later than a girl my age ought to be out. I come padding into the house, all caution and quiet, and there you are, dear old dad, still awake, much to my chagrin, reading a book. . . . Here we go."

The familiar constriction had already come into his throat. He was able only to nod and watch as she removed her shoes, advanced tentatively into the room. He lowered his eyes to the book, the words on the page a blur.

"Oh!" she cried in mock alarm. "Daddy! I thought you'd be in bed by now, asleep."

He readied himself, comfortable in the role. He snapped the book shut and put it aside. "Where the hell have you been? It's three o'clock in the morning."

"Is it really that late? Guess I lost track of the time. I'm sorry, Daddy. I'll just get on to bed, then. Good night, Daddy." She came to his side, planting a quick kiss on the top of his head. Her breasts, so full and reminiscent, fell forward inside the white blouse.

He spoke to her in a voice harsh and laced with an anger born in another time, another place. "Look at you, dammit! Wandering around half-naked in the night. What the hell do you think you're doing?"

"Oh, Daddy, just having fun. Dancing, that sort of thing."

"Don't lie to me. Look at you, about to come out of your blouse."

She clutched the fabric over her chest and ducked her head, girlish and repentant. "We can talk in the morning, if you like."

"We'll talk right now. Don't tell me dancing. Who were you with?"

"A boy I know. A nice boy. We were talking, and I guess I lost track of the time."

"Talking."

"Right outside. In his car, just talking."

"You expect me to believe . . . out there? In the street? Parked in a car with a strange man. Acting like—you're becoming a slut!"

"It wasn't that way."

"Like your mother."

"Nothing happened."

"Don't lie to me. I can tolerate almost anything except your lies. What did he do to you? You allowed him to kiss you? Well, didn't you?"

"Just a kiss or two, there's no harm—"

He slapped her and sent her spinning to the floor. The blow, though expected, surprised her by its force.

"Hey," she protested. "Not so hard. That was the agreement, not so hard."

"Kisses and what else? Did he touch you? Where did he touch you? I want the truth."

She was on her feet, her cheek crimson, her blouse hanging open, her breasts exposed. She went on with the performance. Always the professional, proud of her work.

"All right, if you really must know. Yes, he touched me. I wanted him to touch me."

"Where?"

"My titties." The word amused her, made her want

to laugh, but she was respectful of the rules of the game and intended to play out her role in it. "He touched my titties." She struck a pose in front of him, without defiance, every line of her body imploring him for understanding, forgiveness, begging him to expiate her sins.

"Like this, he touched you like this?" His hand went onto her breast, kneading her flesh, feeling for her nipple.

Her eyes rolled shut and her head swung back and a small moan sounded deep in her throat.

"A daughter of mine," he said hoarsely. "Acting like a whore. Is this what you let him do?"

"He wouldn't stop. I knew it was wrong, evil, but I couldn't stop him."

"You didn't want to stop him, like your mother. No discipline. No sense of right and wrong. Then what did he do?"

A sob and a tear; a real tear. "He touched me here."

She sank to the floor, putting her hand between her legs, prayerful and abject.

"You dirty bitch!" He took hold of her dark hair and pulled her over onto her back. He slammed his hand against her vagina, rough and hurtful.

"Easy, luv," she admonished.

"He played with you! You let him play with you!"

She made it back up to her knees, a look of defiance on her finely featured face. "Yes, yes. I let him do whatever he wanted to do."

"Bitch!"

"I touched him."

"What?"

"Yes, I touched him down there. Like this." Her

hand came down on Sharps's penis, fingers closing tightly.

"No!" he cried in anguish.

"Yes, I did it. And I rubbed it."

She stroked him with consummate firmness and skill. He groaned and fell back on the love seat.

"And then what happened?"

"I don't want to tell you any more."

"You will tell me, you must."

"You can't make me."

"The hell I can't!" He dragged her, hands rough and insistent, across his knees. He raised her skirt, exposing her neat, round bottom. He spanked her. Harder and harder. "You will tell me everything."

"Hey! Easy goes. You are hurting me."

He kept pounding at her.

She broke his grip and made it back onto the floor, jerking around to face him. "Okay, you want to know what I did. What I wanted to do. What I loved doing and what I pray he'll let me do again? I sucked him. I put him in my mouth and sucked him just the way he liked it. With my lips soft and my tongue caressing him. I sucked him till he came."

"No!" Sharps cried. He was on his feet, fumbling with his belt, his fly, dropping his trousers. "You didn't!"

"I did, Daddy darling. I kissed it like this. And licked it like this. And then I sucked it like this. . . ."

Sharps, unable to speak, his jaw clenched against the battering sense of self-revulsion, the unbearable horror of what he was allowing to happen to him, fell back on the love seat, helpless before her raw need.

Watching her head bob up and down over him, seeing himself disappear into her mouth.

"Oh, don't," he muttered. "Don't stop. Please don't."

Nor did she, until he was finished.

Back at his hotel, Sharps showered, letting the steaming water wash over his skin, soaping up and scrubbing with a stiff brush, scraping the scent of the woman away. Only when he felt clean again did he rinse off. He dried himself and donned a white robe made of toweling material, courtesy of the hotel. In the living room of the suite, he mixed himself a drink—Absolut vodka and orange juice. He took a long swallow when the phone began to ring. He let it ring and drank again. Whoever it was needed Sharps more than he needed them.

4

*D*EVLIN bought the blue Jeep in Chicago, along with a set of racks for the roof. He located an army-navy store and bought some good, practical ski clothes. A couple of sets of long underwear, wool socks, and a heavy sweater; plus a first-rate body suit made out of nylon and spandex—jet black. None of it was very fancy, without designer labels and the higher prices that went along with them. A navy watch cap for his head and a pair of well-made ski gloves.

Chicago. How much it had changed since last he had visited. The year of the Democratic convention, 1968. What a tumultuous time it had been. High on grass most of the time, hardly ever sleeping. Attending meetings, seminars, concocting strategies that would achieve their political ends. End the war in Vietnam.

Bring the troops home. Elect a president who would truly have the people's interests at heart. When he closed his eyes he could hear the incessant din of the chanting crowds in the parks and in the streets, students, most of them. And the legions of Mayor Daley's cops wearing helmets and swinging clubs.

"Pigs!" is what they called the cops. "Pigs!" Trying to make them seem less than human, despicable creatures not worthy of respect, not capable of decency. "Pigs!" All their enemies were pigs, while they, the young people, were honorable and righteous, making the Second American Revolution, makers of a new world.

He recalled the oaths they had hurled at the cops. And the pretty, docile girls in granny glasses and long dresses had whispered to the men in blue about love, about lovemaking, about peace. And had offered the cops sandwiches made of human excrement.

What fools they had been. What naive and too often insidious fools. What had they hoped to accomplish? That didn't happen until four years later, and it was Richard Milhous Nixon, mortal enemy of the youth of America, who finally pulled off that trick. He said he had a plan to end the war, a plan that took four years to implement. Four years and all those deaths. And when the end did come, it was chaotic, mindless, death-giving, and vicious. Devlin knew all about it because he had been there. Hammering with his rifle butt at the frantic, frightened Vietnamese who struggled to climb aboard those last choppers.

Chicago in sixty-eight and 'Nam; impossible to reconcile the two. Idealism. Hope. Dreams of a better world had taken him to Chicago. What was it that carried him to 'Nam? Bitterness. Frustration. Guilt over all those who died while he was safe at home. Or was it simply his knees?

Those knees.

Those skier's knees.

He refused to contemplate his knees. Not now, not ever, if he could help it. There was too much pain attached, real and fancied.

He turned his thoughts back to that earlier Chicago. To the campuses he had demonstrated on and the cities he had marched in. To the speeches made, the songs sung, the girls he had loved. No, not love. Very little of that. Lust is what he'd been full of, lust and the need to run up a score, to prove how much of a man he was away from the slopes, without skis.

And all of it, the talking, the marching, the bravado; what had they accomplished? Except divide the country. Cause the deaths of a lot of people, foreign and domestic. And spread sufficient grief around to last a couple of generations.

Some revolution. A chance to sound off. To get off on adolescent rage. To get laid and get high. As if drugs offered any kind of an answer for the problems that existed. Drugs; the way he figured it, they had killed more Americans than the VC. And when they didn't kill, they ruined lives, innocent and guilty without preference.

Power to the people!

Sure.

Power to the same people who'd held it and wielded it before all the Sturm und Drang.

Some revolution.

Damn 'Nam. Sounded like the title of a bad rock

song. The memory of it was a never-ending pain. The
madness he'd encountered "In Country." The pur-
poselessness. The killing. Battling desperately to conquer a nameless, numbered hill one day, giving it up
the next, and fighting your way up again a few days
later. Advance and retreat, advance and retreat. Was
that any way to fight a war?

Driving west to Colorado in the blue Jeep listening
to Rodney Crowell wail on the radio. An aging country
rocker, mellowing out in song and style. That was
Devlin's way. "Many a Long and Lonesome Highway," a lament for his dying father, struck an emotional response in Devlin; he too had lost his father.
Something else best not thought too much about.

Nothing made much sense to him anymore. Peace
protestor to gung ho rifleman. Spraying the impenetrable green jungle with his M-14, snapping branches off
the trees, stitching the tropical underbrush with bullets. Hoping to hell he'd hit one of them. One of the
enemy. Where was the enemy? he used to ask silently
of himself.

Who is the enemy? He still wanted to know.

He had enlisted in the winter of 1970, and three
months later he was in 'Nam. Fresh meat for a squad
pretty much decimated by a VC ambush only three
days earlier. Nobody spoke to him. Nobody asked his
name. Nobody wanted to know his name. It was expected he would do his job until some slopehead took
him down. He would die alone and unmourned, unknown to any of his fellow soldiers.

Close, but no cigar. He made it all the way back to
the world, reasonably intact, marked by a scar from
an AK-47 slug along his left hip and carrying a Purple

Heart and a Silver Star in his duffel. He lost the medals in a crap game two days after returning to the States. The scar was his for life.

The knees did it. Steering the blue Jeep up a gradual incline on Route 82, heading into Independence Pass, he put the blame on his knees. The knees had propelled him to 'Nam. Not patriotism, surely. Not some sudden love of battle. No deep and private need to prove his manhood to himself. None of that; just the knees.

As if by punishing himself he punished most that part of himself that had been so vulnerable. So traitorous. So feeble in dispatching their duty. The knees had betrayed him when he most needed them. They deserved punishment. And eventually death.

Chicago and the Jeep. They brought back too many memories; mostly empty, mostly bad. Until he made it up into the Rocky Mountains, into the thin clean air and the pristine vistas, the high peaks already capped with white. He imagined ridges and peaks and ranges beyond the first one, gentle valleys, long, rigorous hills defying men like himself to ride them all the way down. How good it would be to strap the skis on again. To hit the slopes. To come alive in his heart in that special way that only skiing could bring about. He pressed down on the accelerator, and the blue Jeep leaped ahead toward Aspen and the joys that awaited him, 7,908 perfect white feet above the World.

This time everything was going to be all right.

In New York City, Geneva Sharps lunched at La Grenouille. A business lunch, some might have called it. A clutch of wives, the wives of very successful, very important businessmen-husbands. The Ball Committee of the Organization to Sustain Unwanted Children (OSUC). The ball, an elaborate affair designed to raise a few hundred thousand dollars for "their girls," as the members of OSUC liked to call the children. All the tickets had been sold, all the money had been raised, they were told over lunch, to polite but sustained applause.

A light lunch, as usual. A fragment of lemon sole. The vegetable plate. A small salad, dressing on the side. The women oohed and aahed over the presentation; the colors, green and orange and white. And Perrier and a wedge of lime. That was the sort of lunch it was, in keeping with the meticulously kept slender bodies of the ladies. Geneva yearned for a couple of lamb chops but chose not to confront this season's culinary convention.

Lunch over, she went shopping on Madison Avenue. A half dozen pairs of pumps in various colors from Henriques. Two cashmere turtlenecks at the Sweater Lounge. A pair of tan driving gloves from the Leather Loft. An hour in the art galleries, looking but not buying. By five o'clock she was ready to meet Lulu Henderson, her most recent best friend.

Geneva ran best friends in and out of her life like trains into Grand Central Terminal. Each had her chance, each was allotted a specific slice of her existence, until each wore out her welcome. Geneva had a brief tolerance for other people's shortcomings, for their idiosyncrasies, for their bursts of independent action and thought. She looked for perfection in people, as in objects—paintings, clothing, automobiles—and was inevitably disappointed.

When she first encountered Duncan Turner Sharps, Geneva believed he was perfect. Exotic to look at, a swift, brilliant mind, and much wealthier than any man she had ever met before. He seemed ideally suited for her, able to provide for all her needs and desires for the rest of her life.

How disappointing he'd proved to be. In so many different ways. Duncan had grown into an unbearable burden. Ponderous. Odious. Fearful. No matter how far from home he kept himself. His not-to-be-ignored presence on earth irritated and worried Geneva, knowing that he might appear with neither warning nor reward, superseding her plans, her social obligations, imposing his wishes on her, demanding her time and physical presence without regard to her preference. He issued orders like a drill instructor, expecting immediate obedience. He directed insults her way, an art that he had brought to a high and painful degree.

She preferred Duncan away rather than at home. Distance, at least, brought some tranquillity and a modicum of freedom to her life. Although she understood that her activities and whereabouts were often under scrutiny by his employees and paid spies.

Suzanne Brody, for example. The Wicked Witch of the East, was how Geneva characterized her. Duncan's executive assistant, his right hand, his close associate, his most dependable employee. Pared down to the bone, Geneva viewed her as being bloodless, sexless, all efficiency and dedication in Sharps's service. Suzanne Brody gave femininity a bad name.

Geneva loathed her. Loathed all of the life she lived. The world of badly prepared meals in chic, overpriced restaurants, of mean-spirited gossip and all that empty work for charities that had a life of their own in the grasping hands of professional fund-raisers, who, in the end, she was sure, pocketed most of the money raised.

Most of all Geneva loathed Duncan Turner Sharps.

Lulu Henderson, on the other hand, she found tolerable. Lulu was slight and weightless in appearance and intellect; a diverting sight in a bathing suit with that ridged, bony chest and scrawny arms and thighs that failed to meet, no matter how protectively she clasped her legs together.

Lulu looked better in clothes. By Armani and Calvin Klein ("I just adore dear Calvin"), by an Italian woman named Gina and a Dutchman named Kurtt. Suitably concealed in expensive clothing, her body masked off from view, Lulu was almost pretty, in a pointed, mousy sort of way. And almost clever. Which suited Geneva much more than those fraudulent intellectuals who completed her roster of friends.

Lulu discussed her husband, whom she was crazily in love with. Her two children, whom she was crazily in love with, the town house they had just purchased in the east sixties, which she was crazily in love with. By the time they parted, Geneva had her fill of affection and the salutary effect of love on the human digestive tract.

She hurried over to Third Avenue to a bar with a green neon shamrock flickering in the front window. Inside, the greasy scent of cheap cuts of corned beef and brisket brought sentient memories of her childhood, of her parents and the constant struggle for money that guided their mutual existences. Those were not the best of times, and she excluded the memories from her consciousness with practiced dispatch. At a table midway along, she found the man she was looking for. Massive of head and shoulder, he sat hunched over a ham on rye bread, dripping mustard, and drinking from a tall glass filled with beer.

"Mr. Shipley," she began.

He remained in his chair, mouth crowded with food, managing somehow to make himself understood. "Mrs. Sharps," he said with a certain amount of deference. "You want I should order you some food or something?"

"No, thank you. I don't have a great deal of time, Mr. Shipley . . ." The scent of the greasy meat made her slightly faint, gave her a headache. Or perhaps it was Mr. Shipley, his shirt in need of changing, his tie stained by unknown comestibles earlier consumed. "If we can get to business . . ."

"Sure, I get it." He slid a large manila envelope across the table. "In here is contained the official reports of my field operatives. Plus some pictures, photographs of the subject male and one or two of the subject male's encounters with certain named females, which we have identified. There's also an audiotape which is very unique and explicit, if you catch my meaning."

"I believe I do."

"You got a lock on this one, Mrs. Sharps. All the evidence you need that would stand up in a court of law."

"Where?" she said.

"What? Oh, where? There was the last encounter in London, England. Another in Rome, Italy. In Milan, which is also in Italy. And Geneva, Switzerland. That last one, it's kinda funny, wouldn't you say? Geneva being your name and all. The one in London, I got to tell you, Mrs. Sharps. The subject male has got a few games I've never before run into, if you catch my meaning."

"Will it be necessary to continue the surveillance, Mr. Shipley?"

"I certainly enjoy doing business with you, Mrs. Sharps. The money's swell and you're pretty easy on the eyes. But to tell the truth, you got it all. Anything else is gonna be more of the same."

She nodded and took out her checkbook. "I think you'll find this covers everything."

He shoved himself erect, wiping his mouth with a paper napkin. He offered her his huge, fleshy hand in a fleeting handshake.

"Nice doing business with you, Mrs. Sharps," he said to her back as she hurried away, the manila envelope clutched to her breast.

Peggy Pearce looked him over. Those round violet eyes were unafraid, penetrating, lingering here and there until satisfied with what she had seen. It was a test. He was being probed, body and mind, nothing left untouched, nothing unexamined. He was almost disappointed when she failed to ask for his vital statistics.

"Henry Ricketts," she crooned in a voice that caressed and at the same time stoked his resentment. "People call you that, Henry?"

There was a nastiness to the way she made it sound. As if something were wrong with him, with his name, some built-in flaw he'd never be able to correct. All of it said with a buttery spread of a smile. "Hank," he said, a little more aggressively than he intended. "Call me Hank." She was one hell of a good-looking woman, and stacked. How long would it take to turn her on?

She spoke without haste. Relaxed in a booth along the west wall of the Sunset Tavern. She had insisted that they meet without Evan Larson present, establishing her own preeminence in the situation. She drank coffee out of a mug, he worked on a Jack Daniel's with water on the side. He smoked, nervously and too much, she thought. She made no wasted motion, her eyes steady and measuring.

"Mr. Larson," she said, "tells me you're a good man, Hank. Experienced. Smart. Dependable. With balls of pure brass."

That made him feel better. Relaxed. Compliments, with a built-in bedtime message. That placed them on the same ground, all even. Partners-to-be. "Pure brass and big," he boasted, looking into those violet eyes, putting her on notice of who he was, what he was. Women like Peggy Pearce, they always got the message. A fullness in his crotch, growing bigger; he reached down to shift himself into a more comfortable position. Dress right, dress!

She saw the gesture. Read him loud and clear. All alike, these men, brains dangling between their legs. Each convinced he was the subject of every woman's wildest sexual fantasies. If he only knew. If *they* only knew. But she wasn't going to disillusion him. Much too early for that. Let him revel in his dreams, build up his hopes, place himself willingly at her service. Time enough for him to learn the truth of their connection later on.

Not that he wasn't attractive. One of those golden

boys, eternally tan, forever youthful. His eyes were
sky blue and crinkled only a little at the corners,
enough to make it interesting. His hair was golden, too
golden, the color found in some drugstore bottle. All-
American boy. Superficial and not nearly as smart as
he thought he was; God's gift. Keep thinking it, pal.
Keep sniffing around; as long as you obeyed orders.

"Okay," she said. "Now I know, you're smart and
you're brave."

He missed the irony. "You got it, Peg."

She disliked the diminutive. All right for now, but
in time she'd put him right about that, about all of it.

"Mr. Larson say what this was all about?"

"He said you'd explain."

"House jobs."

"Ah," he said, as if the heavenly light of wisdom had
broken over him.

"Rich people's houses. I am talking big rich."

"Good." He made it sound as if he'd given the project a great deal of thought, come to a profound decision.

"Jewelry, mostly. Cash, where we find it. Silver.
Small items, mostly."

"Fur coats? Those kind of people—"

"Fur coats."

"Paintings. People like that, they put a lot of dough
into art. I am talking about millions . . ."

It was time to lay down the ground rules. "No paintings. They're too hard to deal. If they're worth a lot,
then everybody knows who owns them. You can only
sell them on consignment, and we're not into that. So
we leave them be. Nobody is going to get rich in a sin-

gle shot, Hank, that must be understood and agreed to from day one."

"Sure," he answered slowly. Things would change, he assured himself; nothing stayed the same. The important part of this was it put him back in play, in the middle of the game. Later he'd take over, do things his way. "Whatever you say, Peg."

"What we're discussing is, I'm talking about steady work. A long-term project. Jobs done at carefully selected intervals."

"And you do the selecting?"

He was catching on. "I do."

"Always?"

"I'm open to suggestions. But the final decision is mine. Any objections to that arrangement?"

"Me? No. Not a one."

"Bother you working for a woman?"

"Why should it?"

"You'd be working *for* me. I say where. I make the plans. I say when. And I make the payoffs."

"As long as I get my share, fair and square."

"You will." A look of indecision came onto his face, and she responded immediately. "You've got a problem, Hank. Okay, let's have it."

"Two people, you think that'll cut it? I mean, I'd say we need a couple of more recruits. Another inside man and a driver, unless you're coming along."

"I'll provide information. Floor plans. Timing. Everything goes off like clockwork."

"When I go in on a job, I like to have some muscle at my back."

"Unless it's unavoidable, no violence."

"Oh, I'm with you. But better safe than sorry." He

gave her his best, most winning grin. "Never hurts to have a friend who can throw his weight around."

"No weapons," Peggy cautioned. "No guns, no knives, nothing."

"I agree. Just some tough guy to protect my back."

"I'll discuss it with Larson."

"I know a guy perfect for the job."

She considered the suggestion. She'd hoped to enlist three men previously unknown to each other. Men of separate interests who would never form an alliance to oppose her. But Ricketts was right, they needed some muscle. Just in case. Still . . .

"Somebody reliable?" she said.

"You can depend on this character. A hard rock. I worked with him from time to time. We traveled around together. We skied together. . . ."

"Okay, when can I talk to him?"

"All it takes is a phone call."

"Make it, then. I haven't got all day."

Sam Daly debated over whether or not to pick up the telephone. He let it ring, watching it with considerable foreboding. As if it were a creature alive and dangerous. Curry, he told himself. Or one of his henchmen. Trying to determine if he was still in town. Once he answered, they'd be on their way. Tough guys with unforgiving manners. Beat him to a pulp, they would, or even kill him, if Curry was sore enough.

No matter. In a couple of hours he'd be out of here, and they'd never catch up with him. No way they could know what his plans were. Which way he was going or by what means. His bag was packed, and he was ready to move. A few more minutes and he'd be gone.

Let 'em know how close they came, and missed. Guys like Curry always fell short when they went up against guys like Sam Daly.

He picked up the phone. "Yeah?"

"That you, Sam?"

The voice was familiar. "Who wants him? I think he's already left." Why take chances.

"Sam, that you? It's Hank Ricketts."

He recognized the voice. "Hank, this is a bad time, Hank. I'm about to split out of here."

"Got a problem?"

"No problem. Just enough of Denver. Why you calling?"

"I'm on to something good. A steady lineup of jobs that should pay real well."

"Nah. Like I said, I'm out of here."

"In Aspen, Sam. Plenty of good skiing. Plenty of cooze, all easy pickings."

"The two of us?"

"There's this woman. She cases the targets, sets it all up."

"You know her for a long time?"

"She's good. Would I tell you wrong, Sam? Evan Larson's involved at this end, remember Evan?"

"Yeah. I don't know. I'm booked out of here in a couple of hours."

"We can talk about it, can't we? We can get together at the airport, have a cup of coffee, kick it around. You don't like the setup, you're on your way. Otherwise, we hit the high country and fun and games. Remember the ball we had that season in Lake Placid?"

"Yeah, that was okay. All right, the airport. In one hour exactly."

"Exactly."

Arlen "Red" Hamilton, senior senator from the state of Colorado, sat in his champagne-colored Datsun 280-Z, on the street adjoining the athletic field. The grandstand was shabby, and the field itself was in need of resodding. Not that Hamilton gave a damn; he had voted against every education bill that had come along during his eleven years in the United States Senate.

He filled the cab of the Datsun, a large, well-fed man with a great round paunch and thick, silvery hair of which he was inordinately proud. Once he had been thin, solidly constructed, and his hair had been a rich coppery tone. All that was in the distant past, though many of his friends still called him "Red."

They began pouring out of the school, students anxious to put academics behind them. The boys full of swagger. The girls; had the girls been as beautiful and as sexually provocative when he was in high school? He thought not. Great looking, every one of them. What in God's name did they feed them nowadays? All those delectable young tits, all those sweet round asses. . . .

The human traffic thinned out, most of the students gone on their way. They came out of the school now in pairs. Or alone. In no hurry, these. As if they departed their classrooms reluctantly. A girl came his way. Tall, splendidly proportioned, able to pass for an older woman. He watched her come and go. Not at all what he had in mind.

The next one was exactly right. Had she been made to order, she couldn't have been improved upon. Barely over five feet tall, with a tight, compact body on display in jeans worn tight over the hips and a glistening red baseball jacket. Her cheeks were flushed from the chill air, and her eyes glittered. Her mouth . . . oh, her mouth. Lips slightly parted and wide, just wide enough. She was within six feet of the Datsun and about to pass on, when he spoke.

"Hello . . ."

She paused, gazing at him without apprehension. "Oh, hi. I know you?"

"Not really. I hoped we might remedy that."

She nibbled her lip. Sweet lip, so young and full. He was mesmerized by the way her mouth moved when she spoke. "They warned us about strange men hanging around the school. . . ." There was a sly light in her eye.

He cleared his throat. The nearness of her youth and half-formed beauty made him faint with excitement. He longed to tell her of his confused emotions, of the images that crowded his mind, the things he wanted to do. To her. He said only, "I've seen you before."

"Oh."

"So in a way, we're not strangers."

She held her ground. "You're funny."

"I am?"

"Not ha-ha funny. Different funny."

She considered her next course of action and took a step, a single, tentative step. But she did not leave. "Different is not necessarily bad," he said, a pleading note in his voice.

"You do this often, hang around school? Trying to pick up girls?"

"You don't understand. The point is, I noticed you. What an incredibly attractive young woman, I thought. I wondered what you were like. So I spoke to you. Is that so wrong?" She made no reply, and he rushed ahead. "Am I making you nervous?" Any emotion would be acceptable, any emotion could be exploited.

She took a step closer to the Datsun. If she felt nervous, it didn't show. "What do you want?"

"You get to be my age, you wonder about young people. What they're like today, I mean. So different than when I was your age. What's your name?"

"Judith," she said easily.

Encouraged, he said his name was Charles.

She smiled, full of disbelief, a delightful spread of those luscious lips, a show of teeth strong and straight. She had never needed braces, not this one.

"Charles is not your real name." She was challenging him.

"Does it really matter?"

"What are you after, Charles?" Said as if she knew, *knew,* the answer, as if she had penetrated to those dark, shameful recesses of his being. As if she understood his every bent need, those sinful needs.

He swallowed before he spoke. Ached with longing and the need to speak of that longing, to tell her bluntly and crudely what he yearned to do to her. Not quite yet. He said in a diffident voice, "Care to go for a little drive? It's a nice day, and—"

There was fire and temperament in her eyes. "A ride with you? In your car?"

He could only nod, mute and miserable before her.

"I don't think I can trust you, Charles." Another smile, a sweet taunt. "A girl like me, a young girl. And you a grown man. Mature. Big. Strong, I'll bet. You've really been around, I'll bet. Are you famous, Charles? I mean, is that why you won't tell me your real name? I think you must be famous. And rich, that Z really costs. Are you famous, Charles?"

"That's for me to know and you to find out."

She'd never heard it before and laughed with innocent delight. "That's good. I have to remember it." She repeated it, getting it right the first time. "Tell me your real name, Charles. Show me your ID. You show me yours and I'll show you mine."

He opened the door on the passenger side. "Get in."

She slid in beside him, cheerful and charged with the spirit of adventure. "Where are you taking me, Charles? Some place quiet and private, right? You got a spot all picked out?"

He got the Z started and under way.

"If you don't have a good place," she said as he turned into the first street that would take them away from the school, "I know exactly where to go. . . ."

Silver!

BY 1876 Colorado became a state, part of the inexorable Manifest Destiny of the United States. Three years after that a group of prospectors pitched their tents around a spring frequently used by the Indians. A baker's dozen of them began to scratch at the earth, hunting for silver, staking their claims as if the mountains were theirs to be taken and violated.

The Utes watched. And were dismayed by what they saw. Trees were cut down. Ugly gashes were inflicted upon the sacred land. Game was killed with wasteful efficiency, and those not killed were frightened away. Around the campfires of the Utes the alarm was sounded. Their future as a people looked bleak unless something was done to put an end to this desecration of the mountains in which they lived.

The young warriors attacked and killed eleven white men. Later they ambushed an army patrol. Word of these "massacres" seeped down out of the mountains along with the news that silver had indeed been discovered in the high land. Politicians and press lords, millionaires and those who hungered to become millionaires, grew agitated at these cowardly attacks on the free enterprise system. They cried out in protest against the savagery of the Indians, they made speeches claiming that this was war, pure and simple, against the flag, and all that was good and true in Western civilization. They demanded the government take steps to put the matter right. Kill the Utes, was the cry heard across the land. Extract vengeance from the "heathens" who prevented "real Americans" from getting on with the "Lord's real work."

"The Utes must go!"

And go they did. By force, by deceit, by the power of numbers and the repeating rifle. There was silver to be dug out. Honest toil by honest men. Fortunes to be made and reputations enhanced.

Rich men bought up every claim available and discovered ways of acquiring many that were not available. The business of America was business. No small band of Indians, no single, stubborn miner, could be allowed to stand in the way.

More men came. Powerful men with lots of money and a politician or two in their pockets, insisting on their share of the silver pie. Tough men, motivated by ambition and greed, inventive and amoral. That is, they were claim jumpers.

Shafts were thrust into the mountain. Tunnels were dug. The ore was brought forth in one-hundred-pound balls, wrapped in protective covers made of cowhide, and rolled down the steep slopes. Donkey trains carried the ore to Leadville.

Six years later the Denver & Rio Grande Railroad put a spur up into the rugged high country, and the small community could now claim easy access to the outside world. A man named Clark Wheeler, a man with a good eye for the way things should be, came along. He took a long look at all the trees and their trembling leaves and saw that as an omen of things to come. He renamed the town. He called it Aspen.

5

GENEVA was glad when Sharps arrived home. Not pleased to see him, but anxious to talk to him. She meant to deliver the message face to face. Eye to eye. See his reaction, revel in the surprise he would feel, the shock and dismay. Shake the sonofabitch up, more than a little. That was her intention.

Sharps was an impressive figure, larger than life. Self-absorbed and icily contained. She thought of him as a primal force of nature, leaving uprooted the trees of life in swaths of desolation, always untouched by the havoc and pain and suffering he caused. All his life Sharps had listened only to the demonic inner voices that propelled him on his way, as if he alone mattered. All persons and objects who failed to measure up, who

failed to provide profit or immediate gratification, all
who opposed him, were swept away. Human beings
were of scant concern to Sharps; random creatures to
be used and abused, devoured or destroyed, when
they stood in the path of his self-serving juggernaut.
All that would come to an end, at least as far as it concerned Geneva.

He announced that he'd be out for dinner. "Business," he told her, as if that resolved all questions,
ended all doubts. He shaved, carefully around the mustache that gave him an exotic, ominous look, then
showered. Back in the apartment less than an hour and
on the move again. A perpetual-motion machine.
Drawing on an inexhaustible supply of energy, never
sagging, never showing weakness. That was his way,
to keep going, tenacious and irresistible, wearing
down his competitors, his enemies, to outlast them all,
always to survive. In the end, to triumph.

"I need to talk to you," Geneva said. She watched
him dress himself. He was meticulous about his
clothes, about his appearance. He presented an elegance in public, and in private he offered the casual
vulgarisms of a men's locker room.

"Let it the fuck wait."

He worked a silk jacquard tie into the collar notch
of his Turnbull & Asser shirt. White collar and cuffs
to match, each with three pearl buttons. The body of
the shirt was striped in muted lavender and purple,
a thin line of black every few inches. He slipped into
his suit jacket. Double-breasted wool in a nailhead pattern, with peaked lapels. Tailored especially for
Sharps by a master tailor in Rome, only a few steps
from the American embassy.

"It can't wait," Geneva insisted.

He shot his cuffs and eyed his wife, whom he had not seen in nearly a month. He smoothed his mustache.

"All right, let's have it, if it's so important."

She went into the dining room and he went after her. She seated herself and he took a chair an arm's length away. She slid the manila envelope in front of him.

"You may want to look at that."

"Whatever it is, I don't have a lot of time for games. So spit it out, what's on your mind?"

"I want a divorce, Duncan."

He stood up and buttoned his jacket. "Fuck that noise." He was in motion again, on his way out.

"I mean it, Duncan," she said in a low, firm voice. "Our marriage is a disaster in every way. Certainly we're not in love. We don't like each other very much. There's no reason for us to be together anymore."

He pulled up and turned to face her. The downward pull of his mustache appeared to bring his other features along, sullen and brooding, chin sinking almost to his chest. "We seldom are, in case you haven't noticed."

"It can be civilized, amicable . . ."

He turned again to leave.

"Please, Duncan. Look at what's in the envelope."

"I don't give a shit what's in the envelope. Doesn't mean diddly to me. There's gonna be no divorce, not now, not ever."

"Why?"

"Because it's in my best interest to have a wife at this time in my life, and you're as good as any." His small eyes glittered, his lips thinned out. He was bored with this pointless exchange.

She gestured toward the envelope. "I've had you under surveillance, Duncan. For months detectives have been watching you. Here and abroad." She withdrew the thick, typewritten report and the photographs, dropped them all on the table. He showed no interest. "I won't go on living this way, Duncan. I'm not your private property. I won't tolerate—"

"Shut up!" he bit off.

"You don't own me."

"The hell I don't. Bought and paid for."

"I am going to hire a lawyer, sue for divorce. Cruelty. Adultery. Incompatibility. Those pictures prove—"

He hit her then, with an open hand, sending her sprawling to the floor, legs askew. Shaken, pained more by the blow to her dignity than the force of the slap.

"You bastard!"

She was halfway up when he hit her again. Once, twice, putting her back on the floor, eyes beginning to tear, her ear and cheek stinging.

"There's gonna be no divorce. No fucking lawyer. What you'll do is whatever I tell you to do. Here it is. Get yourself packed, you are leaving for Aspen in the morning. Open the house. Get it cleaned. Ready for me when I get there. When it's all done, then you can put your ass up on the mountain and ski your way down. Ski. Skate. Sulk. Doesn't matter what. As for a divorce, you can just forget all about that."

She made it up to her feet, confronting him with fire and temperament in her eyes. "You can't stop me. Unless you kill me, and you're not going to do that. I will file. I will get a divorce. I will make you pay—"

This time he hit her with his clenched fist. The punch landed on her right breast, and swift circles of anguish went pulsing down into her body. She stumbled backward, but he shuffled after her with the smooth aggressiveness of a good welterweight. A left rocked her head, and a short right hand put her back on the floor. He studied her for a second, then kicked her with the point of his brown suede walking shoe, handmade off a special last by a Milanese bootmaker. She rolled, certain that at last he intended to do her mortal harm, her back to him. Another kick landed on her thigh.

"Tomorrow," he husked out, his breathing noisy. "Tomorrow before noon. You're out of here. Otherwise . . ."

She remained on the floor for a long time, locating the primary sources of her pain. Checking to see if anything was broken. Convinced no permanent damage had been done, she made it into her bathroom, where she stripped off her clothing and inspected her reflection in the mirror. Bruises had already begun to form on her cheek, her breast, her thigh. A thin moan of despair dribbled out of her, and she stumbled back into the bedroom.

She began to pack. Warm clothes, clothes suitable for the high cold air of Aspen. How long, she wondered through the pain, before she would be fit to ski again? At the same time, she made up her mind. Convinced of what she had to do. This time there was no doubt. No questions. No more second thoughts. Just work out the best way to do it, she told herself, the simplest, safest way. And get it done.

6

PEGGY Pearce made Devlin out to be a special man the first time she saw him. Even at a distance he had the look of a champion. She made the connection three days after she returned to Aspen.

Snow began falling that Sunday night and continued for seventy-six hours. Fat, slow-moving flakes that blanketed the Rocky Mountains and closed down Independence Pass; and by the time the snow stopped, a solid base for the skiers had been created. Word swept across the United States: Aspen was ready. Another ski season had begun.

The morning after the storm abated was bright and clear and shining, the mountains sheathed in white and unmarked. By eleven o'clock the lifts were in motion, and before long skiers were racing down the flanks

of the mountain. Peggy Pearce spotted Devlin just before noon. She had started her first run of the day
when the skier in black came *whoosh*ing by, leaving
her in his white-plumed wake. His form was perfect,
strong and controlled, his movements crisp, always
thrusting forward. Later she saw him again riding the
lift back up, and even in the chair, swinging gently, he
seemed an integral and essential part of the environment.

Two days later she saw him for the third time, wearing a shabby blue robe and rubbing his hair dry with
a bath towel, coming out of the hall bathroom in the
rooming house in Glenwood Springs. She introduced
herself, and they shook hands.

"I saw you on the mountain the other day," she said,
wanting him to know that she'd noticed him, wanting
him to know that she was impressed. "You ski real
good."

"Thanks." He was used to compliments about his
ability; but only he knew that he was merely a shadow
of his former self, his body mired in mediocrity while
his spirit still soared in the past. People were so easily
impressed with form, unaware that he rode those
sticks downhill on shaky underpinnings.

"All in black, right?" she added. Flatter him, make
him think—whatever it pleased him to think, as long
as things went her way. "You in competition?"

"Used to be." The direction of the conversation left
him melancholy, and he moved off toward his room.
Women; so many women. All sizes and shapes, all
complexions and ages, all nationalities. Ski groupies
crossed all boundaries in their need to get it on with
the top men of the mountains. This one, in a striped

body suit, was more beautiful than most. Dark hair and violet eyes provided a dramatic look, contained behind a protective scrim, as if she were consciously concealing some essential information about herself.

She trailed after him, allowing him a comfortable space cushion. "You're good," she said. "Better than anybody I've seen lately."

"Thanks again."

"You're new here." She said it hoping he would reveal more information about himself. He only nodded. She pressed on. "I was out of town for a few days. Guess you moved in while I was gone."

"Guess so." He was giving nothing away.

She assessed him openly. A big man, lean and inherently graceful, despite the small, stiff way he had of walking. A mincing walk, as if he were concerned he might step on something odorous or afraid of dealing himself a severe injury. She wondered about that. Men who skied with the kind of abandon he had shown on the mountain, they were seldom afraid of very much. What, she asked herself, made this guy go?

"I'm on my way to get some coffee." She looked up into his face. Those gray-green eyes, veiled and careful, searching for something. He was, she admitted grudgingly, even more impressive close up, despite a nose that could have been improved on. She flashed him her best smile. "Come on along. Unless you've got all the friends you need in Aspen?"

"I'll need a few minutes to get dressed."

"I'll wait."

She knew a place. Limited menu, but good food, tasty and not too expensive. He ordered the pea soup with bacon bits and a melted-cheese sandwich. "I don't have much time."

"Heavy date?"

He grinned, boyish and winning. "Just a job. I work at the Aspen Sports Association."

"Very fancy."

"Rich clients. High membership fees. Low salaries."

"Sounds typical."

"I need the paycheck."

"Don't we all. I clean houses." She decided that she'd have the pea soup, also. It was thick and well seasoned, and she crumbled some saltines into the bowl before she began spooning it into her mouth. "The thing is, Aspen's become a rich man's playground. People like us, ordinary people, working people, we can't even afford to rent a furnished room in Aspen. There's plenty of work, okay, but at the low end of the pay scale. Most people scout around for ways to earn an extra buck or two."

"So you're a housemaid?" he said.

"Not exactly." She explained how the cleaning service worked. What her role was. How she had frequent and unlimited access to the biggest, the best, homes in Aspen. "You'd be surprised at how careless some of those people are. They leave things around—jewelry, even cash—as if nobody would dare to rip them off."

"Maybe nobody would."

She attended her soup. "You know better than that."

"Good thing you're not so inclined."

"Maybe I'm not," she said.

"Not what?"

"Not as straight arrow as you seem to think."

He stirred his soup, eyes averted, determined to make no response. What the hell did she take him for? He was no virgin looking for his first score. Setting him up this way. Still, he was curious; and he conceded her a certain level of smarts. She had yet to reveal herself in any way that might be damaging.

"Soup's good," he said.

"There's better restaurants around town."

"There's better restaurants in every town."

"But expensive."

"Everything costs nowadays."

"The trick is to be able to get your hands on some money. Real money."

"Tell me about it," he drawled.

They ate without speaking until the soup in his bowl was almost gone. He drank some water as if to rid his mouth of the taste. She was watching him; he smiled.

"Over in Denver, I've got a connection," she said at last. "This man, he has many business interests. He buys things and sells them. All sorts of things. Cash on delivery."

"And no questions asked," he said quietly.

"No questions. No bills of sale. Just good old American money."

"Are you sure you've got the right guy?" he said conversationally.

She nodded once, still eyeing him in that speculative way she had. "Let's say—hypothetically, of course . . ."

"Of course."

"Let's say if somebody wanted to do it. A couple

of sharp characters, they could rip off a house in the morning and get rid of the stuff in Denver by the middle of the afternoon, be back in Aspen that same night, cash in hand."

He put the spoon in the bowl and pushed it away. He'd had enough.

She hunched forward, studying his reactions, talking swiftly, softly. "Let's say these guys had detailed plans of each house. Every step worked out. I am talking about houses that are unoccupied."

"What if they're not?"

"Guaranteed. Occupants out on the mountain for most of day. No alarm systems. Or one that can be quickly neutralized by an expert."

"If you happened to have an expert at hand."

"For the sake of this conversation, let's say such an expert was easily within reach. And another guy, equally experienced in this sort of work. A strong, hard guy."

"Muscle, you mean?"

"In and out in ten, maybe fifteen minutes at most. Very selective in what they help themselves to. Items easy to carry. Easily turned in to cash. Nothing that is too difficult to move."

"Sounds too good to be true, and when it sounds too good to be true, it usually is too good to be true."

She didn't crack a smile. "If you're afraid . . ."

"Only a fool doesn't know when to be afraid, and I'm not a fool. I don't know. It could all turn bad. Just one little thing goes wrong."

"Like what?"

"Like one of the marks—he puts a move on the mountain and the mountain fights back. Down he goes, all shaken up. He comes home early, along with his wife and the kiddies. There are your friends with their hands in the cookie jar."

Her laughter was meant to be disarming, full of assurance. "It could happen, I've considered it. But with a third man, a really good driver—someone nervy and patient . . ."

An ironic twist to his mouth, and he said, "Somebody with a Jeep."

"The vehicle of choice in these parts. The town is loaded with them. New ones, old ones, all colors. Means a fella could fade into the landscape, one of many."

"Ever done time, Peggy? I have. Oh, not important time, but enough. All time is hard time when you're inside. I am not going back."

"Nobody blames you for that."

"This expert of yours and the goon . . ."

"That's a harsh word."

"Santa's little helpers, if you prefer. You have to be able to trust them."

When she failed to respond to his little joke—not even a smile—his uneasiness increased. No sense of humor. People who couldn't laugh at themselves were often too smug, too confident of their infallibility, too dangerous. This situation, they were strangers, had met less than an hour ago, and here she was hitting on him for some B&E's. Didn't speak well for her discretion. Could be Peggy Pearce was the weak link in this operation, the flaw that would bring it all down on whomever she enlisted. "You see, there is always a problem."

She answered deliberately. "Hey, listen! I like that.

That you're on the cautious side. Careful, thorough, that's what's needed."

He couldn't help himself, that insatiable curiosity of his. He had to know more. "These two guys?"

"They're okay, I tell you. They come very well recommended. By the man in Denver."

"The fence?" She nodded and waited for his next objection. He was hungry, nibbling at the bait, doing a little dance of self-deception. "There are so many variables."

"Risks can be minimized."

"But not eliminated."

"I'd be lying if I said they could. I am talking about a clean operation. Well planned, well executed."

"These guys, they work? I mean, have they got straight jobs? Covers."

"One is a ski instructor over in Snowmass. The other a part-time bartender. Nobody lets go of the job. We are legitimate people. And after a score, nobody flashes the money around. Nobody keeps any of the take for himself or his girlfriend. By the way, you got a girl?"

"Nobody."

"Poor Dev." He had the sexuality, the vulnerability, of a movie star, leavened by an underlying shyness. She'd known many handsome men, good lovers, some of them; but there was something special about this one. "A person could put together a tidy little nest egg, Dev. A season up here, a job every once in a while. The numbers add up. Come spring, a person could be very well off."

He ran it through his mind, what she'd said, what she was offering. They were relative strangers, yet he felt he knew a great deal about her. She was smart, no doubt of that. And gutsy. Very few women would have been able to put together such a scheme, very few men, for that matter. And get this far with it. He approved of the way she was turned out. Not so much her looks as the way she presented herself. Stylish, but without flash. Hardly any makeup. Doing nothing to attract unnecessary attention. It was her fingernails that convinced him. They were the nails of a serious person. Buffed, but without coloring. Conservatively trimmed and clean. The nails of a woman convinced of her attractiveness, rejecting artificial aids. Everything in place. Well organized.

"Tell me again," he said. "Two men?"

"For the inside. One in the car."

"Where do you come in?"

"I come up with the houses. A floor plan. A schedule for the people. When they're in, when they're out. Where they put their stuff. What to look for. Nothing left to chance."

"One thing about these other guys—will they be carrying?"

"You mean weapons? Absolutely not. Brains and, if necessary, fists. Nothing else. Nothing can go wrong."

Devlin knew better than that. Murphy's law; if it could go wrong, it would go wrong. Nothing was foolproof. Nobody could anticipate every possibility. Still, the chance for some substantial amounts of easy money appealed to him. He needed a cushion until he could connect with another Barbara. Somebody not so calculating and remote. Somebody not so much like himself.

"Why me?" he said at last.

"You're a good man, I can tell."

"Don't be too sure."

"I'm not too sure. I'm never too sure. But I'm willing to take a chance. What about you? Try it one time. You can always back out."

"Without recriminations?"

"No problem."

He was sure he was making a mistake. But the temptation was too great, the possible rewards too glittering to turn down. She was offering so much that he wanted. So he took the bait in his mouth, along with the hook.

7

HE first call went to a Washington lawyer who functioned mainly as a lobbyist for the natural gas industry, the airlines industry, and the handgun industry. Known for his contacts and influence in the District of Columbia, this lawyer was frequently asked to perform services large and small—and always private—for political operatives who had fallen upon bad days. This was one of those days for the senior senator from the sovereign state of Colorado.

The call woke the lawyer, who, being an early riser, went to bed no later than ten o'clock each night. It was almost midnight when the call came. Naturally the Washington lawyer was irritated by this interruption of his slumber. Even angry, though he would never have admitted it. Presenting an even-tempered per-

sona to the world he inhabited was the lawyer's trade-
mark and, in his own view, one of the primary reasons
he had survived for so long in this nest of political vi-
pers.

The Washington lawyer struggled up from a very
pleasant dream to answer the senior senator's cry in
the night.

"Of course I know who this is," he answered, taking
a second or two to make a positive identification. "No,
of course I wasn't asleep," he lied graciously.

He was accustomed to such calls, used to the desperate notes and accents in each caller's voice. Politicians suffered from every one of the human foibles,
plus a few refinements on each theme. Trouble in one
form or another drew them like iron filings to a magnet
and, if the force field was not surgically removed, ter-
minated their careers in despair and disgrace. Men deserved better, the Washington lawyer believed.

"I got a problem, Fritz," the senior senator whispered into the phone.

As if he were the only one, the Washington lawyer
reflected. Politicians were up to their elbows in problems. Either financial or sexual.

"How bad would you say it is, Red?"

"Ah, Fritz, pretty bad, I'd say. The officer here says
very bad."

"Police officer?"

"I'm afraid so, Fritz. I'm being held."

"Why, Red? What are the charges?"

"It's embarrassing to have to tell you. . . ."

"Give no consideration to my feelings, Red."

"Statutory rape, Fritz. Isn't that ridiculous, a man

of my stature and status? As if I could do a thing like that. It's some kind of a terrible mistake."

"Without a doubt, Red. Have you been booked yet?" The Washington lawyer understood that police procedures, when it concerned politicians of a certain standing, went along with utmost deliberation and concern. Cops made it a point to cover their big blue butts at all costs.

"Booked, Fritz?"

The senator from Colorado, the Washington lawyer decided, was an idiot. "Booked, Red. Taken your prints? Your picture? Charged you formally and read you your rights? Slapped you into a cell, Red? Booked."

"No, I can't say that they have. They've been keeping me in a small room. Awful-smelling place, Fritz. Enough to turn your stomach. You'd think they'd keep the place more sanitary. Please, Fritz, if you can get me out of here, I'd appreciate it."

The Washington lawyer made soothing, clucking sounds over the phone. "Is there an officer nearby, watching over you?"

"Watching over me, yes."

"Put him on."

"You want to talk to him, Fritz?"

"Now, Red. On the telephone."

"Yes. Here he is."

A heavy voice rumbled over the wire. "Detective Lieutenant Otis Stringfellow here. Who is it I am talking to?"

"Fritz Golub, Lieutenant. I understand you're detaining my client on some trumped-up charge."

A sigh. Lieutenant Stringfellow was familiar with

the drill. All politicians gave him a royal pain in the ass.
"Want me to spell it out, Counselor?"

"Please."

"Here's how it goes. Your client was discovered in
his car, a Datsun 280-Z, champagne in color, parked
behind a twenty-four-hour convenience store on the
west side of the district. In a loading zone, Counselor,
which attracted the attention of the officer in the patrol
car who was making his rounds. The officer, in the performance of his duty, shone a light into the Datsun,
and there was your client in a compromising position.
His privates exposed to the night air, with the girl
doing him orally, if you follow."

"I follow."

"Seems your client had picked up the girl outside
her high school this afternoon and had been with her
ever since. Driving around from one spot to another.
Parking lots, dark streets. Even a municipal parking
garage, according to the girl. Doing her every chance
he got."

"That's it? A man had sex with a woman, another
consenting adult, and you people make a federal case
out of it? Shame, Lieutenant, shame."

"Yeah, well. Most of the time, who gives a shit,
right? I had a nickel for every dame gets plowed in
a parked car, I'd be fishing in the Caribbean off my own
boat. Only this time, this girl, is a little on the young
side. A minor, you might say. A high-schooler. Turns
out she's only thirteen years old, Counselor. I'll give
you this, she looks a lot more'n that. There's a lot of
her, and it's all prime. And nobody is claiming she
wasn't out there of her own free will. But thirteen,
Counselor. How you gonna get around that?"

"Thirteen? For sure, Lieutenant?"

"We checked. I seen the birth certificate myself."

The Washington lawyer exhaled. "What procedures did you follow, Lieutenant?"

"The usual. Notified the victim's parents. Make that singular. Father hasn't been around for years. The mother works nights waiting tables in a Greek diner. One of them kind, the same brown gravy on every plate they serve. I got to tell you, Counselor, the mother is radically pissed off and wants to bring charges."

"They haven't been brought yet?"

"No rush, this kind of thing."

"You believe, Lieutenant," the Washington lawyer said, selecting his words with care, "that there's room for compromise in this situation?"

In a voice mistrustful and ill at ease, Lieutenant Stringfellow replied, "Complaint or no, Counselor, the girl is a minor. Charges can be brought. But the case is mine, Counselor. Nobody else is involved."

"You strike me as a level-headed, pragmatic sort of man, Lieutenant, and that should be good for my client. It's the mother who concerns me."

"The lady could be a problem. You know the type. Old before her time. Not much education. Never any dough. Works like a dog just to stay alive and keep food on the table for her and the girl. She's awful angry now, Counselor. Full of bitterness over the way her little girl's been treated. I reckon that when she calms down she might be open to persuasion, see things in a different light."

"You've been very helpful, Lieutenant. There is a call I must make. A couple of calls. If my client can be kept as comfortable as possible, as private as possible, I'd be extremely appreciative."

"I'll do what I can."

"No reporters, definitely."

"No sweat."

"I'll be along as quickly as possible."

"Look forward to meeting you, Counselor."

The Washington lawyer hung up, then dialed a number he had long committed to memory. The majority leader of the Senate came on the phone. He listened to the Washington lawyer before he spoke.

"Dumb bastard. Overburdened with cock and short-changed on brains. I've got half a mind to let him take the fall."

"Can't say I blame you. Except for the repercussions."

"Yes, the repercussions. No reason for me to be directly involved."

"No reason at all."

"I'll make a call, to Colorado. They'll have to make a call or two. Somebody'll get back to you before morning. This one is going to be on the expensive side."

"My thoughts exactly."

The Washington lawyer brewed a fresh pot of coffee and sat in the breakfast room of his Georgetown house waiting for the phone to ring. When it did, he answered.

A woman's voice, clear and charged with energy, spoke. "Mr. Golub?"

"Who am I talking to?"

"Suzanne Brody is my name. I am executive assistant to Mr. Duncan Turner Sharps."

Sharps. The Washington lawyer was impressed. The middle of the night and somebody had managed to reach Duncan Sharps on this matter. What was Sharps's interest in Arlen Hamilton?

"Yes," he said. "Go on, young lady."

"Word has reached Mr. Sharps that one of your clients is experiencing a problem."

"Seems so. An expensive problem."

"Can you put a price on it?"

"At this point, it's only an educated guess. Half a million should do it." When he received no immediate reply, he said, "Is that too steep?"

"The dollar amount is irrelevant. As long as matters are put right."

"They will be."

"Good. Take care of things, Counselor. Mr. Sharps will be responsible for all expenses incurred. Oh, by the way, Mr. Sharps would like to set up a meeting with your client. On Monday of next week."

"I'll see to it."

"Take down this phone number." She recited the number distinctly. "That's it, then, Mr. Golub. I imagine you've got a long night in front of you."

"Yes, I have. Good night, Miss Brody. Thank Mr. Sharps for me and Senator Hamilton. . . ."

But it was too late; she had already hung up.

Ellen Haskell looked shriveled and diminished in a cheap cloth coat the color of dead leaves. Her complexion matched the coat, and her cheeks were sunken. The lifeless glaze of defeat was in her empty eyes. Lieutenant Stringfellow, a man of massive proportions, ushered her into an interrogation room and withdrew with his official dignity intact; he understood his function from start to finish.

The Washington lawyer rose and waited for Stringfellow's departure before he offered the woman his hand and a smile that announced he was truly pleased to meet her.

"Mrs. Haskell," making it sound like a distinguished title handed down over the generations. "My name is Fritz Golub, and I am a lawyer."

She looked him over, making her disdain clear. She measured him in parts, as if looking for concealed weapons. All done with the veiled, sharp acuity of someone who recognized the dangerous accoutrements of power and wealth on sight. She lowered herself into a straight-backed oak chair and addressed the wall.

"His lawyer, I suppose."

"Well, yes, Mrs. Haskell. But my concern here is a fair and equitable solution to this difficult situation."

She made a discreet sound of disbelief and eyed him obliquely. "You aim to get him off, ain't it so? Set him loose without a single damned thing being done to him. After what he forced my little girl to do."

Golub arranged his face in a sympathetic expression, kept his voice low and soothing. Never lose sight of your goals, was the rule by which he lived. Never allow emotion to interfere with achieving them. Mrs. Haskell needed some stroking, okay. He'd stroke her.

"I assure you, madam, I sympathize completely with your feelings and the feelings of your daughter. Judith is her name, isn't it? A lovely name. So biblical."

"Is that some kind of a crime? I'm a great believer in the Bible and its teachings. The word of God written

down by the hand of man. You think that's dumb, that
I'm dumb, people like me, believing in the Lord. No
prayer in schools and all that. But going to college
don't make somebody smart about a lot of things."

"Oh, I agree."

She put her eyes on him as if seeing him for the
first time. "You a Jew, Mr. Golub?"

He hadn't set foot inside a synagogue—except for
weddings and funerals—since his Bar Mitzvah, nearly
forty years ago. His wife had been a lapsed Catholic,
his children raised without much thought to religious
training. An irreverent answer popped to mind: "My
father and mother were Jews, but I'm an American."
He swallowed the words and remembered going to the
synagogue on the Lower East Side of New York to
be with his father on Yom Kippur, the Day of Atone-
ment. The old men, unshaven, rocking back and forth
as they prayed, the smell of all those stale bodies; once
it had been an unpleasant memory. Now he recalled
it with pride and affection.

"I'm a Jew," he said softly.

"People of the Book," she grumbled. "I thought you
people knew all about justice and injustice."

He blinked away his memories and pushed aside the
momentary flush of guilt. He was a hired gun, brought
on to do a job; this woman was nothing to him.

"Let's talk about Judith. She's the only one who
matters in this terrible affair. We all want what's best
for her. To protect her."

Her suspicions again aroused, Mrs. Haskell jerked
around in her chair. The lawyer's soothing manner, his
considerate words, made her uneasy. He was not present on her behalf, that much was clear.

"Too late to protect her now."

"Not really. We all know what's going to happen when this case gets to court."

Alarm spread through Mrs. Haskell's system, and her heart beat more rapidly. The courts were another bureaucracy designed to intimidate people like her and defeat them. Justice was something smooth, rich lawyers like this one obtained for their clients. She saw only more trouble ahead.

"What's gonna happen?"

"Judith will have to testify, naturally. Bear witness."

"She ain't no fool. She can do that."

"Of course she can. But you know those criminal lawyers. That's who will represent my client, a big-league criminal attorney. The best legal talent money can buy. A courtroom whiz. Sharp and tough and experienced. He'll be forced to put Judith through an emotional wringer, in pursuit of his legal obligations. All those questions—

" 'Have you ever had intercourse with a man before, Judith?'

" 'Did you do it with my client of your own free will?'

" 'How did it make you feel, taking my client's penis in your mouth?' You see what I am saying?"

"You bastard! All you guys with money are bastards."

"Hear me out, Mrs. Haskell. All I'm telling you is what could lie ahead for Judith. If you go to trial, that is. A good lawyer will explore Judith's background in detail. He'll introduce her school record. How does she do in school, by the way? He'll drag in people who know her. Teachers. Students. Neighbors. Old boyfriends. 'Have you ever had sex with another man, Judith? With this boy or that one? With a teacher?' You see what this can lead to?"

"It's not fair."

"No, it isn't fair, Mrs. Haskell. But it's the way the system works."

"Always against poor people."

He let her think about it before speaking again. "There must be some way to settle this without going to court. Without exposing Judith to the rigors of a trial. Without tearing down her reputation and honor. Why not soothe her pain? Why not find a way to satisfy your very righteous anger, Mrs. Haskell?"

She longed to shout at him, tell him where to go with his calm manner and honeyed voice. But he was too much for her. *They* were too much for her. And always would be. She blinked and said, "How?"

"Let's say no charges are brought. Let's say my client could walk out of here today, free and clear. In return, certain arrangements can be made to your and Judith's advantage."

So, she addressed herself silently, it's finally come around to it. To what both of us were aiming at from the start. No charges, no courtrooms, no public display of dirty linen. Just a fair business deal; the American way.

"How much?" she said harshly.

"I am merely an agent in this matter, Mrs. Haskell. What would you say to fifty thousand dollars?"

The amount surprised her; more than she'd anticipated, less than she'd hoped for. She was tempted to accept his offer lest he withdraw it. Instead she produced a mirthless cackle. Tears began to flow, and she wiped her eyes with the sleeve of the cheap coat.

"Poor is only poor, Mr. Golub. Not dumb. We are talking about a United States senator here. We are talking about the sexual abuse of a girl only thirteen years old."

"I'm sure you can use the money . . ."

She waved him to silence. "More than that, I need it. Need it to get me a house in a decent part of town, Mr. Golub. Need it to furnish the place and buy some decent winter clothes for me and Judith. Need it to live on. For a long, long time, Mr. Golub," she ended slowly, raising her eyes to his for emphasis.

Still smooth, he smiled warmly. "I'm afraid you've misjudged my client's financial worth. There is no way—"

"I figure there's more involved than just one senator. Somebody brought you into this quick enough, and lawyers like you don't come cheap. There's others behind the scenes want all this finished without a fuss. Even I can see that. Big numbers, Mr. Golub. I want to listen to big numbers start coming out of your mouth. Otherwise—I'd enjoy seeing your client's fat ass rot in the slammer. Maybe while he's in there he'll find out what it feels like to be raped. . . ."

"Mrs. Haskell," Golub said, the words riding a sibilant exhalation. "Mrs. Haskell. No need for that kind of talk. I'm convinced that two reasonable people can work this out somehow. In fact, I'm positive we can do so right now."

Mrs. Haskell sat back in her chair and folded her small red hands in her lap. He was made abruptly aware of an inner strength in the woman and a surprising amount of dignity.

"The numbers, Mr. Golub. The big numbers. . . ."

Low gray clouds moved in over the Rocky Mountains, presaging more snow. The sleek Gulfstream came diving out of them as if anxious not to be caught aloft when the storm began. It skidded to a stop on Sardy Field. The flight attendant helped Geneva climb down, saying he'd see that her luggage was sent on to the house. He watched her walk toward the waiting car. She was, he told himself admiringly, the best-looking woman he'd ever seen. What would she be like in the sack, all that lithe, cool beauty, so self-contained? He tried to imagine her in the throes of sexual excitement. A silent lover, he'd bet, accepting but giving very little back. Always cool, always aloof. A disappointment. And the boss's wife. Which meant Don't touch. Don't even think about it. Unless she asked for it. Which she hadn't even come close to doing.

Legally the house belonged to Sharps Industries. Another device relieving Sharps of the direct financial responsibility that ownership brought on. The company had bought the house, paid for the necessary refinements and refurbishments, purchased the necessary furnishings, paid all the monthly bills. It stood on a rocky incline looking down on the town, only a few yards from a paved, two-lane road. With the additions, the house contained just under six thousand square feet, and Sharps estimated it would bring about fifteen million dollars on the open market. Not that he had any intention of selling; especially not now.

A phone call ahead had put the house in working order prior to Geneva's arrival. Food had been delivered, the phones connected, the power turned on, and the heating system at work. Suzanne Brody had made the call to the proper people in Aspen. She was someone Sharps could always depend on to get things done right.

During those first few days back in Aspen, Geneva kept to herself. She lounged around the house watching TV or reading, soaking in the hot tub out back in the pool room, nursing her bruised body back to health and giving her equally wounded spirit time to heal. She spent much of the time reviewing the details of her life with Duncan Turner Sharps. She concluded that ultimately the benefits of being his wife were few and relatively inconsequential; the drawbacks were many, painful, and lasting.

His business interests kept them apart. But somehow his absence placed her in an even more restrictive environment. It was as if, by bearing his name, she was disqualified from developing an existence of her own. She understood that many people found her attractive because she was Sharps's wife; and even more rejected her for the same reason, unwilling to be tainted by the connection.

When they were apart, she was relatively at peace. But his influence floated over her like some poisonous, dark cloud, always threatening to do her in. Close, he was equally dangerous. That most recent beating was only one of many. And hardly the worst of them. Once she had been hospitalized for three days and on another occasion required full-time nursing until she was able to fend for herself. His lack of regard for her was manifested by insults and mockery in public and private, the scorn he heaped upon her, his manner constantly contemptuous and dismissive.

Nothing in her life before Sharps had prepared her for this kind of treatment. Always, no matter how bad her life was, there were moments of joy and freedom, brief intervals during which she had been able to summon up a modicum of self-respect. Sharps had changed all that.

So she immersed herself in the hot tub, perspiration coating her smooth brow, sipping Gilbey's gin over ice from a tall glass and plotting a way out of her dilemma. Getting ready for the fulfilling future she was convinced lay just ahead.

8

"*JUST* coffee."

Devlin watched the waitress walk away, categorizing her as he so often did with women. This one was "working class," strong of feature and figure. A little thicker through the middle than he preferred, but with good boobs and a fine, round fanny. Young, attractive, and, he supposed, smart. At least educated, like so many young people around Aspen. An English major from Smith or Mt. Holyoke, he decided. Certainly she had earned her master's by now, possibly a Ph.D. from Columbia or Stanford. One of the better universities, that's for sure. An athlete, from the easy way she moved; a good skier. Not that it mattered. There were thousands like her scattered over the alpine slopes of America, hustling for a buck so they could spend their spare time skiing. All the right credentials, he reminded himself. All the wrong emotions.

Devlin taunted himself; how dare he sit in judgment of someone else! A ski bum by definition and deportment. Feeding off the sorrows and weaknesses of other people, mostly women. Accepting whatever was offered, helping himself to whatever remained. Anything to pay for an all-day ticket on the lift. Anything to free him up for a few more hours on the slopes. Get him through another twenty-four hours of his life. Anything to keep him from going straight, growing up, becoming a man at last.

"Eat a real breakfast," Peggy Pearce urged him. Full of false parental concern. Claiming the rights of a friend to intrude, and they were not friends. Not even close. Touching the knuckles of his right hand with her fingertips as if some intimacy existed between them. As if they were lovers. Which they most definitely were not.

"Most important meal of the day," she persisted.

She sat across the table from him in the Pancake House West. Hank Ricketts on her left. Sam Daly sat next to Devlin.

"You are what you eat," Peggy said, backing it up with a thousand-watt smile, open and encouraging, showing off all those perfect white teeth.

Devlin had come to a conclusion about teeth. At least, teeth in Aspen. From one end of the Roaring Fork River to the other, nothing but large teeth, evenly matched, blindingly white. Every tooth carefully attended by the same orthodontist, he began to believe. He reached back in his memory; had he ever had a dentist for a friend? Did anyone ever have a dentist for a friend?

"I never met a kid who wanted to be a dentist when he grew up," he said aloud.

They stared at him. Peggy with her shrewd violet eyes. Hank Ricketts, eyes cool, a faded blue, and impenetrable. Sam Daly, glowering under a lumpy brow, a wild, undisciplined man.

Devlin had known them for a week. Seven days of taking meals together, skiing, drinking in the bars at night. Seven days in which to mark their flaws and their strong points, to characterize them, squeeze them into square holes or round ones, all to confirm his perceptions. Or were they biases? Devlin was willing to concede a certain predisposition to error on his part. An alarmingly frequent failure of judgment. Hell, his entire life was marked by a series of boots and bobbles. Mistakes not learned from and seldom rectified. Could it be he was a lot less smart than he believed?

"What?" Ricketts said.

Devlin grinned to take the edge off his words. "Baseball players, a lot of kids want to grow up to be baseball players. Or cops. Or astronauts. But nobody dreams about becoming a dentist. Nobody."

"Yeah," Daly said after a brief interlude. "I suppose."

"Is that what you wanted to be?" Ricketts said. "A dentist?"

"Who, me?" Devlin said. "No, I never had any ambition."

The waitress brought the coffee.

"Eat something," Peggy said. "Breakfast's the most

productive meal of the day. Gets your energy into high gear."

Devlin produced his most seductive expression, giving her the full power of those sea-green-gray eyes, lowering his voice a notch. Never confront people head on; it was a motto to live by. A smile, an amusing remark, a soft word; whatever it took to get you through the day. Treat every woman as if you were aching to get into her pants; another motto in Devlin's collection. And when you had 'em hooked, zap 'em.

"Say, some bran cereal with milk and fruit," Peggy said. "Or a couple of eggs, if you're not concerned about cholesterol."

"Coffee'll do me fine." It was always something, when they were together. Peggy going on about food. Or nosing around about Devlin's love life. Issuing instructions on how to dress so as not to attract attention, how to act, the penultimate authority. Going over the first job a dozen times, as if none of them had a brain in his head.

Breaking and entering, he thought; not brain surgery.

Watching him, Peggy was impressed. No nervousness in his manner, no irritability. There was a gravity to Devlin she had seldom encountered in a man, a certain weight, a shadowed elegance. He smiled a lot, but she perceived little joy in his face, and when you looked closely you could almost see the skull under his weathered countenance. He made a pass at his unruly hair, a vain effort to keep it in place and off his smooth forehead.

"Look," Daly said. "We here for the job or to bullshit about eating and dentists? Boy, what a bunch! Let's get on with it."

Devlin decided to keep a close watch on Sam Daly. There was an unstable quality about him, and he seemed to float free, unconnected to any reality Devlin could identify. Daly, he had come to believe, was operating on a wavelength known only to himself. An oversize package waiting for a chance to explode. A threat to them all.

"Okay," Peggy said. She checked her wristwatch, which told the hour in all twenty-four time zones and was water resistant up to three hundred meters. Peggy was proud of that watch. "Who wants to make the call?"

"Big deal," Daly said. "Making a call." He swaggered to the far end of the restaurant where there were two pay phones on the wall, next to the rest rooms. Devlin almost spoke to Ricketts then about Daly. They were a team, had been friends for a long time. Asshole buddies. And what about Ricketts and Peggy? Were they a pair? Lovers, maybe. Devlin wished he had taken more time to make up his mind about this group, before he had agreed to join them.

Peggy and Ricketts and Daly. Were they all sharing the same bed now and then? A ménage à trois? Devlin didn't care, one way or another. Except for one thing he had learned—weird sexual arrangements almost always meant weird people with weird notions of how to get things done. Trouble was you never knew where such people were coming from or intended to go. Devlin had developed his own blueprint for living, crooked as it was; compared with this crowd he was straight and steady.

"Nervous?" Hank Ricketts said, a slight taunt in his voice.

Devlin glanced his way, eyes opaque and aglitter. "No more than is appropriate."

"Sam says we should go in loaded."

Devlin answered, almost too quickly. "We decided on it, no guns. Otherwise, count me out."

"Chill out," Peggy said. "The deal stands."

Sam Daly returned to the table. "Just like you said, Peggy. An answering machine."

She looked at her watch again. "On the button. A family that skis together, stays together. Let's go, guys."

The men rose and looked down at Peggy, who remained at the table. "I want to finish my breakfast and I'll take care of the check. See you later. And, by the way, good luck."

Ricketts made a rude kissing sound and winked before leading the others outside to where the blue Jeep was parked.

First job.

The Burnside house, put together of native stone and redwood, and an abundance of glass glittering in the morning sunlight, looked as if it had grown naturally out of the snow-packed edges of Aspen Mountain. From the wide, angular deck, the town spread out like a toy Alpine village, splashed with color: blue, red, green, here and there a dab of yellow.

The blue Jeep stood, solemn and staid, on the scenic overlook nearly one hundred yards away with a clear view of the valley and unobstructed sight lines of the house. Its three passengers were oblivious to the sparkling beauty of the day, their thoughts only on what lay ahead.

"I keep waiting for the front door to open," Hank Ricketts said. "For somebody to come on out."

"Nobody's coming out," Sam Daly muttered, making no effort to conceal his annoyance with his friend. "Only the machine answered when I called. Nobody's home."

"They could've come home. While we were on our way up here."

"You losing your nerve, Hank?" Daly said. "Is that it?"

"Fuck you."

Daly cocked one big fist. "Talk to me that way, I'll flatten you, friend or not."

"Cut it out, you guys!" Devlin snapped from his place behind the wheel. "Peggy cased the place. She tracked the family for a week. Not once did they break out of their pattern. So, what're you gonna do, sit here crapping in your pants or go on in? Which is it? We do it or we give it up. Which?"

"Nobody said a thing about giving up," Ricketts answered. "I say we do it."

"Right now," Daly said.

Devlin got the engine started, and the Jeep rolled along the road. A light snow had fallen during the night, and the delicate powder had formed a thin crust on the asphalt, crackling under the weight of the wheels.

Daly taunted his friend. "Suck it up, Hank."

"Stick it, man."

"In your eye. We gonna hit the slopes after?"

"Talk to me after."

Up the driveway of the Burnside house and around back, the Jeep turned to facilitate their getaway. Devlin switched off the ignition. He sat back and flexed the muscles in his legs, hands still on the wheel.

"I hope Peggy's right," he said. "About the alarm."

"No alarm," Daly said. "Peggy said no alarm, and she is one smart chick."

"Yeah," Ricketts said. "Only people make mistakes."

"Oh, shit," Daly said. He climbed out of the Jeep, looked back at Ricketts. "You coming or what?"

"I'm coming."

Once out in the cold air, Ricketts seemed to revive, his normal aggressiveness restored. He led the way onto the back deck. The back door had nine small panels of tinted bottle glass. Without any hesitation, he swung an elbow, shattering one pane. A quick reach for the lock and they were inside the house.

Neither of them spoke, briefed by Peggy and following her detailed instructions. The master bedroom suite was on the second floor. They located a jewel box in one of the closets, and Daly emptied its contents into a plastic garbage bag he was carrying for the occasion. They tossed clothes around, emptied drawers, until they found a stash of bills. Ten minutes had expired and they were finished upstairs. They made one swift sweep of the rest of the house, finding nothing of value, and then were back outside and into the Jeep. Devlin drove carefully on the return trip to Glenwood Springs, glad that it was over.

Devlin ran the "mine dumps" an hour later. Back in the days when silver was dominant in Aspen, the miners shoved the slag and other rubble from their diggings down the mountainside. The result: one half-open gash after another through an aspen forest that at times approached the vertical. Unexpected rises that launched a skier into space, forcing him into choreographic leaps that demanded a built-in sense of rhythm and a certain grasp of aeronautics.

Devlin took one dump and at once launched himself into an abrupt swing to his left. Another dump, and another, and another sharp angle, this time to the right. He gloried in the battle, his legs fighting the uneven ground beneath the snow, gloried in his conquest of the hill.

His last run was at the Back of the Bell. Here the bumps were tighter and the gullies between them even narrower, more dramatic, allowing less time for a skier to make his choices, allowing fewer choices. Here there was barely room enough to finish off a turn, less time to bring speed to a manageable level.

The air, biting cold, turned his cheeks numb and put tears in his eyes. His skis put first tracks in the fresh powder. There was an intrinsic counterpoint to this run, the mountain fighting back harder this time. Trickier. A wily old opponent that kept him dropping at high speed in an unending series of changing images. Green of the trees that loomed up in his path, much too close, the white of the earth itself, the sudden glimpses of distant blue sky. It all blended together as the mountain tried its damnedest to cast him off. Except for the rough sibilance of his skis slicing through the snow, he heard nothing. Only the lofty silent disdain of those tall peaks, full of their own eternal majesty and power.

He reached bottom, his body pulsating, his hands and feet tingling. He almost screamed aloud in celebration of his triumph over the mountain. At least this time. The one, he thought, the true Rocky Mountain high.

This was why he had come to Aspen. This was what his life was all about. And then he reminded himself: the mountain, it was a good place to die.

9

H E senior senator from Colorado sat in the rear seat of the limousine, as far from Suzanne Brody as he could get. Not that he found her unattractive. Or in any way repellent. Not a bit of it; she was a sleek and beautiful woman, fashionably and expensively turned out, with a sharp mind.

She had to be smart. Nobody stupid would have lasted for very long with Duncan Turner Sharps. He knew Sharps only by reputation; a brilliant businessman, brilliant and ruthless, the kind of man who, when he wanted something, went after it with a single-mindedness rare in the human species. There was much to be admired in Sharps; but the senator's instincts told him to be wary of the old pirate, to watch him every minute and never, never, turn his back to him.

A pirate is exactly what he'd heard Sharps was. A pirate and a cutthroat, possibly even a murderer. Not that he gave much credence to that kind of talk. After all, look what some people said about him.

"Flight okay?" Suzanne Brody said. Her manner was professional, a pleasant, controlled expression on that alabaster face.

A cool one, the senator had decided. Not at all his type. Which put her in a very elite company: those few women who failed to excite Arlen Hamilton's extremely excitable libido. He eyed her obliquely; not enough meat on her bones, but the legs were good. Strong, slender ankles and good calves, sheathed in well-fitting panty hose. The senator had a longing for the good old days, for garter belts and stockings, for that indescribable thrill of sliding your hand up a woman's leg and onto a warm, naked thigh. Ah, well, nothing stayed the same.

"Good·flight," he said. "Excellent. The crew took care of my every need. Well, almost," he ended with a reflexive, flirtatious drawl.

Suzanne Brody never noticed, staring straight ahead.

Sharps was doing her, the senator decided. A quickie on the office couch, whenever the old man was in the mood. He heard those rumors, too. The old man was married, not that it mattered. Red Hamilton had never let any of his wives get between him and a fancy piece of tail. He wondered how Brody would react if he whipped out the old all-purpose tool and put it up to her mouth. Not that he intended to find out; no sense taking chances with Sharps. You never knew how those wheeler-dealers were going to react.

"Would you care for a drink, Senator?" Suzanne Brody said. She opened a panel in the back of the front seat to reveal a gleaming, well-stocked bar. "Scotch, vodka, brandy?"

"A tot of brandy to nullify the winter chill."

She filled a crystal tumbler almost to the rim. Just the way he liked it. Could they have met before? He was about to raise the question when she spoke again in that crisp, efficient way she had.

"Here's the schedule, Senator Hamilton. I drop you at your hotel so you can freshen up, change clothes if you like, rest for a while. At eight, a car will be in front of the hotel to carry you to Mr. Sharps's apartment. Please be downstairs on time. Mr. Sharps puts a high premium on his time. He doesn't like to waste any."

An annoyed response brought some angry words onto the senator's tongue. Who the hell did this broad think she was, talking to him that way! Issuing orders like he was some flunky, trained and housebroken. Fuck her and her orders, and he meant to tell her so.

But not right now. Sharps had become too important to chance offending him. A vital member of his constituency; the senator had learned only that morning that Sharps owned a house in Aspen.

He knew what Sharps had already done for him. Sprung for a substantial number of dollars on his behalf. Greased more than a few squeaking wheels that might have caused him a great deal of damage. Gotten him out of that stinking jail and out from under the threat of that stupid woman, mother of that sweet child. Oh, he owed Sharps a lot.

And now Sharps had invited the senator to pay him a visit in New York. Commanded him, actually. Which meant that Sharps was after something in return—quid pro quo—the unwritten law of political life, engraved in every politician's psyche, a lasting admonition. When a man of Sharps's wealth and power called, Arlen Hamilton always responded. After all, what was a United States senator for, if not to service his most important supporters?

"Punctuality," he said to Suzanne Brody, "is one of my strongest virtues."

Brody made a small humming sound in the back of her throat. An indication of acceptance or displeasure? Recognition or revulsion? Red Hamilton couldn't have cared less. Let's face it, no matter how beautiful she was, or smart, or fashionable, she was still only one of Duncan Sharps's flunkies. A well-paid gofer.

"I don't suppose you'd care to say why Mr. Sharps asked me to come?" he said, working over the brandy.

"Mr. Sharps asked me to meet you, Senator. He didn't share his reasons this time."

This time. He made note of the qualification. Meant to establish her own importance in Sharps's eyes—an occasional confidante. Executive assistant. A woman of some power in her own right. There was more to Suzanne Brody than he had first suspected; a glossy overlay of intimidation. A professional extension of Duncan Sharps, and Sharps could be, Red Hamilton had been told, an extremely frightening man. He finished off the rest of his brandy.

Brody refilled his glass without being asked as the

limousine went through the Midtown Tunnel into Manhattan's streets. The snow that had fallen during the afternoon had changed to rain as the rush hour began. The streets turned sloppy, rutted with graying slush, cars fishtailing in the messy gloom. Pedestrians picked their way gingerly around, and occasionaly through, pools of black water, deepening at stopped-up drains. New York in winter, the senator observed, was an unappetizing place to be. Suzanne Brody drew his attention once more.

"Mr. Sharps asked me to inform you, there's a gift waiting at the hotel. A small surprise, he said. Welcome to New York."

A surprise. The senator enjoyed surprises. Especially when they were expensive and handsome. A gold watch, for example. Or a diamond-encrusted ring. Sharps was evidently a man who did things with style, a classy individual to whom cost was never a consideration.

Red Hamilton crossed and uncrossed his legs, silently urging the driver to go faster, anxious to get to the hotel.

The hotel was only a few yards off Park Avenue, conservative, expensive, and discreet. Not even a bronze plaque announced the building as housing a hotel; and the blue-and-white canopy was unmarked.

An assistant manager greeted the senator at the door, and a uniformed bellman carried his leather weekender inside.

"We've been looking forward to your stay with us, Senator Hamilton."

"Thank you."

"You've been checked in, and, if you wish, I'll escort you directly to your rooms."

Rooms; plural. Go with Sharps and you went first class, all the way. He turned to bid good-bye to Suzanne Brody, but she had sedately withdrawn. With an invisible shrug he trailed the assistant manager into a polished-brass-and-mirrored elevator.

The bellman was waiting at the door of the suite when Hamilton arrived. The assistant manager preceded him inside.

"If you'll allow me, sir." He switched on the lights, indicated the bedroom and the bath, showed the bellman where to put the senator's luggage. "I hope you enjoy your stay with us, Senator." He bowed slightly and then was gone, no waiting around for a tip. Again, Sharps's classy hand. The message was clear: when you were his guest it never cost you a cent.

There were cut flowers in the sitting room of the suite. And a bowl of fresh fruit. Against one wall, a fully stocked bar. He helped himself to another brandy and only then noticed the pale blue envelope trimmed with white propped up against the ice bucket. It was addressed to him.

Play the tape and enjoy the modest welcome gift. My car will be waiting at eight. We'll dine at my place. Just a light supper and a touch of business.

No signature, but of course it was from Sharps. He looked around. Across the room, the focal point of a small sitting group of club chairs, the television set. A VCR rested on top, and on top of it was a single videotape. The senator inserted it into the VCR, switched on the power, and settled down with his drink to watch.

The first shots were of a football game in progress, and for a moment or two the senator believed he was watching his beloved Denver Broncos at play. Soon he realized that the players were too slight to be professional, not even large enough to be college men; this was a high school game. And with that recognition, the camera cut to the stands, the crowd on its feet and animated. Next, to a squad of cheerleaders, knees pumping, arms athrust, young faces happily engaged. And in close-up one of the cheerleaders, a pretty child with a smooth, relatively undefined visage. All eyes and pouty mouth. Again the entire pep squad, boys and girls alike; the boys in spotless white trousers, the girls in short, pleated skirts and sleeveless blouses.

Another cut; the cheerleaders·had formed a human pyramid, and on silent command the pyramid broke apart, the various human elements bouncing to their feet. The senator edged forward in his seat, captivated by the girls; short skirts flounced above their hips, revealing satiny underpants; their breasts jiggled enticingly under the blouses.

Beauties, every one. Female perfection. Unspoiled by time and the corroding effects of life on the planet. That's the way the senator thought of it. His throat thickened, and he imagined one of the girls naked, his hands on her, here and everywhere, his mouth coming down on one proud young breast. The thought, just the thought of it, caused him to grow heavy and larger.

The pep squad went into a routine. They danced, they pranced, they whirled and spun around. They shuffled and they leaped, they did handstands and cartwheels, filling the senior senator's eyes with bottoms and crotches and boobs that were never still. They ended in sedate formation, kneeling and standing, chanting in unison, crying out for the victory they so deserved. All that beauty . . . The tape flickered to an end.

The senator suffered a mild pain in his chest. He had to remind himself to resume breathing. He inhaled, he exhaled, he shifted his engorged penis to a more comfortable position. He squeezed it with affection and admiration, proud of its ample proportions. Not bad for a man in his sixties. He stroked it lovingly and allowed his mind to wander. Not much of a gift, that tape, but one he should be able to utilize over and over. He swallowed the remainder of his brandy and got ready to unzip his fly.

"Hi, there!"

The senator's head came around like a shot. His eyes widened. His lips worked soundlessly, spread in a smile of genuine welcome. Standing ten feet away, stretching as if she'd just awakened from a satisfying nap, was one of the cheerleaders from the videotape. So it seemed. She wore the identical costume. Short pleated white skirt and sleeveless blouse. He gestured at the television set.

"You're one of them." He wanted her to be.

She didn't disappoint him. She nodded coquettishly, advancing unhurriedly, hand outstretched. Her grip was pleasantly firm, her round pale eyes untroubled and shining.

"You must be Arlen?"

"Most folks call me Red." He lurched to his feet, sucking in his belly.

Her eyes went lower. "Oh, my, Red," she cooed. "All that from looking at a tape? What a terror you must be with the real thing."

"Are you the real thing?" He spoke automatically; this, then, was the surprise. Expensive, naturally. Carefully chosen and prepared for the occasion. But paid for nevertheless. "I mean . . ."

"I know what you mean. You think I was hired to play a joke on you. But I'm no joke, Red. You mind if I call you Red? I am a member of the pep squad. Midwood Valley High. Didn't you recognize me in the tape? The girl on the far left most of the time. I guess you didn't get a good look at me. Jenny and Sally Ann, they're the ones get all the attention. Jenny's so pretty, and Sally Ann with those great big . . . oh, you know. . . ."

"I'd've put you up front. Smack in the middle. Star of the show."

Her smile stretched out. All that white outlined by those glistening scarlet lips. She retrieved her hand and took a single backward step.

"You're sweet, Red. You truly are. I'm Patricia. My friends call me Trish."

"May I call you Trish?" A hooker, of course. No doubt about it. Twenty, maybe. Maybe even older. But right for the part and user friendly. A nearly perfect substitute. The senator craved the real thing.

She must've sensed his doubts. "I'm a sophomore," she said in a sweet, high voice, her face a youthful mask of innocence. "Back in Ohio, that is. Mr. Sharps had us flown in for tonight."

"Us?" The senator sat back down and examined her with the swift expertise of a connoisseur. Round breasts in outline under the blouse, nipples in stark relief, a narrow waist and flaring hips, those bare strong legs, the skin velvety and without blemish. He would go along with the game. Invented by Sharps, all moves designed by Sharps; but Sharps had only a small idea of what Red Hamilton's requirements were.

"Momma and me," Trish explained. "Momma is going to see a play on Broadway tonight with a friend of Mr. Sharps who was kind enough to escort her. And here I am. Mr. Sharps said he didn't want you to be left all alone in a strange hotel room when you arrived. He said it wasn't very friendly." She giggled and ducked her head. "You don't believe word one of what I'm telling you, do you, Red? Can't say that I blame you for being a little paranoid. I would be, too. But I got to tell you, that Mr. Sharps, he certainly is one who knows how to get things done. He's got people who work for him just about everywhere, it seems. And the way Mr. Sharps gives orders and tosses his money around, he's bound to use it all up before long."

"Not much likelihood of that. Are you actually a high school student?"

"Oh, yes, for real. Want to see my ID? It's back in the bedroom in my purse. I can fetch it if you want."

"That's all right."

"I wish I wasn't. In school still, I mean. But Momma says I got to get an education, go on to college. Says that way I'll meet a finer class of boys and get to make a better marriage. Momma means marry a boy whose daddy's rich, I guess."

"Your momma wants the best for you."

"I believe so, too. That's why I do what she says."

"Always? You always do what your momma says?"

"Oh, yes, sir, always. Well, almost always. Still don't believe me, do you, Red? Okay, I'll prove it to you. Just you run that tape again. I'll point out where I am in the line, and you can freeze the frame and see for yourself."

"That's not necessary."

"I just don't appreciate being called a liar, and all."

"Did I say that?"

"I can tell what you're thinking." She clapped her hands. "I know what. I'll do a couple of tricks for you. That way you'll see that I am honest to gosh a cheerleader. Fact is, Red, there is a very excellent chance that I am going to be named captain of the squad in my junior year. Most of the kids think so. I am that popular and good, and that is something doesn't happen all that often. You ready, Red?"

The bulge in his pants had not gone away. If anything, it seemed harder, larger, the nearness of her making him light-headed. Fifteen years old. So lovely, so tender, so perfect.

He nodded. "I'm ready, Trish."

She performed a school yell, exhorting an unseen student body to the heights of enthusiasm in support of an imagined team. Her arms snapped out in precise movements, her head whipped around, long golden hair flaring out, jerked back into place without warning. A quick sidestep and an even quicker retreat, a practiced pirouette, the short pleated skirt whirling up to her waist. The swift, pounding steps, the herky-jerky thrusts and recoils, a succession of gyrations that caused his brain to tip and yaw, his pulse to race, never quite convinced of what his senses reported.

Red Hamilton blinked and wet his lips. Now you see

it, now you don't. Reality and illusion. What to believe? What the hell was going on? Had he seen her that way? Wearing nothing under the pleated skirt? An image of youthful nakedness had been seared onto his brain. Déjà-vu. He ran the film backward in his mind. Again the skirt went up. Higher and higher still. Those strong young thighs rising and falling to some unheard-of beat and a glimpse of—ah, sweet Jesus H. Christ Almighty! Her words brought him back.

She was poised on one knee, arms outstretched as if seeking applause, that tiny skirt sedately in place. She was breathing rapidly and smiling at him.

"How was that, Red?"

It took a massive effort to summon up an answer. "Very nice," he managed.

She stood erect. "Want to see more?"

He nodded this time.

"I love being a cheerleader," she said, moving into position, getting ready to start. "What I really want is to be a professional dancer. You know, in Las Vegas in one of those clubs. I'd be willing to start small time, if I had to. Go-go stuff, like that. You ready?"

More than ready; he nodded again.

She did another cheer, standing with her feet together, hardly a move. The last syllable left her mouth, and she went into a series of cartwheels that carried her from one end of the living room to the other. No doubt about it; she was naked underneath, crevices and cracks flashing across his line of sight like some elusive forest creature. Mound and round. Tightest, roundest ass he'd ever seen. Then she was on her feet again, advancing his way, an uncertain turn to those lush scarlet lips.

"You see, I told you. I am on the pep squad. Believe me now?"

"I believe you."

"Apologize," she said with a mock pout. "As much as saying I was a liar."

"I'm sorry." He drained the last of his brandy and went after more. "Want a drink?"

"Momma made me promise, no drinking till I was past twenty-one."

"That's right, and you always do what your momma tells you to do."

"Always."

"And what did Momma say you were to do here? Here with me, now?"

"Just to be nice to you and to watch my manners, that's all."

"You always go around without underpants on?"

"Not always." She had taken up a position an arm's length away from him, bare feet planted solidly on the expensive broadloom that covered the floor. "You enjoyed my little show?"

"Very much."

"How much?"

"A lot, really a lot."

She inched closer, fingers curled under the hem of the skirt. "Wanna look again, Red? One more time?"

"Oh, yes, please."

"Beg for it."

"I am begging you."

"On your knees."

He went to the floor, hands clasped prayerfully. "I am begging."

"Yes. You are begging." She lifted the skirt. "See for yourself."

Sucking air, a groan of pleasure and despair trickled across his lips. Smooth and white, she had shaved every vestige of her sexual hair away. From the senior senator's point of view, she might have been ten years old. Or less. He gasped at the pristine beauty of it all. A lowering wail of desire escaped him as his head went forward, lips coming to rest on her. Inhaling the sweetish, sweatish scent of her. Tasting her. And finally toppling into the dark void so generously offered.

For the moment, gratefully lost.

10

THE apartment occupied two floors of one of the best buildings on Park Avenue. Once it had been two separate apartments, inhabited by two different and socially correct families. Convinced of their natural superiority, they had lived quietly on monies passed on by their ancestors, laboring mightily never to attract attention to themselves.

Duncan Turner Sharps had turned all that around. He purchased both properties within six months, transforming them into his Manhattan home and power base. The result was twenty-two rooms of varying dimensions and shapes, each designed for a specific purpose. There was a small suite of offices out of which Sharps could work, when it so pleased him; computers and a bank of direct telephone lines put him in immediate touch with his headquarters in the Wall Street area. Space had been set aside for a brace of secretaries and a medium-size room for meetings and conferences. There were nine bedrooms, each furnished in a distinctive style, three sitting rooms, a library, a music room, a room that contained two handmade pool tables and a small grandstand for onlookers. There was a television room with a large-screen projection system, plus two smaller—but not small—screens. There was an art gallery—actually the corridor leading to a bedroom wing, its walls hung with Renaissance paintings, none of which Sharps cared for; they had been purchased on advice of a decorator with a penchant for the period and an art historian who insisted they were an excellent investment in a rising market. Sharps never looked at the paintings, and his wife, Geneva, preferred the brighter, lighter work of the Impressionists.

The senior senator from Colorado was lifted by a private elevator to the sixteenth floor, where he was met by a white-jacketed servant who took his coat and hat and led him into a hexagonal entry chamber. On the walls, a number of Directoire portraits of people the senator thought were odd-looking, even foreign; not at all his style. Down a long hallway into an office. A somber, expensive room—Sharps's room, he decided at once—with mahogany paneling on the walls, a Biedermeier bookcase filled with old volumes, some small antique tables. A dark green rug with an immense eagle carved into its smooth pile covered the floor. Black leather sofas and two large wing chairs covered with green tapestry formed a seating area around a working fireplace.

In front of curtained windows, a Victorian partner's desk behind which Sharps had placed himself in a black leather swivel chair. He observed Arlen Hamilton's entrance across his steepled fingers and remained seated until the servant had withdrawn and closed the tall, paneled door behind him. Only then did he come out from behind the desk, placing a cheerless grin on his mouth, the thick mustache barely disturbed. His handshake was without enthusiasm, and he dropped into one of the green chairs, telling Hamilton to sit where he pleased; he allowed himself to sink into the deep luxury of one of the leather couches.

"I'm so glad we could meet at last, Mr. Sharps," the senior senator started out.

Sharps grunted softly.

The senior senator felt compelled to continue. "Your reputation precedes you, and—"

Sharps grunted and shifted his position. The senator embarked on a different tack.

"This most recent unpleasantness, I owe you a debt of gratitude—"

"A debt," Sharps muttered. "Yes, you do."

"Well, whatever, I mean, all you have to do is tell me—"

"I'm planning to build in Aspen," Sharps said. His tilted eyes darted here and there, never settling. To Arlen Hamilton, he had the ominous look of a western gunslinger. Wandering along the far edge of sanity, needing only the merest slight to set him off on a murderous path.

"Another house?" Hamilton inquired.

"Don't be a fool, man." Sharps tugged at the corner

of his mustache. "I have a house large enough for a small army now. I brought you here to talk business."

"Of course," the senator said swiftly, alarmed by the flaring temper Sharps showed with so little provocation. Hamilton was an important man with important commercial interests of his own. A politician of accomplishment and standing in the nation's capital, sitting on several committees and chairing two key subcommittees. Yet in the presence of Duncan Turner Sharps he felt insignificant and unsure of himself, intimidated by this strange and hairless apparition of a man. He longed to let loose his resentment, to strike back, to tell Sharps to shove his high-handedness. Instead, all he did was say, "How can I be of help, Mr. Sharps?"

"You acquainted with a man out there name of Marlon Ayres?" It was less a question than a statement of fact.

The senator said yes, he did know Ayres. "Everyone knows old Marlon. Used to be one of the most important ranchers in the state, a few years back. Even tried his hand at politics and served a couple of terms in the general assembly. A real maverick, Marlon, never know which side of the fence he'd land on. Turned his ranch over to his sons some years ago, and the boys promptly sold out to some developers who put up a whole lot of fancy-priced, chintzy tract houses. Old Marlon, he hasn't said word one to those boys since. Says he was betrayed by his sons. Says he had a responsibility to the land, a sacred trust, I heard him say one time, and that he's been betrayed. Exactly his word, betrayed. Still owns some property in that area, if I'm not wrong."

"You're not," Sharps said dryly. "Smack in the middle of Aspen. Within walking distance of the ski lift and downtown. I want that parcel."

The senator spoke without thinking. "Oh, well. I don't think so. Marlon has an almost mystical attitude about the land, about his land. After what his sons did, I expect he'll hold on to any property he has and make sure that after he dies it's held in trust by some environmentalists or folks like that. No way he's going to sell to you or anybody else."

"Try not to be any dumber than you are, Arlen. The man is on the brink of selling at this moment. Do you think I called you in to make small talk and pass the day? My information on this matter is excellent, accurate, and recent. Ayres has been in touch with a pair of builders from California as well as a Japanese consortium. The builders would like to put up some luxury homes—around four, five million each one—the Japs are talking indoor shopping mall."

"Oh, my God!"

This time Sharps's grin was thin and full of self-satisfaction. "Won't that raise up a shit-storm in Aspen, an honest-to-God shopping mall!"

"The town isn't going to go for it. Never, never. There are built-in restrictions. Covenants. Laws. Limitations established by Planning and Zoning and—"

"All academic," Sharps broke in. "I am going to put up a hotel on the property. Summer and winter, every room will be full. At three, maybe four or five hundred dollars a night."

"Oh, I don't know. You see—"

"With a casino."

"Oh, my God!"

"A gambling casino."

"Gambling! In Aspen! Oh, Mr. Sharps, not to sound negative, but that can never happen. You see—"

"You're being negative."

"The thing is, statewide and locally, the opposition . . . so many groups against the idea."

"Don't want to hear what I can't do."

"It's illegal. Prohibited by state law."

"Laws can be repealed. Changed. That's why you're here."

"I can't do that. I—"

"Listen, Hamilton. I'm told you are the single most powerful elected official in the state. You know everybody, you know where the bodies are buried, you know the weaknesses of people, you know how much it will cost to buy a mayor or a senator, even a governor. Tell me what has to be done to get it done."

"Marlon, he won't sell for—"

"Leave Ayres to me. If money isn't enough, pressure of one kind or another will be. Everybody can be reached. The man is old, worn down. In the end, he won't be able to refuse me." He ran a hand over his naked pate. "As for the rest, the strings to pull, the politicians to buy, the palms to grease, that's where you come in."

"I don't think I want to be involved in this one, Duncan. It's more than I . . . It's not right for me."

"It is exactly right for you, Senator."

The senior senator mistook the low, milk-fed tone of Sharps's voice for weakness. And supposed the businessman was simply going through the motions now.

"There are things you don't understand, Duncan." Hamilton spoke with conviction, sincerity, with the persuasive skills honed during thirty years in politics. "People out there, they aren't about to allow a casino in the valley. Don't think you're the first to come up with the idea. They're all against it. Virtually unanimous. Say it would turn the place into another Las Vegas. Another Atlantic City. No, I know those folks, I'm one of them, and I can assure you they ain't going thataway." A twang and a drawl had come into his voice that he had labored so hard to dispose of years before. It was all Sharps's fault; the businessman made him feel like an insecure adolescent once again.

Sharps responded aggressively, always on the attack. "You will convince those that need convincing."

"Now, Duncan, that's going to put me on the wrong side of things. Be too much of a political liability comes next election."

"Do it," Sharps said without emotion.

"I've tried to explain, I can't—"

"Do it."

"Legislation would be in order. That means the general assembly would have to be convinced."

"Convince them."

"So many people in opposition."

"Buy them. Threaten them. Exploit their weaknesses. Whatever it takes."

"I can't compromise my position."

"Do it, Arlen."

"Or my beliefs."

Sharps, in a voice deceptively smooth, almost a caress, said, "About the girl . . ."

The senator's throat constricted; his penis shriveled, his sphincter tightened, his mouth went dry. "Girl?" he got out with an effort. "What girl?" The man in front of him had undergone some subtle, terrible transformation, turned into a cold threat where only friendship had existed before, an overt power coming into play; and danger, so much danger to himself. Sharps had rigged the game, changed the rules in midcourse.

"Trish." Sharps made it sound like an oath. A foul and despicable personage. Some disgusting creature of a foul, lower order. "Trish is only fifteen years old."

Hamilton arranged a worried mask on his fleshy features. A grimace of anguish and regret distorted his full mouth. His eyes grew moist and melancholy.

"She was a professional," he heard himself say. "Bought by you. By that Suzanne Brody, most likely. Your executive assistant. Just pretending. I knew it was make-believe, a kind of fantasy. No need for me to say how much I appreciate your generosity, Duncan. Your discretion . . ."

"Her mother was waiting for Trish in the lobby."

"Her momma, she called her. I thought it was all part of the act."

"There was no act."

"Come on, Duncan. Tell me the truth. How old is she, really? I'm guessing twenty, at least. There was a maturity about the girl. . . ."

"Fifteen years old, with a birth certificate to prove it. Brought east by her mother on holiday. When she learned a United States senator was staying at the same hotel, she tried to get an interview for her school newspaper. High school, Arlen. Apparently the girl has ambitions in the field, wants to become a journalist. Seems she had contacted one of the secretaries in your Washington office, who made this appointment for her. . . ."

"There was no appointment, there wasn't!"

"Yes, there was. The secretary resigned this morning, Arlen. Went to work for some obscure outfit based on Guam. Or she will, after an extended vacation in parts unknown."

"You did this! You set me up! You bought off one of my employees!"

Sharps glanced at the watch on his wrist. An Audemars Piquet, eighteen-karat gold, it gave the time, the day, the date, the phases of the moon, designed for him and handmade. "By now Trish has broken down, confessed all to her mother. How you assaulted her."

"I never did."

"The mother is a shrewd, practical lady. She had a physician examine the girl. He has determined that she not only had intercourse, but that she'd been treated roughly. A specimen of the semen has been sent to a laboratory for analysis. Identification is possible through such forensic medicine. But of course you knew that?"

"She started it. Approached me. Half-naked, showed herself to me, her privates . . ."

"That child, Arlen? Who is going to believe that?" Sharps smoothed his mustache. "Especially after that business in Washington. What was her name? Oh, yes, Judith. Now this. I'd say you have a serious problem, Arlen."

"You did this to me! You set me up!"

"Nonsense. The facts are all there. Witnesses. People ready to testify. Denial won't alter your embarrassing record, Arlen."

The senator sank back on the couch. All strength was drawn out of him, all ability to struggle; he wanted to weep, to beg Sharps for mercy.

Sharps delivered the coup de grace. "Rape and assault. Two incidents within days of each other. An incorrigible threat to our nation's youth, people will say." He went to the bar set up in the far corner of his office and filled a glass with Jack Daniel's. He brought it to Hamilton, urged him to drink.

"Please," he whimpered.

"You're a married man, Arlen. You have children of your own, with lives and careers of their own, grandchildren. How will they feel if this comes out?"

"Why are you doing this to me?"

"You have a reputation to protect."

"What do you want of me, Mr. Sharps?"

Sharps allowed himself a generous smile. He sat down opposite the senior senator, his manner gentle and compassionate. "My suggestion is that you enlist in this noble campaign of mine. Your efforts on behalf of my casino will certainly result in substantial benefits to us both. You'll make a great deal of money, Arlen. More than you ever made before. And you'll make a new and energetic friend: me. With a particularly powerful base backing your political ambitions. Nothing will be positioned beyond your reach, Arlen. Not even the White House."

"You mean it? Me? President?"

"Why not you? Gerald Ford became president. Jimmy Carter, an unknown Georgia politician. And Dan Quayle is only a heartbeat away from the job. Dan Quayle, imagine it? Why not you, Arlen."

"You think it stands a chance, the casino, I mean?"

"With your good offices."

"No harm in trying, I suppose."

"No harm at all."

The senior senator felt the confidence flowing back up into his body. His strength returning, his courage. Gambling in Colorado? Longer shots had come to pass in political life. You had to know what buttons to push, which hands to shake, what favors to bestow.

"About the girl?" he dared to say.

Sharps cracked his knuckles. "An insignificant matter."

"The mother?"

"As good as taken care of." Sharps extended his hand. "Do we have a deal?"

The senior senator could hardly contain himself. "Oh, yes, a deal, Duncan. Once I give my word, you can depend on me."

"Good," Sharps said, freeing his hand from the senator's hearty grasp. "I'm going to do exactly that."

11

RESENTFUL.

Bitter.

Furious and full of unrestrained loathing. All those emotions darted around in Geneva Sharps after her husband's phone call. Nothing new there, she reminded herself. All her feelings for Duncan these days were negative feelings, had been for a very long time. Feeding off his meanness, nourished by her sense of helplessness.

The call had come in the middle of the night. Jarred her out of a sound sleep. Startled and alarmed her, brought her to wakefulness cursing the desperate cravings and anxieties that had entrapped her in this poor excuse for a marriage.

The man was a bully personified. A tyrant. A slave

master. Controlling people with his wealth, with his power, with the bruising pain of his lumpy fists.

No more of that. She was nobody's slave. No one's servant, subject to Sharps's whims and intrigues and sudden eruptions of rage and violence. No more would she offer him a target to beat into submission. He had plundered her soul and her flesh for his own satisfaction, without concern for her needs. No more would she suffer the humiliation and the pain. She deserved better treatment. Deserved a better life. More than he would ever give her.

Respect and concern and attention; she yearned for them all. And love.

Love in all its many-splendored dimensions. The kind of love that enhanced a woman, made her glad to come awake in the morning, made her greet each day as an adventure full of surprise and reward. God, how she craved that love, the love that drenched a woman in emotional comfort and pleasure and, yes, passion.

How long had it been? Since she had been truly aroused, elevated to that sublime level at which she transcended her own flesh, to become one with another human being? How long since she had been at the mercy of that passion, at the mercy of ministrations freely given, pleading for release from a bondage that promised total freedom?

Duncan Turner Sharps. Known from border to border. From coast to coast. Aboard all the ships at sea. One of America's living treasures. A man of his time. A doer of great deeds. A fabulous wheeler-dealer. In whose presence there was the illusion that no poverty existed in the world, no ugliness, no one doing without. Beloved of the tabloids, of the gossip columnists, of all who pandered to the bitch-goddess, Success. Duncan Turner Sharps.

She hated the man.

Off with his head.

Consign him to hell, to eternal flame and torment.

Her own reaction was grimly amusing. A woman scorned. Worse than that. A woman left alone, mocked, awakened in the middle of the night and commanded to perform tasks for her master. A puppet dancing to the orders of the man on the other end of the string.

Naked, she climbed out of bed, put on a long, white terry-cloth robe. The weight and substance of the robe was reassuring, though the house was warm and comfortable. The house was heated according to Sharps's instruction. Had the heating system gone awry, a backup burner would immediately cut in so that barely a degree was lost.

"Fucking Rocky Mountain winters!" Sharps had complained after closing on the Aspen house. It had been something Geneva wanted. Putting her close to the slopes, allowing her to spend much of her time skiing. Sharps told her she was nuts to go sliding down a hill, risking life and limb, submitting herself to the cold. "Not gonna get me to freeze my butt." He had insisted on that backup system, had it installed two days later. The first of many alterations in the house, made mostly to suit its new owner.

A designer had been hired. Brought in from London to make the changes Sharps wanted, to decorate the rooms. Paint and wallpapers were selected and applied. The floors were scraped and stained and varnished or covered with expensive broadloom. An occasional Oriental rug was introduced for color and, in the words of the designer, "for visual excitement." Additions were built; the glass room that contained the lap pool and the whirlpool, a sauna, a suite of offices, and a greenery filled with living plants. When all of it was done to Sharps's satisfaction, when all the furniture had been delivered and suitably arranged, when the kitchen was fully stocked, the closets hung with suitable clothing, only then did he agree to install himself and his wife on the premises. That had happened a full twenty-two months after the closing, in the final days of the ski season. Seventy-two hours later Sharps flew out for a meeting in Lisbon that, he said, "was going to mean some really impressive bucks."

Geneva stayed behind.

The pattern of her life with Sharps was now very well established. His extended absences, whether from Aspen or New York or the summer cottage on Block Island, were frequent and came with little warning. Soon-she began to look forward to his departures; his absence, at least, allowed her some semblance of privacy and peace.

In the Aspen kitchen, a kitchen created as if for a four-star restaurant—polished steel and mirrored surfaces—she poured coffee from a machine that produced a perfect cup every time, a machine that never failed to deliver. Better than a cook, that machine. Certainly better than a wife.

"Take notes," were the first words Sharps had spoken over the phone. No thought that she might have been asleep. No query as to the state of her health. Or the condition of her emotions. No interest in what she had been doing. Or not doing. Or would do the following day. Nothing about her life mattered to him. Nothing about her mattered. As long as she was at hand when he needed her. "Take notes."

"You woke me," she complained, still thick with sleep.

"That's okay, you're not asleep anymore. Got the pad and pen?" There was always writing material near the bed, alongside every phone in every one of their— make that *his*—residences. So that his orders could be inscribed and thus never misunderstood or forgotten. Word for word, that was how she had been instructed to put them down.

"I've decided to make a party," he began again. "New Year's Eve. Got that? A hundred people, maybe more. My secretary is preparing a guest list which she'll fax on to you in the morning. Check it out. They'll be coming in from all over. People important to me, so arrangements will have to be made. Transportation, sleeping accommodations—"

"You mean here?" she interrupted. "At the house?"

"I decided against that. In the condos I own or whatever. Look into that. What I want you to do is make up a list of locals. People who matter around that town. The mayor. Planning and zoning people. That kind. Also, you met any movie stars?"

"No. Should I have?"

"Well, the place is loaded with them. This actor fellow, Nicholson, he has a house in Aspen. And John Denver. That other guy, plays a cop on TV—Johnson something. People like that, to dress up the evening. Also, some of your skiing friends."

"I don't have any skiing friends."

"Meet some. Young ones, good-looking ones. I don't want the place to look like an old soldiers' home. Lots of pretty young women. You better get on the invitations in the morning. Also the food and booze."

"Duncan, I am here by myself. This is going to be a lot of work, all those people."

"Hire someone. If you didn't have that phobia about having people in the house . . ."

"It's not a phobia."

"Some servants, you could have help."

"When will you be home? When can I expect you?"

"Home? You mean out there? I don't know. I've got a lot on my mind right now."

There was always something more pressing than being with her. Something more urgent and more profitable.

"Take care of things," he ordered roughly. Duncan Turner Sharps treated everyone the same: badly.

"It's your party. Shouldn't you be here? Shouldn't—"

The phone was dead in her hand. He'd hung up. Good old Duncan, he never changed.

She added a jigger of brandy to her coffee and carried the cup into the pool room at the back of the house. Underwater lighting cast an eerie green glow around the glass walls. She touched a switch, and forced air jets came on in the sunken hot tub. She sipped coffee and watched the water bubble and swirl. A dozen people would be comfortable in its roomy confines. She tested the water with a toe and, satisfied, placed the cup on the floor and shed her robe.

Geneva was tall with an athlete's strong shoulders. She was heavy-breasted and shapely, without being delicate, long of leg. She lowered herself into the tub, stretching out, allowing the water to rise to her chin. She put her head back and closed her eyes and emptied her mind, until alien images began to float into place.

She touched one breast and then the other, fingers light and tantalizing, her nipples rising to the touch. Circles of sensation descended into her torso, and soon her hand trailed after them, coming to rest between her fine, round thighs.

Her fingers moved. And a vision faded into view behind her eyelids. A man, features vague but pleasing to look at, hovering over her, leaning her way. She made an effort to see him clearly, to engrave his ideal face in memory, to identify him. One thing: the man she had conjured up, her creation, perfect in so many ways, the man who so skillfully aroused and pleased her in that warm, wet interlude, in no way resembled Duncan Turner Sharps.

When he woke the next morning in his New York apartment, Sharps felt unrested and irritated, though he had slept for a full four hours; he seldom required more sleep. He searched his mind for the source of that irritation and very quickly fixed on his wife. Damn Geneva, always presenting him with petty annoyances and problems; the nature of the beast, he decided. The woman was a continuing burr under his skin; her mere presence in the world had begun to get on his nerves. He simply couldn't depend on her to get done what he wanted done. He put in a call to Suzanne Brody.

"How soon can you get over here?" he said without preliminary.

He wanted her at the Apartment, as it was known around the executive suite of Sharps Industries. "I could use an hour," was her reply.

"Thirty minutes," he said before he hung up.

He used the time to shower, to shave—his face and the sides of his head where a thin silver stubble showed up each morning. He was wearing gray flannel slacks and a black silk shirt, open at the collar, by the time his executive assistant came through the front door, the only one of his employees to have a key of her own. Brody never used the key when Geneva was at home, sensing Mrs. Sharps's disapproval of the arrangement, refraining from giving offense or creating a problem for her boss.

She went directly to the kitchen at the back of the first floor of the huge apartment and filled two oversize white mugs with coffee. Black, both of them. Then she proceeded with the coffee to Sharps's private office. He greeted her with a soft grunt and accepted the mug without a word. He leaned back in his chair and swung his feet up onto the edge of the desk, looking past Brody to the far wall, where an eighteenth-century Dutch painting of pink, red, and white carnations hung. It was a restful rendering, the subdued colors pleasant to contemplate from time to time. He checked the gold Audemars Piquet; twenty-five minutes had expired since he had phoned Brody. The woman was a marvel of efficiency. If she had been a man, he'd have long ago elevated her to a vice-presidency, put her on his board of directors—a mere concession to corporate fashion; he *was* Sharps Industries, after all—and raised her salary by triple at least.

As a woman, however . . . He eliminated the subject from his mind.

"Let's talk Aspen."

She reached into the leather envelope she carried, withdrew some typewritten notes. "My sources indicate that an Arab investment group has been nosing around, looking for land."

"Saudi Arabia?"

"They're based in Tunisia. A man named Abdul el-Haramani is the most visible."

"Never heard of him."

"Just the tip of the sand dune. . . ." It was meant to be a small expression of wit; when Sharps failed to respond, she hurried on. "Another conglomerate. Purely financial this time. I hear they want to build a hotel, also. Something large and garish. I managed to get a look at some preliminary architectural sketches—looks like one of those old jukeboxes, all flashing lights and shiny chrome."

"Dammit! What I don't need now is another player. How serious are the Arabs?"

"They've been scouting around for land in Aspen, but they've made no offers, nor have they talked to any of the owners."

"Not Ayres?"

"Not yet."

He trusted her judgment. "You think they will?"

"It's likely. That parcel of his is eminently desirable, easy access to all of the downtown area and the ski runs. You said it yourself, Mr. Sharps, the location can't be beat."

She sat without moving, nothing showing on that finely boned pale face. There were moments when he suspected she was mocking him, finding him a source of private amusement. But for the most part, he chose to believe that there were elements in her makeup that continued to elude him. So many questions that he had about her remained unanswered; none of them relevant any longer when it came to her employment. She played an increasingly vital role in his business life every day; he depended on her as he did on no one else. Certainly not Geneva.

"I have to make some moves," he said. "The Japs are in this up to their eyeballs. And some group from California, talking shopping mall. Now the damned Arabs."

"How can I help?"

That's what he liked about Brody. Right to the heart of the matter. No shaking and baking. No false modesty. Just, How can I help? She was a lot like he was when he was a young man scratching and clawing for a handhold. Only by the time he was her age, he'd made it big. Was a man on a mission.

"I want to make a party."

She understood at once. "In Aspen."

"On the nose. New Year's Eve. A couple of hundred guests. My secretary's got a list. Geneva's out there now, she's supposed to add to it. I want movie stars. Lots of beautiful young people to dress it up. Everything first class. They'll be coming from all over the country. I'll fly 'em all in, house 'em wherever we can. Maybe it's too complicated for Geneva to pull off by herself."

She picked up on the suggestion. "I'll take care of it."

"The party, the guest list, the booze, food, getting the house shaped up."

"Everything, Mr. Sharps."

"Right, everything. Except Ayres. He gets the personal touch. Crotchety old bastard, wants to control how the land is used, even after he gets rid of it."

"When do you want me to leave?"

"Today."

"I'll need a day or two to tidy things up at the office."

"All right. As soon as you can. You can stay at the house with Geneva. Give her a call, tell her you're coming."

She chose her words with care. "If you don't mind, Mr. Sharps, I'd prefer staying at one of the condos. Allows me more freedom of movement, there'll be people in and out, you understand—"

"Whatever. Make your own plans." He grew thoughtful and massaged his burnished scalp. "This guy Hamilton, the senator. He could be trouble, the kind of tastes he's got. Let's keep him under control, feed his appetites, if you have to. Just keep him on track."

"Will do." Then: "Mrs. Sharps, she knows I'm on the way?"

For an extended moment, she thought he hadn't heard the question.

"Keep in touch, Suzanne."

"Yes, sir."

"And as for Geneva, she's not about to give you any trouble. She'll do as she's told. Okay?"

The answer didn't please her at all. There was bound to be conflict between her and Geneva Sharps, sooner or later. And when it came, she suspected her own position would be shaky and impermanent. Still, the only thing she said was, "Yes, sir," which signaled the end of the meeting.

12

D E V L I N went down.

He started early that morning. Riding the lift to the top of the mountain. Urging it to go faster, intrigued by the height at which he found himself, as if doing this for the first time.

Alone in the lift chair, legs dangling, blinking against the exquisite bite of that chilling Rocky Mountain air, sensing his body's reaction as if never before. He had to repress a sudden impulse to leave the chair, to leap out into space, to hand himself over to the rugged white peaks. To be alive as never before in the face of his own imminent demise.

Was that all it was, then, this skiing. This love affair with heights. This obsession with the mountain. Any mountain. Mountains in France and Switzerland, in

Germany and in Spain, in Canada, in Peru. Racing downhill, turning himself into a projectile hurtling ahead in competition against time, against himself, against the dormant but always dangerous mountain.

Why?

What did he hope to find?

What did he hope to prove?

On that run, questions and doubts cluttering up his mind, he went down.

If only there had been a clock on him. The run of his life, it was. The thrill suddenly returned to skiing. All restraints lifted. All fears wiped away. Going faster than he'd ever gone before. How he longed to believe it. To believe that all the physical ailments had miraculously been healed. The strength returned to his once battered knees. The resilience. The body memory that took over in moments of stress, when a skier crossed over the line, beyond self-control, beyond his limitations.

He worked the poles with all the strength he could muster. Slamming them down into the snow. Finding that iota of extra power and thrust that made him go faster. Faster still. Faster than he had been capable of skiing twenty years earlier when all the triumphs appeared to be his to take. When all the glory and gold belonged to him. The adulation of the crowds. The victory of his will over the mountain. He had beaten the best of the world's skiers.

Outstanding competitors, every one. The French. The Swiss. The Germans. Especially that Basque with his compact, explosive style. For that delectable slice of time—too short, too short—he had been as good as any of them. Better. Oh, yes, better. Proud of his ability, proud of his focus, proud of the things he could command his body to do. Without doubt in those days. Without thought. Without even a twinge of fear. King of the Mountain . . .

All that went through his mind as he made that Aspen run, the mountain falling away under his skis in an almost vertical drop. Convinced that at last he had put it all together again. Had discovered that which he had lost so long ago. His mouth opened in a silent cry of ecstasy. To laugh aloud. To exult in this sweet, isolated flash of glory.

And then he fell.

There was no notice. No single thing that went wrong. His legs had kept their strength. His boots were firmly bound to the skis. He ran into no unexpected, concealed obstacle. Just a fall. The skis losing their edge, he would later decide. Going out from under him. Dropping him heavily, sharp pain stabbing into his left shoulder, the impact reverberating along his spine. He spun out of control on the white surface, limbs flailing, giving himself over to the pull of inertia, concerned only that he might be propelled into the treeline. At last he slowed to a stop.

He lay without moving. Mentally examining his body. His limbs. He swallowed, tasting for blood. Nothing was broken. No blood. No sharp pains that would have indicated some organ torn or shattered. No paralysis. No permanent damage.

Except to his pride.

And the fragile hope that he had regained his youthful skills. He cursed his foolishness. His childish belief in miracles. There were no miracles on the mountain, only the harsh reality that sooner or later knocked every skier to the ground in ignominious defeat. It was time, he told himself, to give it up. The dreams, the fantasies, the hope for a deliverance from mediocrity. He had been denied forever.

He lay on the crispy white blanket that covered the slope, willing himself to sleep. Hoping to give himself over to that healing darkness without pain or disappointment. To drift into the void. But even that satisfaction was denied him, and before long he began to wonder if anyone had seen him fall, witnessed his humiliation; put down by the mountain, by his own failure of discipline, by his lack of nerve. He could almost hear the mocking voices of his peers, the laughter this spill would engender in Aspen's gathering places. He shivered, more in fright than in cold, and forced himself to sit up.

After a moment he climbed to his feet. He checked his skis. They were still clamped securely to his boots. His ankles were fine, and his knees; at least as good as they would ever again be. He took the poles in his gloved hands and rolled his shoulders, forward and back. A throbbing came and gradually departed, the pain acute enough to emphasize his mortality.

Not so long ago he would have been shocked at such a thought. Death had been only a vague presence then, its ominous being a threat to other beings, those less well equipped by nature to avoid its terrors. Devlin had been designed to win out over all his enemies, immune to normal ills and hurts, able to overcome even the most exotic dangers. He had been born to win.

Until that day long ago when life turned to shit in front of his face.

He got himself turned around and started back

down. Wary of the mountain this time. Of its traps and tricks, the lumps and bumps that plagued all skiers. He went slower this time. Cautious. Searching ahead. Maintaining control. Accustomed to public loving and praise, he wallowed in a private despair, beaten by the searing memory of what he had once been and was no longer.

Changes had to be made. Essential alterations of memory and vision that would make him greater, into some finer, more noble being than he had ever before been. What sort of person could that new self be? He felt a rising desperation for an answer, for a hint of things to come. But it would be a long time before he discovered an answer.

The Aspen Sports Association (ASA) was a sleek and polished operation, all gleaming steel, black leather, and floor-to-ceiling mirrors. Each morning two dedicated workers with an eye for detail and a love of minutiae went to work polishing the metal parts of the complex body machines and cleaning the glass of the tiniest mote that might get in the way of any member's view of himself. Or herself. Reflected perfection, that was the nature of ASA. It said so in its new, slick, four-color sales brochure.

Membership in ASA cost a great deal, a fact that severely limited its ranks, as was intended. Nevertheless the club produced a solid profit each year for its owners, a group of Swedish investors.

Carefully modulated, unobtrusive music provided a soothing background, softening the metallic click of the moving parts of the exercise machines. Otherwise the air was still, faintly scented to mask unpleasant odors and suitably conditioned, the temperature regulated according to the seasons.

In this tranquilizing atmosphere, the members progressed without haste from one machine to another, attending to specific muscle groups, aiming to attain an idealized version of a man or woman, clinging to a youthful appearance, if not youth; striving for everlasting good health, hoping for everlasting life.

Each member followed a regimen plotted out according to body type, age, physical condition, and stated personal goals. All under the careful guidance of an experienced trainer; or so it said in the sales brochure. Members came in a variety of sizes and ages and shapes. Trainers were always young and lean and sinewy, their bodies exuding good health and boundless energy, objects of envy and desire.

Devlin was a trainer. Following a morning of ferocious skiing, the refined, restrained confines of the sports palace was a pleasant change. He went from station to station, observing, offering suggestions, support, always putting his own finely muscled body on display. This afternoon he wore black nylon shorts and a red cotton tank shirt. And an encouraging smile that revealed those great white teeth of his.

For a prescribed number of hours each day he sought to help his fellow man, and woman, to work harder, practice discipline—"No pain, no gain," he told them cheerfully—and strive to be the very best they could be. In return he received a modest salary and rather substantial tips; most of his clients were well-to-do, as he thought of them. Rich, in some cases, he guessed. Men tipped him the most. As if by so doing they established some kind of superiority over him, not evident in the way they looked. The women were more circumspect with their money, careful not to spoil him. Avoiding even a hint that they might be trying to buy his favor.

Some of them tried. To pay for his flesh. To buy his body, for an evening or for the longer term. Few of them were daring enough or insensitive enough to make the offer directly and openly. Instead there were dinner invitations or quiet evenings of music and conversation and whatever else seemed in order. Payment, when it was offered, was in the form of gifts: a gold chain, perhaps, or a hand-knit sweater, or a gift certificate in one of the more expensive shops in town. Once there had been an envelope containing ten crisp, new one-hundred-dollar bills, the best gift of all; although the lady in question had left town the next day, her husband leading the way.

Few women got to Devlin. Beautiful girls and women had been a constant in his life since he was a boy, and he had learned early on that some of them would go to extraordinary lengths to get him into bed. For the most part it had been fun. A natural extension of his life on skis. Across the United States, in every ski area, across Europe, an army of desirable and compliant women waited for the athletes to complete their runs. Parties, dinners, a night on the town; all an inevitable part of après-ski. In the midst of this feeding frenzy, there was Devlin, always able to claim the lion's share.

Until he began to lose interest. Body and mind, he grew exhausted by the pace, by the succession of interchangeable lovers, the hung-over mornings that found him in strange beds with strangers. He had begun looking for a connection with more permanence. Someone like Barbara. But that had meant a year away from his beloved mountains, a year off skis, a year among Palm Beach's inbred, boring population, full of hypocrisy and a misplaced idea about their importance in the current flow of life in the good old U.S. of A.

Devlin decided to take a sabbatical from women. From love and lovemaking. To rest himself psychologically and physically. He convinced himself it would be no worse than if he were to give up cigarettes; and no less salutary. Oh, the constant craving was there in the beginning, the repeated reminders of past pleasures and delights, and always that hope for a new foray into the unknown. But he stood firm against temptation, holding to his resolution. A changed man. Until he saw Geneva Sharps for the first time.

She noticed him, too, that first afternoon at ASA. And made him out for just another stud, one of so many around Aspen. A little shopworn, a little older than most, but still a prime physical specimen. He would be good with that lithe, muscular body, a world-class bedroom athlete. She recognized a boldness in his glance, in the insolent pelvic thrust when he was still; all leavened by an incipient wariness. As if he were searching for the direction from which a lethal attack would be launched.

He would be good. In that practiced, self-conscious way men like him always were. His body movements meant to extract a maximum amount of gratification for himself, providing pleasure and satisfaction only incidentally. How many had there been before? Athletes, actors, businessmen; so damned full of themselves, locating themselves at the center of the universe, while using and abusing any woman who happened to enter their uneven orbit.

She had no reason to believe that this man, this stud, would be any different from all the others. How much concealed baggage did he carry? Packed to overflowing with deceit and betrayal, an overriding self-interest. She needed a man with strength and courage, with the determination to help her fulfill her monumental dreams.

Would he love her, this man?

Was he capable of loving; love, more than anything, was essential to her plan. He would have to believe in her totally. Give himself over to her needs in preference to his own, her desires, her ambitions. More than anything, he would have to bend to her will.

Go slow. The words were emblazoned in her mind. They leaped out at her like a roadside warning sign alerting travelers to a treacherous stretch of road.

Curva peligrosa. The sign on a winding mountain road in Mexico had pleased her eye. Her ear. Stayed with her as some kind of an invisible talisman. *Curva peligrosa.* Dangerous curves ahead.

She continued doing sit-ups on a padded bench, hands clasped behind her head, twisting her torso as she came up into a sitting position. The muscles across her middle began to ache, but she kept going.

This time will be different. This time had to be different. This one, with those calm gray-green eyes, the even set of his sensual mouth, the confident way he held himself; he would be ready for her, to accept what she had to give and to give what she had to have. He would measure up in every way. Be able to stay the course.

Don't force the issue. Let her eyes meet his, let him look at her all he wanted, let the seed be planted. Allow time for it to take root and grow. Allow the plant to ripen to maturity; and then she would reap the harvest.

Go slow.

Finished with the sit-ups, she moved over to another of the gleaming machines, attending her upper body. Eyes fixed in space, she breathed deeply, breasts thrusting and receding under the pink leotard she wore. Counting reps.

He watched her openly. No ski bunny, this one. No jittery postcollege girl out for a one-week fling. No refugee from a dull job in a dull town looking for adventure and rescue from the doldrums of her daily life.

The profound, provocative look of maturity in her magnificent face and figure. In the steadiness of her gaze. He had seen her look at him, that measuring glance, unafraid, turning away only when she'd seen enough. She looked fantastic on the bench as she lifted and pulled, her torso strong and fleshless, her full woman's breasts outlined under the pink nylon, the nipples in sharp relief. She, Devlin decided, had it all.

More than beautiful. There was an almost sullen cast to her face in repose, her pale eyes unblinking, her mouth in a perpetual pout. With considerable trepidation, he went over to where she was exercising, unable to stay away. He looked her over at close range in an unhurried appraisal, making no effort to conceal his admiration.

"I've been watching you," he began. He gave her a fleeting grin.

She never missed a beat, working her back and shoulders. This was a woman who knew how to take care of her body. Good muscle tone, good definition, her skin taut and tawny.

"I noticed," she said.

Another grin, and a pass at his hair, failing to keep it in place. "I'm Devlin," he said. "John Thomas Andrew Devlin. The Irish Catholics are big on a lot of names, homage to everyone in the family who has gone before."

She interrupted her workout and mopped her face and neck with a towel. Her eyes lifted to his, allowing him to see nothing that was on her mind.

"Lots of names and lots of children."

"My folks discovered birth control at about the same time they gave up on the Roman church. I'm the last of the long line."

She shifted onto a mat on the floor, doing leg-ups. Raise them about twelve inches, spread them deliberately, then back again, ankles touching, and lower them to the mat. Then, again. He was enthralled by the way her thighs expanded and returned to normal, the muscles receding. "It's been a long time since you took communion, then."

He laughed. "A long time."

"Or confessed your sins?" She avoided his glance.

What about her made him so uneasy? That deep surety that announced she held her life in a secure grip. Unshakable in the rightness of her beliefs. Convinced nothing could go wrong, nothing could happen without her approval and cooperation.

"Sins," he said, buying time to collect his thoughts. "Not me. I'm as pure as a newborn babe."

She began another set. Raise 'em up, spread 'em, reverse the procedure. What incredible legs. Coming together in a perfect joining, below that sweet, so softly rounded belly. What would she say if he were to tell her precisely what he wanted to do to her? Here. Now.

"Okay," he said, aware of the boyish uncertainty she created in him. "I've told you my name. Won't you tell me yours, Miss . . . ?" When she failed to reply he said, "Where's the harm in that?"

She weighed her response. "Mrs.," she said. "Mrs. Geneva Sharps."

Married. The wide gold band on her left hand told him that. Told him even more. Studded as it was with finely cut diamonds, all those expensive points of light under a ceiling of neon tubes. Mr. Sharps, whoever he was, did very well, whatever his line of work. Certainly he made a great deal of money. But there was more to a marriage than money.

"I'm the trainer here." One of many trainers, he might have said, and didn't. Anxious to give himself some distinction. To impress the lady. As if a woman with a wealthy husband were susceptible to a part-time trainer in an Aspen sports club. It would take more than that.

She finished the set and leaned back on her elbows, observing him from afar. "You're wasting your talents, Devlin."

He ignored the implication of her words. "These body toys . . ." His sweeping gesture took in all the machines. "It takes more than these to get you in condition, to keep you there."

"Go away, John Thomas Andrew."

"My friends call me Dev."

"Mr. Devlin." She spoke in a toneless voice, and he noticed for the first time a slight, furry rasp. "I have no need of your services."

He refused to accept her lack of interest. Refused to make peace with the notion that he had failed with her. Struck out. Not with Geneva Sharps, this most desirable of women.

"There must be something I can do for you." He put a leer in his voice and learned at once that it was a mistake.

"That will be enough!" The words snapped out of her like a whip. Inflicting pain, drawing invisible blood. "You may leave now, Mr. Devlin." Dismissed. Chastised the way a teacher might chastise a recalcitrant student. Sent from the room. No longer wanted.

Devlin couldn't let go. He was driven to continue talking to her, making a connection, no matter how tenuous. "Most people don't realize how useless exercise alone is," he said. "Proper diet is essential to good health. I could have a menu drawn up. Nothing too radical. Controlled calories and limited fat, easy to prepare, or—"

"No, thanks."

"I've been watching you, and I'm sure you're a skier. As I am. What you should be working on is the treadmill, the stationary bicycle, and use weights on your legs. Bring those muscles to optimum strength. Without—"

"Not interested, Devlin."

"Herbal wrap?" he said, lightening up. "Multiple skin and body treatments? Massages. Yoga classes. Then there's the sauna and the steam room. What do you say, Mrs. Sharps? Want to give some of it a shot?"

She was laughing, and that pleased him. She stood up, tall and magnificently formed. She moved away, and he went after her.

"My husband would not be happy about you hitting on me this way."

He took that as encouragement, subtle but definite. He gave a helpless boyish shrug. "You are a fantastic-looking woman."

"Duncan would strip those beautiful young muscles right off your bones."

Much better. He liked it, her response. There was fire simmering under the ice, and a certain amount of interest. He was sure of it.

"Happily?"

"I beg your pardon?"

"Are you happily married?"

"You're being insolent, Devlin."

He liked the way she said his name. "You haven't answered the question."

She stared at him, and though he held her gaze, he was made uneasy. "Go away and find another play-mate." Each word was enunciated separately, without inflection, missiles spat his way. "Find a pretty child for yourself, someone in your own bracket, Devlin. Take care of your pretty sports machines. I can take care of myself. Now, good-bye."

She settled onto a rowing machine, ignoring Devlin. After a brief, uncomfortable interval, he withdrew.

13

GENEVA Sharps took up residence in Devlin's mind. Her intrusive presence shattered his thoughts. Rocked his concentration and made him uncertain and weak with longing. He visualized her as he had seen her at ASA, moist with perspiration, her body in motion, her vision clouded and watchful. At other times he summoned her up in the mist of fancy, ethereal and pristine, beyond the damage of his carnal appetite. Or he entertained her in the shifting privacy of imagination, accessible suddenly, her flesh writhing to his touch, accepting the grossest of his excesses and returning them in kind.

He lay in his bed, early darkness filling the corners of the room, projecting that classic face of hers on the ceiling. She gazed down at him, a distant vision of per-

fection, allowing nothing of her private self to be seen.
A shifting of features, the eyes glowing hotly, the
finely sculpted lips parted, the tip of her tongue in
sight, coming closer.

Instantly he was hard. An inflexible thrust of tissue
and blood and tension. He quivered and twitched, rising up to meet the vision.

For so many years he had been convinced that he
moved through life with a perpetual hard-on. Half-a-
hard, to be precise, was how he mocked his own sexual preoccupations. For all the sex, the bodily contact,
the exchange of mysterious secretions, for all the
kisses and murmured intimacies, for all of the women,
he had nothing to show. No lover. No companion. No
wife.

Most of all, no child. No living tissue that was both
separate and a living extension of himself. No one to
watch over and nourish and urge on to greater things.
No one to leave behind. Skiing and screwing; neither
left permanent tracks.

He laughed at his own words, his own thoughts; all
affectation. More literary this time than most. Well,
why not? Those first two years in college, he had fancied himself as a writer. Not a novelist; novelists dealt
with impressions and deceits. Not him. He was after
the *truth,* convinced at the time that he had uncovered
that precious and elusive element. Or at least the single road that led to truth.

An investigative reporter is what he would become.
A muckraker of the contemporary scene. A combina-
tion of Woodward and Bernstein; but better, of course.
Ruthless in his pursuit of wrongdoing in government
and industry. Rooting out fraud and and deception, rip-

ping corrupt leaders out of their once safe havens, exposing their failures of nerve and honor to the world.

Writing was a stupid profession. A man alone with his ideas, his reflections; as if anyone cared about what he had to say. What a colossal conceit. Besides, it was too solitary a life, himself and a blank sheet of paper; he had better ways to occupy his time.

There was always skiing. Something he was good at. Better than good. And highly competitive. Victory came almost without effort from the start. And so many satellite rewards; travel to distant mountains, all expenses paid. There was always someone around to provide spending money when he needed it: a coach, a sponsor, an enthusiastic fan. And the women. All those beautiful and complaisant women. All goals were attainable. All men his admirers, his friends. All women his passionate lovers. Life was perfect.

Until . . .

He refused to think about that.

His hand came to rest on his penis. Still a hefty organ, but no longer tumescent. He sat up, feet flat on the floor, torn between guilt and appetite, wishing he had never met Geneva Sharps. Someone was knocking at the door of his room, a controlled, insistent summons. He switched on the reading lamp on the night table alongside his bed.

"Who is it?"

"It's me, Dev."

That deceptively soft tidewater accent of Peggy Pearce. No less authoritative for the extended accents. He had made her out to be a hard nut the first time they met, and nothing had happened since to contradict him. More than just the force behind their little burglary operation, she controlled Hank Ricketts and Sam Daly, and would have controlled him as well, if he allowed her to. *"Eat something. . . ."* Give in to her on even a little thing and he would be lost, his will broken, his destiny in her hands.

"Nonsense," he said to himself. He was stronger than that, more independent, more in control.

"It's open," he said aloud, in a voice forced and falsely friendly, as if he welcomed the intrusion.

She led the way in, Ricketts and Daly close behind. Looking great in a plaid wool skirt and a dark turtleneck that outlined her fine figure. Devlin wondered about her; what she would be like in bed. More than able to take care of Ricketts or Daly, or both of them, if that was her taste. She would be, he conceded, a load even for him.

"What's up?" he said, making himself cheerful.

She seated herself on the foot of the bed with a proprietary display of confidence. "Sam got back from Denver a little while ago. We've been talking."

Daly glared at him, as if finally locating a target for some long-building rage of his. He shook his head from one side to the other.

"Not good?" Devlin said, keeping it amiable.

"Not good," Ricketts echoed glumly.

"These things happen," Peggy said, addressing all three of them. The leader of the band, recharging the morale of her followers. Her energy up, her expression encouraging, her outlook optimistic. She explained in a logical, convincing manner. "Most of the jewelry was fake, paste imitations. There were only a few real pieces. It breaks down to about three hundred dollars for each of us."

"Hardly worth the effort," Ricketts droned.

Devlin wondered about his partners' trustworthiness. The three of them, they seemed close. He, on the other hand, stood outside, almost a hired hand. Still, either he kept his faith in them or he ended their arrangement; and that might present problems he was not ready to confront. Be careful, he warned himself. Be smart.

"Thing is," Sam Daly said petulantly, "I could've used the cash."

"Couldn't we all," Devlin said.

"Which is why we're here," Peggy put in. "I've got another job lined up."

"More profitable than the Burnside house?" Devlin swore at himself for speaking out. "Not that it's anybody's fault." He tried to make amends.

"Whose fault you think it is?" Ricketts punched the words out pugnaciously. "These things happen."

"Maybe," Peggy Pearce offered, those violet eyes unwavering, "you think you could do a better job of lining up the marks, Dev? Maybe you'd prefer to—"

"No, no," he answered quickly. "I'm not complaining."

"No problems?" she said. "You're sure of that?"

"No problems."

"No doubts?"

"Thing is," Daly put in, "Evan Larson is not about to come up with good money for paste."

"No fence will," Peggy said.

"Those things happen," Ricketts said again, his manner milder, more conciliatory this time.

"Right," Peggy said.

"Right," Devlin said with an enthusiasm he didn't feel.

"Okay," Peggy said, apparently satisfied that they were all in harmony. "Let's get on to the next one. You know who Jerry Cross is?"

"The movie star," Ricketts informed them. "Big-time guy."

"That's what I oughta be," Peggy said conversationally, but meaning it. "A movie star. Picture in all the papers. Interviewed on television. All that money flowing in."

"You oughta be," Ricketts agreed. "With your good looks and that figure of yours."

"It takes more than that," she said.

Devlin nodded solemnly. "Some talent, some craft, a lot of hard work."

"A lot of luck, is what." She bit off the words, earnest and grim. "Knowing the right people, connections. Being in the right place at the right time."

"Right," Daly said. "You're better-looking than most of those bitches on the box."

"Better," Ricketts said.

"About Jerry Cross?" Devlin said.

Peggy slipped easily back into her role of strategist and leader. "We have been doing his house for nearly six weeks. Cleaning it twice a week, since he got back to Aspen. I know it inside and out."

"Tell Devlin about the chick," Daly said.

"Cross has got a new girlfriend. Half his age, a baby-faced blonde. They ski all day, and I figure they get it on all night. Cross is no spring chicken, either. He better take care or this babe will give him a coronary before long. The point is, he can't get enough of her, in the sack or out. Poor sucker must spend all his money on her. Presents, expensive presents. You name it, she's got it. Rings, bracelets, pins, earrings, necklaces. Diamonds, rubies, emeralds. At least one long strand of black pearls and about a dozen watches, the cheapest one must've cost twenty-five grand. I guess she figures Cross is a regular money machine, the way she treats the stuff. No safe, she leaves the stuff around like it was dirty laundry. All over their bedroom, in the bathroom, a couple of jewelry boxes on a shelf in one of the closets. And cash. One day I walked in on her helping herself from a bundle of green. Must have been ten thousand bucks, maybe more. All in hundreds."

"Ripe," Daly said.

"Exactly. Ripe and ready."

"When do we hit 'em?" Ricketts said.

"They're on the slopes every morning by ten, never miss a day. Tell you the truth, old Jerry is pretty good on a pair of sticks. We go in early and take our time. Make sure we don't miss anything. Make a real haul."

"When?" Devlin said. His pulse was racing, and fear lodged in his chest like a swollen glob of acid. Sooner or later things would go wrong. Sooner or later one of them would make some terrible mistake. No matter how careful they were, events had a life of their own. He didn't want to be caught, didn't want to spend a considerable portion of his life behind bars. But some unnamed compulsion prevented him from letting go. Not yet.

"Day after tomorrow," Peggy said. "That gives us time to go over the floor plan, scout the exterior, so you get a fix on the way in. Competence," she added, "that's the key. And thoroughness. Nobody goofs, right?"

"Right."

14

*T*HE next night they played poker. Ricketts and Sam Daly. It was Ricketts who found out about the game, from a bearded man in the bar where he'd stopped off for a beer or two that afternoon. Turned out that the heavy man—his name was Hiram—had served at the San Diego Naval Base, same as Ricketts had. But at different times.

Bond enough for Hiram to mention the game to Ricketts, invite him to play. Hiram said it was okay if Ricketts brought his friend along.

"Always room for another player."

Kickoff time; eight o'clock. On the second floor of a two-family house on Original Street, only a few hundred yards from the western edge of town. Outside, a few flakes had started their slow drift earthward. Inside, it was warm, a modest room set up for the evening. A poker table surrounded by chairs. A refrigerator in one corner, and a narrow table stocked with liquor alongside. You paid for your refreshments as you helped yourself, cash deposited in an old coffee jar. Beers were two dollars each, hard liquor three. Soft drinks were a bargain at a buck a can. There were the makings for those who wanted a sandwich.

The rules of the game were few. Dealer's choice. No wild cards. Dollar ante. Dollar minimum, five-dollar limit.

"Just a friendly little game," Hiram explained. "The cards talk. No cutthroat. No raise after a pass. Got it?"

Three hours into the game, Ricketts was holding his own. Sam Daly was a hundred and fifty ahead. And feeling no pain. He was drinking steadily, his confidence ballooning, his recklessness increasing on every deal. Twice he pulled to an inside straight and lost each time; heavily. Once he kept raising on a four-card flush and didn't draw the fifth card he needed. Once he ran a bluff with a pair of deuces in his hand, betting up the pot, raising whenever he got the chance. He lost to a trio of ladies. By the fourth hour Daly was even, and an hour after that he was in the hole for two hundred, nearly all the money he had.

He turned to Ricketts. "Lemme have a hundred, Hank."

The man running the game—big and brawny, with a brown beard that reached halfway down his chest—rocked his oversize head. "No loans in the game, fella."

"Nobody told me that," Daly protested.

"Rules of the house."

"Since when?"

"Since we began playing, two years plus ago. It's your deal, fella. Deal or pass?"

Daly dealt. His fingers were slow, clumsy, and he flipped the cards without concern for where they would end up. One or two of the players objected mildly.

"Fuck off," was Daly's response.

The brown-bearded man cleared his throat. "This here is a polite game, fella. No need for that."

"Fuck you, too."

"Sam, deal and shut up," Ricketts said in warning.

Daly finished the deal. Five-card draw. Jacks or better. Three players passed before the pot was opened for two dollars. Daly swore under his breath but stayed, as did the other men at the table. "Cards?" He dealt the man on his left three cards; he had asked for two.

"I only want two," he objected.

"No big deal," Daly said. He flipped the third card to Hiram.

"Just give me one more," Hiram said.

"You only want one?" Daly said. "That's what you got, one card."

"I want two cards altogether."

"You want two, say two, dammit."

Hiram swept the second card into his hand.

Daly dealt to the next player, and the rest of the deck came fanning out of his hand across the table, some of the cards fluttering to the floor.

"Okay," the bearded man grumped. "The hand is dead. The pot stands, and the deal is moved along. Let's play cards."

"Fuck that noise," Daly objected. "I'm finishing the deal."

"The hand is dead," the big bearded man said. He placed his cards facedown, his hands resting easily on the table.

"The hell with that. You don't run my life." Daly swept the cards back toward himself, along with much of the pot.

Hands separated him from the money. "This son-ofabitch is drunk."

"Or crazy."

"Or both."

"Don't have to be sober to take on you motherfuck-ers," Daly bit off.

"Come on guys," Ricketts said, eyes darting from one inflexible face to another. "Take it easy. None of us wants any trouble."

The bearded man shoved himself erect. "You're welcome to stay," he said to Ricketts. "Your friend is out of here."

That did it for Daly. He launched himself across the table, hands clawing for the big man's throat. The big man took a single sidelong step, driving one big fist into the back of Daly's head, sending him to the floor. He went after Daly with extreme calm, taking hold of him at the neck and at his waist, propelling him struggling and swearing out the door, down the single flight of stairs, heaving him into the street.

"Show up again, soldier, and you may get hurt."

Without a word, Daly charged. Fists pumping, he beat the bearded man back against the wall. Hiram, appearing out of the doorway, got his arms around Daly in a solid bear hug. The bearded man bore down, one fist cocked. Before he could let fly, Daly kicked backward, catching Hiram's shin; it sent him staggering backward. Daly ducked the blow coming his way and unloosed a flurry of punches. Both men went to the ground, punching and clawing at each other, grunting whenever a blow landed. Hank Ricketts, trying to separate them, took a heavy fist on the temple for his trouble.

It was a policeman on routine patrol who finally ended the fight. The brawlers, virtually punched out by the time he arrived, were no match for his strength and skill. Grasping Daly's long blond hair with one hand, twisting his arm behind his back, he slammed him up against the trunk of his prowl car. The force of the blow knocked all breath out of Daly and he slumped down, relieved when the cop dumped him into the backseat of the cruiser. The cop turned his attention to the bearded man.

"What's this all about, Smitty?"

"Ah, just a little mix-up, is all." Smitty worked his jaw and found it serviceable.

"You want to press charges?"

Smitty tested his short, thick nose. No apparent break. His breathing was almost normal.

"A little misunderstanding, is all," Ricketts dared to say. "No damage done."

"Yeah," Smitty said, smoothing his beard. "No damage. Only don't bring that guy back again. He's got no manners."

"Sorry," Ricketts said.

"See that he gets to bed," the policeman said. "And stays there." Drunks, fistfights, abusive skiers desperate to find a good time; they occupied too much of his shift, made for too much paperwork. He opened the door of the cruiser and beckoned to Daly. "You're out of here, mister. Get tough on my shift one more time and I'll book you myself."

A chastened Sam Daly trailed Hank Ricketts to where they'd left the car. He was fast asleep and snoring when they reached Glenwood Springs. And Ricketts half carried him upstairs to his bed, cursing every step of the way.

One look told Peggy Pearce all she had to know about the night before. She had summoned the men to a meeting in her room. Daly, bruised and battered, grinned sheepishly and tried to make light of the fight.

"You should see the other guy." It was meant as a joke; nobody laughed.

Devlin, concerned about his own safety, felt compelled to speak. "This is bad stuff. Now a cop knows you. Knows both of you."

Ricketts nodded gravely. It had been stupid and senseless, as if Daly had been looking for trouble. But they were friends, and he refused to turn on a friend. Unless it became absolutely necessary.

"Everybody has fights," Daly said.

"Not me," Devlin said, exaggerating to make the point. "This can put every one of us in jeopardy."

Daly listened only to what he wanted to hear. "Maybe you ain't got guts enough to fight."

"Stop it, Sam," Peggy Pearce said firmly. "Dev is right, attracting a cop's attention this way. Not very smart."

"Okay, okay. I'm sorry."

"Sorry's not good enough," Devlin insisted. He

shifted around to face Peggy squarely. She was their acknowledged leader, the brains behind their every move. Surely she could see the difficulties that lay ahead if Daly were allowed to act in this careless manner. "Sam's a loose cannon," he said aloud. "As far as I'm concerned, it is over. . . ."

"Up yours," Daly snarled, leaning as if he meant to attack.

"Chill out, guys," Peggy said. There was no way to get rid of Sam Daly without risk to her plans. And she recognized Devlin's desire to cut short his role in the enterprise. She could afford neither loss. She was in this for the long haul, and as in any business organization, minor personnel problems arose from time to time. It was her responsibility to smooth out the rough spots. "Here it is, guys. Sam was wrong. He knows it, we know it."

"I said I was sorry."

"Devlin's got a point, Sam. The cop does know you, but that isn't fatal. He must break up a dozen fights a night. What I want is to be sure it won't happen again. Sam? Do I have your word on it?"

"Sure."

"I'll keep him on a short leash," Ricketts said.

"Dev?" Peggy said. "We need you. I need you. All of you. Screw up one more time, Sam, and you're out. Out with us, out of Aspen. That go down okay with you, Dev?"

He agreed reluctantly. "One more time."

"Sam?"

"No sweat."

"That's the way it is. We're a team. One for all and all for one. Okay?"

"Okay."

It wasn't perfect, she told herself. But she'd never encountered perfection anywhere in her life. This was the best she could get for the time being; it would have to do.

15

SUZANNE Brody tipped the scales.

Not by anything she did or said. But simply by her unannounced appearance at the Aspen house. At nine-thirty the morning after she flew in, the same time she would have arrived at the Sharps Industries office in New York, had she been there. Suzanne had early on in her career recognized the value of punctuality, of the impression it made on her employers. It was one of the first of many lessons she had learned; it was not the last.

Geneva opened the door to Suzanne, an oversize cup of coffee in her hand. Surprised to see the other woman, she suppressed her reaction. What a beauty she was, was the first thought that entered Geneva's

head. She corrected herself at once. Not beautiful.
Much more than that and, at the same time, much less.

Standing there in the penetrating winter morning,
she appeared to have been painstakingly chipped out
of the palest Italian marble, polished to a high gloss.
Shining bright and cold. The alabaster skin fell
smoothly from perfect cheekbones to an equally perfect jaw, lean as an axe edge and quietly accusatory.
Her eyes were immense, fixed, and enigmatic.

And dressed all wrong, but making it right somehow. That willowy figure was wrapped in a long sable
coat and soft black leather boots, a silk Armani scarf
keeping her soft black hair in place. Ready for a stroll
along Fifth Avenue, Geneva remarked to herself. Still,
an engaging package. Suzanne Brody was one of those
fortunate women who could commit no fashion faux
pas, setting styles rather than victim to one. She belonged wherever she was, dressed however she
pleased.

She offered her hand to Geneva in a handshake
swiftly ended, lest the contact be mistaken for something more intimate, of a friendship to come. Her unexpected appearance made Geneva feel diminished.
Less Sharps's wife, less the lady of the house, almost
an intruder on the premises. Illegitimate and definitely
ill bred. Her marital authority undermined by the other
woman's presence. She let none of this show.

"How nice to see you." As if this were the culmina-
tion of a long-standing appointment. "Won't you come
inside."

A fixed turn to her mouth, Suzanne moved past Geneva into the two-story entrance foyer, at home and
in charge at once. She might have been a long-lost an-

cestor of the Russian nobility, Geneva thought wryly, or a descendant of Norman queens. The way she held herself, erect and full of pride, but without awkwardness, taking in her surroundings with a kind of regal authority. A quick glance at the tall windows over the front door. A more leisurely assessment of the Impressionist paintings on two of the walls, an admiring inspection of the long red-and-orange-and-yellow Moroccan rug.

"This is a marvelous house." Suzanne advanced without invitation into the long sitting room, once three smaller chambers. "Who was the architect?"

Geneva withheld any reply. As Sharps's executive assistant, Suzanne knew everything there was to know about the house. She had given final approval to the designer, had final authority over his work, his choices of furniture, drapes, carpets, everything. Sharps, for all the money spent on the place, couldn't have cared less about the house. His interests—his only real interests—lay elsewhere.

The Aspen house, much like Geneva herself, was little more than another acquisition. Perfect in every way. Sleekly beautiful and occasionally helpful. Sharps's homes, his cars, his wife; all were meant to indicate how successful and powerful he had become. Each his to do with as he wished. Until, and unless, he chose to dispose of any of them. For reasons known only to himself and always to his profit.

"Mr. Sharps," Suzanne Brody was saying, "asked me to come out here. It occurred to him that you might need some help."

"Won't you take off your coat?" Geneva said politely.

Brody hugged herself and showed her small white teeth. "When I warm up. How do you tolerate the winters out here?"

"Help with what?" Geneva said, seating herself, finishing off her coffee, placing the cup on the marble-topped table nearby. She knew the answer before it was given.

"The party, naturally."

Naturally. Sharps had never treated her as an adult human being. Never recognized her as someone competent and dependable. The New Year's Eve party was obviously too delicate an assignment to trust to a mere wife. A wife, after all, was a chattel, an acquired bauble meant to decorate Sharps's arm on occasion, a prettified appendage to be trotted out when required. Shown off to Sharps's advantage like his Rolls or his Mercedes, like the glittering watch on his wrist, like his custom-made clothes from the world's most prestigious tailors. Otherwise she was kept tucked away in the backwaters of his existence, an animated encumbrance that only made demands on his attention and slowed him down.

How surprised he would be should he learn of the Plan, as she had come to call it. Surprised at how meticulously designed it was—all that attention to detail—the careful way she was approaching its execution. Much as Sharps himself might have done. Going over every aspect of the scheme, refining every move, leaving nothing to chance. Taking all the time she needed. Omitting nothing. Oh, yes, Sharps would have been surprised. Even proud of her and startled at her daring.

In a way, that was the best part of it; Sharps was

going to find out all about the Plan. Give her the added satisfaction of driving home to him her always denigrated intellect and organizational skills. By then, of course, it would be too late for Sharps to spoil things for her. By then he would no longer control her.

"Oh, yes," Geneva said sweetly. "The party."

"Mr. Sharps was kind enough to send me out here on his private plane."

"Now nice for you."

Suzanne allowed the sable coat to drape halfway down her back. The house was warm, a little too warm for her taste. In New York she kept the heat in her co-op apartment on the Upper East Side on the cool side. Cool and stimulating.

"I brought an amended guest list along." She smiled. "I was sure you'd want to go over it with me."

"Duncan has utmost faith in you, Miss Brody, and so do I."

"Please. Call me Suzanne."

Geneva offered no reply. She waited, hands folded in her lap, an expectant curl to her lips. It was Brody who broke the silence.

"I thought we could collaborate on the project. . . ."

"The party, you mean. How businesslike, to see it as a project. I suppose it is, though. A corporate endeavor, no different from signing contracts or buying some company on the cheap. You don't require any help from me, Miss Brody. I know you'll handle everything to Mr. Sharps's satisfaction."

Suzanne Brody had anticipated a certain amount of antagonism. She would have preferred a neutral situation, but a resentful Geneva Sharps would in no way deter her from her duties.

"About the invitations, are they ordered yet? No matter. I'll want the printer to add the new names to the list. The number of people to be invited from New York and and Washington has been expanded. Also, about twenty invitations have to go out here in Colorado: Denver, Boulder, Colorado Springs. It's all dressing, of course."

"Of course."

"Meant to help your husband close this deal."

"Deal?"

Suzanne Brody ignored the question, words tumbling out of her now in a purposeful flow. "Mr. Sharps explained to me about your phobia when it comes to full-time help. . . ."

"There is no phobia."

"No matter. I'll arrange for the appropriate people, which is more efficient anyway. Relationships don't develop. Personnel problems are kept to a minimum. Cleaning people. Caterers. People to serve. There's going to be a great deal of food, you see."

Geneva nodded slowly.

"There's the matter of housing. I'm sure you haven't had time enough to make any suitable arrangements. I'll take care of it."

Geneva understood that she was being treated like some dim-witted child. Unable to do anything, unable to comprehend what was being said. So be it. She had learned a long time ago that people tended to underestimate her intelligence, and in response she had turned herself into a kind of reflecting glass in which people—in particular, Sharps—would see only their own wishes and desires. Leave her to fulfill her own needs, to live her own life. It had become an immensely valuable tool in her hands. Perhaps even a weapon.

"Then there's no need for me to be involved?" she said, a grace note of hope in her voice.

"Please call me Suzanne. No. No need at all."

"What great luck, that Duncan thought to send you."

"He said you'd be relieved."

"Relieved, yes. You'll be staying here at the house? With me?"

A shudder went through Suzanne Brody. To spend any more time than was absolutely necessary with this spoiled, empty-headed creature was abhorrent to her. "Mr. Sharps made one of the condos available to me. It will allow me privacy, and I'll be able to work at all hours. But we'll be in touch, if you like. . . ."

"Whatever you say."

"To exchange ideas."

"About the party, you mean?"

"Yes."

"I'll have to think about that."

"You'll let me know if there's anything you want me to do."

"You're so kind, Miss Brody."

Geneva ushered Suzanne Brody out, remaining on the wide, wraparound porch with its gingerbread trim painted white. She watched the other woman drive away in a car hired for the occasion, embracing herself against the cold. She had intended to go skiing this morning; now she was not so sure. She wanted to think about what had just transpired, reflect on how, if at all, Suzanne Brody's presence might influence the Plan.

She was about to go back inside when the old blue Jeep came rolling without haste along the road. The driver turned her way, the weathered, rugged face cocked and full of recognition. The Jeep went faster until it disappeared down where the road turned into a stand of tall pine trees. It was all so quick, so unexpected, seeing him away from his natural habitat. There was no doubt: John Thomas Andrew Devlin.

Devlin.

Dev.

What the hell was he doing up here?

16

DEVLIN was immobilized with fear. He waited and ruminated, going over every possibility. He considered and dissected every fractured moment of time and was unable to come up with an answer. It was his fate to fail, he accepted that. He deserved no better for linking up with such as Ricketts and Daly, with pretty Peggy Pearce. Placing his destiny in their unsteady hands. But did it have to happen this way? The terrible timing of it. A second or two and that fleeting glance her way. She had recognized him, he was sure of it. She knew.

She knew!

Everything had gone so well that morning. They were in and out of Jerry Cross's house within minutes. That is, Daly and Ricketts were, Devlin waiting in the

Jeep in the turnaround behind the huge, rambling structure. They had gone in with speed and assurance, following Peggy's blueprint.

"There's a simple alarm system," she had reported. "On the doors and the windows. The power source is the same line carrying electricity into the place. All you've got to do is throw the master switch in the circuit breaker. . . ."

They had all recognized the problem with that. "That means we've got to get inside first," Ricketts said with dismay.

"You're not going to believe this," she said. "The box containing the circuit breakers is on the outside of the house. Alongside the back deck. Next to the entrance to the kitchen. Clear it and there's nothing in your way."

She was right. Right about everything. About the jewelry scattered over a dressing table in the bedroom, about the additional rings and bracelets in boxes in the closet, about the pieces resting on the sink in the bathroom. They even found two diamond-and-topaz rings in the kitchen. Inside a fur-lined men's boot in the closet, they came up with a stash of one-hundred-dollar bills; $12,500. Jerry Cross believed in keeping a substantial amount of cash on hand.

On their way out, Daly helped himself to a bottle of Johnny Walker Red. He closed the kitchen door, and Ricketts reactivated the alarm system, leaving everything as they had found it. Almost.

Minutes later they were back in the blue Jeep going past the huge green Victorian house with the white trim. Only Devlin paid attention to the golden-haired woman standing on the wide porch.

He replayed it all in his mind, focusing in on every detail. Trying mightily to convince himself that Geneva Sharps had not recognized him, and failing every time.

By now she would have put it all together. She would have learned of the break-in at the Cross house, a not-so-distant neighbor. She would have listened to the reports on the radio, heard gossip, she might even have spoken to Cross himself. And she would have remembered the carefully driven blue Jeep with Devlin at the wheel. It took no Sherlock Holmes to make a coherent picture out of the pieces of the puzzle. Devlin, she would know, was one of the burglars.

Geneva Sharps. So incredibly beautiful, all that sensuality, the sweet perfection of the woman; all transformed into a great and immediate threat. She knew about him now, knew too much, more than he would ever have revealed.

There was only one smart thing to do: remove himself from the danger. Leave Aspen at once. Flee for distant parts. Change his identity and lie low. Hide out. But something irresistible kept him in place. Unable to depart that Rocky Mountain paradise. Unable to separate himself from Geneva Sharps.

It was all so stupid. Self-defeating. Geneva Sharps was nothing to him, and he was even less to her. Another woman in a massive, open-ended catalog of women. Another body to pleasure himself with. Another sexual triumph. And suddenly this stranger had become a threat to his life and to his freedom. It was vital that he remove himself from the danger.

Still he remained. Spending a great deal of his time alone in his Glenwood Springs room. On the radio, he listened to Waylon Jennings and the Oak Ridge Boys wail "Ain't Livin' Long Like This." And Johnny Cash. And Roy Acuff. The music offered little relief. He avoided Peggy Pearce and Ricketts and Daly. He kept away from his usual dining and drinking haunts. He stayed off the slopes and told the people at ASA that he was too ill to work. He needed time to make sense of things. To figure out how to deal with this situation.

Days went by, and when the police failed to appear—sent by Geneva Sharps—he became more confused. Surely by now she had figured out his role in the Cross burglary. Surely by now she had reported him to the law. Surely by now they had tracked him to ASA and from there to this address. Why the holdup?

He considered every possibility. He speculated. He plagued his mind with questions, created imagined situations, answers that always failed to satisfy. Except for one: Geneva Sharps wanted something from him, something she could not get if he should be put behind bars. Of course; Geneva wanted him as much as he wanted her.

Fortified by this conclusion, he ventured forth on the fifth day after the Cross job. He skied that morning but felt uneasy on the mountain, out of sync with the slopes, as if he no longer belonged. He gave it up early and headed over to ASA, where he was greeted warmly and put right to work. He expected Geneva to show up momentarily, to come on to him, to invite him into her bed. It never happened.

That evening he searched for her in the bars and restaurants along Cooper Street and in a few less grand establishments on the side streets. No sign of her anywhere.

Had she left town? Departed Aspen for parts unknown for reasons having nothing to do with him? Had he only imagined her as a danger to him? Had he perceived her as a lover only in his fantasies? He wasn't ready to give up. He drove past her house. The lights were on, but no one was visible through the curtained windows. He parked the Jeep and started up to her front door, only to lose his nerve and hurry away.

That night, unable to sleep, he touched himself, that ever-present image of Geneva floating into view. He saw all of her in the darkness, a taunting display of her magnificent flesh, always out of reach. A silent, mocking laugh. Doubting his manhood. Questioning his ability to please her. Challenging his courage. The tension grew unbearable, unrelieved, his body joining her in conspiracy against him. So alone, he was. So afraid. So aware of some unnamed disaster about to take him down. There was nothing he could do but wait.

So he waited. For the inevitable. For what he yearned desperately to possess and for what he feared so very much. She would have to come after him.

And she did, that Wednesday afternoon when she presented herself in the main exercise room of the Aspen Sports Association. She seemed at home among the mirrored walls and the shining machines all dedicated to good health and strength, to physical fitness and leanness, to the enhancement of one's appearance and the ever-vigilant restraint of aging.

He watched her for a long time. Studied that perfect face, hoping to discover some imperfection, some blemish, anything to make her more accessible and so less desirable. He found nothing.

Her movements were strong and determined as she went from station to station, revealing no sign of weakness. And not even once did she glance his way. What was she after? What did she want? From *him*?

She flexed and stretched. She bent and lifted. She pushed and she pulled, her body an animated aphrodisiac for Devlin. Her legs were bare, smooth, tiny golden hairs glinting on the insides of her thighs, thighs that reached under green cotton shorts that clung to her buttocks, that gathered at the crotch. Devlin felt himself shift and swell, begin to harden.

Oh, Mary, Mother of God! Help me. . . .

This woman possessed him, inhabited him like some evil spirit, and he lacked the means to battle her successfully. The distant taste of her flesh lined his mouth. The scent of her—she would smell sweet and so very female—clogged his nostrils. The heat of her idealized flesh encased him, drew him deep inside her until he realized he would find no peace until he possessed her.

She was, he understood finally, his only hope for earthly salvation. She was everything he'd ever wanted in a woman, and she scared him as nothing before had scared him. She was his only hope and his inevitable downfall. He summoned up all his courage and made himself go over to her.

She worked a climbing machine with grace and power. Sweat stood out on that magnificent brow and on the back of her neck. The tank top she wore clung to her back and her sides, accentuating the fleshless perfection of her torso. That was it, Devlin reminded himself, she was perfect. That, and something else. Something more. Something he had yet to isolate and define.

"Mrs. Sharps," he started out in his best professional style. Give her no cause to send him away.

"Devlin." Her legs continued to pump, simulating her ascent on a flight of stairs. Great for the thighs, the hips, the lower midriff.

"You were on the rowing machine the other day . . ." Keep it cool, disinterested; only trying to help, Mrs. Sharps. "You might want to give the low tow pull a shot next time. It can be doubly effective."

"Thank you, Devlin."

A rush of words cluttered up his brain. A thousand clever phrases to capture her interest. Make her laugh. Convince her of what a fine and noble creature he was. God's gift to women in general, to her in particular. Never had Devlin felt so tentative, so inarticulate, so lacking in self-worth. He scouted his internal landscape for something to say. Anything.

"Free weights," he managed. "Try free weights. There are some super exercises that will build up power at the same time they increase your stamina, take care of all of your cardiovascular requirements. If you like, I could work up a personalized program. . . ."

She ceased climbing. "I think not," she said, leaving no room for further argument. She moved on to the next station in her routine.

Helpless and brooding, he watched her go. Never had he longed for a woman this much. Never had a woman so terrified him. There was nothing he wouldn't do to have her. Absolutely nothing.

There were, however, a number of possibilities he had overlooked.

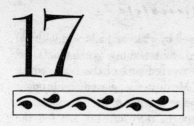

17

T H E state chairman of the senior senator's political party owned a ranch on thirty thousand acres in the southwestern part of the state. The main building was a stately structure with the architectural serenity and columns of a Virginia plantation house. It contained twenty-eight rooms, an indoor pool, and two bowling alleys in the basement, and it required the attention of half a dozen servants to keep it clean and in working order. The state chairman referred to it as the Ranchhouse, presenting himself as a man of simple and agrarian virtues. To this end, on the fifty-two-foot planked table in the dining room—the chairman liked to call it his "mess hall"—he insisted on offering full jars of ketchup, mustard, and A-1 Steak Sauce.

The chairman received the senior senator in the sun

room, a space enclosed by glass and adorned with old wicker chairs painted white and live green plants. An Arabian prayer rug covered part of the floor, which was made of brown Mexican tile, glazed and brought to a high gloss by one or another of the servants each morning. A maid brought refreshments and left the two men alone.

"You were in New York." The chairman mentioned it as if in passing, stirring lots of sugar into his black coffee.

The senior senator poured some brandy from a nearby bottle into his. "You heard about that?"

"And about your little escapade back in the federal district."

Arlen Hamilton was not surprised. Nothing of any weight or gravity got by the state chairman. He was a man with many listening posts around the United States, a man who performed many favors for many men, a man of influence and subtle power. He showed no embarrassment.

"I intended to get around to thanking you, Ralph."

"Duncan Turner Sharps was the point man on that affair, Red. He's been scouting around for a way to put me in his debt, and that little incident managed to do it. Can't say I'm glad about it, but there you are."

"I'll make it up to you, Ralph. I swear I will."

"Keep your concern about little girls to our education system, Red, and that'll do it. Your cock's gotten you into scrapes before this."

"I know, I know. I give you my word."

"Now about Sharps. He brought you up to the big city. What's he after, Red?"

"Nothing special." He watched the state chairman

light up a cigar, blow clouds of blue smoke. "Man is one of our constituents, Ralph."

"You and him becoming asshole buddies, Red?"

"I wouldn't say as close as that. Just that he means to do some good work in the state."

"Meaning make himself richer, you mean?" The chairman emptied half his cup in one swallow. He was a large man with a considerable girth and big, round shoulders and long arms. He had been an outstanding athlete while a student at the University of Colorado, and that trim athlete remained inside his swollen body, as if waiting to be called upon again to perform. His movements were slow, ponderous, his gestures truncated by the effort they demanded. His small eyes missed nothing, and his brain was quick, retentive, and capable of assimilating large and diverse amounts of information. He spoke in that hoarse, intimate way that many large men had, concerned about disturbing those within earshot. "I'd say your Mr. Sharps yearns to change himself over into another Donald Trump."

"I don't know, Ralph. Doesn't seem to have Trump's need to be in the public eye."

"Too smart to expose himself, is what you are saying. A man puts himself center stage, you can depend on it, Red, folks will be throwing things. Bouquets, maybe, and sooner or later rocks. Happens to them all, Trump'll find out. Maybe your man, too. Owns a house in Aspen, I've been told."

"Trump does?"

The chairman moved around in his seat, a determined shift of poundage. He sucked his cigar; it had gone out. He relit it, smothering a cough. He'd known Red Hamilton for nearly thirty years, and as far as he

could tell, the man had failed to add one scintilla of
smarts to a severely limited intelligence; he'd found
a home in the U.S. Senate.

"I am talking about your man—Duncan Turner
Sharps." The chairman wished Hamilton would get on
with it. He'd asked for this meeting, traveled all the
way from Washington so they could talk face to face,
as the senator had put it. That could mean only one
thing: Arlen was after something. A political favor. Access to some easy money. Normal and healthy urges.
Granting favors was what the chairman did best; the
essence of his job. Scratch my back and I'll scratch
yours. He drank the rest of his coffee and smoked his
cigar.

"Yes," Red Hamilton said. "Sharps is an outstanding addition to the town, to the state."

"Some of the time."

"True. Business keeps Sharps on the go most of
the time. Man has business all over the world, as far
as I can tell. But his wife is in residence. . . ."

"During the ski season. The word is she is an excep-
tionally fine looking woman."

"A beauty, from what I'm told."

"You haven't met her?"

"Well, no. Fact is, I've only recently met Sharps."
Hamilton wished he hadn't said that, calling attention
to that small unpleasantness back in the district.

The chairman showed no interest in resurrecting
that. "Younger than Sharps?"

"Oh, yes. Considerably."

"Half his age."

The senator felt called upon to defend Sharps. "But
he's a man of authority and limitless energy. On the

go constantly. Probably takes a younger woman to keep up." He laughed, a skittish sound. The senior senator was not a man of much confidence; many of his colleagues in the Senate intimidated him, made him feel as if whatever he did or said were being offered up under false pretenses. No matter his accomplishments, he continued to feel unworthy, fraudulent, waiting for the axe to fall. "We all like a youthful companion now and again, wouldn't you agree, Ralph?" Another mistake; he was going to have to learn to curb his impetuousness, his obsessive need to run off at the mouth.

The chairman cleared his throat and contemplated his cigar. "No more scandals, Red. People are fed up with the indiscretions of their leaders. The party is fed up. It would be a shame to see one of our more esteemed members so tainted and thereby cut off a career of some stature and longevity."

Red Hamilton shuddered. There was no way to misunderstand the message being delivered; the seriousness of it. He nodded, all the acknowledgment required.

The chairman was satisfied. "About our Mr. Sharps, Red. What is he after? How may I serve him?"

The senator explained the situation; a hotel to be built.

The chairman held forth with the usual objections— zoning problems, popular opposition, the strain on the community. "These," he ended, "are problems that can generally be dealt with. Where is the land he's after?"

"Marlon Ayres's property."

The chairman had heard that Ayres was ready to

sell, that he was entertaining a number of offers. Good for Ayres. He knew Ayres to be a man of honor and principle; therefore troublesome. Ayres was insisting that his land be put to use favorable to his beloved Aspen. Simply put, Ayres wanted to know what the land would be used for. Who would control it. And how it would affect the town in which he had spent so much of his adult life.

"Marlon can be difficult to deal with."

"Sharps is aware of that. He figures to deal with the old man himself."

"The arrogance of wealth," the chairman mused. He had encountered men like Duncan Sharps more than once in his long career, men who believed they could overcome all obstacles by damping them down with money. But for all of its many wonderful properties, the chairman understood that money possessed only limited use. It could buy only those things, those men, that money could buy. Still, if Sharps was prepared to offer his largesse around, he was ready to help relieve him of the burden. A familiar warning flag fluttered in the back of his mind. There was something more to come. "What else?" he said. "Sharps doesn't need my help to deal with Marlon Ayres. A hotel is not much more than a local problem."

The senator tugged at the loose skin under his chin. "A casino. Sharps wants to put in a casino."

"A gambling casino? In this hotel of his?"

"That's it."

The chairman laughed, a choking, sputtering exhalation that sent his cigar flying. It landed on the coffee table, soggy and unlit; he let it lie.

"So that's why you're here!"

"Mr. Sharps is a man of taste. Of impeccable judgment. I have his word—"

"Does Marlon Ayres know about this?"

"I doubt it."

"I doubt it, too. Sharps is too smart for that. Ayres will never turn his parcel over for a gambling casino. Unless he doesn't learn about it until too late."

"That could happen, I suppose."

The chairman located another cigar and bit off the tip, ran his tongue around the edge, and inserted it in his mouth. "There was a king in ancient Greece," he said, firing up the cigar. "Maybe it was Rome, makes no difference. Held up his hand and commanded the sea to stop, the waves to stop. My Jewish friends call that chutzpah. Your pal, Sharps, he's got plenty of chutzpah."

"I have great faith in Mr.—"

"Faith my fat ass, Red. State law says no gambling. It's illegal. Sharps says let's make it legal, which is why you are up here, dancing around me like some Indian shaman working up a rain cloud. Well, Sharps's got as much of a chance of getting it done as that shaman does."

"I don't see why—"

"I'll tell you why, dammit. Atlantic City's a cesspool of poverty and slime, excepting a couple of blocks along the boardwalk. And Vegas is pure honky-tonk. What do you think, Merv Griffin and Trump get their pictures in the papers, so nobody in those places is mobbed up? Spare me the bullshit, Red. Once Sharps pulls this off, the wise guys won't be far behind." He looked away, clouds of smoke spreading out around his massive head. When he came around again, his face was closed, the little eyes glittering out of folds of pale skin. "Up and down the state, the pressure against him will be enormous. From the state house to the locals in Aspen. All those environmentalists. Every other weirdo with a cause. The Godmongers, every fundamentalist preacher within a thousand miles is gonna get a hard-on for this one. Not to mention every greedy sonofabitch on the other side. Does Sharps have any idea what a project like this will cost?"

"Money is no object to Mr. Sharps."

"A thousand pockets to be filled and a thousand sweaty palms to be crossed with silver." He maneuvered around in his chair, looking for all the world like a larger-than-life-size Buddha, his great belly hanging forward. "The kitty will have to be fed. Fattened. Gorged."

"Mr. Sharps understands the practicalities—"

"Starting right here, Red."

"Mr. Sharps understands—"

"Does Mr. Sharps understand that while you may run with the ball, I do all the serious blocking, the down-and-dirty work in the trenches?"

"I told him nothing can be done without your approval and assistance."

"Let me tell you, Red. This will be a big-time battle. Lots of blood gets spilled. Lots of dead men. Lots of wounded. It's going to cost a lot to get it done and then patch up all the hurt feelings after. . . ."

"No limit on funds."

"Front money is in order."

"Sharps's exact words—he wants a number."

"A big-time operator, your Mr. Sharps."

"I would say so."

"How would a million strike him? Cash. In fifties and hundreds. All old bills."

"I'll have to make a call."

"Tell Sharps that's for openers. A show of good faith."

"I understand."

"Make sure Sharps understands—the million, it'll take a hell of a lot more than that before we're through."

"Oh, Mr. Sharps, he understands everything."

18

T H E phone rang and Geneva hesitated before picking it up. As she feared, it was Sharps. For a split second she expected him to announce a change in plans, to order her back to New York or to join him elsewhere for another display of marital hypocrisy.

"Brody there?" he started out, impersonal and serrated, using his voice like a weapon.

"I haven't seen her since she arrived. And how are you, husband mine? Well, I hope." The sarcasm was wasted on Sharps.

"She on top of things?"

"I told you, I haven't seen her. Miss Brody and I are not close."

"Well, you should be. You could learn a lot of good stuff from her. Brody is good at what she does."

"I was under the impression I was to make this party, Duncan. After all, it's happening in my house—our house—and I am the lady of the house."

"Wise up, Geneva. Brody is a pro, knows what she's doing. She gets paid to get things done. You're my wife."

"A fine distinction."

"What's that supposed to mean?"

"Any further orders, Duncan?"

"She wasn't at the condo, Brody, I mean. You hear from her, tell her to call."

"I'll do that, if I hear from her."

"Yeah. And don't forget to do your part. Invite some of those friends of yours."

"I have no friends, Duncan. I go skiing by myself. I work out at the gym by myself. I dine by myself, usually at home. I read books, Duncan, and that is the most solitary of activities. But don't fret, I'll ask around. I'm sure between Brody and me we can round up a dozen or so pretty young things for you and your pals. I know how highly you prize professionalism. What would you say to some pros? Some prosties, hookers. That way you can be sure your business associates will get laid without any difficulty."

Sharps considered that briefly before discarding the idea. People in Colorado might not understand his using prostitutes. If it got out . . .

"Forget it. Just do as I said. Clear?"

"Clear, my darling."

"I'm in Chicago, on business. A few more days, I'll have it all cleaned up, I'll be out there. Just stay on top of things."

Geneva slammed the dead phone back into its cradle. She raged silently at the fates that had brought her to this. Being Sharps's wife had to be the worst job in the world. No matter how much money he provided, she was still vastly underpaid.

Madness.

Certifiably insane, all of them.

Infected by some incurable virus that would take every one of them to the brink of personal disaster and over the edge. Mass hysteria.

Otherwise rational men and women dropping down the side of a mountain on a pair of flimsy sticks. Rushing for no good purpose to the bottom of a hill so they could go back up again and repeat the stupid process. What possessed them to spend their days riding an open chair lift to the heights in bitter cold in order to put life and limb in severe jeopardy? It was, she decided, the most dubious of pleasures. A warm bed and a stiff drink would serve each of them more profitably.

Suzanne Brody stood at the bottom of Aspen Mountain, taking it all in. She wore stretch pants with a black and white diagonal stripe, a heavy wool sweater with a Mondrian-like design, and a windproof shell in a pale green. A blue stocking cap with a yellow tassel and ski gloves completed her outfit. All courtesy of Duncan Turner Sharps. All expenses paid, this assignment. Including a suitable wardrobe; Sharps insisted that his people fit right in, no matter where the job took them.

That was Sharps's way. Free with money, making sure everything, everyone, around him went first class. World-class hotels wherever she went, four-star restaurants, and chic and expensive clothes that allowed her to be comfortable in any environment.

Money was a yardstick to Sharps. A way of measuring himself and his accomplishments against other men, and to make more of it, in large amounts, he was willing to spend it in large amounts.

Brody had learned from Sharps. Like him, she always had a substantial amount of cash on hand. It provided her with a sense of comfort, aware that the sight of green opened all doors, smoothed all paths, provided for a richer and easier life. Of course, where Sharps kept thousands of dollars around, she kept a few hundred. She had known him to keep fifty thousand dollars in cash in a desk drawer. And once he had shown her a suitcase containing, he said, more than half a million.

"Makes me feel good," he had told her. "Just to look at the stuff. To touch it. I love the smell of money, it's like nothing else. Distinctive, and it stays with you for a long time."

Money was how Sharps counted his victories. Money was the measure by which he compared himself with other men. Other entrepreneurs. Men like the Hunts or Forbes or some of the unpublicized billionaires he knew about. All powerful figures, the kind of men who got things done. They were a select group, on a level above Sharps. But not beyond his grasp. He yearned to join that elite group, to make himself their equal. Even more, Sharps hungered to be the best.

First of the best.

King of the hill.

Numero uno.

Two years before, in Milan, working on a deal for an auto design house, competing with a West German company, he'd had what the doctors had labeled a "cardiac incident." Not life threatening, but a warning.

Suzanne Brody had been with him, working alongside him for long hours each day, into the night. She'd been there when the incident occurred. She had been the one to summon help. She'd heard the doctors tell Sharps, "Slow down. Take holidays. Enjoy your money, Mr. Sharps."

He had laughed at them. Work was what he knew, what he did, the only thing he could do. It provided all his pleasure, all his satisfaction; it kept him alive. And if it killed him, it was the way he wanted to go. Besides, he had no time for rest; he intended to beat out those Germans.

The doctors had persisted, and Sharps heard them out. When they were finished with their warnings and their predictions of doom, he gave them his ultimate argument.

"Imagine what it must be like to be heavyweight champion of the world, gentlemen. To be the best at what you do. Better than anyone else in your line of work. What a kick in the ass that must be!"

"That is what you want," one of the doctors said. "To become a prizefighter? At your age?"

Sharps had grinned at the man, a stingy grin, aware that the learned men around his bed had no insight into what made him what he was.

"Champion of the world!" he had crowed. "Champion of the whole goddamn world!"

Witness to the exchange, Brody knew at once that she intended to remain close to Sharps. To watch him in action. To count his triumphs, and her own. To follow him on his way up to the top of the mountain.

She turned down an offer from a German publishing house with an American subsidiary. Six months later she had been invited to become CEO of one of Hollywood's biggest studios. There were other offers; she refused them all. She wanted to be there when it happened, when Sharps made his biggest moves, when he became number one. Champion of the entire world.

She lifted her gaze back up to a point high on the mountain. A single skier began his run off the high altitudes. A dark figure speeding toward the abyss. Soon he came into focus, and she was captured by his sudden twists and changes of direction, the daring leaps. She cheered him silently, urging him on to greater displays of skill and daring. Without warning he went down, windmilling down the slope. She felt betrayed, as if he had seduced her with his skill only to fall short of completion.

Sharps had never betrayed her. Never promised more than he could deliver. Often delivered much greater prizes than she had dared to hope for. Win or lose, Sharps always put the fear of God into his competitors. His opponents. His enemies. Of course they were enemies, standing as they did between Sharps and what he wanted. Obstacles to be overcome. Bruised and battered, finally destroyed. There was that about Sharps; either you were with him or against him. No neutral ground existed.

She started away from the mountain, no longer concerned with the fallen skier. Injured or not. Alive or dead. His failure was complete and no longer of consequence to her.

It was then she spotted Geneva Sharps, on her way to the lift. Skis carried easily across one shoulder, poised, and sartorially splendid in ski clothes that appeared to have been specially designed for her elegant figure. A stab of envy brought Brody to a stop, watching the other woman. So much accrued so easily to the Geneva Sharpses of the world, in return for so little. What did Geneva do to earn the rich life she had? What had she ever done, beyond being born with the right kind of looks, the right kind of body?

Suzanne recalled her early adolescence. All her friends attained puberty before she did. Their bodies blossoming, growing fuller than hers; she had yearned to be just like them. She longed for the menstrual cramps they complained about. She dreamed of growing breasts swollen and womanly; instead her chest remained flat and uninspiring. She might as well have been a boy. And when finally her breasts had come, what a disappointment they were. Diminutive eruptions that weren't worthy of the name and inspired no lust in the boys she knew. All those years ago, and she was still ashamed to show her body to another person. Locker rooms were anathema to her and bedrooms torture chambers, except in the dark. Always the darkness.

Expensive whores, that's what women like Geneva were. Not much different from the cheapest of streetwalkers on Lexington Avenue. Married whores earning their way on their backs.

She sucked the chill, pure air into her lungs. Clearing away such thoughts. Self-pity didn't become her. Nor did critical thoughts about Geneva. She was, after all, Sharps's wife, and Sharps always had a reason for the things he did and the people he assembled around him. So it had to be with Geneva. Besides, such petty jealousy could only get in the way of the work she had to do. Impair her efficiency. Cause mistakes. And Duncan Turner Sharps would never stand for that.

The condo Sharps had set aside for her use—he owned seven such apartments in Aspen—performed double duty. A place to live in comfort and privacy and a work area. There were two bedrooms, but one served Suzanne as an office. She'd had desks and files moved in, a computer, an electric typewriter, and some chairs and desk lamps. Telephone lines were connected and a fax machine hooked up.

She began by entering the names on the guest lists into the computer, along with addresses and telephone numbers. Then she ran off copies of the master list.

She called in the printer. He brought samples of stock, typefaces, and ink with him. It took nearly two hours for her to make her final choices. Then she handed him a copy of the master list.

"How long to get these run off?"

"We're backed up at the shop," he apologized. "It may take three or four days to get to them."

"That won't do. I want a sample invitation on my desk by this time tomorrow. I want the complete lot addressed, stamped, and delivered to me for mailing forty-eight hours after that. No later."

"That's impossible."

She handled it the way Sharps would have done. Smoothly, with a wise smile, but with strength, insisting on getting his way. "You're an experienced printer. The best in town, I was told, which is why I came to you. You can do it."

He hesitated. "I'd need another day or two. . . ."

"Hire extra people. Pay your workers overtime. Double time. Whatever it takes to get it done."

"There are a couple of people available," he said, considering what changes in scheduling he'd have to make. "This could be expensive."

"Whatever it takes. Meet my deadline and there'll be a bonus in it for you."

"I'll be back about this time tomorrow," he said just before he left.

Thirty minutes later the caterer arrived. Three buffet tables were decided on, with an extensive variety of foods, hot and cold, to be served continuously beginning at nine o'clock until such time as the last guest departed. That, it was pointed out, would mean extra equipment, extra help, additional amounts of food, and much, much higher costs.

"Do it."

"I'll prepare a menu for your approval by tomorrow afternoon."

"Today, at two. I'll be waiting for you here."

"At two. About the liquor?"

"An open bar, open all night. Every conceivable liquor. And wine, a good variety of good vintages, red and white. And champagne."

"I'll call my distributor at once. I'll want to get into the house, to make my table setups, the bars, etcetera. You'll want flowers, of course."

"Of course. Be at the house at three this afternoon."

"Are you sure Mrs. Sharps will—"

"Just be there. Someone will be on the premises to admit you."

"At three, then."

And a cleaning service. She interviewed three different services; Peggy Pearce, for Apex, was last on her list. She was immediately impressed with the violet-eyed young woman, at the confident air, at her obvious intelligence, at her startling dark-haired beauty.

Suzanne Brody had come to prize beauty above most other qualities. It was rare, precious, gave unlimited pleasure to an observer. Beauty in art, in fashion, in people. It was a unique element that raised one human being above all others, a gift of nature that could not be bought or taught or otherwise acquired. It excited interest in strangers, it brought attention, affection, love; it quickened the pulses of all in its delicate presence. Peggy Pearce had been so blessed.

Suzanne listened to her outline the services offered, impressed with the confident way she handled herself. She was experienced, and flexible, able to accommodate the special needs Suzanne insisted on.

"I think you ought to go through the house, make sure you know what's required."

"I can do that this afternoon, if you like."

"No, the caterers are coming. We'll make it tomorrow at two o'clock. I want a thorough job. No dust balls under furniture. No cobwebs in the basement. Nothing out of place."

"I'm sure I can satisfy you."

"Let me know how many hours you'll need for the first cleaning."

"How large is the house? How many rooms?"

"I don't have an exact number. You count them. But it's a big house. Here's the schedule so far. The caterers will start bringing in their equipment on the morning of the party. That will take most of the day. Which means you've got to do the final cleanup the previous afternoon, complete. Nothing overlooked."

"I may need a double crew."

"Arrange it. Whatever you need. After the party, a cleanup will be in order."

"New Year's Day?"

Suzanne considered that. Too many hung-over workers, too many other complications. "The day after that."

Peggy made a note. "Anything else?"

Suzanne rose and extended her hand. Peggy took it. Peggy's grip was dry and reassuring, the handshake of a well-centered woman. Suzanne liked that. She liked Peggy Pearce. A lot.

19

O BSESSION was transformed into desperation. Concentric circles of longings and desires dulled his ability to think clearly. He could no longer separate his emotions, was no longer able to know which was the greater, his passion or his fear that she would inform the police. Each day saw his terror enlarged, his frustration sharpened. Nothing helped; not even Peggy Pearce.

She arrived in his room without invitation or warning. Boasting about the success of the Cross job, of the riches each of them could expect once Sam Daly returned from his visit to Evan Larson in Denver.

"I've been on the lookout for other suitable targets." His lack of energy was unlike him, she remarked to herself. His lack of interest in her personally or in their professional partnership. She understood that she was at the center of their enterprise. She was the glue that kept them together, the force and the intelligence that made it work. Without her, without her drive and ambition, the shaky alliance would shatter into separate—even warring—parts. "I've got a couple of new assignments. There's one in particular . . ."

Devlin wasn't interested. He sat on his bed, a pillow behind his head, his legs stretched out, smoking and drinking Chivas Regal. The year with Barbara in Palm Beach had improved his taste in Scotch.

"You drink too much," she told him, voice full of disapproval. At the same time she was careful not to offend him; she had not come here for that. She sat on the edge of the bed next to him. "Gonna ruin your looks," she added with a small smile, hoping to take the edge off her words. "A handsome man like you, you're just about perfect-looking."

In reply he took another drink, straight from the bottle this time. What did she want? Why didn't she go away, leave him to his despair?

It was true, about his looks. Beginning to show the evidence of wear and tear, a vaguely sardonic look, the creases and seams, the brow full of furrows, a map of Devlin's past. Full of strong angles and thrusts, of secrets concealed behind the gray-green eyes, a hint of uncertainty around that sensual mouth. It was a fascinating face, scored with mystery and a reminder of the failures that had helped form it. Devlin's face was the right face for him.

"Are you feeling okay?" She allowed her hand to

come to rest on his knee. "Something on your mind, Dev?"

He almost told her about Geneva. That she could connect him with the break-in at the Cross house and through him connect all of them to the job. But some built-in safety device was at work in him; to tell her was to increase the threat. There was no way to be sure just how Ricketts and Daly would respond once they learned of the danger. They would perceive him as the source of that danger, and rightly so. Daly was a man of violence and would have no compunction about killing Devlin.

"A little under the weather is all," he told her.

Her fingers closed on his knee. "Is this the one?"

It was an intrusion, touching him that way, asking about the knee. He had told her nothing. How could she know so much about him? He supposed his reputation had caught up with him; it had before. People had heard a great deal about him, his skiing prowess, in the months before his time of despair. Still, she had no right to push past the social barriers he had so carefully erected over such a long period.

Her fingers had advanced onto his thigh, stroking, squeezing, exploring. "So strong," she said. "Harder than any man I've ever known. I can see what made you so great on the mountains."

Wrong, he commented to himself. What made a man great was never visible to the naked eye. It always came out of those regions of privacy and personal power that belonged to him alone. Greatness was born of drive and sacrifice and the pain of practice and repetition. Greatness was born in the dark places of a man's soul, and it could be talked about endlessly and almost never understood. Greatness was always in the act, never in the conversation. What was it Hemingway had said: "Only the matador knows what's it like to be in with the bull." Only the great ones had the right to know.

Her hand had managed to find its way between his thighs, and her closed face was alarmingly close. She touched him, and he almost cried out against the violation.

He swung his feet to the floor and took another pull out of the bottle. He lit another cigarette. He hadn't smoked for almost eleven years, resuming a month after moving in with Barbara. Now he was up to three packs a day. Sixty tubes of poison every twenty-four hours, less sleeping and skiing time. How many nails did it take to seal a coffin? Another drink. It didn't help; his mouth tasted like a sump hole.

"You don't want to talk about the knees," she said. "I understand."

"This is no good." He stood with his back to her. How many times had he made love to women without passion. Wanting only the rewards they brought along with them. How often had he performed on demand. On cue. An actor in a familiar role. He longed for feelings that belonged only to him. Private emotions and desires. That he could give freely or withhold, as the mood moved him. He wanted to care for somebody, finally. And to be cared for in return. Love, love. The word inadequately described the unattainable.

She came up behind him, arms circling his waist, hands fumbling with his belt. "Let me get you in the mood."

Panic rose in him like a dark, spreading cloud. He

desperately searched for a way out. "What about Hank? Sam Daly?"

That elicited a girlish giggle. "It's not what you think. Anyway, nobody owns me. I do what I want with whom I want."

He freed himself. "There's something you deserve to know." He came around in that awkward, top-heavy way of his, facing her, all sincerity and regret. His aversion to her was palpable, and he was anxious to put distance between them.

"Ah, Dev, you a little kinky? Sounds good to me. There isn't anything too far out I haven't done. There isn't anything I don't do great."

"It's not like that."

"You turned queer on me? Is that it?"

"I haven't been with a woman in a very long time."

Her laugh was a low, dark sound back of her throat. "You know what they say, they say it's like riding a bike. You never forget how."

"I can't do it, Peggy."

Her expression hardened, and her voice took on a cutting edge. "You mean you don't want to. With me."

He gazed into those violet eyes with all the openness he could muster. Without guile. Without duplicity. "You're one of the most beautiful women I've ever seen. It's that I can't. *Can't,* that's all."

She stared back in disbelief. "Can't do it?"

He nodded once, abject and apologetic.

"Can't get it up?"

"I'm afraid so."

"You gotta be kidding."

"I wish I were."

She retreated a step or two, a better vantage point

from which to look him over. "A fantastic-looking stud like you. People think you're getting it on with half the women in town. You're not putting me on?"

He shook his head.

"You talked to a shrink?"

"I tried that."

"A sex counselor?"

"My first move."

"And nothing worked?"

"Nothing."

"Wow."

"Yeah."

"What a waste."

"I'd appreciate it if you kept this to yourself."

"You can depend on me, Dev." She eased her way over to the door, hand on the knob. "I couldn't figure how come you never put a move on me."

"Now you know."

"Too bad," she said before she left. "All that swell advertising and no merchandise on the shelf. . . ."

Devlin searched for Geneva's name in the telephone directory; no Sharps were listed. He tried Information; the number was unlisted. He told the operator it was an emergency; she said she couldn't help him.

He continued to drink Scotch and smoke and pace the room, caught up in the seductive, suffocating sense of a pervasive loneliness. Fear and longing mingled and became as one, neither distinct in his cluttered consciousness.

He went out into the cold white night. A light snow was falling, and he pointed the blue Jeep into it, driving aimlessly, ending up on the streets of Aspen, assaulted by the late night sounds of laughter and gaiety. In them he could hear the faded echoes of his youth, half-remembered dreams, the numbing memories of all that he had once longed for, all given up without a real struggle. All that was lost.

He drove on. Out of the sparkling alpine village. Away from all the good times. The carefully cultivated prettiness. The mountain quaintness. He found himself on a gently climbing road. *Her* road. Even in the darkness he recognized it. He went past her house, turned around and came back. Twice more, three times, he drove past the house. Not daring to slow down, lest he be found out for a fool, a coward, a lust-ridden man-child.

Choking on recriminations, he parked the Jeep. Turned off the ignition. After a minute or two he let himself out and marched up onto the covered porch that ran around the house. He stepped silently, placing one foot carefully after the other, determined to attract no attention.

He peered through a window; nothing. Farther along, another window, looking into a long, lighted room, seeking some indication of Geneva's presence. Still nothing. A floorboard creaked underfoot and he advanced to a more compatible footing.

Breath rose out of him like holy smoke out of some ancient basilica. Short puffs that signaled his growing fear, a rising apprehension that he might be discovered, found out for the fool he was, mocked and dismissed like the shy and frightened child he had once been.

He was ready to leave. He took a single step when he saw her standing in the half-light of a tall window.

She wore a long robe, closed at the throat, her features frozen into an expressionless mask. She was pointing a pistol at his middle.

"Who are you?" Her voice was empty of emotion, her hand was steady. "What do you want?"

He opened his mouth to speak, but no words came out.

"Come closer, into the light. So I can see you." It was all said in a commanding voice, vigilant and unafraid. He did as he had been told, and after a moment she recognized him, said his name aloud. "Dammit! I might've killed you." The pistol was still pointed his way, and it occurred to him that she still might.

"I tried to call you."

"The number is unlisted."

"So I discovered."

"And you decided to visit?"

A casual conversation between casual acquaintances meeting by chance. So polite and civilized. If only she'd put the gun away.

"I keep thinking about you."

"What a fool you are." The weapon never wavered. A single massive spasm gripped her as if her body had recognized how cold it was before her mind caught up. She lowered the pistol to her side. "I'm going to freeze out here." She went around the side of the house, and he trailed after her, a chastened retainer. She opened a door and indicated that he was to precede her inside. He did, and she followed. The sound of the door closing was ominous, solid and final, much like the slamming of a quality car door. He heard the latch click into place, and all at once he was sorry he had come. Sorry he was in her house.

She placed the pistol into a Regency commode trimmed with gold paint. "There are guns all over this house," she said, as if informing herself of something forgotten. "Guns of all kinds. Pistols, rifles, shotguns. Military weapons. One of my husband's hobbies. He collects things—cars, paintings, wives."

"Wives?"

"I'm number five, and God only knows when he'll decide to trade me in for a younger model, prettier, sexier, someone more up to date. I need a drink," she ended, striding to the bar built into an alcove at the far end of the long sitting room. She poured some sour mash into a short glass and drank some of it. "You drink, Devlin? What would you like?"

He'd had his fill of alcohol for the day. Enough in the last day or two to last him a week. "I drink, but nothing right now."

She came around in what appeared to be a succession of plotted steps, a military maneuver in half-time. She studied him over the rim of the glass.

"Pretty dumb, showing up here like this."

"Your number is unlisted," he reminded her.

"That's Duncan. He has a mania for keeping his name out of sight of the public. He's sure some maniac is lurking about waiting to kidnap him. Or kill him."

"The hazards of the rich and famous."

She finished the sour mash and put the glass aside. "That's better. Why are you here, Devlin?"

"I had to talk to you." He was encouraged; she hadn't ordered him out of her sight. Hadn't sent him away with scorn and anger. His fear dispersed, and the familiar macho confidence began to seep out along his nerves. "It was important that I see you again."

"Important to whom?"

The question put him back on his heels, in a defensive position. "To me. I keep thinking about you."

"You're repeating yourself, Devlin." She gave nothing. Allowed no softness to creep into her voice. No gestures that might bring him closer. No subtle glance of encouragement. Nothing to let him know if she welcomed his attention or his presence. "Why?" she said. "Why do you keep thinking about me? Surely there are more interesting subjects for your attention. World poverty, for example. Or the homeless in our cities. The violence among the young. The topics that seem to engage so many Americans of your social class."

She was mocking him. Underscoring the absurdity of his position. Making him aware that they came from different and irreconcilable worlds. Telling him that he could play no part, however insignificant, in her life. Not now, not ever.

He grew desperate to reach her, to force her to take him seriously. "You know about me," he dared to say.

"What is so special to know about you, Devlin?"

"You recognized me that morning, the day Jerry Cross's house was robbed."

"Oh, yes, the robbery."

"You saw me. Driving the blue Jeep. You were on your porch when we went past. We were coming from Cross's house."

"You've come to confess, is that it? You're a burglar, breaking into people's houses while they're out skiing. Go to the police, tell them of your illegal activities. They say confession is good for the soul, and the cops will put you behind bars. Confess and be punished. This is no jail, Devlin. At least not for you."

What made her tick? It wasn't as if she were afraid of him. She knew he hadn't come to harm her. Nor did she wish to cause him any trouble; that much was clear to him, now. What was her game?

"I expected you to go to the law. I kept waiting for them to come after me."

"You should've run for it."

"Something kept me here."

"Something magical and mystical?" Again that sarcasm coated with sweetness.

"Why didn't you turn me in?"

She shrugged and clutched the long robe at the throat. "Same reason you didn't run."

"Something magical and mystical?" There was no sarcasm in his voice.

"What difference does it make? I didn't tell, you didn't run, and here we stand like a pair of damn fools."

"What are you after, Mrs. Sharps? What do you want from me?"

She spoke in a low, slow way. "You are a lucky man. If my husband had been here, he'd have put a bullet through your head and enjoyed it. Duncan is very big for killing. Animals, mostly. Life for Duncan is one constant hunt for bigger conquests, more trophies for his wall. My husband has an entire room in this house and another in the apartment in New York filled with the heads of creatures he has killed. Water buffalo, moose, a full-size lion stuffed and terrifying to see, but very much dead. A polar bear turned into a rug. God knows what else. There's even a skull of some Asiatic animal, complete with horns and polished to a high gloss. Are you interested in killing, Devlin?"

"No."

"That's one for the living. Duncan destroys people the way he destroys animals. Destroys their businesses. Their reputations. Their lives. Anyone who opposes him. Anything to win. Anything to get his own way . . ." Her voice trailed off, and she offered him a wan smile.

"Just imagine if he had been here this evening. Called upon to defend hearth and home, his life and his property, and, incidentally, his wife. What an opportunity that would have presented him. He would have shot you, Devlin. Blown you away, as the saying goes. And savored the bloody memory for the rest of his life."

"It never occurred to me that he might be home."

"Next time—" Another shrug. "If such an insane notion ever enters your head again, restrain yourself."

"Next time," he repeated without emphasis. What was there about her that made him so uneasy? The moment rang false, as if it had been carefully scripted, rehearsed, and cast. What was his part in all this? What was expected of him? Conflicting messages went through his brain like a school of darting minnows, distracting, and always beyond reach. She wasn't to be trusted, he told himself, and made a move toward the door.

"Do you swim?"

The incongruity of the question set his nerves on edge again. She laughed at his reaction. "There is a pool in the back. Indoors, naturally. I was about to go for a swim when you materialized in the night, Devlin.

Today was such a busy day, I never got out on the slopes. My body craves the exercise. This way . . ."

He went after her. The length of the living room, the dining room, a huge pantry with cupboards floor to ceiling, and through the gleaming metal kitchen. The pool room came as a shock. So large, and complete with hot tub and massage tables, with half a dozen professional-level exercise machines. What had driven her to ASA?

She went to the edge of the lap pool and dropped her robe. For an extended moment she stood naked, frozen in place. A magnificent creation by an inspired artist. Devlin could not remember ever seeing anyone—anything—so precise, so perfect, so beautifully crafted in the image of God.

She launched herself in a flat, racing dive into the pool. She was a strong, confident swimmer, reaching the far end with only a minimum of effort. She stood and faced him, breasts gleaming in the soft green light.

"You do swim, don't you, Devlin?"

"Yes," he managed to say in a voice strangulated by fright and desire, confused in the way young boys are confused the first time with a woman. So full of craving and so terrified of the reality that so suddenly confronts them. "Yes, I swim."

"In that case, what are you waiting for?"

20

*N*O other woman compared with Geneva. All others faded into the recesses of memory. Fairy tales recited long ago, unreal encounters, flickering images in a movie seen once and only dimly recalled. No fullness to any of them. These were no sentient beings, full of laughter and sadness, opening themselves to the possibilities of life. No flesh to be caressed and enjoyed. Only shadows in the mist.

How sweet she was. Immersed in the lap pool, she was softly submissive, giving herself over to him, accepting his caresses, returning his kisses. Her sweetness sweetened him, made him tender and caring. Until gradually she was transformed, inflamed, her passion fueled by his. She became a wild creature, unfettered by convention or inhibition, possessed by a feral hunger that could not be satisfied. She teased and tantalized him, taunted his early restraints, and challenged him to match her soaring desire.

Eventually they made it out of the water onto the padded matting that covered the pool room floor. Limbs entwined, they rolled over to the whirlpool, tumbling into the agitated hot water, afloat in a great, comforting womb.

Her fingers fluttered across his skin. She probed, she stroked, she drew blood with her sharpened nails. She licked the blood into her mouth, soothing the hurt parts with concern and compassion. She presented her breasts to him, and he suckled contentedly on those rose-colored nipples. She guided his hands across and around and into her body. She commanded his attention here and there. She settled down upon him until his huge hard penis reached high up into her belly.

Time was spent unnoticed. Light bent and fragmented. The world consisted only of that single glass-enclosed chamber, cloaked by the night. A madness took hold of him, his passion infinite, harsh, and insistent. He felt dislocated, unconnected with anything familiar, out of control. Until at last they came together in a cataclysmic burst of sound and pounding flesh; her presence bore down on him, and he fell back under her. Unable to move. Used up. Worn out. Defeated and glorying in his defeat. And victory.

As if to signify that victory, she twisted away from him, arms lifted to the sky, and let loose a chilling cry of triumph. She too had gotten what she wanted.

Presently she spoke. "No need to ask, is there?"

"No need."

"Never," she murmured against his cheek.

"Not even once?" A bantering note in his voice.

She understood the question. "Not even one time—with one of the hundreds of women you've had."

"Thousands."

She stroked his chest. "Somebody younger than I am. Some very firm and superb young girl?"

"It's never been better than it was with you. Not even once."

"That's how it was for me. The best. I can't describe it, how you made me feel."

"The way I feel, and I don't know anything about you."

She stood up, looking down at him, her thick sexual hair matted with perspiration, her thighs streaked with his semen. He put his face between her thighs.

She took a backward step.

"Don't you want me to?"

"No. Not now. Not yet."

"But you want me to?" he insisted.

She went over to the lap pool. "I want you to, when I'm ready."

He came up onto his knees. "I want to. I want very much to."

She laughed and dove into the water, stroking to the far end and back again, standing in water up to her breasts. "What a hungry boy you are."

"A boy, I haven't been called that in years."

"There's a quality about you . . ."

"Childish?"

"Youthful. As if you're still not fully formed."

He remembered Barbara and Alain; Alain was a boy,

and suddenly he felt emotionally exposed and vulnerable.

"Ah, Dev, I meant no harm. I like that about you, your youthfulness, that unspoiled quality, a kind of innocence."

It occurred to him then for the first time that he had never felt fully grown, mature, an independent, self-reliant man. By any measure he was middle-aged, and still it was his juvenile side that so often prevailed.

"Look, I'm not a child, don't treat me like one."

"No, my darling, you are definitely not a child. And I'll never treat you as one. That's how Duncan sees me, as a naughty, recalcitrant, troublesome child who frequently has to be chastised. Taught her place. Punished. Maybe it's his age. He's so much older than I am."

"Do you have to talk about him?" Devlin could not remember when a woman's having a husband troubled him. Images of Geneva in the arms of Duncan Turner Sharps crept into the forefront of his brain, and he set himself against it, willing her to be unmarried.

"He's a very real part of my life."

"But not of this, you and me, now. This belongs only to us."

"What a romantic you are, Dev."

In answer he dived past her into the lap pool, jack-knifed and slid back up against her body, kissing her as he went. They embraced, and he arranged his mouth on hers, lips soft and needy. She took his tongue into her mouth.

"Oh," she said. "What is happening to you? You do have a voracious appetite."

"Only for you."

"Liar," she murmured against his cheek. "A few days from now, a week. Someone else will appear. You'll hardly remember me. Another female who couldn't resist you. Another easy lay."

"It's not that way."

"You'll forget my name, and if we pass in the street, you won't recognize my face."

"I could never forget your face."

"Never. Not ever. If only I could believe that."

"Believe it."

"It doesn't matter, Dev. I'm willing to settle for whatever you are willing to let me have. It has to end soon, anyway." She tucked her face against his chest.

"Why?" That possibility had never occurred to him. "Why does it have to end at all?"

"It's my husband. He's due in Aspen any day now. Once he arrives . . ." She let it hang; there was nothing else to say.

"No." His vehemence caught him by surprise.

"There's no way to change the facts, my darling. Once Duncan shows up, he'll take charge of my life, use me the way he's always used me. Ordering me about. Debasing me in private and in public. Forcing me to do the things that please him. Turning me into his whore . . . another of his possessions."

"Ah, baby," Devlin said softly. He felt a great and abiding tenderness with this woman. For her. And he would allow nothing and no one to hurt her. The depth and honesty of his emotions startled him, affirmed what a vital part of his life she had become in such a short time. "Let me take care of you, baby. Let me take care of you. Whatever it is, I'll make things right for you." He meant it, he believed it, he intended to do it.

If only she felt the same.

They could not bear to be apart. They showered together. Soaping and cleaning, tasting every inch of each other's skin, putting lips and tongue to every crevice, paying homage to every orifice, every shadowed place. They spoke of the miracle of being together. Of finding each other. Of loving each other; neither said the word aloud in the beginning, neither dared to.

They went to bed, her bed. The silk sheets crisp and cool, the mattress substantial under them, a comforter forming a tent for warmth and in a sudden, surprising need for modesty. They made love in a quiet, old-fashioned manner, an act so dramatically different from their earlier bouts of animal passion that it sanctified what he felt, what they had become to one another.

But in the still recovery time he grew troubled. He lay where Sharps had lain. He had taken her where Sharps had taken her. He had listened to her moans and the small, sharp cries of delight and desire, wondering if she had moaned for Sharps this way, had cried out for him. He grew uneasy and irritable and climbed out of the bed, searching for a cigarette.

He stood at the window smoking, peering out between the curtains. Daylight had spread over the mountains, the upper reaches still encased in a thin drape of fog. In his mind he was atop the highest peak, able to see forever, one range after another, clad in virginal white, unmarked by a human presence. This was when it was best on the mountain. Any mountain. Aspen or Crested Butte. Pas de Chèvre. Or the West Face in Squaw Valley. Or the Parsenn at Davos. In his mind he stood poised on the highest, most inaccessible of ridges, the tips of his skis pointing the way over the edge. The morning wind whistled in his ears, and his pulse raced in visceral anticipation. Then he launched himself, making first tracks where no one had ever gone before him. The perfect run. The perfect mountain. All these years of searching, and failing every time.

She called to him, summoning him away from his dreams. "Dev. What are you thinking?"

He remained at the window. "Just looking at the mountains."

She came up behind him, arms circling his waist, cheek against his strong back. She was struck anew by his athlete's physique, the powerful torso, the lithe limbs, muscles defined and flexing at the slightest movement. She needed all this trained power.

"My darling," she said. "I want to know everything about you. Your most private thoughts."

He turned to face her. They kissed lightly, a renewed, reassuring intimacy. "I'm all right," he said.

"You seemed melancholy, standing here, looking out. As if you'd lost something out there."

He was touched profoundly by her sensitivity, by how insightful she could be. He kissed her eyes. Her nose. Her mouth.

She drew him back to the bed and fit herself to him, back to front, like a pair of perfectly matched spoons. She lifted his hands to her breasts and allowed her eyes to flutter shut.

"Would you rather be up on the mountain now? Getting ready for that first run?"

"There'll be other mornings."

"I wish I could ski with you."

"Well, let's do it."

"And risk someone seeing us together? A woman by the name of Brody is here. She works for my husband. If she saw us—I don't think I want to take that chance."

"Does that mean we have to spend the rest of our time together in bed?"

"Would that be so bad?" She teased him.

He pretended to think it over. "Not so bad. But it ain't skiing."

"Oh, you . . ." She drove an elbow lightly into his belly. He grunted and laughed. Then, more seriously: "Are you a good skier, Dev?"

"Good enough."

"Better than just good, I bet."

He hesitated before answering. "I'm a great skier, Geneva. At least, I used to be. One of the best in the world."

She came around to face him. "I think you mean it."

He nodded. "That was a long time ago. That's what I was meant to be, a skier. A champion. That's what my father taught me to be. Back in Vermont, where I was born. Surrounded by hills and all that snow. My father had me on a pair of skis almost as soon as I was old enough to keep myself erect."

"Tell me about your father, Dev. What kind of a man was he?"

His face closed up, the gray-green eyes lidded, clenched against the attempted intrusion. Until he was struck by the impulse to share his past with her. To tell her who he really was and what he had come from.

"My father was almost fifty years old when I was born. He never wanted to be married, never wanted a family. He was a victim of the Depression. He used to tell me how it was, without work, without money, scrounging for enough food to stay alive. He lived in hobo camps and rode the rails from town to town looking for a job."

"It must have been terrible for him."

He felt ill at ease on her silk sheets, protected by the warm comforter, so strangely at home in this millionaire's house. His father had never made love to a woman like Geneva Sharps. Had never wallowed in such luxury. Guilt and anger made him want to share it with her.

"He was a special kind of a guy, my father. Gargantuan in his appetites, Dionysian in his laughter, unpretentious. Always seeing the possibilities of life, despite all the damage it had done to him."

"And your mother?"

He frowned, the flow of thoughts broken by the question. His mother . . . He selected his words cautiously, uttered them without stress or color. "She was much younger than my father. A beautiful woman, which is why he married her, I suppose. She had wanted to have children, a family. But once I came along all that changed. Being a wife was too confining for her. Being a mother too demanding.

"She dreamed of becoming an actress. Singing and dancing on Broadway. She loved musical comedy. Once in a while I'd see her dancing around the house, singing sometimes, even pretending to be acting a role in some play."

"She must have been a gifted woman."

"Unfulfilled gifts. She never tried . . ."

"She had a hard life. Raising a little boy . . ."

"She should've tried. She grew stunted by disappointment and defeat until . . ."

"Until?"

"She disappeared one day. Just like that. I was seven years old, and when I came home from school she was gone. No warning. No explanation. Nothing but the emptiness where she used to be."

"Poor Dev."

He shook his head as if to clear it of befogging memories. "My father, he wept when he found out. It was the only time I ever saw him cry. He went to his room and stayed there for an hour or so, and when he came out his eyes were dry. He said we had to act like men. Be strong and be brave, and the next morning he took me out on the intermediate hill not far from where we lived and insisted that I take it, top to bottom. When I did it, he clapped me on the back and told me I could become a world champion, if I had the nerve and the will. He said he would teach me, and he did. Taught me everything I know. Everything he knew. How to win. What it took to win. The discipline, the character, the endless hours going over things on the slopes. He was a man, my father. A real man."

"How good did you become?"

"When I was eleven, I began winning competitions. Against older boys, even against grown men. Medals, ribbons, trophies, all of that. I entered tournaments all over New England. In high school, I was the best

skier in my school. The best in the state. When I out-
grew the local competition, my father began sending
me to other venues around the country. Somehow he
managed to scrape up enough money to send me to
Europe. When I was sixteen I was skiing in
Klosters. . . ."

"And sleeping with all those fantastic European
girls?"

He stared at her, forced away from one set of memories to another, forced to alter his mood. "There
were girls. And women, as well. They're part of the
ski scene."

"All heroes have got their groupies."

He'd never thought of it that way. Lumping all the
women he'd known into one silly category. Groupies
were those fatuous little creatures who hung around
rock bands and football players. The women he'd
known . . . he wanted to believe they had come to him
because he was special. An individual. That even when
the encounters meant nothing, some residual value remained.

"Maybe you're right," he conceded.

"Tell me about Klosters, the skiing."

"I won the downhill by three full seconds. And I
came in second in the giant slalom. I should've won,
but my concentration was not too sharp that day."

"Those things happen, I suppose."

Did she care, he asked himself, or was that just an
automatic response? How hard it had become for him
to trust another human being. It was as if there were
no certainties, no psychic handholds to cling to any
longer. It had been a very long time since his expecta-
tions had corresponded to his experiences. A sense

of displacement swept him up, and he clung to Geneva for fear he would be cast off again into an empty, lonely void.

He spoke in a flat, toneless voice, putting the words out one after another. "An hour before the slalom I received a phone call from my mother. From Vermont. I hadn't seen her or heard from her in all those years. And there she was, on the phone, efficient and businesslike, calling to tell me that my father had had a massive coronary and was dead. A phone call and he was gone. So you see, during the slalom . . ."

She quieted him with a finger. "Hush, my darling."

"Was I wrong? To compete that morning? It's what my father would've wanted, I told myself. Was I wrong?"

"It's all right."

"I still don't know."

"It's over now."

"I'll never be certain."

"Don't think about it anymore. It's over."

"I want you to be right."

"Trust me, my darling."

That was the key, he reminded himself. To trust another human being. "I do," he said. "I do trust you."

She was up against him, clinging tightly to him, mouth against his chest, delivering tiny kisses, the tip of her tongue moist and warm against his skin. "You're so beautiful, my darling. So perfect. I feel so safe in your arms."

Which is what he wanted, to please and reassure her, to protect her.

She knelt before him, eyes fixed on the heaviness of his manhood. He shifted, moved, as if a separate life existed between his legs. "Are you always like this? Half-hard and ready?"

He could make no answer.

She cupped his testicles, embracing their pendulous weight with her fingers, unloosing sensations of pleasure up into his groin. He rose to fullness as she watched, trembling with excitement, agleam in the soft early light. She touched him tentatively with her lips, a tender kiss, and then drew him into her mouth, looking up at him at the same time.

Her head bobbed back and forth in a primitive rhythm, a muffled crooning back in her throat. This was for her, done out of her own needs, gaining a secret sort of nourishment from his power. As if in response to his thoughts, she murmured, "For you, my darling. My present to you."

He knew better than that.

21

THEY nourished themselves with imported cheeses and English water biscuits, on Polish sausage and Mexican fruit, all washed down with a chilled pouilly-fumé from Sharps's collection of French wines. They ate while soaking in the hot tub and waited for the strength to return to their drained bodies.

She touched the scars on his left knee, lifting his leg out of the water for a clearer, more convincing view. She kissed her way along the twisted, crimson route.

"I want to know about this."

In the past he had always brushed aside such inquiries, treating them as intrusive and bothersome. Not this time; he was unable to deny her anything.

"It was at Lake Placid. I was training for the Olympics, making a run I'd made a hundred times before. Going at three-quarter speed, practicing my technique. There was something buried in the snow. A small branch of a tree, a rock, maybe an empty beer can. I never found out what. It doesn't matter. Whatever it was, it took me down. The leg turned on me, the pain sharp and lasting.

"At first they said it was nothing, the doctors. A bad sprain, they said. Rest and rehabilitation would take care of it. When that didn't happen they took another look. This time they said it was a grade-three disruption of the medial collateral ligament. A few months' rest. No skiing, no workout. Just take it easy.

"Next they discovered cartilage damage. They cut me, and when they told me I could, I went back to work, building up the strength on the knee. I took a few trial runs, and everything seemed okay. Until the knee went out again. I went through the entire procedure one more time.

"Finally I was back in shape. I went over to Sugarbush, back home in Vermont. Nothing very fancy, nothing too hard. An intermediate trail, the kind of thing I used to eat alive. The knee held up. It's just that this time, the other one went on me. Blew out like it had been booby-trapped.

"The doctors said I shouldn't worry. Surgical techniques had advanced rapidly. They could rebuild the knee until it was better than ever. They were wrong. I can still ski. I can still make it down the side of any mountain there is. I can still get up a pretty good rush along the way. Once in a while I can even fool myself into believing that I'm as good as I used to be.

"I'm not. I never will be.

"My competitive days are over. I don't have the strength in the legs to win. Nor the speed. And there's always the fear that at any moment the knees will go out on me again."

"Poor Dev."

"Thing is, I was a lock for the gold that year. The downhill and the slalom. Everybody knew it. You could bet the house on it, the wife and kiddies. No way I was going to lose. Nobody came close to my times. Two gold medals. Do you have any idea what that would have meant? I would have turned pro. Demonstrations, endorsements, TV appearances; there was even a movie waiting in the wings. All of it went with the knees.

"Can you imagine what it means to be the best? Best in the U.S. Best in the world. Better than the Austrians. Better than Jean-Claude Killy, even. Number one. Until my life turned to shit. The rest of me is fine. In great shape. Better than ever. But I'm hostage to the knees. . . ."

"Maybe—"

He cut her off. "Don't say it! There's no chance. It's over. I can never be what I was then. Never be the best again. That's all in the past. Dreams of long ago, adolescent dreams. Maybe that's all they were—dreams—and none of it ever really happened. Maybe I was never as good as I remember."

There was a hushed intensity to her voice. "You are better than you know. The best man I've ever known, in a hundred different ways."

He managed a small, sad smile. "We haven't done it a hundred ways."

She matched his smile and kissed him. The phone began to ring. She ignored it.

"Aren't you going to answer?"

"It's probably Duncan with orders for me to carry out. Or one of his lapdogs. That executive assistant of his. In any case, I don't care."

An expression of renewal, of discovery, faded onto her face. Without makeup, the golden hair combed straight back off her brow, her skin glowing, she was bright-eyed and youthful. Her head went back when she laughed, her long neck graceful and smooth. She enjoyed his naiveté, she told him. In a world corrupt and venal, so cruel and ill-mannered, he had somehow managed to retain his innocence.

The word surprised him. "I lost my innocence a long time ago, I told you that."

Wine on her lips, she kissed her way from his mouth to his lap, inhaling the distinct manly odor of him. "There's the smell of chlorine on you."

"Your pool."

"I love the way you smell. The taste of you, after you've been inside me. The scent of your sex, your sweat, everything. The way you fill up my mouth. And when you're ready to come, the tension in your crotch, all your muscles becoming harder, until you explode."

"No one's ever been as good for me. It's as if you are my first woman."

"Who was she?"

"My first woman? That was a million years ago."

"Tell me about her." She nibbled at the hairs on his thighs, tugging, setting her teeth and tearing half a dozen hairs out of their roots. When he protested, she licked the hurt place lovingly. "I want to know everything there is to know about you."

"Her name was . . ." He paused. "I still remember, Mrs. Colby. My God, I haven't thought about her in years."

"How old were you?"

"That first time? Fourteen. No, fifteen. We were at the shore. On Cape Cod. Wellfleet, I think it was. For a while, we went every summer for two weeks. I loved being with him for those two weeks. Swimming, fishing, taking long walks on the beach, challenging the breakers."

"And Mrs. Colby."

"She had the cottage next to ours in a small development in some piney woods. She had a son about my age, and I used to swim with him now and then, play ball with him. His name was Arnold, and he was a bit of a nerd. At least that's how I viewed him back then. Arnold became a lawyer, and he's become a public defender in New Haven or Providence, somewhere in New England."

"And you got it on with Arnold's mother."

"More like the other way around. My father drove up to Boston and I stayed behind. I stayed at the cottage most of the day. Alone. Something caught my attention. Movement outside the side window. The side of our cottage faced Mrs. Colby's cottage. There she was, showering the sand of the beach off herself. Each cottage had its own outside shower."

"She was naked?"

"She had taken down the top of her bathing suit and was directing the stream of water onto her breasts. I had never seen a woman's breasts before. Fully exposed. No more than ten or fifteen feet away. They filled my eyes, pale and shining from the water, the nipples huge and pink. I couldn't believe my luck, seeing Mrs. Colby this way. It was one of the most exciting events of my life, almost as good as a perfect ski run. I could hardly breathe. I was hard as a rock."

She laughed and kissed his thigh. "I know all about how hard you can get. What happened then?"

"Nothing. Mrs. Colby pulled her suit back on and went inside her cottage. But the image remained in my mind, vivid and immensely provocative."

"I'll bet."

"The next day, when I saw Mrs. Colby leave the beach, I did the same. My father thought I was sick and wanted to come along. I told him I felt like taking a nap, that I hadn't slept too well the night before. When I got back to the cottage, I sneaked a look out the window, and sure enough, there was Mrs. Colby, half-naked under the shower. It made me crazy with lust. . . ."

"Which has remained with you ever since?"

He barely heard her words, his mind reaching back, reliving that special moment.

The boy, John Thomas Andrew Devlin, summoned up every ounce of courage he possessed and hurried out the front door. He circled around back, coming up between the two cottages, coming to a dead stop only a few yards away from Mrs. Colby.

Sensing his presence—her back was to him—she came around deliberately. Her bare breasts, shining in the late afternoon sun, pointed at him accusingly. She appraised him without urgency, then very slowly brought her hands up to shield herself.

He protested his innocence. "I didn't know anybody was here. I had no way of knowing. I'm sorry. Sorry." Ducking his head in shame and embarrassment, he hurried back into his cottage.

Minutes later Mrs. Colby was at the door. Her bathing suit was firmly in place, a towel wrapped strategically around her for added protection against his prying eyes and sinful thoughts.

"I think we should have a little talk," she announced.

He could only stand immobile, eyes cast down.

"Give me ten minutes," she went on. "Then come to my cottage."

He made the short walk on unsteady legs. His mouth was dry, and his palms were lined with perspiration. He anticipated only the worst, the worst being that Mrs. Colby felt impelled to inform his father of his transgressions. She hadn't believed his protests, had seen right through the implausible screen he had erected. She knew him for the pervert he was.

She admitted him silently and indicated that he was to sit on a small sofa against one wall. The towel was gone, and the swimsuit, replaced by a modest red-and-yellow sundress that ended at midthigh. She took up a position in front of him, a thoroughly intimidating creature.

"About what happened . . ." She made a vague gesture that was intended to include the outdoor shower.

"I'm sorry. It was an accident. I didn't think that anybody was out there." The lie was transparent to his own ears. Weak and futile. There was no denying the awful creature he was.

"Have you done that sort of thing before?"

"Oh, no!" That she could even suggest such a disgusting possibility was horrifying. Frightening. A threat of monumental proportions. Those things he did to himself; she couldn't know about that. No one could. He performed certain acts in clenched privacy, lest anyone discover the extent of his depravity. *Father, forgive me, for I have sinned* . . . How many Hail Marys had he said, how many rosaries? How he feared the fires of hell and the wrath of Father Dunleavey, and of his own father.

She said in a low voice, "I would feel terrible if anyone ever found out."

No words came out of him.

"Now, John, you've got to give me your word. Your oath. Do you swear it, that you'll never inform another living soul of what happened out there today?"

He managed a single bob of his head.

"Say it."

"I give you my word."

"Swear it."

"I swear it."

She exhaled and allowed herself a pleasant smile. She was a pretty woman, a little larger here and there than she wanted to be. But on balance, satisfied with herself.

"You swear, John Devlin, that you will never tell another person that you saw Mrs. Colby's bare titties?"

"I swear," he said again. And in that split second of time he understood that some subtle, unnamed change had taken place. The balance of power had shifted only slightly, yet sufficiently to make him know that he was no longer in danger. Fear began to drain

away. Replaced by a slight curiosity, an awareness that
Mrs. Colby had become a little unsure of herself.

"I want you to tell me something," she said after
a moment.

"Yes?"

She wet her lips. "Did you like them?"

He knew what she meant; he nodded.

"Better than other titties you've seen?"

"I never saw another woman that way."

"That surprises me, a pretty boy like you."

The fear had been supplanted by nervousness,
aware that he had crossed over into territory unex-
plored by him and alien in its demands. What now?

Again that little smile of hers. "Well, at least you
didn't get much of a look. I mean, it was a pretty short
look, after all."

He almost confessed that he had seen her before
through the cottage window. That he had looked at
length and at leisure, studying every bit of those great
breasts. He clamped his mouth shut.

"Well," she said. "As long as I've got your word.
That you'll keep our little secret. In that case, I don't
mind too much that you had your little look. No damage was done, was there? And to tell the truth, I'm
kind of proud of my titties. Do you think I'm terrible?"

"Oh, no, Mrs. Colby."

"Believe me, more than one man has tried to get
his paws on them. Men love to do that, you know, cop
a feel."

He didn't know what to say; he said nothing.

She said, "I suppose you've touched plenty of girls.
Their titties, I mean."

He was appalled. "Oh, no!"

"Poor boy. What a shame. A good-looking young fellow like you." She paused, went on in a sly, suggestive manner. "Bet you wouldn't mind getting a look at mine one more time. Or am I wrong?"

Yes or no? What answer responded to the question? He wasn't sure and so said nothing.

"Give me your word," she said, leaning his way, so large and intimidating. "Tell me that you'll never tell. As long as you live. Swear."

"I already did swear." Levels of fear until now unknown, and trembling, took him in its grasp. "I swear."

"No one is allowed to know. No one."

"I won't tell." He had turned the corner on excitement, gone past temptation and desire, drifted out of coherence, into a suspended state of perplexities and enigmas. Reason had departed, and he seemed to be floating purposelessly through a great golden dream. "I won't. Never."

"Good. . . ." She was no more than an arm's length from him when she unbuttoned the sundress, pulled it aside so that she was completely exposed.

Young Devlin's throat constricted, breath coming in harsh, desperate gasps. His mouth was dry and his brain spun wildly, giving rise to brief magical images. Her breasts loomed up before him in pale, shimmering magnificence, those nipples pointed toward the nether regions of his soul. And at the periphery of his vision, that dark and mysterious patch out of which had sprung legend and lie, calling forth a riot of doubt and contradiction. He wanted, he needed, he had to have. He dared not confront that dark heart of her womanhood directly, dared not reveal the extent of his madness, his psyche twisted out of shape, his cock inflated to such mighty proportions that it pained and embarrassed him.

She took his hands. "Touch me." Her directions were an example of clear thinking translated into concise, hard language. Only an idiot might have failed to understand. Or deny her. *Touch this firmly, harder with the palm of the hand, quick, birdlike movements of the finger. One finger.* Sounds came out of her, and words eventually, the words running one into another, muffled and thick. "Sweet boy. Oh, so nice for Mrs. Colby. Up and down. Here. There. Side to side. Oh, yes, sweet boy. Faster. Harder. Yes. Not quite so fast. Not quite so hard."

She was a demanding taskmaster, an outstanding and remarkably patient teacher. He was an apt, anxious, always willing student.

"Don't stop. Whatever happens, don't stop. Don't stop."

The thought had never occurred to him.

"And then what happened?" Geneva Sharps had been moved by the recitation, unable to resist its sensual lure.

"Then?" Devlin made light of the memory. "We got it on."

"You put it in her?"

"She put it in."

"And you loved it?"

"It ended so quickly."

That drew a small laugh out of her. "My, how you've changed."

"Mrs. Colby insisted we do it again. . . ."

"Until you got it right?"

"Something like that."

"You didn't protest."

"I'd've done it all day, all night, all week. I was insatiable."

"You're still insatiable, a sex maniac."

"Every woman should have one."

"Is that it, then, you're my sex maniac."

"As long as the grass grows and the rivers flow."

She was delighted by him. "How lucky you are to have found your true calling in life."

His eyes clouded over and a vague vision of the snow-coated mountains appeared on the screen of his mind. After skiing, he amended silently. Always a distant second to that.

She failed to register the change in his mood. "You'd be surprised how some men are. Some can hardly ever perform to their satisfaction or mine. Others, ungiving, demanding, never concerned about their partner."

How many men had she known? The question startled him; he had never considered it before, not until Geneva had such information seemed worth knowing. Guilt and shame, like twin scolds, berated him for his hypocrisy and superficiality. He was compelled to make up for such unworthy thoughts.

"Whatever you want," he said. "I want to give you."

"Right on, my darling. Just keep being the sex maniac you were meant to be. . . ."

He obliged her.

"You never answered the question," he reminded her. They lay next to each other in his bed, in his room. She had insisted that they come here. She wanted to

see where he lived. How he lived. Be able to visualize
him in these surroundings when they were apart.

"I want you to make love to me in your bed. Am
I being unreasonably romantic and sentimental?"

He drove her to the house in Glenwood Springs in
the blue Jeep. Took her up into his room via the back
staircase that led from an alcove adjoining the kitchen,
away from prying eyes. They sipped an inexpensive
Chianti out of plastic water tumblers and nibbled at
garlic chips and cheddar cheese and made love. The
sheets were damp with their sweat and his semen and
rough with the crumbs of the chips. Later he smoked
and reminded her that she had yet to answer his question.

"What question?" She had ignored it, hoped he
would refrain from asking it again. Now she wondered
how much she could let him know without pushing him
away. She made up her mind.

"I haven't always lived a good life."

"Certainly I haven't."

"You're lucky, you knew your father. He loved you,
and you have your memories. My father was a drunk,
and he died in an alley outside a detox unit in Fresno.
Out in the valley in California. I guess he had come
for help, but it was too late. He was dead when they
found him."

"I'm sorry."

"My mother? Like yours, she simply disappeared
one day when I was ten years old. I'd rather not remember anything about her. I kicked around from
uncle to aunt to cousin to foster homes during the next
few years. Always working for my keep. Doing laundry. Cleaning the house. Doing stoop work in the

fields. Living like a donkey, doing donkey's work. Anything to have a place to sleep and some food to eat. My uncle, my father's brother, he was the last member of the family I stayed with. He showed up in my room one night, forced himself on me, and came back every night after that.

"What he did was wrong. Evil. And when I couldn't stand it anymore, I helped myself to a steak knife from the kitchen and when he came to me that night I sliced his cheek from ear to jaw. He threw me out of the house with just the clothes on my back."

"The bastard."

"Yes. But I was on the street. There was the occasional job, terrible jobs that paid badly but kept me alive. And always men trying to get into my pants. I won't lie to you, more than one did. After a while, you get tired of fighting. You long for a warm bed. A good meal. A few extra dollars.

"I was fifteen and waiting tables in a diner in Oakland. I met a boy. Actually he was a man, in his twenties, and we became engaged. He loved me and I loved him and we were going to be married. On the day before our wedding, two men robbed an all night convenience store. A police car came along and there was a shootout. My fiancé was killed in the crossfire. He had gone into the store to buy a pack of cigarettes. His parents managed somehow to convince themselves that it was my fault, and they refused to let me attend the funeral. But I went to the grave the next day and cried over him and left some flowers. That night I left Oakland.

"I moved on with my grief and little else. A meaningless job here and there, until the boss hit on me.

Or his wife thought he did. Either way, I was out again. I headed south and ended up in Los Angeles. I was pretty, I guess, and men kept telling me I ought to be in movies. That they could get me into this studio or that one. I was young, but not stupid. Oh, there were men, a few of them. But not so many. Men, but no movies. I lived with my poverty and without hope. Until I met Duncan Turner Sharps."

"He rescued you."

A peculiar expression came into her eyes, a glint of suspicion and distrust; in time he came to recognize it for what it was, but not then.

"Yes," she bit off in a tough, aggressive way. "He rescued me." Her expression softened. "You want me to go on?"

He nodded.

"Okay." There was resignation in the single word as if something terrible would result from her words. She filled her lungs with air and went on. "Sharps gave a party. Sharps believes in parties, as a means to an end. The end, naturally, is to put more money, more power, in his hands. Sharps is convinced that liquor and music and lots of pretty young women make for a successful party. And ultimately a successful deal.

"A friend brought me with her. I can remember how out of place I felt among all those wealthy and sophisticated people. I was still in my teens and afraid and suspicious of everyone I met.

"During the evening I met Sharps. That is, he approached me. What a dramatic-looking man he was. Head shaved clean, a great curving black mustache that made him look like an Oriental potentate. He has small eyes, nearly black, intense. And his voice is granulated, almost a monotone, hypnotic and powerful.

"He took me off to a small, book-lined room and we talked. He did most of the talking. About business. About politics and politicians. About money, the benefits of being wealthy. About the exercise of power. I was fascinated by him."

"And then he took you to bed?" Devlin said with considerable bitterness.

She let him wait for her reply. "I'm trying to tell you, Sharps is different from other men. He never touched me that night. Never raised the issue of sex. Most men talk about little else. We just talked through the night. Talked and drank champagne. In the morning, he sent me home in his chauffered limousine. He treated me terrifically well that night. And for a long time afterward."

"When did you see him again?"

"Not for weeks. One night, late, he called and asked me to go to an all-night hamburger joint with him. Another time, he took me to Disneyland. The bullfights in Tijuana. Once for an all-day outing on his yacht. He sold that yacht," she ended with regret.

"And still no sex?"

"You have a one-track mind, Dev."

"End of track is just around the bend."

"Okay, cut to the sex. Sharps's way. Expensive and brassy, glitzy. He had me flown out to Las Vegas for a weekend. Turned out he was dealing for one of those big hotels on the Strip. He never missed a trick, not Sharps.

"I had a suite of my own. A car to take me around. And ten thousand dollars in cash for gambling money.

Sharps has a thing about cash. He loves the look of money, the smell of it, I guess. Once he showed me a suitcase filled with one-hundred-dollar bills, neatly stacked and counted. Half a million dollars. Said it was just a reminder of how far he'd come. Half a million or five million, it made no difference. All he had to do was make a phone call and the money was delivered. He always keeps large amounts on hand."

"Isn't he worried about being ripped off?"

"I asked him once. He laughed at me. Said no one would ever think a man could be so dumb to keep that kind of money in his house. Besides, if somebody did try to rob him, Sharps would shoot him. Sharps would enjoy shooting a human being."

"What happened to the ten grand?"

"I lost it all."

"And he demanded payment?"

"Poor Dev, such a small mind. No, Sharps simply handed over another ten thousand. Told me to enjoy myself. We flew back to Los Angeles together. In his private plane. To his house in Bel-Air. We had a light supper and he told me how much it meant to him to have me along in Vegas. That's when he kissed me for the first time. And then he took me to bed."

"Trumpets and a roll of drums."

"Don't be nasty."

"Maybe I'm jealous."

"It's important that you understand. I did it with Sharps because I wanted to. I liked him. Then. He treated me very well. In bed and out. And a week later, he proposed marriage to me. Said I could have anything I wanted, the best of everything, as long as I remembered that I was Mrs. Duncan Turner Sharps and acted accordingly." She paused reflexively. "So we were married and lived unhappily ever after."

He said nothing for a long time, and neither did she. It was as if both of them were talked out, emptied of words and drained of emotions. "You think I married him only for his money, don't you? And that puts me out there with the girls on the street. A high-priced hooker, isn't that what you're thinking? Maybe you're right. Maybe that's what I am. Nothing but Sharps's whore, and you're so pure and fine you can't tolerate my being that."

He took her by the shoulders, shaking her, fingers digging into her flesh. Hurting her. "Don't you get it! What I am. How I feel about you."

She recoiled as if struck, not by the words, but by the force with which they had been said. "Don't say anything you'll be sorry for. You don't have to say anything."

"I want you to know."

"Only if you mean it. Only if it's the truth."

He touched her lips gently, close to her, trying to convey his deepest feelings by his presence. "I love you, Geneva. I know now that I've never before loved anyone else. I never will." His kiss was tender and affectionate.

"There's so much you don't understand. . . ."

"We have the rest of our lives to talk. . . ."

"Oh, no, I have to explain, how it is about me and Sharps."

"I don't care about him. Only about you."

"Oh, yes, my darling, and I care about you. But it matters to me that you know. As soon as I married Sharps, things changed between us. It was as if someone had drawn a shade and shut out the sunlight. He made me live in darkness, letting me out only when it suited him, for his own twisted purposes. I don't love him, I never did. He's crude and demanding, he's rough and selfish, a monster. A deceiver. My jailer."

"Then why . . . ?"

"Why did I marry him? He wasn't like that before the wedding. He concealed his true nature. Or maybe I just couldn't see it. I was so alone then, hustling just to survive. Afraid of what I might become. Afraid of what I'd already become. He offered everything I used to dream about—wealth, safety, someone who would stand between me and the ugliness of life. This man— he was nearly forty years older than I when we met— so sure of himself, so exotic and exciting, he offered me sanctuary, a place free from fear and despair. He seemed to know all the questions as well as the answers. What a joke." She laughed a small, bitter laugh. "I told you, he collects things—guns, paintings, cars, antique furniture. I was one of those things. And ownership for Duncan means license, freedom to inflict pain and humiliation. Oh, he can be so charming when he wants to be, turning it on and off at will. But he's a devil. He taunts me, insults me in front of other people, he beats me . . ."

"Leave him."

"A hateful man. More than once he's taken a whip to me, a great black ugly thing. Or his leather belt. He's bloodied me and loosened my teeth, blacked my eyes. He's battered me and afterward locked me in a closet, naked, without food or water, for days at a time. And when he wants me, he takes me. Uses me roughly and without consideration."

"Leave him."

"He is the ultimate corruption, truly a monster. More than once I ran away, with just the clothes on my back. He sent men after me. Big, powerful men with empty eyes. They found me and brought me back to him. He whipped me, he punched me, he did unspeakable things to me."

"Enough, don't say any more."

"I want you to know what he's done to me. There are times, when it was in his business interests to do so, he used me to generate profits. . . ."

A fine anguish had settled over him, as if her pain superseded his own, as if living his life through her, experiencing the wonders and torments she had experienced, living life in rough translation. She continued to speak, almost a stranger in that moment, aloof and enigmatic and set apart. He struggled to bring her back into focus.

"The first time was the worst. Duncan was entertaining, for business purposes, of course. He gave me no warning; a collection of people descended upon the apartment he used to own in Milan. A Swiss banker, an Italian industrialist, a Sicilian Mafia chief, some others. Without their women. If they had women. Without their sedate, correctly turned out, middle-aged, middle-class wives and lovers."

"And Duncan?"

"And me. Duncan turned me into something I wasn't that night. Something I had never wanted to be. Becoming his wife, it was my chance to live a decent life. To be a proper married lady. Conservative, dull, attracting no particular attention to myself. A faithful wife. And I always had been. That wasn't enough for Duncan. Not that night.

"He brought home special clothes for me to wear."

"Clothes?"

"Yes, my sweet, innocent love. Clothes. Bits and pieces of lace. Black, of course. A long black skirt printed with white-and-yellow flowers that in a certain light was transparent. The panties he made me wear barely covered me. And the blouse. A delicate Egyptian cotton, also black, and totally revealing when worn without a bra. And Duncan forbade me to wear one. My breasts were completely exposed. To make sure all his associates appreciated my body, Duncan spent a good part of the evening calling attention to it. Making me pose with lights behind me so that they could see through my skirt. Ordering me to stand close to the Sicilian, a piggish little man, so he could touch me, find out what he was missing, as Duncan said. And when he was convinced his friends had had enough of the diversion, he sent me to bed, and soon after that I heard the sound of women's voices. He'd brought in a squad of whores to provide the pièce de résistance to the evening's entertainment. He told me the next day that it had been a very successful evening for him. He'd closed a couple of very big deals. When my dear husband wants something, he gets it. No matter what. He takes no prisoners."

"You're right, he is a monster. I wish he were dead."

"If wishes were facts, my darling, Duncan Turner Sharps would have died long ago, over and over again. But it doesn't work that way," she ended wistfully.

"Come away with me now. We'll go—"

"Hush, Dev. A man like Sharps, all that money and power, the people who work for him, people who are willing to do anything he says. He'd find us. He'd bring me back. And he'd hurt you. Or worse."

"He's not going to hurt you again. I promise you that."

"There are times when I wish it were over, that he would beat me past the point of caring, past the pain, end it once and for all."

"Don't talk that way. If anyone should die—Sharps deserves to die."

"There's nothing to be done. Nothing you can do."

"I don't accept that. There has to be some way, there has to be."

22

SHE appeared at the door of his room in Glenwood Springs late one night. She was trembling, pale, clearly distraught. He embraced her protectively and gave her some Scotch to drink and drew her to the edge of his bed, seating himself next to her.

"What's wrong?" he said when she calmed down.

"I shouldn't have come."

"Of course you should."

"You might not have been here."

"I am here."

"You might have been busy. With someone. Another woman."

He looked into her eyes. "There is no other woman."

"Oh, God, Dev. When I think such thoughts—I try

to put them out of my mind. I love you so much. I'd be so jealous, supremely jealous."

He waited for her to stop, for the flow of adrenaline to slow. In the half-light of the reading lamp, shoulders slumped, hands clasped prayerfully in her lap, she looked incredibly young and forlorn. Without hope. Somehow he intended to give her that hope.

"What is it?"

"He's coming."

No need to ask who. "When?" he said.

"Tomorrow."

"He called you."

"I don't even rate that much anymore. Suzanne Brody is here, arranging for a New Year's Eve party. Another of Duncan's business bashes. My house. My husband. Suzanne Brody's party. She informed me that he was on the way. I'm to meet his plane. More show, the dutiful, caring wife. The image suits Duncan's requirements."

"What are you going to do?"

"What can I do?" A flare of anger at the question. Holding him at fault for not instantly healing her wounds. For not repairing the broken dreams of a lifetime. "I do what I'm told."

The words were a slap in the face of his pride. Of his undeclared longings. Confronted by her problems, he could offer nothing but platitudes and empty phrases. He searched through the deeper regions of his brain for some square, muscled response that would solve this unsolvable situation. What other final proof of his love could he offer?

"This is our last night together," she said.

The finality of those words tore at him like Oriental

throwing stars. A massive spasm rocked him, and his desperation swelled. He felt as if he were choking, and he reached down into a personal reservoir to summon up all his remaining strength.

"There is no way I'll allow that to happen, to stop seeing you. I can't do it, I won't." He turned her face toward him, words stumbling over each other in a rush to get it all out before he lost courage. "Sharps, he's got to go. Out of our lives once and for all."

"He'll never let me divorce him. It's impossible. I know the way Duncan thinks."

"Then we'll have to find another way."

"There is no other way."

"There has to be. We can think about it, come up with something. Something. . . ."

They made love without passion. Without much feeling. By rote, neither of them aroused or caring, a horizontal dance without rhythm or reason. Ending in a relieved whimper. They lay back, not touching, each alone in that awful empty way people are often alone and lonely in bed.

And in that still interlude, all illusion was dispersed for Devlin. All lies crumpling, leaving him to choke on their dust. He understood with alarming clarity how much he loathed the life he'd been leading, how much he loathed the man he'd become. Somehow he would have to find a way to take charge of his future, to make himself over in a new image, to reshape the world in which he functioned. He was always on the edge of things, a marginal player, playing the angles in return for small profits, small rewards. He longed to live a robust existence to his own specifications. He longed to be his own man.

Sharps's wife. Geneva. Everything he had ever wanted in one woman. Her presence replenished the emptiness in him. Her beauty was a symbol of everything that was good and fine. She was his ticket into a world of luxury and ease, an end to worry, the beginning of a new life.

Sharps's wife. She came encumbered. With a husband who was a living danger to their happiness. Sharps had to go. His presence in the world could no longer be tolerated. His wealth and power made him a major and ongoing threat to them both.

Sharps had to go.

"Leave Sharps," he said harshly. "Flat out leave him. Divorce or no divorce. Walk out of that house and come to me. We'll go together. You can do it."

In a hushed but firm voice, she spoke, without denial, without equivocation. "I could, but why should I? All that Sharps has, all that money. I deserve it. As much as he does."

The money, Devlin thought. The Victorian house sitting so majestically on the side of the mountain looking down at Aspen. The apartment in New York. The summer place on Block Island. The Rolls, the Jag, the other expensive cars. The priceless paintings, the gun collection, all those *things.* He wanted all of them. And Sharps's businesses, his influence, his considerable piece of the action. His *power.*

And Sharps's wife.

"Leaving him," Devlin said in an insinuating drawl. "This is not a new idea. You've thought about it many times."

"Many times."

"But you never did it."

"I told you. He brought me back—"

"It's possible to get lost. To disappear. A new identity, a new life, one of billions in the world. You left a trail each time."

"I was never able to do it the right way. Not by myself. I wasn't strong enough."

"You're one of the strongest people I've ever known."

"I need help, the right person."

"The right man, you mean."

"Yes, a man."

"And I'm that man?"

"Yes."

He knew at once that his visit to her home uninvited—was it only three days ago?—had been no accident. She had very cleverly brought him to the point where his passion for her had wiped away all caution, had blinded him to reality, had made him helpless in his desire. She had manipulated him with ease, skillfully, taking him down a path so narrow and precipitous that he could no longer change his mind. There was no turning back. No more was it enough to take Sharps's wife. Not enough to steal her, to possess her, to make her his own. None of it was enough anymore.

Now Sharps had to die.

"If you don't want to help me, Dev, I'll understand. I'll be disappointed, but I'll understand. I want you to know that I love you, I always will, and never more than I do at this moment. Just tell me you don't love me, Dev. Not enough to help me, and I'll understand."

It was in the sound of her voice, the glitter of her

eye, the determined set of that luscious mouth. Sharps's death occupied her mind as it did his own. She profoundly desired it, passionately required that it happen; her husband's death. He had to be killed. Murdered. A murder that he, John Thomas Andrew Devlin, would have to commit.

He pressed his lips to hers. A harsh kiss without warmth or affection. Dry, cool skin smashed flat and hurting against the teeth beneath them. An ancient ritual sanctifying the bonds that held them together. Devlin knew he was doomed.

"About the money?" he said in a practical mode of thought, getting to the heart of the matter. The music had stopped; the dance was just about to begin.

"What about it?"

"How much is there?"

"Millions." A throwaway line, carelessly considered. A coin in the pocket of the very rich; oh, brother, can you spare a dime?

"Give me a number."

"I don't think Duncan could tell you the exact amount. All the property, all over the place. Luxury housing. Hotels. Skyscrapers. A castle in Scotland. Two more in Ireland. Another on a tiny island in a lake in Switzerland. Stocks. Bonds. Factories. All kinds of businesses. All kinds of investments. All kinds of money."

"And if he dies?"

The question was clear; she paddled around it, trying to muddy the waters. "The man is an ox. He'll outlive us all." She brought her eyes around to his, level and full of that deep chill. "I am my husband's heir. It comes to me. All of it. The money, everything."

"All?" he repeated in a whisper. All the money in the world. More than a man could count. Or care about counting. More than a man could spend. Or give away. An endless green-and-gold wall behind which to play, to love, to hide. Safe at last.

"Except for a few minor bequests," she added. "Certain charities. A distant cousin; his only family. Some key employees get token amounts. All the rest goes to me."

"You sound so sure."

"I refused to obey him one night. Refused to costume myself like some European courtesan for the visual pleasure of someone he was doing business with. When I told him I wouldn't play his sick, spiteful game anymore, he beat me. He went a little farther than he intended, hurt me pretty bad. Believe it or not, he tried to make up. Told me he was sorry. Told me that when he died his entire fortune would be mine. That's when he showed me the will. There it was, just as he'd said."

"He might have changed the will since then."

"You don't understand Duncan. He'd've told me if he had. Rubbed my face in it. Oh, no, the will stands."

It was as if all his solidity had evaporated, the weightiness lifted away. She was able to see into the depth of his soul, into the darkest caverns of his mind. "You mustn't think that way."

"Accidents happen."

"Not to Duncan."

"On the mountain. Skiing. A wrong turn and—"

"Duncan doesn't ski. He hates the snow. And all his hunting, only where the weather is warm. Africa. India. Never in the Rocky Mountains."

"Then why a house in Aspen?"

"An indulgence. Skiing, it's all I can do really well. The only thing I care about. Until I met you. Most of the time I'm here alone. But Aspen's a good place for Duncan to make new contacts. Rich people. Famous people. He likes them around. Makes him feel he belongs."

"As rich as he is, what's he after?"

"More. More money. He'll never accumulate enough. Greed and power. My husband is like a pubescent boy saying, 'Yah, yah, yah. Mine is bigger than yours.'"

Maybe that was it, Devlin suggested to himself, the difference between them. Maybe it was that simple; Sharps had a bigger dick, bigger balls, was more of a man. Too much of a man for Devlin to challenge.

She read the fine print of his doubts. "Oh, Dev, is that it? Duncan's too strong for you . . . for us."

Agree, he commanded himself. Admit to her and to himself that he was less a man than he wanted to be. Sever the bonds that tied him to a macho past. Cast himself on her mercy.

Would she continue to want him? Continue to love him? He dared not take the chance. He could not afford to lose her.

"I have a lot of thinking to do."

"Yes," she said, shifting away, putting some distance between them, her manner casual and indifferent. "Do what you must do, Dev. And so will I."

23

T H E mayor of Aspen was slender, recently turned forty, with a voice carefully cultivated and a salt-and-pepper beard to match. His hair was wavy, and he wore it pulled into a braid that fell down across his shoulders.

He lived in a new house that had been meticulously constructed to resemble an old house, painted a muted mustard color with a dark blue trim. The house was worth more than twenty times the amount it had cost to build, a financial fact that gave the mayor a lasting appreciation of his economic acumen. The mayor lived in the house with his significant other, a pair of neutered cats, and a grizzled English bulldog. From his bedroom window he had an unobstructed view of the Roaring Fork.

This mayor had a B.A. from the University of Chicago, an M.A. in French literature from Princeton, a Ph.D. in art history from Yale, and a law degree from the University of Virginia. During the winter season, he spent every morning on the mountain. He was an indifferent skier who wore a headband with a Navajo design he had knitted himself and aviator glasses, tinted amber against the glare.

By ten o'clock he was in his office, his body atingle with fitness, his brain alert, ready to take charge of his municipal duties. He was an earnest man, hard-working, and there were those who insisted that he was the best mayor Aspen had ever had. He denied, when asked, that he felt any need for more material wealth than he already possessed. He also denied he entertained any ambitions for higher political office.

"I'm happy where I am," he liked to say with an in-genuous bobbing of his hairy chin, and there were few who dared question his truthfulness.

The state chairman of the party, himself a career politician, and a student of human character and appe-tites, knew better. The mayor had a hard-on for the governor's chair.

So it was that he skipped the skiing on this particu-lar morning for breakfast with the state chairman at the mustard-and-blue house. They dined on breakfast burritos and eggs, scrambled with hot sausage, red chili, and a bland Mexican cheese. And plenty of strong coffee.

On his second mug of coffee, the state chairman said, "I'd like to get your opinion—political, not per-sonal."

The mayor swallowed. "Not a chance."

"You're sure?"

"I'm positive."

The state chairman could not remember when he had last been positive about anything. Not if it included human beings. Their behavior was a constant surprise, though never a shock, and he had learned to anticipate the unexpected, no matter the point spread.

"I'm not so sure."

"You know this town, Ralph. Almost as well as I do."

The state chairman brought out one of his large cigars. He bit off the tip, licked it lovingly, and fired it carefully. Clouds of blue smoke rose up around his immense head.

"I know you, Norman. You're an ambitious man—"

"I wouldn't go that far."

"—with a fix on the state Capitol. Well, I am here to tell you that I can virtually guarantee you the party's nomination next time around. Leo's about had it. Ready to call it quits, plop himself down on that farm of his. There are only a couple of lightweights standing in the wings, Norman. Nobody you have to worry about."

"Ah, Ralph, you know me. I'd go along, if I could."

"Then go along, Norman, and get along."

"I could say yes to you. I could promise that I'd railroad this thing through. What's the use? The opposition will be broad and deep. There's Planning and Zoning to begin with. And the environmentalists in the general assembly. There's all those citizens groups. Greenpeace. Green Party. Green this and green that. Every time a builder wants to break ground for some project, the picket signs come out and the petitions are dumped on my desk, signed and attested to. Let's not kid each other, Ralph. A gambling casino in Aspen is one very large crackpot idea."

"Duncan Turner Sharps is behind this idea."

"Sharps? I'm impressed, only he should know better. Somebody's got to tell him how things stand."

"Sharps is not the kind of man who takes rejection gracefully."

"Tough tittie, is all I can say."

"Unless . . ."

"Unless what?"

"Unless the respected mayor and all other disinterested parties were to approve the project, point out how beneficial it could be to the town, to the surrounding towns, to the entire area."

The mayor brought forth a small plastic bag half-filled with marijuana. He rolled a joint and offered it to the state chairman. He refused it.

"Too early in the day for me, Norman."

The mayor lit up and sucked hard. "First-rate shit," he said admiringly.

"What would your constituency say, the mayor in such a flagrantly illegal act?"

The mayor laughed. "My constituency consists of some of the biggest dopers in the Western Hemisphere. Actors, writers, ski bums and bunnies. Everyone of them would ask me who I deal with." Another toke. "You were about to tell me the ways in which a casino could help this town."

"Make a huge addition to the tax base. Provide lots of cash to spend on town projects. Highway maintenance. Snow clearance. Lengthen the airport runway one more time. Maybe even subsidize the cost of a lift ticket for the permanent citizenry."

"And make Sharps richer than he already is."

"Make a number of people richer. Would it offend you, Norman, having a numbered account in the Bahamas? I don't think so. A substantial amount of bucks deposited every month. Guarantee a comfortable old age, my friend. That, and your pension as a retired governor. Can't call that chopped liver, as they say back east, Mr. Mayor."

"You think it could be put through, a casino bill?"

"With me behind it, I believe so. With you giving things a shove here in Aspen, well, that won't hurt. All you got to do is give us a nod, Norman, and you're on your way to becoming a rich man."

The mayor thought about his significant other. She considered Aspen to be just one step short of Paradise. Not perfect, but close. A gambling casino, she would point out in that sensible, pedagogical style of hers, would attract tourists. Men in plaid Bermuda shorts during the summer and their women in shapeless cotton dresses. Buses carrying them in year round. Neon lights and slot machines. Plus the serious gamblers, the hard-eyed men who would do anything in order to win. And the representatives of organized crime, those burly men with pinky rings and pointed shoes. No amount of police vigilance would keep them away.

Taxes would go up in order to pay for the increased police force required. The enlarged fire department. The road maintenance crews, the sanitation department. Aspen would become a city, the sort of urban blight the mayor's significant other loathed. No, the mayor told himself, no way he could go along on this one. He told the state chairman so.

That drew a frown. "You'd make a good governor, Norman. A very handsome governor and a very rich one. Don't throw it all away for a principle you don't even believe in."

His mind made up, the mayor leaned back in his chair, utterly satisfied with himself and his righteous decision. He sucked on the remainder of his joint.

The state chairman arranged a benign expression on his broad face, concealing his true thoughts. This mayor was an arrogant young man who had just made a very serious mistake. Never shit where you eat; it was a rule the state chairman lived by. It was a lesson Norman had yet to learn. But he would learn, sooner or later, and in a most painful fashion.

Bad Times in Ute City

 S *ILVER* turned Aspen into a bustling, thriving community. Affluent and ambitious. Almost civilized. A Sunday school was organized. A glee club came into being. A literary society.

News of this picture-book town in the Rockies traveled swiftly. Word of new and rewarding opportunities spread across the continent, and newcomers began to arrive. Jerry-built miner's shacks were no longer sufficient for these people to live in. Real houses were in demand and were built. Victorian houses with wide porches to sit on in the summertime and steep roofs that encouraged the snow to slide off of its own weight. A telegraph line was brought across the mountains, and soon after that the first telephones began to appear.

The most recent immigrants demanded entertainment and culture, the sorts of activities that had filled their evenings in their hometowns. The result: an opera house was built. And the Row sprang up; elegant houses with elegant private pleasures for the gentleman at his leisure, the gentleman with an abundance of money in his poke. Elegant madames ruled over teams of young women who, for a price, offered affection and tenderness to those in need.

In 1889 the Hotel Jerome was opened for business. A charming place of style and comfort. And why not. Visitors showed up in Aspen to do business, to buy and sell, to share in the flow of profits coming up out of the mines. Ten million dollars' worth of silver was shipped each year.

Mammon prospered, and soon so did man's spiritual life. Ten churches came into being to do God's work among the eleven thousand citizens. Three schools were opened and three banks, a hospital, six newspapers, and a courthouse to deliver punishment to evildoers when justice was not within reach.

Four years later disaster arrived. Congress repealed the Sherman Act, which demonetized silver. Businesses shut down. Banks failed. Mines were sealed. Built on the seemingly eternal worth of silver, Aspen was shocked to discover that nobody wanted the shining metal anymore.

The town shrank. A dwarfed version of its former healthy self. Set down alongside the Roaring Fork in splendid isolation. Ignored and neglected, forgotten by the world beyond the mountains. Just as the twentieth century was born.

The new century brought about changes that would

result in a minor revival in Aspen. Skiers began to learn of the wondrous possibilities of Aspen Mountain, and they began to dribble into town. A ski run was cut to accommodate them and a boat tow was constructed, and before long trains began running people in from as far away as New York City. New shops opened and restaurants and rooms were let, and optimism ran high in the valley. Things were looking good.

Until the Japanese attacked Pearl Harbor, plunging America into war. Once again Aspen slid out of the public consciousness, hibernating in the war years that followed.

THE Gulfstream made a smooth landing. A welcoming party of three stood in the cold while the plane taxied from the end of the runway to where they waited. Geneva, in a ski parka and dark glasses, standing separately from the other two, in no mood to make small talk. Suzanne Brody, looking slim and elegant in her sable coat, a cashmere scarf wrapped around her head and face so that only her dark eyes showed. And Arlen "Red" Hamilton, slapping his hands against his chest in a vain effort to stay warm.

The plane came to a halt twenty yards away, and moments later Duncan Turner Sharps climbed down to the tarmac. Red Hamilton rushed forward to greet him.

"Duncan, how great to see you again."

Sharps shook the senator's hand and moved past him to where Geneva stood. He draped an arm across her shoulders and gave her his cheek for a kiss of greeting. He guided her toward a waiting limousine, speaking to Suzanne Brody.

"How's the party coming?"

"We're making good progress, Mr. Sharps. The caterer's in place. We're serving veal tidbits with a French—"

"The invitations all out?"

"Every one of them, Mr. Sharps."

"Acceptances. Certain people are vital to me."

"Jack Nicholson sent his regrets. He's in Bangkok making a movie, that's what his secretary said. Bette Midler has a concert scheduled. Otherwise—"

"You invited Marlon Ayres?"

"I called him myself, and had the invitation hand-delivered."

Sharps paused outside the limousine. "What about you?" he said to Geneva. "Those people I told you to get. How you doing?"

"It's taken care of, Duncan."

He inspected her face for some sign of deceit. "How many?"

"Five or six."

"Not enough." Sharps got into the limousine. He waited for the others to join him. "I want this to be an outstanding affair. Get more people," he ordered Geneva. Then he leaned back and closed his eyes. He had a great deal on his mind these days.

The Coyote, down Gallery Street, within sight of the Elk's Club Building, had the worn, permanent facade of an adobe hacienda. Inside, the floor was red brick worn smooth and the walls were faded stucco in need of painting. There were dark beams in the ceiling and plain wooden tables scattered about in front of the long wooden bar.

For the most part the patrons of the Coyote were somber, serious drinkers who chose to pursue their habit in the relative privacy of these shadowed, pacific confines. There were four booths against the western wall in the rear room. It was in one of those boothes that Devlin was being interrogated.

"Piss off," was Hank Ricketts's reaction.

"Piss off," Sam Daly echoed.

Peggy Pearce sat silent, violet eyes lidded and wary. The chemistry wasn't there. That secret ingredient that would have made them into a close-knit group. A team. With a single goal. Working like a finely tuned machine. Perhaps it would be better if they ended the relationship, each one going his or her separate way. That could be more troublesome over the long haul; no telling which of them might begin running off at the mouth. Telling too much to the wrong person. Making them all vulnerable to arrest. They had to stay together, bonded at least by common fears. Besides, she wasn't ready to give up.

"You might have mentioned it, Dev," she said in disappointment.

Devlin felt no anger. Only resentment. His personal space violated by these people whom he perceived as strangers. "How'd you find out?" he said again.

"Followed you," Ricketts answered.

"Whataya think," Sam Daly said. "A town this size, you ain't gonna get away with anything. Never spotted me, did you? Shows how dumb you are. That's one of my specialties, following people."

"Geneva Sharps," Peggy Pearce said. "Her husband's a very rich man."

"A really hot pistol," Ricketts added.

"You spent two days with her," Peggy said. "Two days in her house."

Devlin was struck by the incongruity of the situation. These three tracking him, marking his whereabouts, his activities; claiming some right to his personal life. "What in hell is wrong with you? How dare you follow me! You want to know something about me, just ask."

"That Mrs. Sharps," Daly said. "What a dandy. Great in the sack, I bet."

"It happened by accident," Peggy Pearce said, trying to put a pleasant face on the matter. "Sam just happened to spot you driving around one night."

"Figured I'd see what you was up to."

"My private life is my private business. You had no right."

"Is she?" Ricketts said with a wide, malicious grin. "Great in the sack, I mean?"

"Sure she is," Peggy said in an almost offhanded sort of way. "Good enough to fix a broken cock. Isn't that so, Dev?"

Ricketts was puzzled, curious, and said so. "What's that supposed to mean?"

"I hear Sharps is worth half the dough in the world," Daly said. "A dame like that, she can set you up for life."

"Lucky Dev," Ricketts said.

Peggy Pearce persisted. "The old tool back in working order, is it, Dev?"

Devlin kept himself from confronting her. "Her husband, he's the one with the money, like you said, Sam."

Daly grinned in reply. "I'd be happy with half the leavings of that pair."

"Not our Dev," Peggy said. "Leavings aren't enough for our Dev. The way I see it, Dev's after the whole ball of wax."

"That it?" Daly enthused. "You got her to where she'll dump her husband for you, Dev? You gonna marry the dame? Christ Almighty, you'll be rich."

"She's just a friend." The words were hollow to his ears, without meaning. Whatever it was between them, Geneva and he were certainly not friends. Not by any definition he could conjure up. Where was she at this minute? What was she doing? What was Sharps doing to her? His penis grew heavy. Crotch to crotch, maybe that's all it was, scratching the old itch until the day it went away. "Her husband's away a lot and she gets lonely."

"Sly Dev," Ricketts drawled.

The waitress arrived with another round. Dev waited until she went away before speaking again. "Is that why you asked me here, to talk about Geneva Sharps?"

"Geneva," Daly said. "Nice name."

"As for me," Ricketts said, "I like the way you do things, Dev. Bang the mark and case the house at the same time. Very smooth. You must know it inside out by now."

"Forget it," Devlin snapped. "It's not like that."

"How else could it be?" Daly said cheerfully.

"About the house," Ricketts said. "Alarm system? Safe? Big as it is, must be loaded with goodies just waiting to be snatched up."

"Biggest strike yet," Daly said.

"Forget it," Devlin answered.

"The way to go," Ricketts said, "is you get the Sharps dame out, over to your room, Dev. Screw the ass off of her for an hour or two. That way we'll have plenty of time to clean the place out."

Tension lined Devlin's throat. He swallowed some more beer, buying time to clear his mind. His eyes raked the trio and saw nothing there he could appreciate.

"I don't think so," Peggy said. "Dev's got something else on his mind."

"Yeah, what?" Daly said.

"Something better?" Ricketts suggested, shifting forward so as not to miss anything.

"Sure," Peggy said. "Better. Our Dev, he's smart."

Devlin lit a cigarette, puffed briefly, and snubbed it out. He swore to quit again, at least to cut down. "Okay, I'm going to tell you the truth. . . ."

"Won't that be nice," Peggy said with contrived sweetness. "The truth."

Devlin went on. "Geneva, it's serious with us. Very serious."

"Meaning what?" Ricketts said, not liking what he'd heard.

"Meaning," Peggy said, "that Dev intends to cut us out."

"The hell you say," Ricketts said. "You stumbled

into the honey pot, you came up with a prizewinner, found yourself a piece of rich, married cooz. Okay, Dev, good for you. Chalk one up for our side. Only it's got plenty to do with the rest of us, man. We are together, remember?"

"A team," Daly put in.

"That's right, a team. We do jobs together, and this looks like one of the best. Serious with the dame cuts no ice with the rest of us."

"We are going to hit the Sharps house," Peggy said, leaving no room for argument.

Devlin's mind raced. "Her husband's back in Aspen. Arrived today. They're planning a big party, people coming and going in that house night and day. It's impossible."

"Nothing's impossible," Ricketts said.

"Nothing," Daly said for emphasis.

"We can wait," Peggy said. "Meanwhile, Dev, you keep an eye on things for us. Draw up a floor plan of the house, leave out nothing. Where they keep things. You know the drill. Make it that much easier when we do go in."

"No," Devlin said.

"Yes," Peggy said firmly.

"Tell you what," Ricketts said expansively. "You want out, okay. Peggy, Sam, and me, we'll handle the job itself. Hey, if it bothers you so much, don't take your cut. Nobody's gonna force unwanted money on you. But with you or without you, the job gets done."

"I said no." Devlin clenched his fist at the edge of the table. "No."

Daly grinned tauntingly across the table at him. "Go

on, Dev, take a shot at somebody. Give me any excuse
to turn your face to mush."

"Ease off," Peggy said, and to Devlin, "The job gets
done, with you or without you."

"Which is it?" Ricketts said. "In or out, Dev?"

Devlin answered without thinking. "Out."

"Out it is," Ricketts said. "After you deliver the information we need on the house."

"One more thing, Dev," Peggy Pearce said with no
change of expression. "I'd like to hear a little more
about this party. . . ."

Darkness masked off the high peaks of the Rockies.
A few snowflakes had begun to fall, and the streets
of Aspen took on the festive, animated look of a holiday greeting card. Christmas lights twinkled on trees
in shop windows, and shoppers were laden down with
packages.

Inside the Silver House, a handful of drinkers were
lined up at the bar, locals without interest in the
nightlife that captured most visitors to the ski resort.
Middle-aged men in thick corduroy trousers tucked
into insulated boots and heavy Buffalo plaid shirts.

At a round table toward the rear, Marlon Ayres attacked a thick western beefsteak, nearly burned to a
crisp, with a ferocity that belied his normally mild manner. Across from him, Duncan Turner Sharps picked
at a filet barely cooked through. He was used to dining
much later in the evening; but Ayres was an early
eater and had suggested meeting at this hour. Ayres
drank Coors out of a can; Sharps sipped a red wine
from a California vineyard that left an offensive after-
taste on his tongue.

"Don't get out much anymore," Ayres said. "Town's changed too much. People say change is the way of the world, and I reckon they're right. Which don't mean I got to like it, which I don't. Or approve of it, which I don't." He raised his eyes to Sharps and spoke around a mouthful of beef. "You're not all that much younger than me, Mr. Sharps."

"Please. Call me Duncan."

"Which don't mean we've lived the same kind of a life. Fact is, I've always worked with my hands. Lumberjack. Trucker. Farmer. Rancher. I ain't sayin' that's the only way to go, but it does let you know what you can do and what you can't do. You a family man, Mr. Sharps?"

"I'm married."

"Children?"

"No children."

"Kids give a man perspective. Cleaning off a baby's butt keeps you humble. Dealing with a kid day to day puts a man in touch with a growing life. Losing a child—I lost two sons, Mr. Sharps; one in Vietnam and another to illness—that is a load of grief, more'n anyone should have to bear. All I've got left now is my oldest daughter and her children. Two little ones. Thing about grandchildren is you can spoil 'em rotten and blame your own child for not raising 'em right." He cackled at his own joke. "They live in San Antonio, which is where I aim to settle once I clear all my business hereabouts. It's as good a place as any, considering the amount of time I've got left."

"You've got all the time in the world."

Ayres wasn't buying. "I'm seventy-five years old, and that puts me on the downside of the hill. Every morning I open up my eyes and thank the good Lord for giving me another day. You might start doing likewise, Mr. Sharps. A bit of prayer ain't gonna hurt your standin' with the man upstairs." Another cackle, briefer this time.

"I'll keep that in mind."

"You do that, Mr. Sharps. Rumor is that you mean to put a hotel onto my property, if I sell out to you, that is."

"That's the truth of it, Mr. Ayres. Which is why I asked you to have dinner with me, so we could kick it around."

"One of them high risers, I suppose."

"No sir, nothing like it. I have a great and abiding feeling for Aspen, its history, the way it looks. What I have in mind is something that fits right in. Two hundred rooms, I'd say. No more than three hundred. Maybe less, depending on the design. Low rise, three stories maximum. In keeping with the local architecture. Sculpture gardens and a glass-enclosed swimming pool. All the amenities. All the luxuries."

"A rich man's hotel."

Sharps hesitated. Ayres was a character, unlike most of the people he dealt with. Tread lightly, he told himself. Give him no cause to take offense. "None of us is in business to lose money, Mr. Ayres. It's the American way."

Ayres chewed and swallowed, spoke in regular, thoughtful phrases. "Makin' money's never been a sin, leastways I ain't never thought it was. It's greed that gets a man off the track, gets him all twisted around so's he don't know where he's bound for or what he's after. I don't begrudge nobody an honest profit."

"Which brings us back to your land."

"Put a television set in every one of them rooms, I'll bet."

"People are taken with modern technology."

"Never watched much of it. Never cared much for what I did see. Bad news, bad jokes, lots of smut. Haven't owned a set of my own in ten years and haven't missed a thing, I reckon."

Sharps chose not to pursue the subject. "Tell you what, Mr. Ayres. I am prepared to close our deal right here, right now."

"Didn't know we had a deal, Mr. Sharps. Not yet, anyway."

Sharps caused himself to laugh, a self-deprecating laugh that said the joke was on him. "I've been known to rush things a little, Mr. Ayres. All right, let's talk business. Yes, I won't try to hide it, I'm anxious to get on with it, finish our negotiations and close the deal. To help facilitate matters, I'm willing to increase payment by one-quarter of a million dollars above your asking price. How does that strike you?"

Ayres nodded sagely. "Never was a question of how much. I tell that to you just as I told it to those other fellas."

A cold knot formed up in Sharps's gut. He managed to keep his temper from breaking out. "What other fellows are you talking about, Mr. Ayres?"

"Oh, there's some Japanese folks showing a lot of interest. Also a couple of people from Mexico City made some inquiries. One or two others. A lot of different folks admire my holdings, Mr. Sharps."

All the possibilities flashed through Sharps's mind. He weighed, assessed, accepted, and rejected, sorting out the winners from the losers; the Japanese, always the Japanese these last few years.

"I'm an American, Mr. Ayres, just like you. Born and bred. My folks go back a couple of hundred years. I'd hate to see some foreigners come along and snatch up another chunk of the good old U.S. of A. Tell you what I'm going to do, match any offer you've had and put it up by another million. That's as good as you're going to get."

Ayres put his knife and fork aside, wiped vigorously at his mouth with his napkin. He filled his mouth with Coors, rinsed, and swallowed. "Like I said, money's not at the heart of it. I just want to do what's right."

Sharps's convictions shrank in the face of this stubborn old man. How to reach him? How to convince him? He intended to find a way. He always did.

25

*I*RINA'S shop was on Mill Street, not far from the Wheeler Opera House. Irina was a Hungarian, complete with accent and an inexhaustible amount of energy. She owned an equally inexhaustible collection of tales of royal and not-so-regal paramours, of husbands rich and poor, of adventures on four or five continents. She knew a great deal about art, about music and theater, about the lives and loves of the rich and famous. All of which she was prepared to discuss fluently in any of the seven languages she spoke.

There was no sign above her shop. No name on the door to attract the attention of the unwary passersby. Nothing except the show that Irina herself put on behind the great front plate-glass window. Irina stepped and skipped, she danced and scuttled, she gestured and fluttered and waved, all the while praising or rejecting or gossiping about her friends and lovers, past and present, customers and long-deceased cousins.

There was in Irina's a constantly revolving inventory of expensive European fashions. One-of-a-kind items brought from the best of the designers in Paris and Rome, occasionally Madrid. No store in Aspen could match Irina's, not in style, not in price. Certainly not in the dynamic presentations of the proprietor.

Irina bustled. A diminutive woman of indeterminate age, she circled her friends—as she was fond of calling her customers—like a wary fox. The bustle was verbal as well as physical, an extension of her inner self, always in tune, always in harmony, always consistent. Irina pinned and tucked, she folded and snipped; she issued commands. Complaints. Compliments. It was a nonstop performance, rooted in all the days of her life. Now she scurried counterclockwise around Geneva, fitting a new dress on Madame Sharps and trying her damnedest to extract an invitation to the Sharpses' New Year's Eve party, news of which had spread around town like an infectious disease.

"Only the best people," Irina chattered. "The very best." Images of social lions and movie stars, of eastern aristocracy and midwestern millionaires, floated around inside her head. Irina loved fancy parties.

She adjusted the gown Geneva was modeling, a silver sheath that glittered in the soft lighting. "Perfect for you, my darling. Perfect for Aspen. Silver, you know."

She tugged at the bodice. "A little lower would be ideal. A little looser, my dear. Show what you've got, I always say, as long as it's in good taste. You have superb breasts, dear child, display them with pride and a reasonable amount of provocation. Be the woman you were made to be. Ah, and here, across the *fanneee.*" It sounded foreign, the way she said it. Exotic. French, most likely. With a Hungarian accent, of course. Irina spoke all languages with a Hungarian accent.

"Marie." She summoned her seamstress, who came complete with tape, scissors, and a supply of straight pins between her lips. "Tighter here, Marie. More shape here. Perfection, perfection. Even beyond perfection. Buttocks round and defiant at all times. The cleft distinct, but full of shadows, a challenge, a mystery. A promise of what remains unseen. You will have many celebrities, yes?"

Geneva recited the names of the movie stars who would be at the party. The industrialists. The entrepreneurs. The political giants. The press lords.

"Ah. Ah. Truly a gala. Most affairs are so dull, so lifeless and without zest."

Geneva offered a discreet smile. "Then you must come, Irina. Duncan would never forgive me if I didn't invite you. You will come, won't you?"

"How can I refuse?"

Neither of them noticed the door of the shop open to admit a tall man who moved on stiff knees, no expression on his seamed face.

"Monsieur?" said Marie, the seamstress. "May I be of some service?"

"Hello, Mrs. Sharps," Devlin said.

She jerked around as if yanked by an invisible strand, alarmed by the sound of his voice. She struggled to regain her composure. "Oh, Devlin. How nice to see you."

"Spotted you from outside and thought I'd say hello."

Irina studied the tall man with a controlled curiosity. Interesting, she told herself. Unlike all those empty blond men one saw around Aspen. This one had a center, a core of passion, of concealed ideas and drives. What, she wondered, was the relationship between these two?

Geneva, her confidence returning, made the introductions.

Irina committed the name to memory—Devlin—and withdrew, taking the seamstress with her.

"I missed you," Devlin said when they were alone.

"Dev, this is insane. What if someone should see us? . . ."

He indicated the departed Irina. "Somebody already has."

"Other people, people here for the party."

"Not seeing you makes me slightly crazy."

"Me too," she whispered. "I tried phoning. You're never home. You haven't been at the ASA."

"I wanted to talk to you, too. To be alone with you."

"Hush. It's about the party; would you like to come?"

"I don't get it. You're afraid someone'll see us together here, and next you invite me to your house, to your party. Your husband . . ."

"There's safety in a crowd. We can talk then."

"Isn't that pushing it?"

"Duncan told me to invite lots of young people.

Handsome people. You are certainly a handsome man."

"Thank you, ma'am."

"I mean it. You will come?"

"I don't know."

"Lots of food. Drink. Come any time after nine. Make it later. Closer to eleven. That way, in that mob scene, no one will pay much attention. I'll expect you, yes?"

His level of uneasiness climbed steeply. "I'll have to think about it."

"Promise me. Or do you have something better to do? A date with some beautiful young girl?"

"Right. Miss World of 1990."

"I'm serious."

"Then I'll be serious. No date. No other party. Nothing better to do."

"Then you will come, good."

He asked himself: Were they functioning on the same wavelength? Full of caution one moment, fearless and willing to take great risks the next. She was not, he decided, to be considered excessively reliable.

"Okay, I'll be there. But when twelve o'clock rolls around, there'll be none of that kissing between us."

"Depend on it." There was no lightness in her reply. "One more thing. You may bring a date. A female escort. To provide an aura of respectability to it all. But no hanky-panky, Dev. It's all just for show."

"I'll keep it in mind."

He was almost out the door when she said his name, bringing him around. "I love you," she mouthed silently, and blew him a kiss.

He nodded once before he left.

*   *   *

On the last day of that year, Devlin finished his shift at ASA. He showered and dressed in the small locker room provided for employees. Some of the trainers were already welcoming the new year at a private party in the main exercise room; Devlin decided not to attend. He tried not to think about the night that lay ahead. New Year's Eve courtesy of Duncan Turner Sharps. Farewell to the old year; he trembled at what the new year would bring.

He feared Sharps. Feared meeting the man, talking to him, perhaps even getting to like him. A man of his accomplishment and stature would likely possess great personal force and charm. Was he man enough to confront Sharps? Conceal his loathing from the man, conceal his feelings for Geneva? Conceal his wish to see Sharps dead?

He decided it would be madness to put in an appearance at Sharps's house. Even in that crowd he would be noticed, his identity established, his closeness to Geneva remarked upon. Geneva would be annoyed with him, even angry, but better that than to risk disaster. No party for him that night. But a strong drink was in order.

The Cat's Meow vibrated with celebrants. Drinkers crowded up against the bar, and all the booths were full. Decorations were strung from the old carved-tin ceiling, and twinkling lights, green and red, cast odd, unsteady shadows.

He spotted Peggy Pearce at the bar, focal point of a group of young men. Devlin turned to leave when she spied him and called his name. No escape was possible. He swung back, watched her come toward him.

"Trying to avoid me, Dev?"

"So crowded here. Figured I'd find a quieter place."

"Where you go, I go." She watched him over the rim of her glass. She was not a woman who lost sight of her goals.

"Sure. Well. Might as well hang in here, then. I thought I'd have a hamburger and a beer and head on home for a quiet evening. Alone."

"Poor baby," she cooed. "Such a waste. Or is it going to waste? Why do I suspect you have no trouble getting it up for the beautiful Mrs. Sharps?"

"For Christ's sake, keep your voice down."

She laughed. "Mustn't fret, Dev. A little rejection keeps a woman like me in line. Teaches humility. A reminder of one's lack of perfection. About the Sharps house . . ."

"Not here."

"I got the job cleaning up. Both prior to the party and afterward. So you needn't worry too much. I've come up with a detailed plan of the place. Still, I wouldn't mind going over it with you, profiting from your keen powers of observation." She batted her lashes at him. "Place is spotless, Dev, bet you can't find a speck of dust."

"I'm not going."

" 'Course you are. I insist you go. A pretty boy like you, you'll be the hit of the ball. And Geneva wants you there, I'm sure of that. To dangle you in front of her husband. If the lady had balls, they'd be made of pure brass and polished to a high gloss. You aren't going to disappoint Geneva, are you, Dev?"

"Forget it, Peggy."

"I can't do that, Dev. A party like this, it might be

the chance of my life. To make some super contacts. Meet some really first-class people for a change. A rich man. An important man. I intend to go, Dev, and you are going to see that I get there."

"And if I don't?"

"Not smart, Dev. Not safe. You don't want me for an enemy. You don't want us for enemies, Ricketts and Daly. Daly's crazy, you know. Homicidal, in my opinion. Keep your distance from that one, Dev."

"You're threatening me, Peggy."

"All I'm doing is trying to get to that party. With you. Afterward you're on your own. I promise you. All debts will be marked paid in full."

Devlin knew better than to argue. Truth was, there was nothing that could keep him from going to the party. Nothing that would keep him out of the Sharps house tonight. And some perverse aspect of his character relished the notion of taking Peggy Pearce along. What was it Geneva had said? "It's all for show." Well, all right. He'd give her a show, a good one.

"Okay, you've got a date. You look your best, your sexiest. Knock their eyes out."

Her lips spread in a guarded grin. "You've got it, Dev. I'll put a real shine on it."

26

T H E party.

In full raucous sight and sound by the time they arrived. A few minutes before eleven, a rock band pounding out an incessant beat over a powerful system of professional amplifiers, rented in Denver and flown in for the occasion. People shouted in order to be heard. Clinking ice cubes added a more delicate subtheme, along with the isolated peal of a woman's laughter.

The noise greeted them like a great, enveloping wall. Painful to ear and psyche alike. A servant took their coats, and Devlin led the way toward a bar at the near end of the long sitting room. The distinctively sweet stench of marijuana floated on the still air. A silver bowl with ornate carved handles containing co-

caine sat on a long trestle table, a few dozen matching
silver spoons alongside in marching order. The coke
surprised Devlin; it hardly seemed consistent with
Sharps's style.

Peggy Pearce, exquisitely turned out in a loose-
fitting satin blouse and a short, tight skirt, could not
keep her feet still, bouncing in time to the music.

"What a blast," she cried happily. "I'm so glad you
brought me."

"Ecstatic," he answered.

"Nasty, nasty." She looked up into his face. "Oh,
I don't care. This is my kind of a night. Dev, as good-
looking as you are, you could be a movie star. A little
offbeat, maybe. A character actor. How I'd love that,
to be a movie star. What a gas. TV, movies, whatever.
I'll bet there's a producer or two in this crowd. What
do you think?"

"Start looking, you'll find one."

She leaned his way. "Check it out, Dev. I still
haven't spotted an alarm system. If you see any signs,
let me know. This is a mark just waiting to be had."

"For Christ's sake, Peggy, not now."

"Right, right. See you later, lover, I'm going to min-
gle. Maybe connect with my movie producer. Have
fun. Remember, we're supposed to be a couple, and
I expect you to see me home. Unless I can do better,
of course." She faded into the crowd, a welcoming
turn to her lips, the violet eyes gleaming with anticipation. Desperate to get on with her life.

"Radishes are the thing."

So said the woman from Beverly Hills. Stick thin
and hollow-cheeked, she might have been a victim of

third world famine, in immediate need of International Relief. A worthy object for a Care package.

She was in fact the wealthy wife of a wealthy corporate lawyer. Chic in an Armani dress. Bejeweled. Every hair tenderly treated and coiffed in a succession of electric curls. Her eyes bulged, her nostrils flared, her chest was a depressed area, and her backside was flat.

"Vegetables," she went on. "Salads. You can't go wrong with vegetables and salads."

"Oh, I couldn't agree more," her companion murmured. She was one of the slender young, not quite as emaciated as the lawyer's wife, but with plenty of time to catch up. She was fragile of bone and narrow of waist and shoulder, and proud of it. "Chef Victor comes to our apartment four afternoons a week." She lived on Park Avenue, and her husband labored on Wall Street in behalf of her father's brokerage firm. "Chef Victor prepares an entire range of suitable foods. Grains, veggies. Steamed, of course. All Cook has to do is pop them in the microwave when Charles is ready to dine."

"Health is so much fun."

"Have I told you about Helmut? He's from Bavaria. Very disciplined, very thorough. My personal trainer. He attends me three times a week. He has the strongest hands. Ingest untainted foods only and fully utilize your body."

"The key to longevity."

"And the good life."

"Exactly."

"You do use tofu, don't you?"

"Tofu. Let me tell you about tofu . . ."

*   *   *

Sharps worked the party. Easing his way from room to room, dapper in a finely cut scarlet mess jacket complete with brass buttons. His eyes glittered, his smooth head gleamed, his mustache had been skillfully trimmed. He showed his neat white teeth in what a casual acquaintance might have mistaken for a smile. He was all business. Introducing himself to people he didn't know. Greeting those he had met before. Allotting his time prudently, according to who might be helpful in the near future.

He came across Arlen Hamilton slumped in a chair in one corner of the entertainment room, looking glum and neglected. "Got a problem, Red?"

"You promised me goodies, Duncan. Super goodies, you said. All I've seen is older people."

"You've got to know where to look. Try the third floor, door at the end of the corridor."

Hamilton came to his feet, life pumped back into his fleshy face. "A prince among men, Duncan. That's what you are, a veritable prince." He leaned and spoke in a subdued, cautious voice. "No tricks this time, Duncan?"

"No tricks."

"No more cameras."

"Enjoy yourself, Red. Maybe we'll talk later on."

"Anything you say, Duncan, anytime."

Sharps barely heard the final words, his mind put to better stuff.

A pink-faced dealer of junk bonds picked his way through the heaving, swelling collection of people into the pool room. The soft green light made him feel that he had arrived in an alien world. Green, he decided at once, was his favorite color. He finished his drink and helped himself to another off the tray of a passing waiter.

"What a brawl," he said to no one in particular. Everywhere he looked he saw handsome men and beautiful women. Not six feet away, at the edge of the lap pool, a young woman with curly hair and round eyes. She was the most beautiful creature he'd ever seen; a closer inspection was in order. He came up behind her and inhaled the sweet, perfumed scent she gave off. The cavities of his skull grew inflamed, and his heartbeat increased. He had an irresistible urge to impress upon her his good qualities; the high level of his success, the full extent of his wealth, his great wit. He tossed off the rest of his drink and dropped the glass into the lap pool. He placed a hand on each of the curly-headed woman's buttocks. He squeezed, he pushed, he sent her flying into the pool.

"Happy New Year!"

Someone clubbed the junk bond dealer between the shoulders with a heavy forearm, sending him after the woman. It must have seemed like a swell idea to a lot of people, who went diving in after them, splashing about happily.

Inspired by this wonderful game, the unhappy and pleasantly drunken wife of a congressman whose district included Aspen shed all her clothes and deposited herself into the bubbling hot tub. Before long she was joined by a number of other naked people pressing against her, hands groping without hesitancy. How long, she wondered cheerfully, had this been going on?

*　　*　　*

The plump man in a meticulously tailored tuxedo was surrounded by young women. Curious, Peggy Pearce pressed closer.

"A producer," one of the women said.

Peggy worked her way even closer until she stood directly in front of the plump little man. The tip of her moist red tongue appeared at one corner of her mouth.

"Scout's honor," the plump man said. He noticed Peggy. He watched the play of the tip of her tongue. He inspected her strong legs, the enticing roundness of her hips, the fall of the satin blouse across her breasts. He smiled.

"Movies?" someone said.

"Music," the plump man said, still staring at Peggy. "Records, tapes, music videos. The works." His glance rose to Peggy's face. The smile broadened. "I don't suppose any of you pretty ladies sing?"

"You're not going to believe this," Peggy murmured.

"Oh, yes, I will. Whatever you tell me, I'm going to believe you."

Suzanne Brody encountered Geneva in the kitchen. In a sparkling silver sheath that enhanced every perfect line and curve of Geneva's body. She looked like she was part of and belonged in the shining stainless-steel room.

Waiters and waitresses carried trays filled with food back to the party and returned for more. Another crew of workers continued to prepare food. Satisfied that everything was proceeding according to plan and schedule, Brody spoke to Geneva.

"No reason for you to be in here, Mrs. Sharps. I've

taken care of everything, and the caterer and his staff will do all the rest."

Geneva stared at the other woman. Angular and dramatic in a short black dress trimmed at the waist and throat with a strip of white lace. There was a coltish quality to Suzanne Brody, and it registered with Geneva, a hint of awkwardness that promised even greater things to come. She was, Geneva acknowledged to herself, a remarkably handsome creature.

"I do live here," Geneva said, but with none of the acerbity she usually displayed toward Brody.

"Just trying to make things easier for you."

"Of course."

"It's your house, it's your party. Why not enjoy yourself? That's what I intend to do."

Why not? A moment later Geneva left the kitchen, determined to have a good time.

Devlin planted himself against the wall and took it all in. There was a sharply defined flow to the party, the participants entering into the scheme of things as if rehearsed, moving this way or that way in distinctly ordered streams of traffic. The women were an impressive group, beautiful for the most part and exquisitely gowned and coiffed, bright-eyed and responsive. Yet it was the men who dominated. The house had the satisfied, almost smug, air of a men's club, the women present on sufferance, sparkling adornments and adjuncts to their lords and masters, brought along to excite and arouse the latent liveliness of the occasion. He was trying to locate Geneva when the bald man materialized out of the human press.

"I noticed you," he began, smoothing his full mustache over the corners of his mouth. His voice was strong and rough, and though his smile was ingratiating, there was a hard veneer that warned this was no one to trifle with.

Sharps, Devlin knew intuitively. It had to be Sharps.

Sharps offered his hand; it was firm and strong, the handshake brief, as if the older man were offended at the touch of someone else's flesh. He introduced himself. "I'm Duncan Turner Sharps."

Devlin was not to be outdone. "I'm John Thomas Andrew Devlin."

Sharps laughed out loud at that. "You've gone me one better, four names to three. What a burden to carry when you're very young."

Devlin refused to play that game. "People call me Devlin."

"Has a good, solid ring to it. I suppose Mrs. Sharps invited you?"

"Yes." Devlin spoke quickly, determined to establish the legitimacy of his presence.

"That was her assignment, to dress the place up with bright and good-looking young people. Well, enjoy yourself, Devlin. Your glass is empty, get another. Some food. Perhaps even a woman. I take it you're interested in women." He left, chuckling, seemingly pleased with himself.

Jerry Cross, the movie star, was surrounded by his fans. He signed autographs and answered questions. Part of the burden a man in his position carried. Clinging to his arm, a pretty young blonde, fearful and wishing she were someplace else.

"Soon," he whispered in her ear. "We'll split soon.

I had to make an appearance. One of Sharps's companies owns a substantial piece of my last picture, and—"

"Tell the truth, Jerry," one of his fans persisted. "What's Barbara Streisand really like?"

Cross gestured to the other side of the long sitting room. "See for yourself. There she is."

The fans darted away.

"Let me find Sharps," Cross said to his blond companion. "And then we're out of here. You've got my word on it."

Devlin worked his way around the main floor of the house. A medium-size room, which looked out on the front porch and might once have been a reception chamber, contained only a billiard table. To his surprise and consternation, Hank Ricketts and Sam Daly were playing.

An inarticulate cry of rage filled his throat as he propelled himself toward the two men. Neither of them showed any alarm. Until Devlin grabbed Ricketts by the shirtfront.

"Cool it, Dev," Daly said, brandishing his cue.

"Let go of the shirt," Ricketts said.

"You damn fools. What are you doing here?"

Ricketts smoothed his shirt back into place. "It's a party, is all. Having some fun, is all. Same as anybody else. Same as you, Dev. We aren't doing any harm."

Daly said, "You seen the trophy room, Dev? Animal heads. Skulls. Stuffed specimens. I tell you, this guy Sharps is a regular killing machine. And guns. He's got a million of 'em, every kind. Rifles, shotguns, pistols.

Even a couple of automatic combat rifles. Some antique stuff, too. Worth a fortune, believe me."

Ricketts grinned. "Look around, man. Lots of first-class quiff on the premises, in case you haven't noticed. Everybody ought to be plowed tonight."

"I want you guys to get out of here. Now."

"Forget it, Dev. Party's just getting good." Daly rolled his eyes. "These folks sure do live high off the hog. Ten minutes in and out and a team like us could come up with a real score."

"Shut up, Sam."

"I mean it. Take a look on the second floor. One whole closet with nothing but fur coats in it. Sable, mink, leopard, even a Siberian white tiger."

Daly chimed in. "The man in Denver has an abiding interest in good fur coats, he told me so."

"Forget it."

"I don't think so," Ricketts said. "Me and Sam, no way we can pass up a deal like this one. Never forgive ourselves if we did. We are going to hit this place, Dev, and soon. Soonest we can."

"Hank, I'm going to kill you."

Ricketts laughed. "Not you, Dev. Killing's not your style. Not in your system. Take Sam here, he has no such scruples."

"Not a single scruple," Daly said.

"So don't jerk us around, Dev. Makes both of us mad."

Devlin, inarticulate with rage and frustration, spun away, trying to figure out what went wrong. When had he lost control of his own life?

*   *   *

Geneva saw Devlin heading for the bar and started in his direction when Sharps loomed up in front of her.

"Enjoying yourself, my dear?"

"You know how I feel about big parties."

"Make the best of it, as you always do. There are some people I'd like you to pay attention to. Let them bask in your beauty—"

"Please, Duncan."

"—and be overcome by your personality. By the way, I was talking to one of your young friends. . . ." He indicated Devlin with his strong chin. "There's something about him. . . ."

Geneva answered without thinking. "No friend of mine. I don't know him."

Sharps revealed those sharp white teeth. "My mistake. They all look alike to me, these skiing types of yours. Clones out of the same genetic laboratory."

"Not mine," she almost cried out. But Sharps had gone, smiling, greeting, even laughing as he went.

Suzanne Brody surveyed Peggy Pearce from a distance before approaching her. She touched the younger woman lightly on the shoulder, bringing her around.

"Miss Brody!" A burst of sound, little more than a nervous exhalation; and then Peggy regained her composure. She had expected Brody to be here, anticipated meeting her; still, it was a shock, as if she, Peggy, were committing some awful social blunder. "How nice to see you again."

"Mrs. Sharps must have invited you. You two know each other?"

Peggy put on her widest, most guileless smile. Her

violet eyes were round and mischievous. "A friend brought me. His name is Devlin, perhaps you know him."

Nothing showed on Brody's handsome, angular face. Peggy found her a little unsettling, that chilling confidence, always in control. And in this alien environment, it was Peggy who was out of place.

"You were talking to Mo Hammaker," Brody said. "The little fat man."

"Oh, yes. The music producer."

"Yes. Hammaker Music, Incorporated. Mr. Sharps owns the company."

"I thought—"

"Hammaker runs it, of course. Mr. Sharps never interferes with any of his holdings, unless the man in charge is incompetent. Or goes for two straight years without showing a profit. I'll say this for Hammaker, he's good at his job. Is that what you're after, a career in music?"

Peggy pulled at her fingers. With Ricketts and Daly and Devlin, she could be strong and authoritative, always in charge. With this woman, she was thrust into a secondary position, always on the defensive. She made an effort to set herself against Suzanne Brody's dominance.

"I wouldn't mind a singing career."

"You're a performer, then?"

"Not really," said Peggy demurely. "Just loaded up with the usual fantasies."

"Looking for some man to put you on the road to fame and fortune, is that it?"

"I guess so."

"Hammaker might be able to do it."

"Well, I'm glad to hear that."

"Sharps could do it even easier, if he wanted to. But that would be out of character for Mr. Sharps. As I said, he never interferes in someone else's bailiwick."

"Then I better take my chances with Hammaker."

Still that pale, impassive visage, in a voice without expression. "Mo Hammaker eats women like you alive."

"The casting couch? What else is new?"

At last a slight show of amusement. "The more things change, the more they stay the same. If you are serious about a career in show business . . ."

"It's always been a dream of mine."

"Sharps Industries," Suzanne Brody said. "In Manhattan. Ask for me. I might be able to help."

"You mean it?"

"I never say anything I don't mean."

Peggy watched her go. So slender, swaying provocatively, so sure of herself, the kind of woman Peggy Pearce had always wanted to be.

In the third-floor bedroom, Senator Hamilton had doubled his luck. Two nubile females. Each more tempting than the other. Both of them glowing with good health, their naked bodies aquiver with excitement. Both of them wanted him. They said so.

The senator shed his clothes as quickly as he could. Which first? What first? One of them answered his questions.

"Make a sandwich!" she cried. Her name was Nini. She was small and precisely formed, perfect in every way. Her face was without a line, and her brain was without an idea. "You be the meat."

"That means we're the bread." The second girl called herself Mimi. She patted the bed next to her and, when the senator took his place, pressed herself up against him.

They might have been twins, they looked so much alike. They were sisters, less than a year apart. Young, but not nearly as young as Red Hamilton liked them. Under the circumstances they would do, do very well, thank you.

The pink-faced junk bond dealer perched on the edge of the hot tub, plump feet dangling in the swirling water. He held his penis in his hand, an offering to any woman who happened to glance his way. So far no takers. But the junk bond dealer was a patient man; he knew how to wait.

Devlin was sorry he had come. Another mistake in a lifetime of mistakes, minor and major. He marked this one down at the bottom of the list, but with excellent possibilities for rocketing up to the top. Just one wrong move was all it would take.

He shouldn't have come. He should have remained in his room alone. Gotten drunk. Allowed the new year to sneak in without his help. The voice of reason nagged at him. Maintain tight control over his emotions, his impulses, his actions. Do nothing reckless or stupid. There were too many ways to lose. To lose everything. His freedom. His life. Whatever possibilities still existed for him. Every step along the way was booby-trapped. Danger lurked in the shadows, ready to strike, ready to take him down without warning. He decided to split and went looking for Geneva, only to say good night. And encountered her husband instead.

"Devlin, isn't it?" A derisive turn of that strong mouth under the thick, curling mustache. "Still haven't found yourself a woman, I see. Taking your time, right? Selective, right? I approve. There are moments in life when the quickest way to attain your goal is to go slow. It's how I handle my business. You didn't say, did you, what your business is?"

"I give ski lessons, some of the time."

"Ah."

That exhalation made Devlin feel as if he failed to measure up to expectation. For reasons he dared not consider, he wanted to impress Sharps, make him know that he—Devlin—was a man of substance and accomplishment.

What accomplishments?

A seducer of older women—easy marks every one—in order to find a meal ticket.

Teaching clumsy boys and girls to slide down a snowy slope on a pair of expensive sticks.

Burglarizing empty houses in league with a pair of small-time thugs.

"I'm also a professional trainer," he tacked on, another notch in a gun seldom fired. What would the man in the scarlet mess jacket think if he learned Devlin was his wife's lover? How would he react if he discovered Geneva was in love with Devlin? What would his response be if he found out that his wife wanted him dead? And so did Devlin. "At the Aspen Sports Association," Devlin continued matter-of-factly.

A rictus of a smile froze Sharps's mouth in place. "Ah," he said again.

"Best sports club in town." Devlin hated himself for boasting.

"I believe Mrs. Sharp works out at ASA occasionally. So that's how you two met."

Devlin's discomfort increased, eyes darting past Sharps, seeking some excuse to separate himself from the other man.

Anticipating the move, Sharps dropped a proprietary hand on Devlin's arm. "You enjoy the work? All those half-naked people . . ." A shiver traveled along Devlin's spine. "A kind of intimacy must occur between a trainer and his subject. The seductive closeness of strangers. I like to call it. You must make out very well, Devlin. With the ladies, I mean." A short, grating laugh, man-to-man stuff.

Devlin made an effort to leave. Sharps held him in place, those powerful fingers closing on Devlin's biceps. "Impressive," Sharps said. "You have an extremely strong arm. A good sign, Dev. Mind if I call you that—Dev? Bodily strength is a positive factor in a young man. Builds confidence. Provides the ability to do all sorts of things. Physical activities, that is. You ever play football?"

"There was never time."

"Of course not. How about wrestling? Or did you box? No, I guess not. Contact sports leave a mark on a man. The usual lumps and scars, of course. But I was thinking about the eyes. A hardness in the eyes. Reflecting an inner toughness. Are you tough, Dev? The kind of tough that allows an otherwise ordinary man to perform extraordinary feats?" He released Devlin's arm. "No matter. Just a garrulous old man making useless conversation."

In the silence that followed, Devlin attempted to stitch into a cohesive whole all that he felt and thought. Sharps frightened him as no one and nothing ever had. An unidentifiable force emanated from the man, a narrow focus that held Devlin in thrall. He longed to flee, to locate a safe hiding place. He couldn't move, and at once he knew, *knew* with a terrifying certainty, that there was no safe place for him. Nor would there ever be.

Sharps continued to speak. His voice had grown deceptively gentle, supported by a suggestive, barbed undertone. "Ever actually hurt anybody, Devlin? Mentally and physically. Not in some childish street fight that ends in a black eye or a bleeding nose. I'm talking about more than that. Broken bones, a ruptured spleen, an eye gouged out; where a man screams in anguish and torment. Put a man to the far edge of his life, ever done that, Devlin? Oh, the satisfaction of breaking another man. Reducing him to jelly, helpless in the face of your manhood. Taking away the last vestiges of his pride and power. Strength and guts, that's what it's all about." Sharps ran his hand over his smooth scalp, eyes never leaving Devlin's. "When it comes to crunch, a man's got it or he hasn't. What about you, Devlin? Are you ready for a gut check?" A short, reptilian exhalation. "No answer expected. What it gets down to, one way or another, winners deliver pain."

Devlin summoned up all his stubbornness, all the resolve he could muster. He refused to let Sharps see how shaken he was.

"That it, Mr. Sharps, you enjoy hurting people?"

Sharps's mood changed. A quicksilver shift of gears.

His mouth turned at the corners, the mustache lifting parenthetically. All harshness had faded away from that vaguely Oriental face, and he put all those neat white teeth on display once more, dazzling and hypnotic, forcing the younger man to smile back.

"The future. Are you reflective by nature? Certainly you consider your future. Catalog your dreams still unfulfilled, measure the chances of bringing them to fruition. Time is so ephemeral, Devlin. Especially for men like yourself. Ball players, fighters, skiers. How quickly you use up your physical currency. Reflexes grow duller, muscles less resilient, the power diminished. You begin to settle. For second place. For third. For simply completing a competition on your feet. Isn't that right, Devlin? Look at all these young men, skiers like yourself, medal winners at one time or another. Hanging out in Aspen or Vail or Breckenridge. Getting by on the droppings of others. The leavings of their betters.

"Until one day a younger crop shows up. Younger, stronger, better looking. Crowding the old-timers like yourself out of the field. There's no retirement plan for aging ski instructors. No annuities for trainers. Not even Social Security for gigolos. My guess is that few of you strike the mother lode. That very desirable, very compliant wealthy widow or divorcée. Most people who have money treasure it too much to let go of very much of it. Haven't you found it so, Devlin? More droppings. Nickels and dimes when hundred-dollar bills are what's needed.

"And there you are. Thrust rudely into your own future. Unprepared. Without a bank account or a job. Without a trusty nest egg to see you through your declining years. Bad scene, no matter how you look at it, Devlin. Could make an otherwise good man tense and irritable. Used up. Running on empty.

"You got a future, Devlin? Is it bright and shiny, tempting you to rush into it unafraid? Oh, well, a smart lad like you, you've undoubtedly lined up a good career for yourself in a stable industry. An outstanding job. Ample salary and bonuses. Outstanding medical benefits. Full retirement plan. A smooth ride to the finish line. Allows you to make plans, that does. Look ahead, shape your own future. Know exactly what kind of life you'll be living in ten years. Twenty. What kind of a life will you be living in twenty years, Devlin?"

Assaulted as he had been by Sharps's words, Devlin felt compelled to fight back yet remained unsure of how to repel his attacker. Everything Geneva had said about her husband was true; he was abusive, a bully, a man who honored no truth save his own. He put on his most ingenuous expression.

"I see you're about to offer me a job, Mr. Sharps."

Sharps was undaunted. "What a novel idea."

"Doing what, Mr. Sharps?" Devlin held on to that single notion with the rare tenacity of a shipwrecked sailor clinging to a sliver of driftwood. "What kind of work could I do for you, Mr. Sharps?"

"You working for me. Now there's something worth considering, don't you think so, Devlin? But in what capacity? That requires some considerable consideration. You come up with anything, let me know. Meanwhile, this is a party. Find yourself some pretty young thing, somebody you can screw in good conscience. . . ."

"I came with someone." What made him tell Sharps

anything? Talking as if they were friends of some standing. Sharing intimacies. He spotted Peggy Pearce in a group across the room. Sharps followed his glance.

"Very nice," he said. "You do have first-rate taste in women, Devlin." And then he walked away.

Devlin was shaken. *Women.* Was it possible that Sharps knew about himself and Geneva? No way, no possible way. Still, Devlin shivered despite the reassuring warmth of this fine, rich man's home.

Geneva watched her husband. He advanced on her, shoulders thrusting before him as if seeking some enemy to destroy. He positioned himself close to her, angled to one side, speaking for her ear only. No intimacy, she thought, only his affection for conspiracy. Sharps loved secrets, the notion that he was privy to information no one else possessed.

"That Devlin," he began. "Complex young man."

Geneva allowed nothing to show on her face or in her voice. Duncan kept returning to Devlin, bringing him up to her. Had he discovered her secret?

"Who?" she said.

"Attractive devil," Sharps said with a hint of glee, as if in some way not yet revealed he could lay claim to a special relationship with Devlin. "Dresses up the party by himself. There's a style to him, a certain reckless way. He must have been an exceptional skier when he was younger. Smart of you to invite him."

That froze her. She searched her mind for the slightest evidence that would link her to Devlin in her husband's mind. Had she committed some egregious blunder she was not aware of? Her teeth ground together, and she made a mighty effort to relieve the tension.

"Did I?" she said, elaborately casual. "I don't think I know the man. He must have come with someone else."

"Of course. You never met, you told me that you never met. How careless of me to forget. All these people, so many I've never seen before. He skis, Devlin does. Expertly, I'm sure of it. Look at him. Half the women in the place have got their eyes on him. All muscles and balls, that one."

"If you say so, Duncan."

"Oh, I do say so. You prefer men who are more cerebral, my dear. Artists, writers, even crass and crude businessmen. Mature, cultured men. And why not? Devlin and I, we were discussing his future."

"Does the young man have a future, Duncan?"

"An excellent question. Exactly what I asked him. What would you say if I offered him a job? If he came to work for me? Train him to do things my way. He might become a valuable property in time."

A penetrating chill settled in behind her navel. "Your business is your affair, Duncan."

"For both of us," he amended. He smiled.

She smiled back at him. "Leave me out of this."

"I imagine I could find some use for him. He's attractive, and strong. Some sort of a general handyman. Driver, bodyguard, someone to carry your packages when necessary, Geneva. What would you say to that?"

"I'll manage without any help, thank you."

"Be nice for you to have someone around the house. Some company for you when I'm away."

"You can be so hateful, Duncan."

"Is that how you view me? Well, so be it. See that beautiful girl talking to the little fat man? The one in the satin blouse. Fantastic, isn't she? He brought her, Devlin did. They came together, they'll leave together. Won't that be nice for Devlin. Rolling all over that hot little number. Admit it, Geneva, that is world-class material."

"You have a filthy mind, Duncan."

"Yes, I suppose I do," he murmured before wandering away.

"No white breads."

"Oh, definitely not, not white."

"Just their absence makes you feel lighter. . . ."

"Transparent, I always say."

"And nothing fermented."

"Natural juices and spring water."

"Quinoa, Job's tears . . ."

"Buckwheat . . ."

"Roasted."

"I sprinkle vitamin powder on *everything.*"

"Very good for you and yours. As far as condiments go . . ."

A middle-aged man in a bad toupee insulted another middle-aged man he had once cheated in a business deal. The second man cursed him. Punches were thrown. One blow dislodged the toupee, which infuriated its owner; he began to weep at the indignity and punched faster. Most of the blows missed.

Two burly young men appeared and separated the combatants. Off-duty policemen hired by Suzanne

Brody to deal with just such a situation. They hustled the battlers off to the kitchen so that their verbal onslaughts wouldn't bother any of the other guests.

Devlin, watching, thought of a question: Did Sharps keep bodyguards of his own on site? It would make sense if he did, all his expensive possessions, all that money in the house. He made a mental note to speak to Geneva about that.

The party flowed. From room to room. From one level to the next and back down again. Deals were launched. Still others were consummated. Arrangements of one kind or another were made. Telephone numbers were handed out, promises whispered, meetings scheduled. Later, most of the guests would boast that it had been a marvelous party. That they had had a marvelous time.

The pink-faced junk bond dealer, naked, worked his little hand under the dress of the wife of a Washington lobbyist. As luck would have it, he managed to locate her vagina, fingering it roughly. She shrieked, more in surprise than distress, and stumbled away, too drunk to know where she was headed.

It took the pink-faced junk bond dealer only a second or two to locate her again, by now sitting in a white plastic chair at the side of the lap pool. He confronted her, thrusting his semierect penis at her face.

She grimaced. "Get that ugly little thing away from me."

Encouraged, he jiggled himself in what he supposed was an enticing way. "Satisfaction guaranteed."

"Pervert."

"You'll love the taste."

"Pig."

He pushed his way between her lips.

Shielded by a self-protecting illusion, he imagined her lips to be warm and moist, her mouth accepting. Thus it came as a mighty shock when her teeth closed down on him in a fierce, powerful clamp. He screamed and tried to force her jaw open. He pleaded for his release. He promised never to do it again. He begged for mercy. And finally he punched her in the eye. She tumbled out of the chair and rolled into the lap pool, paddling serenely away.

The pink-faced junk bond dealer turned pale as he contemplated his wounded pride and joy, at rest in his hand like the wrinkled, useless object it was.

"She bit me," he muttered. "The bitch bit me."

No one heard him over the joyful din.

"I surely do admire the quality of your acting," Hank Ricketts said to Jerry Cross.

The tall movie star accepted the compliment with practiced graciousness. He had learned how to deal with flattery; criticism still gave him trouble.

"You folks been coming to Aspen for a long time?" Sam Daly said. He directed the question to Cross's blond girlfriend.

She felt more comfortable with people nearer her own age. "We love it," she said. "At least until last week. Can you imagine it, somebody ripped us off."

"That a fact?" Ricketts said, full of compassion and understanding.

"A true fact," Cross said. "Came into the house

while we were out skiing and took everything that wasn't nailed down. I'd like to get my hands on those guys. . . ."

"Fantastic," Sam Daly cried. "The way you did in *Blues Long Lost,* right? You were incredible in that picture, better'n Schwarzenegger. I dig it when you go into action."

"Oh, yes," the blonde crooned, "so do I."

Peggy Pearce located the plump music producer. She gazed wide-eyed into his face.

"You are not going to believe this," she began.

"I believe lots of things."

"The coincidence, I mean."

"What coincidence is that?"

"I sing."

"You're kidding me."

"I told you before. People tell me I'm very good."

"Not too good, I hope."

She fluttered her eyelashes at him. "Oh, you. You know what I mean."

"I work with a lot of singers. Help them, I mean. Guide their careers."

"That's what I need, someone to help. Guide me."

He leaned her way. "I have this theory about singers."

"Yes?"

"All singers have one trait in common."

"They do?"

"It's genetics, I'm convinced. Every one of them is compulsively oral, if you get the meaning of my words."

"Is that really true?"

"Singers, they all give extreme head. What about you?"

She presented her most demure smile. "Does that include boys, too?"

Midnight came, announced by a flickering of lights and a tinkling of sleighbells. The ritual kissing began. A woman he didn't know pressed her mouth on Devlin's mouth and then was gone. Seconds later another stranger, her kiss intense and routinely sexual, her tongue stabbing into the back of his mouth. The cloying scent of her perfume made him dizzy, the empty intimacy, the raw need; it all embarrassed him somehow. More of the small-scale fictions in which he had dressed himself. So much talk, so little said, with people he neither knew nor cared for, with women whose beds he had entered so glibly, every one of them at a distance. His memories were without substance; illusions that provided ballast for a life without purpose.

He found an empty bathroom and locked himself in. He sat on the john and smoked and struggled to go down and dirty with the circumstances of his life. What he came up with was an off-key anthem of dependence and disruption, a small-time con man's tuneless lament.

He rose to leave the bathroom and caught sight of himself in the mirror above the sink. The face he saw looked different, only partly formed, a sculptor's failed experiment. The eyes were hooded, full of benign deception, and his mouth turned down, lips pressed together in permanent disapproval. He did not like what he saw and turned away.

He went back to the party, wishing he hadn't come.

*   *   *

Nini labored industriously on Red Hamilton's front. Mimi, with equal fidelity, attended to his back. In the dim light of the bedroom, in the tinted ceiling mirrors, the senator was unable to distinguish one girl from the other. Not that he cared. Interchangeable parts was what they were. Jiggling breasts and clenched buttocks. Insatiable mouths. When would it end?

How many times had his middle-aging flesh responded to the sisters' siren call? Where had he found the strength? How long would his heart hold out? There were moments when it had faltered, missed a beat or two, come very near surrendering to this juvenile onslaught on its valves and chambers. Christ Almighty! These little girls had learned their lessons too well.

The images in the tinted ceiling glass shimmered and shifted about, as though they had begun to melt. Out of the flailing mass of limbs, one dominant shape materialized. Duncan Turner Sharps. Commanding and impressive in that scarlet mess jacket. The shaved head gleaming in the glass. His smallest gesture an order to be instantly obeyed.

"Out," he said.

The senator coughed.

The girls protested.

"Hey," Mimi said.

"Say," Nini said.

"Out," Sharps said again.

One look at that stern, exotic visage was enough. The girls scrambled for safety in an adjoining room. The senator managed to make it up into a sitting position, wheezing and breathing hard. He pulled a pillow wet with sweat and semen over his slack genitals. He smiled apologetically up at Sharps.

"Those girls," he said in awe.

Sharps said, "Let's talk."

"Those two." Hamilton gave one of those down-home, political chuckles that seemed always to work among his constituency.

Its charm failed to move Sharps. "Put on your clothes."

The senator did as he was told. Fully dressed, he summoned up some measure of dignity. He confronted the other man.

"Well, Duncan. Here we are."

"I'm unhappy, Red."

That made the senator nervous. When a man like Sharps was unhappy, he made those around him unhappy. He made an attempt at cheerfulness. "I thought we were doing all right. A few more palms to grease, maybe. I'm ninety percent sure the general assembly is going to swing our way. There are a few holdouts, but over the long haul that shouldn't matter."

"It's Ayres who's the problem. There are other interested parties. . . . Have you mentioned the casino to anybody, Red?"

"Oh, my God, no. I would never do a thing like that. My mouth is stapled shut."

"I hope so."

"Still, you never can tell. More and more people know the truth. You can't tell if somebody spilled the beans."

"No casino means no hotel. Without the one, the rest of the project is a waste of my time and money, a substantial portion of which will go into your pockets and the pockets of your associates."

The senator shifted around in place. Talking about money, payoffs, this openly made him uncomfortable. He had always lived by the unwritten rules of the business, had always been careful to attend to the refinements that protected them all. He said, "There are people of influence who are afraid of mob influence."

Sharps stared. Arlen Hamilton disgusted him. He was greedy and corrupt, but too fearful to put himself at risk. Easily bought, he spent excessive amounts of time indulging his cravings for young girls and in finding ways to cover his ass. But Hamilton was all he had to work with, and he meant to make the best of it.

"I've been doing a great deal of thinking about you, Red. Once this deal is resolved, we should be able to focus completely on the next step in your career."

The senator took a deep breath. "You've lost me, Duncan."

"The Senate is too confining a forum for a man of your infinite talent. You need room to exercise your strength and intelligence, to expand your political capacities. I am talking about the inevitable role for you. The ultimate job. The Oval Office, the White House. I am talking about the presidency, Red."

"Me?" Hamilton felt the flow of weakness in his limbs, along with a sense of hope, of a lost ambition rekindled. "Me?" he said again. "The president?"

"You'd like that, wouldn't you? To become president of the United States."

"It's been a secret dream. . . ."

"Of course, an ambitious man like you. Why not dream."

"I don't really have much support, Duncan."

"Neither did Jimmy Carter, when he started out. But with me behind you . . ."

"A run for the top job, it requires an organization. Good people. Money."

"Money can buy all the other elements, and I can make sure you get that money, Red."

"Oh, Duncan, what a good friend you are."

"Now get back downstairs and circulate. I want to know who else is bidding on the Ayres property. What it will take to get them out of the chase."

"I'll do my best for you, Duncan."

"I'm sure you will."

"There's one more thing, Duncan."

"What is it?"

"Those girls. Keep them away before they kill me."

A bird in the hand . . .

Peggy Pearce didn't dare allow the music producer to get away. She was too hungry for the opportunity he could provide. Suzanne Brody; she might pursue that avenue later on, when she was more firmly ensconced in New York. But the music producer was here and now.

In a bathroom on the second floor, lined with pink and green marble, the plump music producer sat with his pants crumpled around his ankles and his chin on his chest. He sighed. He snorted. He sucked air into his lungs. He peered at Peggy Pearce, on her knees in front of him. "Let me tell you something, girlie, you sing half as good as you blow and there's no holding you back. You'll be a star."

She would have curtsied if she could. "Thank you, kind sir."

The stick-thin woman from Beverly Hills said it. "You reach a certain age, you can't take immortality for granted."

The slender young woman replied with humility, as though she were applying for a job. "How clever of you to say so. Yet there are moments when Charles and I do get an irresistible craving for red meat."

"You don't."

"We do, I confess it."

"Naughty, naughty."

"I know, I know. Isn't it awful. But we do, we do. From Pure Bred Beef, Incorporated, in British Columbia, in Canada."

"I know."

"Specially raised cattle. Fed only whole grains. Their steaks are lean and untainted. Free of antibiotics and all other poisons. Pure Bred Beef, Incorporated, ships by UPS, packed in dry ice."

"If you must. For me, there are simply too many pollutants in the food chain. No matter how careful people are, we never ingest anything that has four legs. . . ."

"Don't I rate a New Year's Eve kiss?"

Geneva spun around, an expression of alarm on her lovely face. "Are you out of your mind! Coming up behind me this way. You scared me."

"About that kiss."

She retreated a step. "Don't even think about it. Go away. I've decided we shouldn't be seen together."

"He knows we know each other."

"What do you mean, he *knows*?"

"It would be unnatural for us not to greet each other, not to talk."

"Duncan *knows*?"

"Of course."

"How? Why? I told him we'd never met."

"I'm sorry. I said we'd met at ASA."

"Damn, damn, damn. Duncan is not a fool. He'll figure it out, that I'm hiding something. Lying to him. Damn, Dev. That was stupid."

"Don't call me stupid."

She set the gears and pulleys of her mind in motion, seeking a way out of the dilemma in which she found herself. Devlin on one side and Sharps on the other, both watching her for some false move, some betrayal of her innermost thoughts. She brought her voice down to a whisper, a verbal caress. "My darling, it's just that we've got to be careful. Duncan is a dangerous man. He has to control everyone, everything. We mustn't take unnecessary chances." She glanced from side to side, a hostess's vapid smile on her lips, making sure they weren't being observed. "I saw you two together. What were you talking about?"

"Small talk. Party talk. He asked about my work. What plans I had for the future."

"Did he offer you a job?"

"A job. No, of course not."

"He might. He will, I'm sure he will."

"He doesn't even know me."

"It's the kind of thing Duncan does. A way of displaying his power. So he can keep an eye on you."

"That's crazy. That's—"

"It's time you left. I'll be in touch in a day or so, as soon as it's safe. We have some serious thinking to do."

"I was hoping we could be alone."

"Out of the question. Now, go away. Excuse yourself and walk away from me while I attend to my duties as hostess. We'll talk another time."

He obeyed at once. He had come longing for attention, affection, some emotion. All he got was indifference. And indifference, he understood at last, was the real killer.

Devlin located his coat and searched for Peggy. She was nowhere to be found. Nor did he see Hank Ricketts or Sam Daly. They had left together, he told himself. They belonged together, a natural threesome. It was time for him to end his connection with them. He was almost at the front door when he heard that harsh, insistent voice.

"Leaving so soon, Devlin?"

It was Sharps, fingering his mustache. He steered Devlin out onto the covered porch.

"Great night, Devlin. Look at the sky."

Devlin looked. Stars everywhere, the air crisp and clean. That's what Aspen was supposed to be about, Devlin reminded himself. Unspoiled days and nights, man competing with himself and the immutable high country. All the rest was shit.

"Very nice."

"Not too cold for you?"

Devlin said he handled the cold very well, thank you.

Something in his manner amused Sharps, and he laughed, brief and brittle. "We will talk again, Devlin.

Exchange ideas. Maybe dinner. The two of us. Soon, Devlin, soon." And he vanished back inside the house.

Devlin experienced a sense of loss. And he realized that he wanted something more from Sharps, something solid and lasting. He made his way down the driveway to where it joined the road. Two police officers in Smoky the Bear hats were huddled together, speaking quietly to each other. One of them tossed Devlin a soft salute as he walked past. On quivering legs, Devlin went the rest of the way to where the blue Jeep was parked. He drove off, wishing Independence Pass were open so that he could go on forever. And never look back.

27

ON the second day of the new year, Sharps called Marlon Ayres and arranged to meet him in the bar of the Hotel Jerome. Any excuse to get out of the house. A crew of people were bustling from room to room, dusting, polishing, vacuuming. A swarm of worker bees performing tasks essential to the hive but producing no product, no wealth. The kind of work he had always loathed. As for the queen bee—Geneva— she had quit the premises early that morning to spend the day going up and down the mountainside. All that energy wasted to no gainful purpose.

Before he left the house, he phoned Suzanne Brody, congratulating her on the success of the party.

"I had a chance to talk to Ralph Gaffney and the mayor of Aspen," she said.

"The mayor, yes. Keep the pressure on that pussy. Everything about him rubs me the wrong way, but I need him. Also the members of the zoning board. We've got one vote out of the three. We must have at least two."

"I'm on top of it, Duncan."

"Check with me this evening," he said before he hung up.

Ayres was seated at a large round oak table in the bar of the Jerome when Sharps arrived. He was nursing a bottle of Coors and talking to the manager of the restaurant. He introduced Sharps, and the manager beat a diplomatic withdrawal.

"I get the feeling you know about everybody in this town," Sharps said in his most jovial manner.

"Was a time when I did for a fact know everybody. Leastways to say hello to. Most of the old-timers is gone by now, but I can still claim a friend or two. You drink beer, Mr. Sharps? Coors is as good as you're likely to get. It's the water separates the beers, folks say. Fact is, except for that, they make it the same way all over." He signaled the bar, and a waiter brought two more bottles.

"Hope you enjoyed the party the other night, Mr. Ayres."

"Quite a do. More folks than I've seen in one place in thirty years. All that sound, all that drinkin' and carryin' on. Can't say some of what I saw I approved of."

Sharps entered a quick disclaimer. "People get out of hand. A party that big, there were lots of people I never saw before."

"I reckon that's a fact." He took a long pull on the

Coors. He smothered a belch. "I take it you asked me here to talk business, Mr. Sharps."

"I have, sir. About your land, have you reached a decision? I'm anxious to close our deal and put my planners to work."

"Jumping the gun a mite, I'd say. Didn't know we had a deal."

Sharps swallowed a cutting retort. The old man had a point; crowding him too much would inevitably backfire. Doing business with Ayres required an eternal balancing act, and one false step could result in failure.

"Got me that time, Mr. Ayres. Guess I'm a little too anxious." His investigators had determined that his strongest competitors for Ayres's property were the Japanese. They were aggressive businessmen, persistent but always polite, playing by rules that they alone adhered to. It was time to raise the ante, put the competition in a game they could not win. "Remember Pearl Harbor, Mr. Ayres?"

The old man's face closed up like a fist, a lumpy hardness that caused a warning light to go on in Sharp's mind; he snapped to a new level of attention. Ayres was shrewder than he knew. Tougher. With the strength and combativeness a lesser personality would lack.

"I ran a company of marines, Mr. Sharps, during World War Number Two. I took 'em ashore at Tarawa and Iwo Jima, where too many of those good boys died on the beach. We fought on Okinawa, and we'd've gone right on into Japan itself, if not for that big bomb they used. I can recite the names of all the men under my command who died, Mr. Sharps. At night I lie in bed and they march across my memory, those brave, forever young men. You bet I remember Pearl Harbor."

"Well, then. Under the circumstances, I'd be a little shy about dealing with those Japanese."

"Mostly younger, the ones I've met," Ayres said in a voice dry and acerbic. "Not a one of 'em ever heard a shot fired in anger. Didn't start that damned war, anymore'n I did."

"Doesn't matter, I suppose, since they seem to be the real winners. Buying up everything they can get their hands on over here. One of our movie companies has gone Japanese. And a lot of hotels and businesses. Why, they even snatched up Rockefeller Center. Won't be long before they start calling the shots coast to coast."

Ayres thought it over, in no hurry to answer. "Not so different, is it, from what we've done. Buying up property and businesses around the world, mines and farms and plantations, shipping. That's what they mean, ain't it, those bureaucrats in Washington, when they run off at the mouth about American interests in this country or that one? Economic imperialism, I think they call it. A fancy name for overseas greed, Mr. Sharps, which I'm guessing you know all about." Ayres swallowed the last of his beer. "Don't matter much to me anymore who was on which side in some ancient war. Gonna make my decision based on my own best interests and what is fair for all involved. That sit okay with you, Mr. Sharps?"

"Wouldn't want it any other way," Sharps said at once. But he was already searching for another way to get this cranky old man to give up his land, to make the deal Sharps wanted. There had to be a way; there always was.

The Ski Capital of the Western World

T H E Second World War almost closed Aspen down forever. Instead it proved to be its salvation. The Tenth Division Mountain Infantry went into training at Camp Hale in Colorado. Ski troopers.

Many of the soldiers were experienced skiers who had put in a great deal of time on the mountains of France, Italy, and Switzerland. It was inevitable that they discover the rewards to be found on Aspen Mountain. They wrote of this Alpine prize to their friends. Some of them even authored articles for ski magazines; the word spread.

Some of them did even more; Friedl Pfeifer, for example, started a ski school.

Walter Paepcke, a businessman, imagined a sporting, intellectual, and cultural center that would attract a variety of people from around the world.

With Pfeifer, he created the Aspen Company and the Aspen Skiing Corporation. He took over the Hotel Jerome and refurbished it. And he replaced the old boat tow with a modern ski lift.

Inspired by Paepcke's vision and energy, others moved to revitalize Aspen. Houses were restored and brightly painted, all in the Victorian mode. New houses were built: imitation Swiss chalets, log cabins, and contemporary structures. Land prices rose as the demand increased and real estate speculators moved into place.

The Wheeler Opera House was reopened. An annual design conference came into being. The Institute for Humanistic Studies was established. In increasing numbers people began flocking into the high valley to be educated, to be entertained, and to ski.

Something important was happening in Aspen, and the rich and the famous, anxious to become part of it, arrived. Rock stars and movie stars, entrepreneurs, world-renowned clothes designers, best-selling novelists; they bought houses or built new ones. The price of an average home in Aspen was put at one million dollars. One extravagant vacation house was said to have cost twenty-five million dollars. Working people, unable to afford the high prices, were forced to live elsewhere, commuting to their jobs, outsiders in their own community.

Aspen had struck the mother lode. And while the few remaining old-timers shook their heads in despair, the rich, chic carpetbaggers transformed the little town into their own personal playground.

28

S H E didn't appear at ASA.

She didn't call.

She had dropped out of sight.

Three days passed since the party. Four days, five. And still no sign of Geneva. Had she left Aspen, departed with her powerful and commanding husband for milder, more rewarding climes? Had she given him—Devlin—up as a weak and ineffectual man, of scant value to her? The possibility caused tremors of frustration and fear to ride down his spine; he could not accept the idea, would not accept it.

He missed her.

Her absence left a void in him that could not otherwise be filled.

Devlin loved Geneva.

He longed to carve the words into the mountainside. To announce to the world his feelings. To impress her with his ardor and his desire. .

Love. That amorphous and most fanciful of human notions. Bereft of reason and logic. A mere biological itch pumped up out of proportion, prettified in romantic garb, enhanced by myth and mystery; he was compelled to scratch.

Twice he drove past her house—Sharps's house, he reminded himself bitterly—not daring to stop, not daring to visit. Unable to take charge of his own destiny. Visions of Geneva drifted into view, the strong, womanly scent of her; he grew hard at the memory. No different from a horny adolescent hot on the trail of his first love.

He went back the next morning and saw her leave, driving a flame-red Isuzu Trooper, short skis fastened to the roof rack. He followed at a discreet distance, arriving at the Ute Nordic Center only seconds behind. She was already gone, out on the cross-country trail. He rented skis and poles and set out after her.

Past Buttermilk, along one of the most beautiful corridors in the Rockies, straining to catch up. Into the Owl Creek area and on through gently descending meadows and groves of aspen trees. On impulse he swung onto the difficult upper trail, where his strength and skill would give him an advantage. And minutes later he spotted her; he pressed forward, closing the gap. He had begun to feel the unaccustomed strain on his thighs when, as if sensing his presence, Geneva paused. He came to a stop alongside her, glad of the respite.

She gazed up at him out of oversize goggles. That

perfect face, cheeks flushed a rose color by the cold, a wool watch cap pulled low over her ears, had never seemed lovelier to him.

"Why are you following me?" she asked tonelessly.

"I missed you. I haven't seen you since the party. Why didn't you call?"

"It's not going to work between us, Dev. I hoped it would, but I was wrong."

"Don't say that. I love you, Geneva."

"Love is not enough. Not for you, not for me. There's too much standing between us, keeping us apart."

"I won't give you up, Geneva."

"You've never had me, Dev. Not really, not the way Sharps does. I belong to Sharps. Sharps owns me."

"You love me as much as I love you."

"Find someone else, Dev. Sharps will never let me go."

"But why? He doesn't care about you."

"I explained it to you. Everything is business with Sharps. A divorce would reflect badly on him. It could be that simple. Or it could be more, more practical reasons. Sharps Industries, for example."

"I still don't get it."

"It's a holding company. A business device. A tax dodge. Sharps Industries holds majority ownership of every one of his projects. No matter what happens— a dip in the market, a depression, a lawsuit—all possible losses are limited to that single company. Sharps is protected. His fortune is protected. The holding company, and control of it, that is the key to his financial well-being."

"What's that got to do with you and me?"

"Very basic stuff, Dev. There are only two share-holders in Sharps Industries—equal partners, fifty percent each. Another legal escape hatch. . . ."

A shred of an idea tickled Devlin's imagination. "You and Sharps?"

"That's it."

"Then there's the answer. Tell him you'll exercise your vote against him and—"

"I tried it once. He almost killed me. Oh, no, I vote the way Duncan tells me to. I sign whatever papers he puts before me, without reading them. I do what Duncan tells me to do. My husband owns Sharps Industries. He owns people, they do as he says. He owns me. Everything he does is business." She told him then about Marlon Ayres. About the hotel Sharps planned on building and about the casino.

None of it made much sense to Devlin, and he said so. "None of it has anything to do with me. Or with you."

"It has everything to do with me, with us. Sharps makes it so." She lifted the oversize goggles onto her brow. A dark purple bruise cupped her swollen left eye, extending almost to her temple.

He bit down on his gloved hand, a low mournful cry breaking across his lips. "Sharps?"

"It's done now."

"No, it will never be done, until Sharps is done. Until you're rid of him. Until he lets you go. . . ."

They lay next to each other in Devlin's bed, careful not to touch.

"I'm sorry," he said.

"It happens."

"Not to me." The irony of the event was not lost on him. That had been his excuse for not making love to Peggy—that he was impotent. The lie had come back to haunt him. So many nameless, faceless women in his past; each time he had performed like a robot, robust and controlled, delivering satisfaction on demand. Yet with this woman, who meant so much to him, he was unable to please her. Unable to demonstrate his manliness.

How often had she listened to a man protest the uniqueness of his failure in bed? How many men had she been with? She had long ago lost count. Poor delicate darlings. One harsh word and the blood drained out of that little tool each of them believed was so special. Skittish little boys, each of them striving so mightily to claim a man's portion of the bed for himself. How few of them ever made it. She stroked Devlin's thigh.

"Rest. Relax. You mustn't try so hard."

"You know what's on my mind."

"I know," she allowed after a still interval.

"It's got to be done," he insisted.

She allowed the silence to grow.

"It's what you want, Geneva. To be rid of him once and for all."

She permitted the word to escape between clenched teeth, a low, slow sibilance. "Yesssss . . ."

"Then that's it," he said, relieved that the decision was made. He had come full circle. To that small, secret plot of her being where she had been even before they had met. He had arrived finally to where she had always stood waiting, waiting for the right man to come along and do her bidding. Rid herself of the terrible burden that Sharps was.

That was Devlin's reason for being. To help her. To please her. To free her at last. And in return she would bring him everything he had ever sought after in a woman, all that he had missed up to now. He would love her forever, and she would love him.

Until death do us part.

He spoke without meeting her eyes. "Sharps," he said with irreversible conviction, "I'm going to kill him."

He failed to notice the sweet smile of triumph on her lovely mouth.

29

T HE Far End.

A restaurant of no particular distinction, nevertheless crowded and noisy. Sharps had chosen it, convinced that anonymity was best found in the midst of a crowd. A succession of medium-size rooms, running from front to back. The center room provided booths with high protective panels; soft amber lighting made it impossible to recognize anybody from more than a few feet away. It was in one of those booths that Devlin joined him for dinner.

Sharps ordered for both of them. A mixed grill with baked potato and an excellent salad served in a large wooden bowl. Devlin drank beer; Sharps ordered a bottle of Beaujolais. Sharps held forth on the quality of the food in Aspen.

"Not nearly as good as it might be. But we're a captive group here. Locked into this valley at this time of year. That's to your liking, isn't it, Devlin? The high isolation. The white mountains. The skiing. The attraction of speeding down a mountainside eludes me."

The food, the beer, the amplified sound of all those voices bouncing off the carved-metal ceiling; Devlin felt the tension drain away, and he began to find some pleasure in the other man's company.

"It was one of the Wallendas," he said. "The circus tightrope family. He said that being on the wire was living. Life itself. All the rest, he said, was waiting. That's how it is for me without a mountain to slide down—just waiting."

"Very good," Sharps said. He cut a square of meat out of the double lamb chop on his plate and chewed energetically. He was a precise man, meticulous, following preconceived paths in all aspects of his life, great and small. "I've given a great deal of thought to our earlier conversation. New Year's Eve. Our discussion of life and its many and varied components." When Devlin said nothing, he went on. "The world consists of two kinds of people—those who make their lives stand for something. Men of accomplishment. The movers, the shakers, the power brokers. And those who do nothing. Those who pass this way and fail to leave any tracks.

"Take hunting, for example. A marvelous activity. A man on his own in the wilderness, dependent on his own limited natural gifts against the speed and strength and aggressiveness of the beast. A good hunter makes things happen. He alters the existing condition of the world so that it favors him. He locates his quarry, and, one way or another, he kills it."

"Not much of a contest. An animal is helpless when confronted by a man with a gun."

"No accident there. It was a man who recognized the need for some kind of weapon. Otherwise he would provide a meal for the beast instead of the other way around. Knives. Clubs. Throwing instruments. Spears. Bow and arrows. Ultimately the gun. Accurate and powerful, remarkably efficient. I have a great fondness for guns. Our superior intelligence provided the edge, Devlin. The cleverness to invent, the skill needed to kill.

"Power. That's what it's all about. Power and greed. The twin results of accomplishment. A man can't have too much power, and when he has it he must exercise it. To allow it to lie dormant is to surrender that power, to let it go to waste."

"And what about greed?"

"A positive force. We're acquisitive creatures, you and I. Look around, see for yourself. People are always collecting objects of one kind or another. The greatest acquisition of all—money. The more you get, the more you want. It's the nature of the beast." Sharps laughed around a mouthful of food. "Add some seasoning. A modicum of discipline, courage, a substantial dose of mental toughness. The qualities that make up a real man. No mistake why I've made it to where I am and others who crave it just as much have not."

"Toughness?" Devlin broke in.

"Yes," Sharps said, massaging his scalp, shaping his mustache. "Toughness. That's the quality that allows a man to do whatever he has to do in pursuit of whatever it is he is after. The tough man does whatever is necessary. The tough man, the truly tough man, lets nothing stand in his way. Nothing."

Devlin waited.

Sharps sat back in his chair, eyes lifted toward the ceiling, clarifying his thoughts before speaking again. "A hypothetical case in point. Have you ever killed another human being, Devlin? I have. A number of men, during the war. How did it make me feel? Damned good, I don't mind telling you. Fighting under battle conditions is the ultimate test of a man.

"You know that. You've been there. In Vietnam. One of my people looked up your record. You're a hero, Devlin, Silver Star, I believe. I salute you, sir. You do know how it makes you feel, killing your enemy. Reinforces the belief you have in yourself, in your own ability to survive. Makes you glad to still be alive and that the other fellow is dead."

"War is a unique situation."

"War is a bizarre situation. Legalizes the killing. They hail you for it. Promote you. Pin medals to your chest. Win enough medals, they give you a parade.

"Killing outside the law. That is a special case. Killing because another man's death will profit you in some way. Kill for money. Or property. Or because you want his woman. Could you kill for those reasons, Devlin? Have you got that kind of toughness? Think about it—you must *decide* to kill. You must plan the act. And finally carry it out. A man needs smarts, he needs determination, he needs guts. Tell me, Devlin, have you got what it takes?"

The question came like an unseen blow, a wallop

that jarred all his perceptions of himself and the world in which he lived. Sharps acted with a feistiness that made it seem he was wired into Devlin's darkest fears and anxieties. He struggled to come up with a suitable response. He longed to measure up to Sharps's standards. He was afraid he might wet his pants.

"What about you, Sharps?" He mustered all the strength available, a show of defiance. But he remained calm; a loss of control would be fatal. "Could you do it? Kill a man in cold blood?"

Sharps sliced a piece of lamb chop away from the bone. A precise little triangle, pink in the center. He raised the fork, using it with a natural gracefulness. A maestro before his orchestra; aware of his own superiority, with a casual arrogance, never missing a beat. "A naive question, Devlin. Men in my position don't do that sort of thing. We hire some young man without scruples or morals to do the deed. Buy the service. Any idea what the going rate is these days for murder? Of course you haven't. A man with balls enough for the act and smart enough to pull it off and get clean away. How much would it take to get you, hypothetically speaking, to commit murder, Devlin? What's your price?"

Devlin finished his beer. His hands were remarkably steady, and his voice, when he spoke, was playful, going along with the game.

"Depends. On who the victim is."

"Good answer. Who? Where? When? Degree of difficulty? All must be factored in. Let's see, as I understand it, most murders take place in the home. Family squabbles between husband and wife, between parent and child, between children. There ought to be a shop for murder. With all the prices listed according to state regulations. Plus any incidental expenses incurred. Transportation. Weaponry. Poison, if that method is preferred. So much for a father. So much for a mother. Children under eighteen cost less, yes?"

Devlin laughed in spite of himself. "Like a Saturday matinee at the movies."

"Exactly. Does the age of the person affect the price? A wife, for example. If I wanted someone—you, Devlin—to murder my wife, the reason is of no consequence. How much for the death of a wife, Devlin?"

That took all the fun out of it. Devlin lifted his glass; it was empty. He examined the lacy patterns left by the foam; no help there. He raised his eyes to Sharps. "A man as rich as you are, Mr. Sharps. The price would be high. Very high."

"That makes sense. But only to a point. Not smart to overpay for a job, sets off an inflationary spiral, and nobody profits from inflation. Too bad neither one of us has the experience—to set a fair price." Sharps put his knife and fork aside, patted his lips with his napkin, sat back in his chair, a brief smile fading across his mouth. He waited, a silent challenge to Devlin to keep the game going.

"Okay," Devlin made himself say. "You are shopping for someone to kill your wife."

"Let's say so. Speculation, of course."

"Still speculating, Mr. Sharps. I'd want to know why. Provide a clearer picture of what I'd be getting into."

"Background material."

"Yes."

"Thoroughness in your work, an admirable quality,

Devlin. Well, let's see what kind of a story I can provide that would satisfy your curiosity. Still hypothetical."

Devlin braced himself in his chair, as if to fight off an attack. Determined to maintain his composure, not to permit Sharps to get to him.

Sharps began to speak. "Geneva was a hooker when we met. Not feasible, you say? On the contrary. Many women, poor but beautiful, have taken that route to launch themselves. The smart ones make successful careers or financially sound marriages. Wealth and power. Neither guarantees wisdom for a man when it comes to a woman. We're all led around by our cocks."

Devlin was conscious of the pounding of his heart. Of a high-pitched vibration inside his skull. He had heard enough. Too much. Yet he didn't dare tell Sharps to end this cruel game of his.

"Yes, a hooker," Sharps said. "Highly priced, highly recommended. Working out of an escort service in San Francisco. Let's say that I had a business conference scheduled. A number of important executives from abroad. There was a party afterward, lots of liquor, lots of women to provide pleasant company. Geneva was one of those women.

"You've seen my wife, Devlin. More than merely good-looking. There's an attitude in her, an intensity, a spine of resolve and stubbornness. Hooker or not, it would take quite a man to conquer her, to tame her, to own her. Can you recognize the challenge? . . ."

Devlin made no reply.

Sharps said, "I invited her to dine with me the next time I was in San Francisco. I went to Paris the following week, and she came along. We spent an increasing amount of time together, and I began to discover that she was a complex and often difficult woman. I grew to admire her.

"One night, after knowing each other for a number of weeks, we made love. I invited her to come back to New York with me. Offered her an apartment of her own, plus a considerable amount of money for her to spend as she saw fit. She turned me down. Smart, my Geneva. A week later I asked her to marry me, and she accepted.

"I married a whore, Devlin. Have you any idea what you get when you marry a whore? You get a whore, of course. Geneva's boffed half the men in New York, by a rough count. Younger men, for the most part. In New York and elsewhere.

"There you are. A man makes a mistake, a bad marriage. He reluctantly confesses to himself that he's a fool. An even bigger fool than you know; I allowed her a certain amount of influence in my business. Divorce her, you say. Not without doing myself irreparable harm. She knows too much about certain of my arrangements. In business, in government, with the military. She's in a position to cause me great and lasting difficulty. She could throw up roadblocks to future sell-offs. To buy-outs. To in-company manipulations. No, divorce won't do, even if she'd give me a divorce.

"There you are, Devlin. Under such conditions, might not a reasonable man become desperate to correct the error? To put things right at last? To the point of hiring someone to kill his wife. Right?"

"Right," Devlin said.

"If any of it were true." Sharps laughed and poured

some more red wine into his glass. "Which we both know it isn't. How could it be, a man in my position?" Sharps took hold of Devlin's forearm in a grip powerful and painful. "A fascinating hypothesis. A game of what if. What magical mysteries the human mind is capable of devising. The human brain is a wondrous instrument, able to create, create, always to create. An infinite number of concepts for a man to speculate on in those lonely moments before he is able to fall asleep at night."

A grim smile shifted the corners of Sharps's mustache. And then he changed the subject.

30

"**T**O hell with them," Sam Daly muttered.

He and Ricketts were drinking Jim Beam with beer chasers in the Downhill Racer, a bar off Cooper Street. At this time of day only a handful of solitary drinkers were in residence.

Ricketts and Daly had been drinking for nearly two hours, and their judgment was dulled, their reflexes slowed. Daly felt all-powerful and immortal. Ricketts was glum and full of resentment, a man shortchanged by life at every turn. Earlier in the week he had seen Peggy Pearce coming out of Devlin's room. Ricketts had hit on her four or five times without success, and yet she was giving it to Devlin, who was a dozen years older and not half so handsome. Why Devlin? Just another broken-down skier. He stared into his drink and saw nothing in the amber liquid that would help.

"I'm as smart as she is," he complained.

"Smarter," Daly insisted.

"And Devlin. Sits behind the wheel waiting and pulls down a full share for that."

"Scared to go where the action is."

"A fool and a coward—who needs 'em."

Daly grinned a self-satisfied grin. "I tell you about Julia?"

"Five times already."

"A hot little number, Julia. It must be the diet—all that chili—makes Mexican women the way they are. Never can get enough. She's their housekeeper."

"Who is?"

"Julia. For these folks name of McKinney. They're heading out to Houston, or some such place, to visit their kid in school."

"What's it got to do with me?"

"With us. Julia's there all by herself. We go in, rip the place off, and get out. Simple as that."

"What about Julia?"

"We wear ski masks. That way she don't recognize me. Tape her up and help ourselves to the goods. From what Julia tells me, the McKinneys are loaded."

Ricketts made an effort to clear his mind. "What about our getaway?"

"We park the car in the driveway. Hey, man, not to worry. In and out in ten minutes, no fuss. Then I'm on the plane for Denver. The fence don't care who he does business with. . . ."

"What if Julia makes trouble?"

"No sweat, I'll bust her chops and that's all she wrote. Whataya say?"

Ricketts shoved himself away from the bar. "Let's do it."

The house was a series of cubes arranged so that they resembled a set of oversize steps climbing toward the highest peaks. A wooden deck angled its way around three sides of the house with a three-car garage tucked under it. Ricketts drove his old Buick station wagon around back. They donned the ski masks and climbed onto the deck.

The maid, Julia, as if expecting guests, opened the back door. There was surprise on her pretty face, but no fear. She looked directly at them, laughing happily.

"*¡Hola!*" she cried. "That is you, Sammy?"

Ricketts had enough and wanted to call it off. With such a bad start, no way it could turn out well. Even with that red-and-navy ski mask, with only his eyes and mouth showing, Julia had made Sam Daly.

But it was too late to stop. Daly shoved the slightly built woman, sent her sprawling back into the kitchen.

"*Basta,* Sammy! Not so rough. Din't I tole you—no rough stuff. Whataya, showing off for your friend or something?"

Daly swore and hit her. His fist snapped her head back, and she went crashing against the refrigerator. She hung briefly in place, before sliding to the floor.

Ricketts felt for a pulse. "Jesus, I think you've killed her."

"That's weird, man. I only tapped her."

"We better split."

"What the fuck, we're here. Let's finish the job."

Ricketts was on his way out the back door. "I'm not taking a murder rap, not for you or anyone, Sam. Stay or come, it's all the same to me."

Peggy Pearce summoned them to her room. She tossed the newspaper at them. On page one, the story of the killing. A police lieutenant described it as a break-in turned bad. "Probably the same crew been burglarizing houses up and down the valley the last few months."

Daly looked directly at Peggy and shrugged. "What's it got to do with us?"

"You guys did this."

"Nah," Ricketts said. "That's not our style."

"Not my style," she shot back. "But it stinks of you, Sam, and your lousy temper. This could bring us all down. If the cops get on to you . . ." Her voice trailed off.

"Nobody's getting on to anybody," Daly blustered.

"Big talk," she said. "You want odds on how long it'll take the cops to get you to open up, Sam? Turn over the rest of us? What you've done is to put us out of business. I'm not taking any chances on new jobs with the cops out looking for a couple of dumb-ass killers. It's all over for us, which is too bad because I had some juicy scores lined up."

"Ah, Peg," Ricketts said. "We lay low for a couple of weeks and then—"

"Forget it, Hank. Take my advice and get out of town. None of us has much of a future around here anyway."

Later, when he and Ricketts were alone, Sam Daly pointed out how well things were working for them.

"With Pearce out, with Devlin out, there's only two shares to split up. And if we ever run into anybody on a job, they'll remember that little Mex and crap in their pants. I think we're on to something good here, really good."

Ricketts was much less sanguine, but he was too smart to voice his doubts.

"He's gone."

"What? Who is this?" Devlin came awake reluctantly, his brain functioning in low gear. The familiar voice roused him further. "Geneva, is that you?"

"Duncan's gone. Overnight to San Diego. He won't be back until tomorrow afternoon. We can have tonight all to ourselves."

Devlin told himself that he'd been sleeping too much recently. Seeking sanctuary in oblivion, avoiding the decisions he had to make. Ignoring the demons that plagued him.

"I'm coming over," she said. "I need you, Dev. To be alone with you. To make love to you. Oh, Dev, I keep thinking about how you make me feel, the things you do to me . . . I'll be there as soon as I can."

He remained in bed. Legs crossed at the ankles, smoking a cigarette. If only Sharps would never return. An accident might claim him. End his life. His plane might crash into the mountains, killing him. Freeing Geneva, freeing himself.

Geneva entered the room without knocking, expecting the door to be unlocked, as it so often was. Expecting him to welcome her, to want her, to accept her without hesitation. She let her coat fall to the floor, a studied gesture that he noted and filed away. She raised her sweater over her head, and it went after the coat, displaying her full, round breasts. She drew off her boots, her socks, the stylishly cut slacks. Naked and humming, she came to him, announcing her need.

"Dev, I'm so horny for you."

"I was at the airport. When Sharps left. I saw you two together."

She sat back on her haunches, dressed now in a protective cloak of irritability. "You were at the airport. What am I supposed to make of that?"

"You and Sharps," he said. "Holding hands. Unable to stop touching each other. Kissing. Very much the loving husband and wife. What am I supposed to make of *that*?"

She almost laughed aloud. Jealous, the poor boy was jealous of Sharps. And at this late date. How sweet. How silly. How absolutely irrelevant. "It's an act. A performance, part of my deal with Duncan."

"Deals. That about covers everything with you. With Sharps. Just another deal. Is that what it is with us—a deal?"

"I love you, Dev." The words came out quietly, with an undertone of threat. "I love you, but I won't be treated badly by you. I don't intend to trade one tyrant and master for another."

"But you don't let go. Not of Sharps, not of me."

She stood up, began to dress herself. "Obviously it was a mistake, coming here."

"I know all about you, Geneva."

"I told you everything there is to know."

"Not quite. Not about the escort service in San Francisco . . ."

A shudder racked her body, and she settled back

down on the edge of the bed, clutching the sweater to her breast. Her eyes grew moist.

"*He* told you. Duncan told you that. What an unholy sonofabitch he is."

"Why didn't you tell me?"

"Look at you. At your reaction. Your expression says it all. I disgust you, don't I? I was a call girl, yes. Some kind of lesser creature. To be despised and cast aside, to be kept at arm's length. Nothing's changed about me, Dev. I'm still the same person you said you loved. Except now you know the worst. . . ."

"I trusted you."

"And I deceived you, is that it? I'm not the pure and perfect rich man's wife you believed me to be. All I am is a common slut. Is that the word Duncan used? Slut? Whore? Hustler? What about you, Dev? Which name do you prefer? Hustler? Thief? Gigolo? Working lonely women for a meal." She pulled on the sweater and stood facing him, her finely boned face flushed with rage. "Sharps, what did he want from you? Telling you that story. What was he after? What else did he say? Did you ever doubt him? Consider the possibility that he was not telling the truth?"

"Why would he lie?"

"Why wouldn't he lie? Sharps lies as easily as most men change their shirts. For reasons that he alone knows."

Looking at her, Devlin saw her differently. The idealized beauty had somehow turned to something less perfect. For the first time he noticed faint stretch marks scoring her belly and a suggestion of flabbiness at her thighs. She looked worn, burdened, and her shoulders sagged. Still, he had never desired her more.

"Sharps," he said, trying to bridge the gulf that separated them. "He made it sound as if he were making it up as he went along. A fantasy. Just a fairy tale plucked out of thin air. But it was plain to see, he meant me to accept it as the truth."

"The truth!" For a moment she was unable to go on, hiding her face in her hands. Devlin almost went to her, to take her in his arms and comfort her, to assure her that he would love her always. He remained in place. "You, Devlin," she said finally. "Sharps. Me. None of us knows very much about the truth. Certainly you don't know my truth. Or the kind of life I've led."

"No more lies, Geneva."

"Why not? What is this addiction to truth? Is that what your life has been—always exemplary, always the truth? You want the truth, I'll give it to you. God knows you won't like it any better. Another version of the same story.

"My father began having sex with me when I was ten years old. Can you believe that, Dev? Ten years old, and I had to keep it secret. Not my secret, his. Until he'd had enough of me and my mother and left us. He ran for it, and I blamed myself, convinced in my child's mind that I had done something wrong, that I hadn't pleased him, and this was my punishment. I swore I'd never fail another man. And there were other men. First my uncle, my father's loving brother, and two of my mother's boyfriends. Others. They sniffed me out and took what they wanted. And I laughed and smiled and did whatever they told me to do. Trying my damnedest to be a good little girl.

"The escort service. Oh, indeed, there was an escort service. It provided structure to my life. Imposed discipline. Taught me what rules to follow. You obeyed those rules, john and hooker, or you were out of the life.

"My time was my own. My money was my own. My privacy was never breached. In many ways, that was the best time of my life."

"Until Sharps."

"Until Sharps. He wooed me. With expensive gifts. With holidays in foreign countries. With his attention. He taught me how to dine in fine restaurants. Which wines to order. What clothes to wear. He paid me for my time. Never shortchanged me by even a minute. Strictly first class, that was Duncan Turner Sharps. And he demanded nothing in return.

"Until he made love to me one night. Made love, Dev. Not banged me. Not screwed me. Not humped me. Made love, as if he really cared, and tough nut that I was, I fell for it. The whole ball of wax, as the saying goes.

"He asked me to marry him. Everything would be forgotten. I could start my life all over again. Clean. Untainted. Free of all guilt. Lock, stock, and barrel, I bought it. I had no way of knowing that it would be me who paid. Over and over again. A higher price every day.

"Yes, I was a hooker. And right this minute it seems like that was the best time of my life."

She finished dressing and was out of there before Devlin was able to formulate his response. Relief and disappointment were what he felt. Gratitude that she had left him, freed him from the awful burden she had imposed. Soon he would leave Aspen, drifting as before, propelled by the currents of his fancy and the events he encountered. Beholden to no one. To nothing.

He didn't need Geneva.

He didn't need anybody.

He had his own life to lead. Without her.

Alone.

The girl in the Stem Cristie was bright and shining, pure blond. Her eyes were round and clear blue. When she smiled, those around her smiled back. She was perched on a tall stool at the bar, short skirt revealing long legs, provocatively crossed. She was somewhere between adorable and cute, Devlin concluded. At her peak, bursting with good health and self-consciousness. Used to the attention of men. Bringing her drinks. Lighting her cigarette. Trying so hard to get into her pants.

Spoiled rotten, was Devlin's assessment. Not much different from him. Seldom having to ask for anything. Accepting it all as his birthright. Because he, like the blonde on the bar stool, looked so damned good.

The evening wore on, and the blonde grew prettier with each drink Devlin poured into himself. She seemed to have put her stamp of approval on one man. One of those all-American studs with a broad jaw and eyes that could see forever. Complete with a crooked grin.

Devlin, high on Scotch and driven by a lifetime of disappointments and failures, decided that the all-

American stud didn't deserve the perky blonde and
her long legs. If not Geneva Sharps, he certainly was
entitled to another blonde in his life. In his bed. Out
of a great collective mist made up of equal parts of defeat and psychic pain, and his simmering rage at Geneva and Duncan Sharps, he made his move. He went
over to where the blonde sat. Waiting, he was almost
convinced, for him.

"I'm Devlin." He spat the words out and showed
her his teeth in a manner harsh and disputatious.

No one had to tell her he meant trouble; the un-
checked aggression, the raw hostility. She'd seen it
before in men, just before they started swinging.
There was a difference with this one, a suggestion of
sadness in those gray-green eyes, the stiff-kneed way
he moved, as if mortally damaged and trying so hard
to remain on his feet. If only he'd showed up sooner;
what to do about the all-American stud? She'd encouraged him, flirted, led him to believe . . . Her round blue
eyes leaped from Devlin's seamed and weathered face
to the all-American stud. He worked a frown into
place.

"What's yours?" Devlin said, pulling her attention
back to him.

"What's my what?"

"Your name?"

"Nancy." How to avail herself of both of them?
Tuck one securely away for another evening. Or
maybe a midday break. Which one would handle post-
ponement more graciously? "You asking me to
dance?" she said with a lilt.

"Hey!"

The all-American stud took a dim view of the way

events were unfolding. Who was this dude? What was he after? The smooth all-American brow furrowed while he processed information in a methodical manner. The answers he came up with were neither positive nor pleasant.

"Beat it, buster," he growled.

Devlin directed all his attention to the blonde. He let his hand fall on one of her long legs. He squeezed. He rubbed. He traced a single fingertip across her thigh at her hemline.

She shivered.

He smiled.

The all-American stud growled. "Hands off, fella."

Only by the grace of God and an extra portion of willpower was Nancy able to keep from uncrossing her long legs for this stranger—what did he say his name was?—inviting him in.

"I'm with . . ." she whimpered.

Devlin's hand went under her skirt.

"Cut that out," the all-American stud demanded.

Devlin's hand had a life of its own; completely out of sight now.

"Oh," Nancy cooed. "Oh, oh."

"Ah, shit," said the all-American stud, grumbling and grunting, shifting into an awkward fighting stance. A long roundhouse of a right came from far out of the west.

Drunk as he was, distracted by the moist warmth between Nancy's thighs as he was, Devlin had no difficulty avoiding the blow. He came around in a crouch, striking hard, in tight combinations. He hit the all-American stud four quick blows to the face. Blood began to flow from the all-American nose and from his mouth, and when he spit shards of teeth went flying. Devlin punched him in the belly, which doubled him up, then popped him a straight right on the jaw. Down he went.

Devlin addressed the long-legged blonde. "Another time, maybe." And then he was out of there before any of the all-American stud's pals could gang up on him. He took the long way round to where he had left the blue Jeep, singing show tunes, telling himself that life wasn't so bad after all. That, all things considered, he was really a great guy. But he didn't believe it. Not for a minute.

31

"*THE* Sharps house!" Peggy Pearce was alarmed and said so. She squinted at Ricketts, then Daly. "It won't work."

"I think it will," Ricketts said. He was pleased with himself and his preparation. From memory he had drawn a floor plan of the house. "Sam and me, we can pull this one off."

"You don't understand," Peggy protested. "Sharps works out of the house. He's on the premises a great deal of the time." She didn't care what they did, once she was out of Aspen. Until then they were a threat to her welfare. Neither one of them would be able to withstand a police interrogation. They would incriminate everybody: herself, Devlin, Evan Larson. They would all end up behind bars. "Another thing," she continued, looking for some way to put a halter on the two men. "All those weapons. Sharps owns guns, he is an experienced marksman. He'll blow you guys away."

Sam Daly let loose a peal of laughter, a rising sound that added to Peggy's fright. "Little sauce to spice things up." He spoke in a delicately tinted voice, pitched high, the voice of a man out of touch with the real world. It was obvious that he was past the point of caring what happened to him; to any of them. Danger was an inexorable attraction to him. Getting caught no longer mattered. Being shot at, or killed, or killing someone else; all of it excited him.

"You guys go waltzing into that house and there is Sharps waiting for you, some kind of a cannon pointed your way. You won't like it. He'll blow you both into the next county."

"Maybe not," Ricketts said without alarm.

"No way," Daly said. "He's an old man. I'll punch him out . . . bang, bang, just like that. We tie him up, we blindfold him, we help ourselves to the goods."

"Jewels," Ricketts said, the word rolling out of his mouth like some sweetish bonbon. "Cash. The gun collection. And furs—I counted nine different coats, worth a fortune."

"The paintings," Daly said with rising excitement. "Don't forget the paintings."

"That's crazy."

"Sam spoke to Larson. He's got a connection with an art guy from Philadelphia. He'll fly out to Denver when we deliver. We are talking big sums here, Peggy."

"I've got a bad feeling about this one."

"This one job could make us all rich," Ricketts said.

"I told you, after the Mexican maid . . . I am finished. You guys are nothing but trouble."

"Suit yourself," Daly said. "Maybe Devlin wants to take one last shot at making some real dough."

"Don't tell me," Peggy said. "You guys are on your own."

Daly's grin was lopsided, a little crazy. "That's the way it's best."

"She's right about the guns," Ricketts said when they were alone.

"We get to him fast enough, it don't matter."

"And if we don't?"

"This job, it's too rich to quit on."

"It could be a problem."

"Not if we go in carrying."

"A gun, you mean?"

"No reason why not."

"We don't have a gun."

"Yeah, that is a problem," said Sam Daly.

Sharps sat behind the desk in the room in the Aspen house he used as an office. Brown leather sofas and chairs, a large Bokhara on the floor, bookcases covering three of the walls, and a display of antique dueling pistols on the fourth. He was dressed in a flannel suit with a shadow stripe made for him in England, a silk shirt with vertical bands of pink and chartreuse, and a dark wool tie. His hairless scalp shone in the natural light as if burnished. His Oriental eyes, with their dirty little secrets, fastened on Suzanne Brody.

"Well?" he said.

"The money was delivered an hour ago. One million dollars in fifties and one hundreds. That much in cash, it's an impressive sight."

Sharps dropped a hand on an imported leather attaché case on his desk. He undid the solid-brass fastenings and lifted the lid.

"Another half million," he remarked. "All new bills. A soothing reminder of what my real worth is. And it sometimes comes in handy in an emergency." He dropped the lid back in place and locked it. "How did he react?"

"Modestly. Either he was in awe of all that money or used to having it around. I couldn't tell which." It was meant as a small display of humor.

Sharps didn't laugh. Sharps seldom laughed, and when he did it was brief, controlled, mirthless. Very little in life amused Sharps. Brody hurried to span the silent gap. "He said he thought matters could be concluded favorably."

"When?"

"Next session of the general assembly. Tacked on to some complicated bill. A bill without sex appeal, was the way he put it. A bill that won't attract much public attention. That way debate is kept at a minimum and most objections can be dealt with in the back rooms. He seems convinced he can arrange for a small majority in the assembly."

"An optimistic man, the state chairman."

"Confident."

"He can afford to be, since it's my money that's doing the job."

"Speaking of money—additional expense money, was the way he put it."

"How much?"

"Five million."

"The man's greed is growing by leaps and bounds."

"He's the linchpin in this affair, Mr. Sharps. A casino in Aspen, it will alter the entire economy of the state."

Sharps made a low, inarticulate sound in contemplation. "Keep working on the local people, the mayor, the zoning people. Without their support . . ." His voice faded into silence.

"Will do. Ralph Gaffney mentioned a referendum . . ."

"No. Must be avoided at all costs. Too many do-gooders around. Animal rights nuts. Environmentalists. Leftover hippies and peaceniks from the sixties. No telling which way they'd vote."

"And Mr. Ayres?"

"I'm dealing directly with him. I'm going to double my offer. No way that old man is going to turn me down. No way."

32

$S\,H\,A\,R\,P\,S$ had dressed carefully for the occasion, buttressed against the cold. Long silk underwear under double-weight trousers, a turtleneck wool sweater, and a flannel shirt. Two pairs of socks inside of lined boots to keep his feet warm. Over it all, a sheepskin coat and a trooper's hat to protect his naked scalp. A long wool scarf was wrapped around his neck, tugged up over the lower half of his face. He didn't want to be recognized.

He positioned himself in the shadowed doorway of an empty shop diagonally opposite the Aspen Sports Association, watching men and women enter and depart. All that energy wasted; work hard, he silently advised those fitness buffs, and then work harder. That's all there is, all that counts. And the payoff is worth the effort.

He stamped his feet against the cold and rocked from side to side, loathing the debilitating weather but willing to deal with it. This, after all, was another detail that required his personal attention.

Devlin appeared. Tall, hunched against the night wind, moving on slightly stiff legs in distinctive, mincing steps. Sharps gave him a short head start before hurrying after him. At the corner he called out, for his ears alone, "Devlin!"

He stopped, not looking back, recognizing the voice, the inevitability of Sharps's presence. He lifted his chin in a conscious act of defiance. "Mr. Sharps," he said.

"Let's walk, Devlin. To your car. Is it winterized?"

"Heated, yes."

"Good."

Devlin directed the blue Jeep aimlessly around town, turning finally toward the airport. He pulled in at the diner. "I could use some coffee."

"Keep driving," Sharps commanded. "It won't do for us to be seen together."

Devlin obeyed. Ten interminable minutes passed before the older man spoke again. "Tomorrow night."

A flood of weakness went through Devlin, and he gripped the wheel tightly for fear he might lose control. Next to him, Sharps sat staring into the passing night, immutable, powerful, righteous. Exercising his infinite authority over Devlin and other men with hardly a word spoken.

"Tomorrow?" Devlin said.

Sharps shifted around in the passenger seat of the

blue Jeep and glared at Devlin. Admiring that perfect profile, sensing the messiness it so successfully concealed. He broke the silence in a low, insistent voice. "Tomorrow night. You're going to kill my wife for me tomorrow night."

Sweat broke out across Devlin's shoulders, and his mouth went dry. There. At last it was said, plainly, directly, impossible to misunderstand. This is the way Sharps did all his business.

"That's crazy. I'm not about to kill anyone. No one."

"We made a deal."

"No. No deal. Just some hypothetical bull about life and death. Just sophomoric jawing about greed. About the exercise of power. Talk, that's all it was."

"A verbal contract is what we made."

"No. I'm not a killer."

"Of course you are. Given the right circumstances. 'Nam, for example. You did a great deal of killing there."

"That was something else, war."

"We discussed it in considerable detail the night of my party."

"Party talk. Liquor talking."

"I don't think so. You understood the full thrust of my words. My intentions. Now to specifics."

"You are crazy."

"You're going to do this for me."

"I . . . I can't."

"Of course you can. You will. You must. That's the point of the exercise, to practice self-discipline under stress. Grace under pressure, is what Hemingway called it. It's the payment; you're disappointed in the amount. No problem. We'll adjust it upward. The money is yours, plus a position with one of my companies. There's always a number of openings available. You make the choice. A lifetime proposition. A good starting salary, medical benefits, and an outstanding retirement program. Life insurance. Paid holidays. Here's your chance to straighten out your life, to go straight. Offers this good don't come along every day."

Sharps's words were an assault, a cascade of stinging blows, dulling his senses, escalating his confusion. He stuttered, rummaging around in his cluttered brain for the right words.

"You want to hire me to murder your wife?"

"That's straightforward enough. Call it a professional assignment. A free-lance job. Call it an investment in your own future. Call it anything you like, as long as you get it done."

"Why?"

The question took Sharps by surprise. "Why? You mean, why do I want Geneva dead? Oh, let's say that she's become an intolerable burden to me."

"Okay. Divorce her, then."

"If only it were that simple. But, no, she's become willful, obstinate, unwilling to go along. She frustrates my business interests, keeps me from growing, from moving ahead. Spoils my plans. You can see that she gives me no choice. No choice." He was breathing hard and took a moment or two to calm himself.

He went on. "Consider the logic of my position, Devlin. Geneva doesn't deserve the rewards of being my wife. Doesn't deserve half my money, my businesses, a say over everything I do. Not after the way she's treated me."

Devlin swung the blue Jeep back toward Aspen. It was time to rid himself of this crazy old man with his delusions of absolute power.

"You've met Geneva," Sharps went on, a contrived note of regret in his voice. "She's a beautiful woman, and very few men can deny her anything. She's shrewd, she's wicked, and Devlin, there's a great deal you can't know about her.

"For example, she denies me the comfort of the marital bed, and has for many, many years. And she flaunts her lovers, taunts me with their sexual capacities, insists I was never good for her. No man should have to suffer that.

"There's more. She refused to have children. Had her tubes tied to make sure of it. Kept it to herself until years after our wedding day. She is using up the best part of my life and a considerable portion of my wealth. Her extravagant whims, her ridiculously expensive baubles, her lovers . . .

"Shall I continue to go on this way, tortured, with no relief in sight? Help me, Devlin. Do this for me and I will be forever in your debt." Out of the deep pocket of his sheepskin coat, he brought an eight-by-ten brown manila envelope. He placed it on the dashboard where Devlin could see it while he drove. "There it is, tool of the trade. Not much good for hunting, but made for close work. This one has no provenance. No previous owner of record. No way to connect it to me. Or to you. I think of it as an orphan weapon." Sharps glanced out the window. They were back in Aspen now, cruising along Durant Avenue. "Make a left at the next street and let me off. My car's only a block away."

The blue Jeep rolled to a stop. "I'm a skier," Devlin said with all the firmness he could muster. "Maybe a ski bum is what I am. Not much good for anything. But I'm not a killer for hire."

It was as though Devlin hadn't spoken. Sharps took his gloved hand in both of his, staring into Devlin's eyes. "Tomorrow night. Be there about midnight. I'll be in my room, in bed, asleep. Or so Geneva will believe. She, I promise you, will be fully awake. This is a woman who requires only a few hours of sleep a night. She'll be in the entertainment center watching a movie on the VCR.

"There's a black leather sofa facing the TV screen. Put the revolver to her head and squeeze down on the trigger. That's all there is to it.

"At the far end of the sofa there is a cube table. Put pressure on the rear panel and it will swing open. Inside, a safe. It will be unlocked, I'll make sure of that. That's where you'll find the money. Twenty-five thousand dollars in cash. Take it. Take Geneva's jewelry, anything else you can carry. Make it look like an ordinary burglary. That's what the police will believe."

Devlin felt trapped, his hand in the other man's steady grip. How strong Sharps was for a man his age—how old was he?—how amazingly fit. How clever and far thinking. Plotting out what seemed to be a perfect crime, a crime planned by the victim herself. Devlin could find no flaw in the scheme; Sharps was too damned smart to overlook a thing.

Sharps was still speaking, providing a step-by-step scenario. "Park your Jeep on the road, pointed down the hill, toward town. Come up the driveway on foot. Keep to the shadows of the trees. Circle the garage and you'll be alongside the pool room. There's a door in the east wall. It will be unlocked. There will be light enough for you to see your way. . . ."

That shimmering green light from the lap pool. Devlin could almost see Geneva naked in the pool, inviting him to join her. The scent of her had been tinged with chlorine, and oh, the sweet, womanly taste of her.

Sharps went on. "From the pool room, into the mud room and a short corridor that leads to the kitchen. That will take you to the dining room and the large sitting room. You'll see two doors, both on your left. Take the first one, the first door. Across the back hallway and into the entertainment center. Enter quietly and she won't hear you. Put the gun to her head and finish her off. Collect your very deserved reward and get out." Sharps paused, looked at Devlin inquiringly.

When Devlin didn't speak, Sharps allowed himself a small smile. "Where will Sharps be? you're asking yourself. Good question. Shows you're thinking right. I told you, in bed. Ostensibly asleep. But the sound of the shot, bound to wake even a heavy sleeper, which I am not, by the way. This is the heart of the plan, to make it look good in the suspicious eyes of the law.

"Bang. I wake up. Still half-asleep. Afraid. I'll call out for my beloved wife. 'Geneva! Geneva!' When there is no answer, I'll get out of bed, put on a robe, and reach into the drawer of my night table for the personal weapon I keep close by for just such emergencies. A Glock seventeen. I'm licensed to carry it in six states. A superb development, the Glock. Made almost entirely of plastic, it's lightweight and virtually

impervious to detection by the devices used for airport security.

"Pistol in hand, I'll go out onto the balcony over-
looking the entrance foyer. 'Geneva!' Still no reply. By
then you will have emptied the safe. Bring along a
small bag for all your treasures. Head on out the way
you came. Hurrying now, you'll make no effort to muf-
fle your footsteps. Will you remember all this?"

"Every word."

"Good. I'll be descending the staircase. Suddenly,
off to one side, a movement. A shadow, perhaps. Or
is it the intruder? A threat to my life and the life of
my wife. There have been a rash of house burglaries
in Aspen recently. One unfortunate young woman was
murdered. As I said, I'll be nervous, afraid. I point the
Glock and fire.

"You'll be nowhere around by then. In the pool
room, maybe outside, on your way to the Jeep and to
safety. No one will see you, Devlin. No one will be able
to make an identification. You're free and clear.

"As for my shot. No need to fret over that. I'll fire
high. While ordinarily I'm an excellent marksman, my
nerves have betrayed me on this occasion. The police
will understand."

Sharps spread his hands, his manner cheerful and
encouraging. "There you have it. Not a single flaw
from start to finish. As long as you follow my instructions. We'll hold the funeral here in Aspen, Geneva's
beloved Aspen. Many important people will want to
pay their respects.

"Let's give it two weeks, Devlin. At which point
someone from my organization will contact you and
offer you a job. We'll have to allow a reasonable period

before you go on the payroll, of course. No more than six months. If you're agreeable, that is. You'll be launched into a new career, Devlin. A new life. A new world. A member of the chosen few. The elite men and women who sit at the top of the social and economic pyramid. The good life will be yours, my friend. Worry free. Are there any questions, Devlin?"

It was etched into Devlin's face. In the truculent tilt of his chin, his unsatisfied suspicion and wariness, the dislike he felt for the other man.

Sharps moved to allay his fears. "Don't you trust me, Devlin?"

Devlin considered his answer. "Don't be silly."

"Neither a yes nor a no. No matter. We're partners, Devlin, from this moment on. Tied together for life. Now, I must leave you. It's about time I was getting home. I wouldn't want Geneva worrying about me. . . ."

33

A MAGNIFICENT object, the revolver Sharps had given Devlin. A .38-caliber Smith & Wesson five-shot with a two-inch barrel. Shining and solid in his hand. Form followed function; an exquisitely crafted blend of aesthetics and mechanics. He sighted along the barrel and tightened his finger on the trigger.

Click.

He reached for the bullets that rested so innocently on the bed where he had dropped them earlier. How devoid of weight, how insignificant they were; how charged with incipient threat. The snubbed nose, the mix of metallic shadings, the power. Always the power. To destroy. To maim. To kill. Flesh torn and shredded. Bones shattered and splintered. Internal organs battered beyond repair.

And, oh, the pain.

The nickeled skin of the weapon gleamed seductively in the light of the bed lamp. Points of enticing light glittered and danced. No more perfect piece of the sculptor's art existed anywhere, he assured himself. No instrument conceived by the mind of man was so efficient and reliable, with such a minute expenditure of energy. No wonder Sharps loved weapons so. He sighted down the barrel once more.

Click.

He whirled and fired from the hip.

Click.

He shoved the .38 under his belt, for fast draw.

Click.

He allowed his eyes to flutter shut. And a vision of danger rose up out of the darkness. His enemy, advancing with intent to do him harm. To kill him. In his mind, he raised the revolver into firing position.

Click. Click. Click.

His eyes snapped open and reality came rushing at him. A rhythmic summons at his door. Feathery, almost, the tapping of meticulously maintained fingernails. He placed the Smith & Wesson under his pillow, and the bullets, and fluffed the pillow. He opened the door.

Geneva.

She stepped quickly into the room, closing the door behind her. Her arms went around him and she covered his face with kisses, mouth coming to rest finally on his own, her lips a miracle of tenderness, her tongue overheated and edgy, never still.

"I can't stay away from you."

He separated himself from her. "Sharps and I, we had a small talk last night."

She cocked her head. "About me?"

"About you. The details don't matter anymore. What's true, what isn't. None of that matters anymore."

She watched him warily, weighing her next move. Had Sharps gotten to him at last? Whose side was he finally on? She commanded herself to an increased state of readiness. Take nothing for granted, not with this man. Not with any of them. "What does matter, Dev?" She said it quietly, careful not to give offense.

Devlin went over to the bed and brought the nickel-plated .38 out from under his pillow, a precious and delicate object. He cradled it in the palm of one hand, as if fearful of causing it damage, causing some terrible alteration to its graceful curves and angles. She pulled away as if struck.

"Where did you get it?"

"Sharps." He told of her of his conversation with her husband, word for word, omitting nothing. "There it is," he ended. "Sharps expects me to kill you."

She squeezed her eyes shut, hands in a prayerful pose. When finally she looked at him again, she was pale and shaken. "Then do it," she said. "Do it now and get it over with. I don't care anymore. If you don't trust me . . ."

"You and Sharps, both of you talk so easily about trust."

"You're right. Maybe neither of us deserves your trust. Maybe neither one of us is worthy of your love or your friendship. You've said that you love me, Dev.

Do you? Really love me? Can't you see what he's doing to us? Driving us apart. He wants me dead, needs me dead. A devil's trick on his part, and you're supposed to be his assistant."

"I'm not as dumb as either of you seems to think I am."

"Then do it, Dev. Come to the house tonight. Just the way Duncan wants you to. He's right, I'll be awake, watching a movie. He's right, I have trouble sleeping. Life with Duncan leaves me empty and miserable. If I'm lucky, if the movie is bad enough, I'll fall asleep on the couch with the film still running. Just walk right in and put the gun to my head, pull the trigger. Blow my brains out, Dev. Do Sharps's work. Just one piece of advice—afterward, after you've murdered me, watch out."

"What's that supposed to mean?"

"Do you believe for a second he'll go through with his side of the deal? Not Sharps. Not my husband. Check the safe, it will be locked."

"He said—"

"I know what he said. That's the way Duncan operates. That's when you'll know for sure that you've been duped, only it'll be too late. Sharps will appear with a gun of his own. . . ."

"You think he means to shoot me?"

"He never misses. He won't this time. He'll kill you as surely as you will have killed me. Only then will he summon the police and tell them he's shot the burglar who just murdered his beloved wife. He'll be properly distraught when they arrive. He may even weep. Sharps can deliver an extraordinary performance when called upon to do so. And while he's lamenting my passing, he'll gloat over his victory. Another deal done in his favor. At the same time, he's gotten rid of a troublesome wife and the only person who can connect him to my murder. He'll be a hero and go scot free."

"Unless I shoot Sharps first. That's the idea, isn't it?"

"It was your idea, Dev. Remember that."

He ignored the remark. "And if I do shoot him, how can I be sure you won't do the same thing to me?"

She waved his words aside. "Oh, I don't care anymore. Do it, Devlin, Sharps's way. Follow his instructions. But no matter what you finally decide, remember that I love you. I'll always love you."

She kissed him briefly, then a more lingering kiss. And without haste, she made love to him, tenderly and at length, refusing him access to her own body. And when she was ready, she went to the door, spoke without facing him.

"Come to the house tonight, Dev. Around midnight. I'll be waiting for you. Sharps and I both will."

Minutes later, suffused in sadness and regret, he began to drink Scotch, like an insatiable infant, straight out of the bottle.

34

"I'VE made up my mind, Mr. Sharps."

"Good. What have you decided, Mr. Ayres?"

Ayres hawked his throat clear. A man who, from Duncan Sharps's point of view, took too long to get to the heart of the matter. *He* was a man who always placed himself strategically close to a deal, ready to close. From where he sat, Ayres still looked like a general under siege, unwilling or unable to break out of his self-imposed trap, waiting for events to catch up with him.

Ayres said, "Never was much for gabbing over the telephone. Prefer to do my business face to face."

Sharps could find no fault with that. He was anxious to make the deal, get Ayres's approval on the record.

What other way could the old man go? Sharps was offering top dollar for his land.

"The Jerome bar okay with you?"

"In twenty minutes, Mr. Sharps."

Ayres was hunched over a Coors when Sharps got there. They shook hands, and a waiter set a Coors in front of Sharps. He leaned back in his chair and examined Ayres. Nothing showed in that ancient visage. It was a poker player's face, an empty mask, with those all-seeing bird's eyes staring out across the table. The cards, Sharps knew, were all that talked in this game.

"Best to say it straight, Mr. Sharps. I have decided not to turn my land over to you, sir."

Sharps kept his temper in check. The old man was running a last-minute bluff, trying to build up the pot. Okay, if that's the way he wanted to play.

"Name your price, Marlon."

"I'll say it again—I ain't gonna sell to you."

Sharps was not a man who gave up easily. "The land's for sale, right? You're entitled to make a profit. Calculate what that is and I'll meet your price." The old man was too prickly, too direct, to be a wheeler-dealer. He didn't know how to hold his cards close to his vest. "Name it," Sharps commanded.

"Thing is, I take a dim view of gambling."

Sharps fought the urge to curse Ayres out, to make plain what an insignificant creature he was next to Duncan Turner Sharps. How dare he stand in the way of *his* ambitions.

He rubbed his scalp. He played with his mustache. He arranged a placating smile on his lips. "What's all this about gambling? I am talking about putting up a hotel. Best of everything. Comfort. Convenience. Satisfaction guaranteed."

"With a casino," Ayres insisted.

Sharps rolled his head as if to loosen the muscles that held it in place. "You've been listening to my competitors. What those people say isn't necessarily so."

"Don't get me wrong, Mr. Sharps. A friendly game of one-eyed jacks or stud poker, I ain't against them. Won and lost my share over the years in my own kitchen. But a casino—no sir."

"I want that land, Marlon."

"A casino is bound to turn this precious piece of God's own country into another honky-tonk, Mr. Sharps. Drunks, drugs, those gangster types. I won't be a party to that."

"Suppose I up my offer another million."

"For you, Mr. Sharps, it's all about money. For me, it's more'n that. And less."

"Gambling's illegal in Colorado." Sharps's voice was high-pitched and thin. He had to restrain the impulse to wrap his hands around the old man's scrawny, wrinkled neck. "No way I can buck that."

"Maybe, maybe not. The kind of money you throw around. Money has a way of getting things done. But not with my help. Not on my land."

"Make it another million, Marlon. Nobody's gonna come up with that kind of money for four measly acres."

Ayres exhaled. "There you are, sir. No matter how hard I try, I can't bring myself to where I like you. Or respect you, sir. There's a mean streak in you, Mr. Sharps. Always got to have your own way, you do. Far as I can see, you are not respectful of these mountains, or of the folks who make their homes out here. No, Mr. Sharps, no. We are not about to do any business, you and me. No siree."

Sharps leaned across the table, his hands clenched into hard, lumpy fists. "Who? Who you selling to? The Japs? Some big-shot developer from back east? Trump, maybe. Or an Arab sheik? I'll match whatever any of them offer. We can still deal, Marlon."

Ayres drained the rest of the beer out of his glass. He stood up and dropped a bill on the table. Sharps watched him walk out into the late afternoon gloom in a rolling gait that made his bow legs more prominent. Ayres never took even a single backward glance.

Devlin paid no attention as the light of day faded from his room. He struggled to remember when he had begun drinking, the hour, the day; it remained a blur in his mind. He emptied the last of the Scotch from the bottle in hand. Had he actually downed a fifth of Scotch without help? He located another bottle on the shelf in his closet, opened it, and brought it back to bed with him.

He put it aside and took the nickel-plated revolver into his hand. The butt fit so snugly in his grasp, finger hooked over the trigger. He sighted into the closing darkness and squeezed the trigger.

Click.

A human head, shaggy and vulnerable, materialized in front of him. Once more he fired, and the head exploded. Brains and blood, bits of bone, filled the air in a widening spray. What remained of the head rocked backward in response to the deadly assault.

He blinked. There was no head. No blood obscuring

his vision. Only the stench of death and the weapon. So terrible and ugly in his fist.

He rushed out into the hallway and made it to the toilet just in time. A rush of sour refuse came rocketing out of his belly. He gasped, he groaned, until at last the spasms subsided. He washed his face with cold water. Weakened by the onslaught, he stumbled back into his room, rinsed his mouth with Scotch, and swallowed. His brain tipped and tilted, and he fell back onto the bed.

Held in bondage by self-pity, he fought to clear his mind. To consider his predicament. How far he had fallen. Brought low by circumstances and events and emotions he still did not fully comprehend. Geneva was the cause of it all. He was helpless before her beauty, the repeated demands and rewards of her perfect body, obsessed as never before by a woman.

Sharps extended the equation. Sharps, who made him feel helpless and weak, of little significance, prepared to do his bidding lest he fall short in Sharps's eyes. What would it take to be accepted by Sharps? To measure up? To be just like him?

Devlin drank from the bottle. So much of his life— too much of it—had failed to leave him proud. The burglaries, for example. The hustles he'd run. The way he'd dealt with women, all those trusting, often loving, women. The bullying and beatings he'd delivered to people too weak to defend themselves against him.

But never killed.

Never murdered on order. Not for love, not for money. Never needed to, nor wanted to.

Another long pull on the bottle. He lay back, head

on the pillow, placing the bottle on the floor. He allowed his eyes to close.

Geneva. Unlike any woman he'd ever encountered. Just her touch caused him to cry out, to quiver in anticipation, to convulse with pleasure. She satisfied him as no woman ever had; and yet he never got enough of her. She had become vital to his continued well-being.

If only Sharps would go. Vanish from the earth. Gone and forgotten. A burden lifted from mankind's weary shoulders.

Sharps was unique. Different, difficult, disturbingly mean-spirited. Beyond Devlin's capacity to comprehend or to cope with. He wormed his way back into the darkest crevices of his brain for a solution. Examining the options still open to him.

He wanted to choose.

The right thing.

His hand fell off to one side, coming to rest on the revolver. Offended by its nearness, he pushed it away. What would his mother think? How odd to think of her now. That woman who had never approved of anything he'd ever done, had never approved of him. How he had longed for her approval.

A low, despairing sound seeped across his lips, and he rolled, as if to escape his memories, back toward that beautiful, deadly presence with him on the bed. And in an otherwise empty moment before he fell asleep, an answer came. *The* answer. And he assured himself that in the end everything was going to be all right. Everything.

35

$\mathcal{S}$ *HARPS* spent most of the evening on the telephone. He spoke to Senator Arlen Hamilton, ordering him to redouble his efforts to influence his colleagues in the general assembly. "I want that gambling legislation," he insisted.

Hamilton said, "I'm trying, Duncan, really I am. I spoke to Ralph Gaffney, and he tells me we're making progress. Only these things take time."

"I don't have a lot of time."

Next Sharps called his subordinates in New York, in London, in Rio de Janeiro, marshaling his forces. He called Suzanne Brody, dyspeptic and peevish, issuing instructions and brooking no dispute.

"Find out what other parcels of land are available in Aspen."

"There isn't much. The demand has—"

"Do it and get back to me. If it has to be, I'll build outside of town. No way shoe clerks and chicken farmers are going to stand in my way."

He slammed down the phone and checked his watch. It was past eleven o'clock; time to shift gears. From its place in his desk drawer, he retrieved the Glock 17. He checked the clip and, satisfied, snapped a round into the chamber. He made sure the safety was on before slipping the weapon into the pocket of his smoking jacket.

In the pool room, he unlocked the door. He went through the house turning off lights. Certain strategically placed lamps would turn on and off during the night, activated by electric timers.

As expected, Geneva was in the entertainment center. Curled up on the leather sofa, modestly dressed in a floor-length robe over a flannel nightgown. She was sipping tea from a ceramic mug and watching a movie: *Ninotchka,* with Greta Garbo and Melvyn Douglas. She had a penchant for old films.

"I'm hitting the sack," Sharps announced.

Without looking away from the TV screen, she said, "Good night, Duncan."

"That's a good picture. I saw it a long time ago."

"Yes. Very good."

He walked out of the entertainment center on slippered feet, and she heard him climb to his bedroom on the floor above. On the screen, Garbo and Douglas were about to kiss; Geneva hardly noticed. She had other, more important things on her mind. This, after all, was the most important night of her life.

*   *   *

Devlin slept fitfully. Thrashing around in protest against the frightening images that inhabited his unconscious, resisting the impulse to wake. In oblivion there was comfort and safety, at least for a while.

A distant sound caused him to stir and mumble in response. The door of the room opened partially, a rectangle of light leading Peggy Pearce to the side of his bed. She sniffed in distaste and wondered what she had ever seen in this man.

"I'm on my way, Dev," she announced.

He made an unintelligible answer.

"I'm going to be a star, Dev. In L.A. This man, he's a producer, he's going to build a singing group around me. I'm going to live in his house, Dev. On the beach, at Malibu. Everything I've ever wanted. No more scratching for nickels and dimes. We're flying out of here tonight, by private jet. I owe it all to you, Dev. Taking me to that party New Year's Eve. I wanted you to know. . . ."

His eyes rolled open, then fastened shut again. "I'm sick," she thought he said.

Mists of stale alcohol rose up from him, and she recoiled. She was about to leave when something shiny caught her attention; the nickel-plated thirty-eight. Her breathing went faster.

"Sick," she murmured. "Sure. Wish me luck, Dev, and look for me on MTV." She backed out of the room, taking the revolver and the five bullets with her.

Some deeper need raised him out of the semi-drugged sleep. He lay without moving, willing the sleep to return, to shield him off once more. It did not happen. Instead, his mind began to function. He recalled Peggy Pearce. What had she wanted?

He swung up into a sitting position in an unplanned movement. His head felt as if it had remained on the pillow. There was a throbbing behind his eyes and a persistent ache at the base of his skull.

He tried to remember; something of significance. His brain refused to respond; memory failed him.

He checked his watch. Nearly midnight. It made no difference, he was going no place. He lurched out of the open door into the hallway, toward the bathroom. Something was wrong. He never left the door to his room ajar; unlocked, yes, but never open. In the bathroom he swallowed four aspirin tablets and let cold water run into the sink. When it was full he plunged his face into the icy pool, shuddering at the shock. He repeated the process twice more before drying himself off, going back to his room.

He stood at the side of the bed, looking down. Something *was* wrong. Something was missing. The gun. Sharps's beautiful gun. He felt for it on the bed, under the pillow, on the floor. It was gone. And the open door meant he'd had a visitor.

Peggy Pearce, come to bid him good-bye. She had Sharps's gun; why had she taken it? She had always shied away from weapons before. Understanding came slowly; she had passed it on to Ricketts and Daly, a last gift to them, providing Sam Daly with the firepower he had always lusted for.

So be it. Relief flooded the cavities of his brain. Without a gun, there could be no killing. Not by his hand. Sharps and Geneva were both safe.

Always had been, he told himself. No way he would

have killed. Not for money and not for love. Two of a kind, Sharps and Geneva. Joined in unholy wedlock. Meant for each other in life and in death. They deserved each other.

The finely crafted, shining .38.

Sam Daly would surely use it, the edge he'd always longed for on a job. He went to their room and knocked; no answer. He tried the knob; the door was locked. He struggled to make sense out of the bits and pieces of information he was able to dredge out of his disordered brain. Gradually it came together.

They were headed for Sharps's house. Where husband and wife, unbeknownst to each other, were expecting Devlin to do their killing for them. Geneva, certain that Devlin could never do her harm. And Sharps, waiting for the murder he believed his money had purchased. Waiting to fire that defensive shot at Devlin, to relieve himself of all unwanted burdens.

Ricketts and Daly. They would do the burglary, they would confront Geneva, and then Sharps. There would be shooting and bloodshed. Someone was bound to be killed. And he, John Thomas Andrew Devlin, would be as guilty as any of them.

36

D ESPERATION drove Devlin. And sobered him. Eased the pounding inside his skull. Donning a ski jacket against the freezing night air, he went out to where the blue Jeep was parked, got it started after a brief battle with the battery, and turned it toward Aspen, driving too fast.

A light snow had begun to fall, and he hunched forward, squinting into the white night, braced for imminent disaster. A woman's laughter came from a house as he went by; he didn't hear it. A cry of anger and frustration. The rich sounds of a Beethoven sonata. He heard none of it.

The Jeep went into a skid, the rear end making a strong effort to catch up with and pass the front. He fought the wheel and managed to make it out of the skid. He went on, determined to reach his destination in time.

In the Sharps house, lights burned behind draped and shaded windows. He left the Jeep on the road and ran up the driveway. He was almost to the house when the first shots ripped through the darkness. Three of them, unhurried, meticulously spaced. He cried out, "Geneva!" and ran faster. Around to the back of the house and onto the deck, into the pool room, advancing more cautiously now. He was in the kitchen when two more shots rang out, a cleaner, more authoritative sound; Sharps's shining .38.

He made himself go forward, stepping tentatively into the long living room, and saw them all at once. Frozen in a tableau of death and life. Hank Ricketts sprawled on his back, limbs awkward, staring sightlessly at the high ceiling. Close by, Sam Daly was rolled up on his side in a fetal position, blood running from a wound above his ear. Near the entrance to the front foyer, Duncan Turner Sharps. Back against the wall, slumped clumsily, bleeding profusely from a hole in his chest.

Devlin hurried to his side. The Oriental eyes were dull, his cheeks drained of color, a pale, spectral version of his former self. When Devlin said his name, some of the old force and fire returned to his eyes. "Geneva," he husked out. "Geneva . . ." And then he died.

Devlin shoved himself erect and looked around. Where was Geneva? Had she too been shot? Had she managed to stumble away from the carnage only to die elsewhere? Her name was the last sound Sharps had made. Was it a plea for forgiveness? Was it a warning? A cry for help? As if in answer, Geneva appeared out of the entertainment center.

Devlin said her name, relief in his voice, in the spread of his arms. "Thank God you're all right."

She raised her chin, and the slight movement froze him in place. Only then did he notice the gun in her hand. Dark and ominous, pointed steadily at his belt buckle; the Glock 17. A quick sideways glance and he spotted the nickel-plated revolver—*his* weapon—still in Sam Daly's oversize right hand.

"You shot them?" he said to Geneva, more in admiration than accusation.

Her lips moved in what a stranger might have characterized as a smile. But there was no levity in her. No warmth, no compassion. She spoke in a voice like dry ice.

"That was Duncan's doing. The poor fools never had a chance. He was ready, you see, with this." She gestured with the Glock 17. "These two, did you send them in your place? Is that it, Dev, you lost your nerve? Who were they after, Duncan or me? No matter, it's done now."

"I made up my mind not to come at all. Not to kill for you. Or for your husband."

"Ah, Dev, what a noble creature you are. An upstanding citizen. A pillar of the community, almost."

"I'm not a murderer."

"Yet here you are. And there's been much killing, careless killing, if not murder. Tell me, how did they get your gun?" Her smile was fleeting. "Sharps's gun, of course. You gave it to them?"

"They discovered it, they took it. By the time I

found out they had it, it was too late. They intended to rob you. I came to try and stop them."

"So much failure, yours and theirs."

Devlin took in the bloody scene, imagined what had taken place in this room. "Sharps surprised them, I suppose, and Daly shot him. Is that the way it happened?"

"Very good, Dev. The way you assess the circumstances, your deductive reasoning, the way you piece it all together. That's what you're supposed to think. That's what the police will think when they arrive." She flicked the Glock 17, indicating he was to retreat, herding him into position not far from the bodies of Ricketts and Daly. "It was," she drawled, "the perfect opportunity. For me, that is. Duncan shot your friends before they had a chance to do any damage. He was standing just about where he is now. When I heard the shots, I came into the room, saw what had happened, and realized that here was my big chance. I knelt down next to the big one, as if to take his pulse, see if he were still alive. I picked up that lovely little gun and put one right into Duncan's chest. I never told you, did I, that I was an expert markswoman. Duncan taught me, of course. The police will find the thirty-eight in that fool's hand. And me with the Glock, my husband's weapon. The weapon that allowed me to avenge his death. I'll make a first-rate heroine, Dev, don't you think? A woman who fought to protect husband and home. Depend on it, I'll make a very convincing widow."

He watched her with fascination. He saw her arm raise up, wrist supported by her other hand, in a classic shooter's stance, deliberately bringing the weapon to bear. It was all so simple. She meant to kill him, too, claim he had been party to the break-in. His time had run out.

He dived to the floor just as she fired. He scrambled up, running as fast as he could. Another shot went whirring past his ear. Through the kitchen, the mud room, along the lap pool, and into the white night. Slipping and sliding as he charged off the deck onto the sloping driveway, falling once, but keeping his forward momentum, until he came to where the blue Jeep sat waiting.

He almost got away. Would have, too, if not for the prowl car pulling into place, blocking his way out of there. And a second car. Flashers spinning, the uniformed officers positioning themselves behind the open doors on the driver's side, pistols drawn, identifying themselves, calling upon him to halt. To raise his hands. Telling him he was under arrest. Reciting his constitutional rights.

He lifted his eyes to the high peaks, so solid and eternal in the night, among God's most majestic creations. Never again would he glide down those slopes. He had made his last run. It was all over.

37

D UNCAN Turner Sharps was buried in Red Butte Cemetery. Two hundred people huddled in the cold of a gray Rocky Mountain morning and listened to an Episcopal priest speak of Sharps's accomplishments, his love of the high country, his admiration for Aspen in particular, and his fondness for the great American outdoors in general. At Geneva's request, Suzanne Brody had composed the eulogy.

There were two governors present, four United States senators, and seven members of the U.S. House of Representatives, plus an uncounted number of lesser political figures. A handful of his business competitors showed up—come, it was said with a certain amount of glee, to make certain Sharps was truly dead and put to ground. Press photographers and television cameramen infested the area around the grave-site, vying for more strategic positions from which to shoot.

Geneva made an ideal widow. Dramatically turned out in stylish black, complete with a flimsy lace veil, she was beautiful, emotional, restrained; cast for the role, a Hollywood producer noted with professional cynicism. At her side during the ceremonies, Ralph Gaffney, state chairman of the party, one hand supporting her elbow. Suzanne Brody was always a step behind, watchful and whispering words of advice, making sure everything got off on schedule.

Afterward many of the mourners returned to the Sharps house and consoled themselves on catered food and expensive liquors. Chairman Gaffney drew Suzanne Brody off to one side of the long sitting room, at approximately the spot where Duncan Turner Sharps had expired. He held a mug of hot black coffee in one hand and an unlit cigar in the other. He smiled down at the pale, slender woman who reminded him of one of those alabaster saints you saw in so many Italian churches. He spoke for her ears only.

"Poor Duncan's passing has left some of us with a number of unsolved problems. There are certain unfulfilled obligations, certain unfulfilled promises. Who will be in charge? some people want to know. Make the necessary decisions?"

"Mrs. Sharps has stepped in as chief executive officer of Sharps Industries. It was Duncan's fervent wish—"

"I'm sure it was. And you, my dear?"

"I do whatever I can to help. That's my role. Until such time as—"

"Yes, yes. Let's be a little more specific. You heard that Marlon Ayres sold off his parcel to a Dutch consortium, and that's a fact. There goes Sharps's hotel."

"Unless Mrs. Sharps decides to proceed with the project. In some other location."

"Is that the way she's going?"

"Time will tell."

"I know of a perfect plot, and it's available. Just west of town. Good acreage. Easy access to roads. Fine views."

"And if one were to dig deep enough, who might one find to be the ultimate owner of that plot?"

He peered into her eyes for some sense of what lay behind her words. How much did she already know? Or was she simply making a good guess? He gave up looking; he found nothing. An impenetrable glaze. An emotional wasteland.

"There's going to be a substantial commission for anyone who brought such a sale about. I can virtually guarantee it."

"At the appropriate moment, I'll mention our conversation to Mrs. Sharps."

"You do that. And one more thing. Those videos."

"Videos?"

"Of Red Hamilton. Naturally you know about them."

"What about them?"

"He—and I—would be grateful to whoever could put them into his hands. No need to give the good man an extended hard time, don't you agree, Ms. Brody?"

"Let's allow that to rest for a while. Until after a suitable mourning period. Until the matter of a hotel and casino in Aspen is finally settled, to the satisfaction of all interested parties."

"Of course," he said with a slight incline of his great head.

"Of course," she said, turning away. "If you'll excuse me . . ."

It was nearly four in the afternoon before the last, most enthusiastic of the mourners finally departed. Suzanne Brody hurried the caterers out of there, ordered the cleaning crew to return the next day. Only then did she seek out Geneva in the small sitting room. Geneva, having been on her feet through the entire day, had settled into a high-backed chair, straight and dry-eyed.

Suzanne Brody approached her tentatively, unsure of her professional future. Working for Sharps had been fascinating, and she'd learned a great deal, but she experienced no sense of personal loss. She would, she supposed, have to find another man of Sharps's stature and attach herself to him.

"Is there anything else I can do for you, Mrs. Sharps?" she said.

Geneva lifted her eyes. A little weariness showed, otherwise she displayed no emotion. "You did very nicely, Suzanne, with the funeral, and you were very good with the press."

"Mr. Sharps taught me a great deal."

"Yes. There was much he taught me. What now, Suzanne?"

"I don't understand," Brody said.

"Your future?"

"I haven't been able to take time out to consider

that. The last few days have been so difficult, so emotionally trying . . ."

Geneva took stock of the other woman. Slender, yes, but without any hint of fragility. She stood with her ankles touching, her arms at her sides, very much the good soldier in a stylish black dress with a thin line of scalloped lace at collar and cuffs. And no jewelry. Absolutely correct for the occasion, yet chic and quietly provocative. The kind of woman men often were curious about, asked questions about, but seldom dared to approach. Geneva stood up and, with no change of expression, said, "Do you swim?"

"Swim." The question surprised Brody. "Yes, I am a good swimmer."

"And champagne? I seem to remember you're fond of champagne?"

Brody nodded once.

"Good. You'll find some Moët in the fridge. Fetch a bottle and some glasses and join me in the pool room."

Geneva was floating in the lap pool when Brody appeared. The champagne was uncorked and resting in a silver ice bucket. She placed it, along with the fluted glasses, on a white metal table and poured. Geneva stood up, accepting a glass. They toasted each other silently and drank.

"Swimming is a great antidote for tension," Geneva said. "Whenever I feel the need I do laps until I'm too tired to do anything else." She drained her glass and handed it back to Brody. "Well. If you intend to join me—get undressed."

Brody could hear the echo of Sharps's voice when Geneva spoke. That crispness of command, the unan-

ticipated stops and starts of authority, the verbal dry-
ness that indicated he knew what you were thinking,
what you were feeling.

"Yes," she said. "I'd like that." She shed her clothes
swiftly, controlled, sure fingers working zippers and
hooks with skill. She stood poised at the end of the
pool, as composed and confident naked as she was
fully clothed.

Geneva looked her over with bold curiosity. That
fleshless torso, those long legs, surprisingly well
shaped and muscular, those erect, round breasts. Almost boyish in concept and execution, in the mode of
a Giacometti sculpture, lacking only the artistic exag-
geration.

"All right," Geneva said. "Come in."

They swam without speaking for nearly forty minutes, cutting through the green water at a good pace,
neither straining to get ahead. Neither falling behind.
Geneva stopped first.

"Enough," she said, climbing out of the pool. She
switched on the jets in the hot tub and wrapped herself
in a large white towel while waiting for the bubbling
water to heat. "You've never liked me," she offered
presently.

Brody kept her distance. "My primary loyalty was
to Mr. Sharps."

"And now that he's gone?"

"I'm employed by Sharps Industries, at the moment. That means I work for you, Mrs. Sharps."

"At the moment," Geneva replied. "You noticed,
I'm sure, all those important executives who worked
for Duncan, Americans, Frenchman, Englishmen,
Mexicans, the lot. At the funeral and afterward. They

were around me like bees around honey. More interested in their paychecks than getting into my pants." She allowed herself a small laugh. "One of the hazards of being a rich man's wife."

"They're frightened. You can't blame them for trying to get on your best side."

"Is that what you want, Suzanne, to be on my best side?" Geneva tested the water with her toe. It was perfect. Everything was perfect, or soon would be. That was another lesson she had learned from Sharps: the rewards of wealth and power. She lowered herself into the tub. "Join me." Another command, encased in velvet, but no less insistent.

Brody did so. She seated herself far enough away so as not to presume anything, close enough to show her independence and her defiance.

"Were you afraid of Sharps, Suzanne?"

"No," she answered, too quickly, and more emphatically than she would have liked. "Maybe a little. He was a dominating man."

"Are you afraid of me, Suzanne?"

She answered without thinking. "Of course not." It was a mistake. There was a smile on Geneva's face, a secret little smile that spoke volumes. Geneva was not to be underestimated. She was a strong woman, clever and perceptive; and, just possibly, in her own way as brilliant as Sharps had been. "Maybe a little," she amended contritely.

This time Geneva did not smile. She cupped her hands and splashed warm water on her cheeks. "You plan on leaving Sharps Industries, I imagine?"

"It seems like the logical move. You'll want your own people around you. . . ."

"But you don't have anything specific lined up?"

Exactly the way Sharps would have reacted, brushing aside all attempts at double-talk. Be careful, Brody warned herself. "Not yet. I thought I'd stay on until you are settled in. Provide any assistance you might need."

"Yes, that would be helpful. There's so much I don't know. The intricacies of the business. How to deal with all that money. The exercise of power. Those men who worked for Duncan, many of them will resent me. Resent working for a woman."

"Fire them," Brody said in a flat voice.

"There. That's what I mean, you have the mind-set of a businessman. You sounded almost like Duncan then."

"Some of your top executives will resign; they won't want to work for a woman. Others will hang on."

"Which ones can I trust? I'm sure you can help me answer that question."

"If you want me to—I'll do my best."

Geneva turned toward the other woman, her gaze steady. "Forget about leaving the company. Stay on. In the same capacity you served Duncan, serve me. More so, perhaps. Whatever your salary is, your bonuses, we can come to an arrangement. Upward, that is.

"I'll be doing a great deal of traveling. I want someone experienced and smart, someone I can depend on and trust. In time, we'll get to know each other better, come to trust each other, appreciate each other. Perhaps even grow fond of each other. So, will you stay on with me, Suzanne? Be my good right hand. My close assistant. My friend."

Brody didn't rush her reply. "I would like that, Geneva." She drawled the name for emphasis, slow and insinuating. "I would like that a lot."

Geneva extended her hand, wet and warm.

Brody took it in hers.

Their eyes fixed on each other, and Geneva leaned toward the other woman, kissed her lightly on the lips. Then kissed her a second time, gentler, warmer, in no hurry to break contact.

"I take it, then, we have a deal?" she said for the other woman's ears only.

"A deal, yes. . . ."

38

A UNIFORMED guard brought
Devlin into a room set aside for lawyer-client conferences. A room of no distinction, with flat white walls
and floors covered with gray tile. There was a gray
metal table with four chairs to match. Geneva, poised
at the head of the table, watched with considerable interest as the guard ushered Devlin to a chair.

"Sit," the guard grumped out. He looked over at Geneva, open admiration in his glance. "Sure you don't
want me to stay in here with you, Mrs. Sharps? Just
in case."

She answered, her eyes fixed on Devlin. "There
won't be any trouble."

The guard growled at Devlin. "Stay in the chair,

man. Mind your manners. I'll be right outside that
door." He withdrew.

Geneva smiled. "Not even a little hello, Dev?"

"Why are you doing this to me, Geneva?"

"Poor Dev. Is it so difficult to understand what's
happened? You're charged with breaking and entering.
With fleeing the scene of a crime. With armed robbery.
And second-degree homicide done during the commission of a felony. Very serious business, Dev."

"I'm innocent, you know that. All you have to do
is tell them the truth."

She lowered herself into a chair at the opposite end
of the table, examined him with interest. "Innocent.
I suppose you are, in so many ways. About that night,
Dev, this is what I told the police. Those two men
broke in—they forced the door to the pool room open.
There were appropriate marks on the knob, around
the lock. Sharps's work, I suppose. He was always so
thorough. The men jimmied the lock, the police told
me, came inside intending to burglarize the premises."
Her expression was apologetic, her manner crying out
for compassion, for understanding.

"I was aware of none of this, of course. I was watching a film on the VCR in the entertainment center.
That room is rather isolated, Dev, very little sound
from the outside can be heard in there.

"But Duncan, according to the police, must have
heard the intruders. He had retired to his bedroom."
She smiled shyly. "I had to confess to the officers and
to the district attorney that my husband and I maintained separate bedrooms. They showed a great deal
of interest in that.

"I heard a hoarse cry. I think that was the phrase

I used—hoarse cry. Duncan calling upon the robbers to halt. Actually, what he said was, 'Freeze, you bastards!' Just like in a movie. There were shots. I rushed into the entry hall, where I found my husband bleeding from a chest wound. Later, I discovered that poor Duncan had been shot twice. Needless to say, I was distraught. Terrified. Dazed, I snatched up Duncan's weapon. It's called a Glock seventeen. I rushed into the long living room, where I found the two intruders. Without thinking, I fired, striking both. Lucky shots, of course. I killed both of them, Dev.

"Then you appeared, the third man of the robbery team. I was in shock by then, and your appearance startled me even more. I fired again—purely a reflex action on my part—and you fled. The rest you know about."

He stared in disbelief at that magnificently formed face, every feature perfect. Skin without blemish. Eyes bottomless and revealing nothing. He was innocent; an innocent, used and manipulated from start to finish.

"You planned it every step of the way, Geneva."

"Mustn't give me too much credit. Those men, for example—Ricketts and Daly—how fortuitous that was. No way I could figure on their coming. It was you I expected, Dev, only you."

"How could you know I wouldn't shoot you? Sharps offered me a good deal."

"Not you, Dev. You cared too much for me to do that. Besides, no way you could trust Duncan. He was too obviously devious for that. Had you executed me, he would have shot you on the spot."

"Which you tried to do."

"What choice did I have, Dev? Can you see it, you and I strolling hand in hand through the rest of our lives? I'd be bored to death in a minute and a half. An ex-jock without imagination enough to stir an idea to life. An aging gigolo. Oh, Dev, you can see that we could never have a future together."

All at once it came together in his mind. He hefted it for substance, he examined it for flaws. "You didn't shoot Ricketts and Daly."

"Don't be silly, of course I did. The police are convinced of it."

"No, no. It had to be your husband. He was waiting for me to arrive, that was our deal. When those two showed up, Sharps was forced to act. He had the Glock seventeen. Seventeen shots, if he needed them. It took only three to take out those two."

"In that case, who could have killed poor Duncan?"

"You did. You picked up the thirty-eight—Daly would have been carrying it—the gun Sharps gave me, the gun they stole out of my room. You arrived on the scene out of the entertainment center, pulled away from your movie by the noise. You picked up the thirty-eight and shot your husband twice while he was off guard. You placed the revolver back in Daly's hand and picked up the Glock seventeen. Just in time to get that last shot off at me."

"And missed."

"I've been thinking about that. It was deliberate, that missed shot. You wanted the cops to have a suspect, to deflect attention from yourself. You wanted a trial, a public show of your grief. You needed a victim, and I was it, from the beginning."

"It's a long reach, Dev. A stretch of logic. The police

prefer simple explanations—shootings in the commission of a break-in. Much more acceptable to the official mind. Nobody is going to believe your version, Dev. Not when the grieving widow bears witness against you."

She was right; she had put it together so carefully. And when Ricketts and Daly appeared unexpectedly, she'd managed to pick up the pieces of her plan, ad-lib around the reality that was unfolding even as she watched. She was good, much better than he'd imagined.

"You've got it all now," he said. "Duncan's money. His power. Your freedom."

"More than you can imagine, Dev." She went to the door, standing with one hand on the knob, looking his way. A perfectly composed picture, staged for his benefit. Something else for him to remember.

"I'll think about you, Dev, from time to time. Even miss you a bit. A handful of regrets aren't much when compared to all that I've gained."

He rose and the movement startled her; he could see her hand tighten on the knob of the door. Then she recaptured her assurance when she realized he intended her no harm.

"Is there any point in asking you to get me out of this, Geneva?"

"I'm afraid not, Dev. You can see how awkward that would be. I'll give you this, though, we did have our moments. In bed, mostly. You are good in bed, Dev, as good as they come. Maybe I'll think about that from time to time and miss you. But no matter. Sooner or later I'll find someone to take your place, someone at least as good as you are."

"You are the bitch of all time, Geneva."

There was a faintly malignant turn to her mouth as she replied, her voice a serrated caress. "Poor Dev," she crooned thinly. "Poor dumb Dev . . ."

Burt Hirschfeld is the author of numerous paperback bestsellers. He lives in Westport, Connecticut.